Slow Boil Rising

By D.T.E. Madden

Slow Boil Rising

Copyedited by Heather Zehring

Cover art and design by Theresa Hertling

ISBN-13:
978-1515259862

ISBN-10:
1515259862

Frog
 thrown into boiling water
 attempts escape

Frog in water
 then brought to boil
 accepts fate

   - After the Apocryphal, 20th Century

Prologue:

As stratus clouds soared across the sky, all seemed calm in the world. Intolerance was an outdated notion; evil had been eradicated once and for all. Bright-chested birds sang, and feral chickens frolicked. Life was peace, and peace was the law of the land. Insensitivity, after all, was illegal.

The year was 0039 according to the new calendar of the Enlightened Era. Acceptance of everyone was the norm of the day and the law of the land. Gone were outdated notions and unacceptably intolerant calendars of a bygone era. Every person had been set free to accept the General Will. Those who had not accepted the General Will were intolerant of others and were rightfully punished for their intolerance.

In the Unified Society of America, 50 stars had been replaced by one star – a bright shining beacon – symbolizing the General Will and the freedoms unique unto it.

Persecutors known as the *Intolerants* ignored the General Will. These evildoers were properly segregated into facilities where they could not harm others, for their hatred and intolerance were not to be tolerated. Society had become a homogeneous conglomerate of accepting free thinkers.

Most of this progress was due to the President, who was now in his 10th term in office. But the court system played its role as well. Speciesism, racism, sexism, and proselytizing religion had been declared evil by a unanimous vote of the Magnificent Court of the Unified Society, and such divisive doctrines were therefore illegal.

The law was very clear. Intolerant individuals must be forced to accept the General Will of free people; they must be forced to be free. Based on the freedoms unique unto the General Will, no one should ever again be persecuted in the Unified Society of America.

Despite society's progress and evolution under the Unified Society, generations-old human tendencies remained problematic. One such tendency, the need to organize society into hierarchies, was rearing its ugly head behind the scenes in the nation's capital. The truth was no one had seen the President in decades. He kept winning elections and responding to his email, but no one had seen him. Well, no one had seen him except for members of the Department of Internal Security, the very agency in charge of protecting him.

As it turned out, the Department of Internal Security was wielding more and more of the President's power on his behalf. This created suspicion in the minds of more than a few power brokers that Internal Security was up to something nefarious. This, in turn, created something of a tinderbox, with divergent elements within the government prepared to expand their power at their rivals' expense.

And as one particularly seditious rumor had it, the Department of Internal Security itself had lost tabs on the President, and DIS leadership was desperately trying to find him.

Now, as most civilians knew, they had it pretty good in the Unified Society.

But they also knew from Department of Free Speech news outlets that not everything was well outside the boundaries of the tranquil North American state. Many countries and many evil leaders had not yet accepted the General Will. Several foreign states flaunted their refusal to ratify the International Agreement on the Abuse of Animals. The Norwegians, especially, touted the fact that they would not cease the wicked practice of slaughtering millions of Atlantic cod. The Norwegians refused to accept the fact that meat eating was highly insensitive toward the fish they were kidnapping and slaughtering. They refused to acknowledge that fish had certain inalienable human rights. Logically, an example had to be made of someone at home who exhibited the same sort of undesirable behavior that made the Norwegians the target of national outrage.

Book I: Pax Tolerantia

The Trial of Reginald Bowperson: 31-32 January 0039

The sound of his roosters woke up Reginald Bowman on most mornings, and the morning of January 31st fell nicely into this pattern. Winter had waned enough in the northern part of the Dominion of Missouri for Bowman to get back outside his home near the banks of the Chariton River and do the work necessary to fill his belly.

He had spent much of the last six weeks cracking his knuckles in solitude inside his home, a home that stood on stilts in a small clearing amid a lowland forest filled with burr oak, hickory, and cottonwood trees towering over mulberry shrubs and sumac bushes. The past few weeks, he only ventured outside to gather the wood he had chopped last fall for his wood-burning stove and to throw corn into the chicken coop that sat nestled in-between the stilts holding up his house.

Those stilts had kept his home safe from many floods over the years. The Chariton River was low this time of year, but it rarely behaved itself for very long into the spring. Unable to hunt or fish, much less grow any crops during the hardest part of winter, Bowman had spent the last several weeks eating preserves and honing his craft by fashioning fish hooks out of tin for both his own personal use and to sell on the black market.

After rolling out of bed on the morning of the 31st, Bowman checked the wall voltmeter that monitored the batteries fed by the solar generators on his roof. He gladly saw that the sun had melted enough snow off his roof for electricity to once again course through the walls and outlets of his home. He made his way into the bathroom and turned on the hot water faucet. After a few moments, *success*! Thanks to a decent solar charge the past few days, his water heater was back in business and there was water warm enough for shaving.

After a few minutes in the bathroom, Bowman had shaved off his light brown beard and felt himself presentable enough to meet his distribution partner in his secret hook-selling operation. His distributor also happened to be his wife, Veronica. Well, she was his wife in every way except on paper. Theirs was a clandestine marriage so Veronica and the kids could reside in public housing on the farm while Reginald maintained his activities in the Uninhabited Zones.

Veronica lived on the designated U.S. farm surrounding a man-made reservoir about 10 miles to the east of his river home. The U.S. farm occupied the fields and hills near the site of Macon, his former hometown. Veronica and Reginald were able to use their hooks to bribe the gate guards on the farm. And she was able to sell her husband's fish hooks to earn extra income for their three children.

But before Reginald would meet up with his wife, it was time for a fried fish breakfast. And that meant he needed to check the trotline he had set up last evening out in the river.

Bowman had readied his canoe next to the river around dusk the evening before, and tied 12 hooks to short strings dangling off one long line he would extend out into the river. He preferred to bait his hooks with worms. After all, he designed his hooks to be the best hooks in the business at keeping a worm intact by having three barbs on each hook. That being said, he only had corn this time of year. After baiting each hook with three or four kernels of sweet corn, Bowman slowly rowed out to the middle of the river. He tied one end of the line to a plastic jug so the jug would remain floating and visible for easy retrieval later. He then tied a rock for weight about three meters down the line to anchor his trotline in place. After letting the jug float and dropping the rock, he rowed back to shore and let his hooks gradually slide into the water. Once reaching shore, he tied his trotline to the same branch on the same tree he had been using for this purpose for nine years.

He knew that some large catfish and grass carp would be finding their way up the tributaries of the Missouri River now that the seasonal thaw was well underway. And with the Chariton feeding into the Missouri about 40 miles downstream, some hungry lunkers might be passing by at any moment.

By setting out his trotline overnight, he'd be able to entice any fish that went swimming by in the moonlight with dangling kernels of sweet corn. Bowman was an experienced outdoorsman and had been at his craft for years. In his younger days, Bowman liked fishing all night long, smoking his pipe and listening to his shortwave radio.

But he was now a couple months on the long side of 30 years of age, and he knew his limits very well. Those limits would easily be tested by fishing all night in near-freezing temperatures. His trotline would give him the benefit of fishing all night without having to shiver in the cold and catch his death.

When it came time to venture outside and check his trotline the morning of the 31st, Bowman dropped a stepladder from the balcony of his house and climbed down. The smell of hickory smoke coming from his chimney was strong this morning, and he could clearly see his breath. Taking a deep breath of the smoky air, Bowman exhaled and quietly said to himself, "Spring is almost here."

As he made his way down the foot-worn path winding through the sumac bushes to the riverbank, he paused about a quarter of the way down and saw what looked like the distinctive, small footprints of raccoons who had been out the night before. They evidently agreed that spring was around the corner.

He took a few more steps before freezing dead in his tracks. One woodland constituency that was normally very vocal about the advent of spring was conspicuously quiet. *Why weren't the birds singing?* Where were the larks? The robins? The jays?

Something wasn't right. A sumac branch snapped in the woods about 20 meters to his left. Bowman turned just in time to see the motion of something large in the trees, which were still bare of their leaves. He reached for his sidearm revolver – damn, not there. He forgot to wear it this morning, and this was no time to be slipping. Bowman turned and ran at full speed back to his house.

Within moments a female voice cried out from his right, "Halt! DETA!" He kept running.

A male voice shouted from his left. "Halt! Department of Equally Treating Animals!"

He kept running. He was just a dozen or so steps from getting back into his house, where he'd arm himself for this confrontation. *Step, step, step.* Bowman could see getting back would only take a few more seconds, when – snap – his momentum suddenly came to a halt. He found himself tangled and writhing on the ground.

A cleverly camouflaged rope net pulled taught between two trees did the halting. He was tangled and caught like a fish on one of his lines.

"Turn away from the sound of my voice!" a male voice called from behind him. Bowman pulled out his filet knife and began cutting at the rope to free himself. Frantically cutting for a few moments, he had his left leg free.

"Turn away from the sound of my voice!" a female voice yelled from his right. Frantically cutting, he had his left arm free.

"Turn away from the sound of my voice!" a female voice ordered from his left. He nearly had his right leg free.

"Turn away from the sound of my voice!" a male voice roared from just in front of him. He looked up just in time to see a can of pepper spray pointed at him with a stream of orange mist headed right for him.

The pain was blinding.

He felt a hood slide over his head and zip ties applied to his wrists and ankles as he heard about four voices congratulating each other.

One of the male voices spoke directly to him. "Reginald Bowman, on your feet." Two or three pairs of hands pulled him up on his feet and turned him to face the man speaking to him. The man continued, "You are under arrest. You have the right to remain silent, but it will harm your legal defense if you do not affirmatively mention, when questioned, something upon which you later rely in your defense. Anything you say can and will be held against you in a court of law. You have the right to an attorney. If you cannot afford one, an attorney shall be provided for you. Do you understand these rights?"

Bowman remained silent a few moments, testing the strength of the zip ties on his wrist.

"Well, then. Take him away, agents. We'll search the residence."

Bowman spent the next day hooded and tied up in what felt like a boat, then a helicopter, then an elevator, then a very cold shower. By the time they took the hood off his head, he found himself damp and naked in a cold, dim prison cell with a neatly folded orange jumpsuit lying on a cot in the cell's concrete corner. After the steel door slammed behind him, he put on the jumpsuit, noticing the words "Department of Coexistence" embroidered on its back.

A glowing sign loomed over the steel door with the words "You are as we describe you" emblazoned in bright orange. Taking a seat on his cot, Bowman gave his wrists a brief shake, placed his hands together with his fingertips touching, then cracked eight knuckles in one motion. His mind raced with thoughts of Veronica. She had to be worried that he missed their meeting. He could only hope she had not ventured out to the cabin to check on him only to run into the same DETA patrol that had picked him up.

The following morning, a Bailiff strapped hand and ankle cuffs to Bowman and silently escorted him to a courtroom where he cuffed him to a chair facing an empty judge's bench. Behind the oaken bench stood two large bay windows, through which Bowman could see the top half of the Gateway Arch. Now with the knowledge that he was sitting in a high-rise courthouse in the Good Louis Habitation Zone, he sat in silence, looking out the windows for about an hour more while camera and lighting crew members set up equipment around him. A kindly looking old man in a grey cotton suit sat next to him and introduced himself. "Hi, I am your defense attorney. My name is Jamesroy. What is your name?"

Then the trial of Reginald Bowperson began in earnest.

"Oye! Oye! On this most enlightened day of the Enlightened Era, all rise in the honorable Court of Justice of the Unified Society of America, Eighteenth District of the Dominion of Missouri. Court is in session, the Honorable Magistrate Mangolada presiding."

The most honorable Mangolada entered the courtroom, robes flowing, with a bejeweled scepter in hand, and thus took the seat behind the oak bench commanding the forefront of the courtroom.

Mangolada announced, "This is the honorable Court of Justice! All must show the proper respect to the Court of Justice of the Unified Society of America, Eighteenth District of the Dominion of Missouri. Behold my scepter, traditional symbol of justice!"

All in the court bowed, trembling before the scepter as Magistrate Mangolada banged it on the oaken altar of justice.

As the echoes of scepter banging subsided, the Bailiff announced, "Honorable Mangolada, we have before us today the case of the Department of Equally Treating Animals versus Reginald Bowman, on this the thirty-second day of January in the year zero zero thirty-nine of the Enlightened Era."

"Reginald Bowman, Bailiff?"

"Yes, your most Honorable Magistrate of the Eighteenth District of the Dominion of Missouri. Reginald Bowman is his name."

"That seems like a rather insensitive name doesn't it? Bow-*man*." Mangolada's jaw shifted side to side while saying Bowman's name.

"Yes, it surely does, your most Honorable Magistrate of the Eighteenth District of the Dominion of Missouri."

"That name, Bow-*man*, would seem to suggest that the only people who are allowed to, or are capable of, using bows, arrows, and other primitive sorts of missile weaponry are men. That name symbolizes gendernormative oppression. This court simply cannot abide such nonsense. From now on, the defendant's name is Reginald Bow*person*."

Nodding, the Bailiff slammed his fist to his chest and declared, "The most Honorable Magistrate Mangolada of the Eighteenth District of the Dominion of Missouri hereby declares the so-called Reginald Bowman to be from henceforth and so on Reginald Bowperson! So let it be written in the record."

Mangolada rubbed the most honorable scepter and moaned a large moan of self-assurance. "That's much better. Now no one will be offended anymore due to that rather crass name."

Reginald Bowperson, still confused from his arrest and immediate prosecution, spoke up. "Please! Your honor, I–"

"You just showed a tremendous lack of respect, Bowperson!" the Bailiff yelled as he threw his elbow into Bowperson's chest, slamming Reginald to the floor, blanketing him in the floor dust that had accumulated through four decades of enlightenment. Dragging Bowperson back up off the floor, the Bailiff growled, "Behold the scepter, you Intolerant! Behold the oaken altar, you Norwegian sympathizer! Call the most Honorable Magistrate Mangolada of the Eighteenth District of the Dominion of Missouri by the full title, fish killer!"

Mangolada spoke, "Let the Intolerant address this most tolerant court."

Bowperson, trying to clean the waxy dust off his Department of Coexistence jumpsuit, pleaded, "Most Honorable Magistrate Mangolada of the Eighteenth District of the Dominion of Missouri, I have been convicted of nothing. I beg of you, please do not change my name, I am Reginald Bowma–"

Mangolada slammed the scepter upon the altar of justice and screamed, "Silence!" before kissing the most honorable scepter and whispering unto the golden rod for five seconds as if apologizing to it. The Magistrate's gaze shifted back from the scepter to the defendant, then back to the scepter, then back to the defendant again.

"Reginald Bowperson, judging by your dusty appearance I must assume you are intolerant – intolerant toward cleanliness and tolerance!" Mangolada declared, looking around the courtroom at the facial expressions of children on field trips, senior citizens, Department of Free Speech television producers, and camerapersons before banging the scepter again. "Oh I'm sorry, Mr. Scepter, I didn't mean it this time, I didn't." Mangolada paused for a while, staring at Bowperson, sneering. The honorable Mangolada then shifted from sneering at Bowperson to staring honorably at the scepter, whispering to it again. The courtroom audience watched in silence as the whispering continued for what seemed like nearly a minute, perhaps more.

"Your honor," Bowperson pleaded, composing himself as calmly as he could in preparation for his well-thought-out argument, an argument he had been practicing since finding himself in a jail cell hours earlier, "I–"

The Bailiff kicked the shackled man to the floor once again. "You sick Intolerant! You're interrupting a very delicate moment."

"It's okay, Bailiff," Mangolada magnanimously declared. "I can see this so-called Bowperson, if that is his real name, is an *Intolerant*. I mean, look at the way he is dressed, you'd think he would try to clean himself up, yet his Department of Coexistence jumpsuit is still covered in dust. That tells me he is a pig and does not clean his house."

"Hooyah!" Defense Attorney Jamesroy cried aloud.

Mangolada smiled with a nod to Jamesroy. "I hereby sentence Mr. Bowperson to pay reparations for past damages to society. Bailiff, calculate his past wrongs indicator."

The Bailiff straightened himself up, grabbed a notebook, and solemnly announced, "Your most Honorable Magistrate Mangolada, we have determined that due to his gender and or heritage, and lying about his name to intentionally displease the court, his past wrongs quotient is an astounding negative one point twenty-one. Negative point four based on his ethno-demographic class and for possibly being of German ancestry, negative point five due to being male, negative point zero one for having grandparents born before the Enlightened Era, and a negative point three for lying about his name. With a past wrongs quotient of negative one point twenty-one, his past wrongs indicator is therefore a whopping one point twenty-one."

Mangolada did the math on the court's specially designed graphing calculator. Using what judges and lawyers referred to as the "Tolerant Calculation of Intolerance to Past Wrongs Reparation Quotient Method," Mangolada multiplied the past wrongs indicator by one hundred and added a percentage sign. The process was complete in under 45 seconds, a personal record. "So this Bowperson would therefore have to pay one hundred and twenty-one percent of his future earnings to repay society for his past wrongdoings."

Bowperson cried out, "But your honor, I haven't even been told what crime I am charged with yet!"

Mangolada scowled. "Simpleton, your sentence is not contingent upon your crime, thanks to the guidelines handed down by the Fairness in Sentencing Act of aught-aught thirty-two. Your sentence is based entirely on the Tolerant Calculation of Intolerance to Past Wrongs Reparation Quotient Method."

Mangolada leaned forward and smiled. Clearly this Bowperson had never attended law school and was ignorant to the simpler realities of the world, such as the Tolerant Calculation of Intolerance to Past Wrongs Reparation Quotient Method. The magistrate continued, "But, assuming for the sake of argument that your punishment is somehow related to your crime, I will humor your ridiculous inquiry with an inquiry of my own. Were you not caught living in an unlicensed structure outside a Designated Habitation Zone? Were you not in possession of contraband weapons and paraphernalia? Were you not in possession of up to three thousand barbed hooks that speciesists once referred to as *fish hooks*? Guilty!" Mangolada banged the scepter again, this time visibly wincing at it.

"Bailiff, you failed to include the zero point nine quotient for having dust on his jumpsuit. This brings Bowperson's overall past wrongs indicator to a two point eleven." Following another brief interlude while Mangolada did the calculations on his Department of Coexistence graphing calculator, the enlightened

Magistrate continued. "Mr. Bowperson, you hereby have to pay two hundred and eleven percent of your future earnings in reparations. This is in order to atone for your evil deeds and the evil deeds of the demographic class to which you belong. Your actions and the actions of those who share your physical traits have hurt our feelings and our absolute morality tremendously. For all of your murderous actions, you must pay your debt. In consideration of the speciesist nature of your crime, your reparations will hitherto go to the Department of Equally Treating Animals."

"Please! I did nothing wrong! I was only trying to feed–"

"You lied about your name, didn't you? And you look dirty, like you have been on the floor, and that shows a lack of cleanliness ... and, and a lack of tolerance for cleanliness!" Almost as if jolted by the word "tolerance," the assembled courtroom spectators roared in approval.

Mangolada continued, "But it is obvious you cannot pay two hundred-plus percent of your earnings, because unkempt, dusty people like you don't work hard enough. I mean, look at you. You are so dusty. This *is* the Court of Justice, does it not warrant the proper amount of respect? You know I love this scepter, for it has been the traditional symbol of justice and fairness these past decades. Because you lack respect for our fundamental and traditional values, like my scepter here, I hereby remand you to the custody of the Department of Coexistence for political re-education. You shall be assigned to sensitivity training and re-education at the Tolerance Corps facility in Freepersonsburg, Not-East Virginia. There, you shall be retrained to serve the General Will of society. You shall become a soldier in our struggle to spread the General Will. However, should you fail to meet this obligation to pay your debt to society, the Department of Coexistence has ways of collecting. I am hereby placing a lien on all of your bodily organs."

"I've got my eye on your spleen, Bow*person*," the Bailiff sneered. "A spleen is a very powerful aphrodisiac."

Department of Protests Regulation 215 Bravo Bravo:

Department of Protests Code 215
The Department of Protests, empowered by the Violence Against Whales Act of 0025 and the First Guaranteed Right of the Constitution of the Unified Society, the guarantor of the right to freeness of speech, is hereby authorized to regulate the size, construction, material, and content of protest signs, songs, or other messages in such a manner that extends to but is not necessarily or unnecessarily limited to the following provisions.

Provision 1: The protection of sensitivities, be they cultural or ethnic or gender or non-gender based.
Provision 2: The protection of children and other things.
Provision 3: The protection of the General Will, and the freedoms unique unto it.
Provision 4: The protection of both sign makers and protesters.
Provision 5: The protection of sensitivities not currently known or discovered but that can be discovered through the fruitfulness of thoughtful and tolerant discourse.

DoP Code 215(B) (Addendum Bravo):

The Department of Protests, empowered by the Violence Against Whales Act of 0025 and the First Guaranteed Right of the Constitution of the Unified Society, the guarantor of the right to freeness of speech, hereby alters Department of Protests Regulation 215 in accordance with Department of Protests Code 215(B) to include Provision 6.

DoP Code 215(B)(b) (Addendum Bravo Bravo):

The Department of Protests, in its wisdom and empowered by the Constitution of the Unified Society and the Violence Against Whales Act of 0025, hereby alters Code 215(B) in accordance with

Code 215(B)(b) as 215(B) failed to include Provision 6 in its structure. This addendum succeeds where the previous addendum failed, through the inclusion of Provision 6. Needless to say, Provision 6 was narrowly tailored and necessary toward fulfilling several compelling governmental interests. We apologize for any inconvenience.

Consent to this and all Department of Free Speech regulations is to be implied by partaking in the regulated activity of free speech.

A Well-Organized Protest: 23 January 0039

In the Dominion of Sacajawea, in the Seattle Designated Habitation Zone, the democratically selected Supervizier arranged a multicultural and demographically correct protest against Norwegian fish murderers and the inherent evil they represented. Supervizier Anderchild addressed the mob assembled at the steps of City Hall. "Norwegian oppressors will rue the day they defy us. They refuse to accept and face the facts, my fellow Societans. They deny that the creator endowed all living creatures with the right to exist in freedom."

On this January 23rd in the year 0039, members of the well-organized mob stood abreast and in file, maintaining proper intervals within their formation. The ability to maintain formation, after all, was the key to any successful Department of Protests-sanctioned event. They held signs, waving them in the rain-soaked breeze. Emblazoned upon the signs, in all the colors of the rainbow, were "Fish have rights," "Freedom and tolerance for all of the creator's creatures," "Accept the General Will," "Respect and Tolerate," and "Death to the Norwegians."

Anderchild turned aside to speak to his prized aide. "If this goes as planned, I may be promoted to the Overseership of all of Sacajawea. But I thought that I had decreed that we would have some signs with 'Anderchild for Overseer' decorated with rainbow-colored letters?"

"I apologize, Sir, but Foreperson Jolly countermanded that order and ordered a middle-management strike at the Michael Moore Memorial Department of Protests sign manufactory in Vancouver."

"I thought I had made it clear that the Michael Moore DoP sign manufactory was not to be used." Anderchild continued to grin and wave his arms to the well-disciplined mob, as they stood, rigidly, at the position of present signs. "We were supposed to get our signs from the Raul Castro DoP sign manufactory in Tacoma."

"Yes, Sir, that technically is true, but the Raul Castro manufactory has had production diverted in order to make signs to be sent to our insurgent protesters in Venezuela. Orders of Foreperson Jolly, Sir."

"Jolly, that dilettante. She has her hands in everything. It's just because she's campaigning to be the Overseer of Sacajawea, too, you know? We used to be great friends, but with Selection Day around the corner, she now has it in for me. Apparently, I am not intolerant enough of the Intolerants to suit her tastes. In any event, my unruly protesters await my words of wisdom, and we shall show that Jolly who's the most accepting and sensitive son of a bitch this side of the Rockies."

Anderchild ceased waving to the mob. "Activists, give your elements the 'Order Signs' command on my mark." He paused, soaking the misted breeze into his lungs. "By the numbers, Order."

"Order!" the activists echoed.

"Signs!" bellowed Anderchild.

At that command, the mob ceased waving their signs and lowered them to shoulder level as per General Protest Order Nine. Anderchild firmly took hold of his red, white, blue, green, yellow, and black podium. Taking a deep breath, he declared, "Fish have rights."

The activists screamed in unison, "Elements, give hooyah!"

The elite formation of protesters hollered in an approval reminiscent of the cackling of crows and the buzzing of hornets.

Anderchild continued, "But there are those who refuse to face facts. They refuse to face the fact that fish have rights."

"Hooyah!"

"They want to deny fish their inalienable human rights. As long as one fish is persecuted, no one among us can be free!"

"Hooyah, honorable Anderchild!"

Meanwhile, about two kilometers away, an unregistered and therefore illegal mob rode on horseback toward City Hall. This mob did not have signs in accordance with U.S. Department of Protests

Code 215 bravo bravo. This mob carried no signs. This mob did not maintain formation; this mob was riding as a gaggle of individuals more so than an elite protest unit. They rode without being in formation, and most certainly without maintaining proper interval or distance from each other. Conspicuously absent was any semblance of a Department of Protests-issued uniform, but most wore hats, and most wore boots. Leading the mob was a man known as El Asno.

"Fish ought to be free to accept the General Will. We must preserve that freedom. Your country needs–" At that, Anderchild received a swift tap on the shoulder from his prized aide.

"Sir, a very disturbing development has occurred. Ubiquitous Camera Command reports an anomaly."

Anderchild stepped away from his silver microphone as the activists ordered the mob to present signs once again. Facing his pale prized aide, as the signs waved in unison, Anderchild gritted his teeth. "What are you saying? I thought I told you I don't want any interruptions during this protest."

"My Supervizier, there is an imminent danger here. Ubiquitous Camera Command has reported that a mob entered the Seattle DHZ on horseback about twenty minutes ago. They're moving toward our direction."

"Are they holding signs in DoP code two fifteen specifications?"

"No, Sir, they are not holding any signs at all, much less signs in accordance with DoP code two hundred and fifteen."

"Well, I am not concerned about two hundred and fifteen. What about DoP code two fifteen bravo?"

"Sir, it is my duty to report to you that code two hundred and fifteen bravo has been replaced with code two hundred and fifteen bravo bravo, and it maintains that DoP code two hundred and fifteen bravo has been modified in accordance with DoP code two hundred and fifteen bravo bravo."

"What the hell does that mean?"

"We do not know, Sir. And last I checked, our legal counsel was going to get back to us."

"Well, you say they are not holding any signs?"

"No, Sir."

"So they are holding signs?"

"No, Sir."

"I think I understand."

"Sir, Ubiquitous Camera Command is giving us a video feed. Look, my Supervizier. They are less than one-and-a-half kilometers away."

"Wait a minute – they don't have any signs!"

"Yes, Sir."

"Yes, yes they have signs? Or yes, no they have no signs? Because I do not see any signs."

"Sir, if they do have signs, they are very small, and illegible, and therefore not in accordance with DoP code two hundred and fifteen bravo bravo."

"Agreed, they are quite likely Intolerants. What do they want?"

"Hard to say, Sir. They don't have any signs."

As the mob grew close, it began to chant. "No more protesters. No more protesters."

Anderchild's aide grew still more pale. "Sir, we've got a disturbing message from UCC. Ubiquitous Camera Command has done a demographic sample in order to ascertain inclusion. The mob is *not* demographically correct."

Anderchild waved to his mob. "Fish have rights!"

"Hooyah!" The sound was a slightly less enthusiastic cackling of crows than before.

"Sir, we have a very non-inclusive mob of likely Intolerants headed toward us. Their signs are not in accordance to DoP code two hundred and fifteen bravo, or two hundred and fifteen bravo bravo. UCC facial recognition scans indicate that the mob is being led by an Intolerant officer carrying the rank of Colonel. His image matches drone reconnaissance photos from several campaigns in the Broadband Rebellions. I'm requesting identity information on the leader, but UCC is giving me an 'unknown' designation on him."

"They definitely are Intolerants then."

"Yes, Sir. Most likely speciesists too."

"Right right right, enslaving horses and having no signs."

"Yes, Sir."

The thundering of hooves and the echoing chant of "No more protesters" became deafening.

"They're here, Sir!"

Anderchild screamed as he ducked behind his red, white, blue, green, yellow, and black podium. "Intolerant Norwegian horse-enslaving racists!"

El Asno: 23 January 0039

On the morning of January 23rd, 0039, a group of about a hundred men and women huddled in the woods just outside the Seattle Designated Habitation Zone. Their gaunt leader dressed himself in a tattered olive military uniform bearing the eagle insignia of a rebel Colonel. Brass fish hooks dangled from his shirt pocket just beneath where the name "El Asno" stood scrawled across his uniform in black ink.

He sat drinking broken orange pekoe tea while watching salmon roast over an ashen bed of birch wood coals. His face was lean and adorned by a dark grey beard beneath his salt-and-pepper hair. "Is the protest happening today for certain, Hackberry?"

"Yes, Asno. Everything looks like it'll be going on. I'm certain," Hackberry said with a slight country drawl.

"We make for City Hall at noon then." Sighing deeply, El Asno ordered, "No signs."

"We will scare the piss out of 'em." Hackberry laughed.

"We will." Asno blew steam off of his tea. "Hackberry, you've served with me proudly. Served the cause very well."

"Thank you, Asno."

"I need to confide in you. There are things you need to know."

"Are you going to finally tell us your real name?"

Asno stood from his log and tossed his tea upon the coals, his voice hissing as the coals hissed. "I have no name, it was stolen from me! I was born in a year that no longer exists. I am Asno to you, am I not?"

"Yes, Sir, I did not mean offense, my curiosity got the–"

"Hackberry, there's a good chance our actions today will cost us all of our lives."

"Asno, we are–"

"Hackberry, have I ever told you about Alliance?"

"No, Asno."

"In my travels, I found a place of exceptional beauty. Both beautiful and austere at the same time. This doesn't make any sense to you. But it will. Remember Alliance, Hackberry. Remember Alliance. Remember this above all."

"I don't understand, Asno."

"Someday you will, Hackberry. Now have everyone saddle up."

No More Protesters: 23 January 0039

"No more protesters! No more protesters!" the mob chanted in a maniacal tone as they approached Anderchild's immaculate protest formation.

Asno rode ahead of the mob, his eyes focused on an invisible object ahead – something imperceivable. "We are here," he said quietly to himself.

"They are here, Honorable Anderchild!" Anderchild's prized aide yelled in horror.

"How dreadful. Would you look at them?" Anderchild indignantly peered over his podium. "They look horrible. How undisciplined. A mob of protesters? Mismatched clothes, signs missing, not even in formation! How can they even expect to get a point across?"

"No more protesters! No more protesters!" they chanted.

Asno raised his hand, palm facing forward, the back of his hand facing those loyal to him, and they became silent.

Asno announced their presence with a belly yell. "Anderchild. Honorless Anderchild! I am El Asno. Your sham of a protest is at an end."

"Where are your signs? You must have signs!" Anderchild's aide cried down from the balcony.

Anderchild's mob stood in stunned silence. Hackberry rode forward, brandished a shotgun, and fired a single cartridge into the teary-eyed clouds that dripped slowly upon the concrete. At the shocking noise, Anderchild's anti-Norwegian mob scattered like silverfish panicked by the ignition of fluorescent light bulbs. The lead pellets from Hackberry's shot scattered upon the steps before City Hall.

Asno yelled, "*That* is my sign!"

Asno's mob began to roar as they waved shotguns, pistols, and pipes. They dismounted, then charged up the steps to City Hall.

At Anderchild's command, the Seattle Constabulary, which had been supervising the orderly protest from carefully selected vantage points throughout the city square, opened fully automatic fire into the surging mob. The doors of City Hall were to be barred, but they were not barred in time. A wave of Intolerants crashed into the door and began to spill into the atrium of City Hall, in the very seat of Anderchild's benevolence, firing, bashing, and destroying.

"Gas gas gas!" Hackberry shouted a warning. "Into the building! To the sound of my voice! To me!" The firing into the crowd had stopped while Seattle Constabulary personnel donned gas masks. Of Asno's original hundred, one in three had made it through the doors of City Hall as a pink smoke filled the plaza. The doors were slammed behind them. The smoke trickled in. Asno was not inside.

Confusion abounded as the unauthorized protesters scattered throughout the corners of the atrium of the building; fire rained down upon them. A few Intolerants managed to find cover; a few had managed to return fire. Two of Hackberry's closest friends in the mob, Leonard and Vargas, had found a stairwell. Hackberry sprinted into it behind them, barking, "Anderchild will be somewhere on the third floor, that is where his balcony is."

Behind them, from the atrium, a scream erupted. "Gas gas gas!"

Hackberry slammed the door behind them. As the three men raced up the stairs to complete their mission, an explosion deafened their ears from above.

Darkness.

Silence.

Concrete dust.

Intolerants of the Offensive Variety: 34 January 0039

"Oye! Oye!" announced Bailiff MacTavish, a proud man with a barrel chest and bushy brows. He sported an orange revolver on his left hip and an orange stun gun on his right. "On this most enlightened day of the Enlightened Era, all rise. The honorable Court of Justice of the Unified Society of America, Eighty-Ninth District of the Dominion of Sacajawea is now in session, the Honorable Magistrate Pierre presiding."

Magistrate Pierre waltzed into the chamber with her robe flowing; it was a black robe with a bright red star upon her chest. "You did say Sacajawea, Bailiff? And not Washington?"

"Yes, your honor."

"Good. I would not want to have to do with you what I had to do with my last Bailiff."

"Yes, your honor. I will never call Sacajawea by its former name, Washington."

"Bailiff, seize the Bailiff!"

"Your honor, I am the only Bailiff here. The other personnel are Internal Security."

"Seize yourself then!"

"Your Honor?"

"Seize yourself!"

Bailiff MacTavish grabbed himself by the wrist.

"By the neck, damn you! The neck. Not with one hand, use two!"

MacTavish obliged, lightly choking himself.

"Good, Bailiff! Now take the Bailiff out into the hall and taze him." MacTavish walked out of the court, waddling with his hands upon his throat, and turned left down the marble-lined hallway toward the 42nd-story window. Pierre set her elbow upon her bench, and leaned her honorable head to her honorable hand, making a cup around her ear. A minute passed, and Magistrate Pierre became impatient. "I'm waiting!"

A buzzing sound echoed from the hallway.

"Well then, let us continue. As you know, I am the judge of this court for the—"

Another buzzing sound echoed in the hallway, this time coupled with barely audible yelps of pain. Directing her gaze toward one of the Department of Internal Security men assembled in the jury box, Pierre ordered, "You, DIS man, go help him out."

The DIS man jumped to his feet with a smile and briskly walked out into the hallway.

Pierre paused a moment and briefly drummed her fingers on her bench. "As I was saying, I am the judge of this court of the Eighty-Ninth District of the Dominion of Washington and so forth."

Another buzzing sound came in from the hallway, this time coupled with loud cries of pain.

"So, Bailiff, what have we got on the docket for today?"

The court sat silent. In the second row sat Hackberry, a man in his 30s, and Leonard, a high school-aged kid. Hackberry and Leonard, the only captured survivors of the unruly mob that had descended upon Seattle City Hall a week and a half earlier, awaited their fate.

"Bailiff?" Pierre snorted.

The door to the hallway slid open as MacTavish slowly walked back into the chamber, hunching over and leaning on the DIS man for help. "I am here, your honor."

"You have tazed yourself, then?"

The DIS man responded, "He did, your honor."

"Well in fairness' sake, your honorship," MacTavish said, straightening his stun gun on his belt, "I missed the first time – instinctive reflex. I beg your pardon, Ma'am. But the second time, my aim was true and I tazed myself in the leg."

"It's true, your honorableship," the DIS man grinned. "And I zapped him one time in the middle of his chest for good measure."

MacTavish unbuttoned his shirt, showing the magistrate a large patch of irritated skin.

"Nice tazing," Magistrate Pierre admired. "Nice tazing indeed."

MacTavish smiled, "Permission to resume my post, Ma'am?"

"Move along there, Bailiff," the magistrate smiled.

The DIS man helped the Bailiff a few steps toward the magistrate's bench, when MacTavish collapsed to the floor and soiled himself, dropping dead from a heart attack.

"Nice tazing, DIS man!" the defense attorney shouted.

"Quite nice indeed." Pierre stroked the red star upon her chest. "A moment of silence for our good Bailiff ... MacDonald? MacDougal, yes, MacDougal. He died for his country, with honor, and tragically, his life was cut short, in the name of tolerance and President Tolerance. Just as we honor Anderchild, who did so much for our people, our society, and culture, and just as Anderchild made Seattle safe for North Atlantic cod through his valiant and selfless dedication, we honor MacGoogle." Caressing the star on her robe and bowing her head, Pierre raised her gaze once again and peered across the courtroom in quiet contemplation.

The DIS man volunteered to drag MacGoogle's corpse out of the doors and into the hallway, and he was so ordered, but not before Pierre proclaimed him to be her new Bailiff. "What is your name, DIS man? For you shall become my new Bailiff."

"My name is DIS Specialist Robertsperson Junior Class, your honor."

"For today, your name is *Bailiff* DIS Specialist Robertsperson Junior Class."

Once the floor was properly cleansed, waxed, and buffed to Department of Coexistence specifications, and the remains of MacGoogle (as his name was to be remembered honorably in death and on a bronze statue outside the courthouse) were sent off to Georges Danton Memorial Organ Extraction Center down the street, the day was nearly half over.

Throughout the day, Hackberry and Leonard sat shackled in their second-row bench. They had been brought before the Court of Justice to answer for the brutal assassination of the democratically selected Supervizier Anderchild and for the murder of his prized aide.

Before the day ended, evidence demonstrated that while the men were ascending the stairs of Seattle's City Hall, and while their companions used illegal gas weapons to gas themselves to death in the atrium below, the two defendants had managed to fire a rocket-propelled grenade from across the plaza outside into Anderchild's airtight office. Thus the rocket incinerated the honorable Anderchild and his staff as they sought refuge from the barbarous rampage of an unlicensed mob below – a mob who had strangely gassed themselves and the horses they had enslaved. These defendants were part of that wicked mob, a mob that did so willfully and wantonly engage in a protest without properly displaying signs or posters in accordance with Department of Protests Code 215 bravo or Department of Protests Code 215 bravo bravo.

After the three-hour trial, Pierre ordered a recess while she contemplated the gravity of all that occurred in Seattle on that fateful day – a terrible day indeed. An anti-Norwegian protest had been disrupted before camera crews had gathered enough footage to display on the nightly news or post on Bureau of Twacebook social news feeds. The rights of fish had been disrespected. A mob of ruffians had assailed City Hall with illegal firearms and unlicensed plumbing, and Anderchild and his entire protest-coordinating staff had been murdered. Only two survivors were taken prisoner from the evil mob, and these two had to serve as an example for the rest of society and all unlicensed mobs everywhere.

Plus, Magistrate Pierre knew she had to make an example of these criminals in order to look strong for the Europeans, with all the international intrigue going on. None of the enlightened European Kings, Emperors, Sultans, or Emirs would ever allow the Unified Society to use their lands as a base for the increasingly likely Norway operation if the Unified Society appeared too weak to deal with internal disobedience. She had reached her decision. Court was re-adjourned.

"Murder, chaos, mayhem, animal enslavement, and chemical weapons aside, such wanton disregard for two one five bravo and two one five bravo bravo is not something this court stomachs lightly." Pierre was indignant. "In a free society such as ours, rules are important. It is important that every citizen know that she or he is safe to protest for the rights of fish or against the tyranny of Intolerants and intolerance. Every person must know that law is law, and rules are rules. And that laws are rules and rules are laws for a very good reason, and perhaps if only these Intolerants had obeyed DoP regulation two one five bravo and two one five bravo bravo, and if only they had made their wishes known in sign or song form, this tragedy could have been averted. But what is done is done, and I too know what also must be done." The magistrate paused briefly, looking at Hackberry and Leonard sternly before continuing on.

"Hackberry and Leonard, you are hereby found to be in conflict with the General Will and the freedoms unique to it. So long as such a conflict exists in your wretched hearts, you may not remain free to disrupt our freedom. You must learn the true meaning of freedom. Having found you guilty of violating two one five bravo and two one five bravo bravo, and in accordance with our Fairness in Sentencing Guidelines, I hereby commit you to the custody of the Tolerance Corps for an indefinite period. In this time, you shall learn to accept the General Will; you shall be forced to become free."

Overseer Jolly: 34 January 0039

"Foreperson Jolly!" Samantha Jones-Jones yelped with joy as she barged through the gold-encrusted doors of the Overseer of Sacajawea's office. "I have most triumphant news, the–"

"*Overseer* Jolly! That is my new title now that Selection Day is behind us, *Agent* Jones-Jones. And I should hope they teach you door-knocking skills at the Department of Equally Treating Animals." She shook her head and smiled.

In the capitol building of Sacajawea, details of the triumphant court decision had arrived. The trial of Supervizier Anderchild's assassins had come to a just and honorable conclusion. The Intolerants who had so hatefully killed one of North America's shining political stars had been brought to justice.

"I apologize, my Overseer." Agent Jones-Jones paused with a smile. "The case of Anderchild's death has been closed! And you are now both without worries and without rival in Sacajawean politics."

"It is about time." Jolly clapped her hands with satisfaction. "You shall have your just reward for your service. A commission to the Department of Equally Treating Animals is not an easy one to attain. But one hand washes the other. Remember that, Sam."

The two celebrated with a handshake and a momentary embrace, settling down from the joy of attaining such respected positions, and having eliminated such a cunning rival as Anderchild through such devious and ingenious methods. After all, disguising an assassination as an unauthorized protest, whose only witnesses were railroaded into the Tolerance Corps for the deed, seemed, in hindsight, almost too easy.

"Jones-Jones, It may not be long before I call on your services again, this time as an official DETA agent. Some obstacles remain in our way if I am to make it all the way to President Tolerance's Cabinet in D.C."

Jolly's office phone rang from behind a stack of unpacked boxes. "Who would have this number already?" Jones-Jones said with surprise.

The phone rang for nearly a minute before Jolly directed Jones-Jones to pick it up, but say nothing.

"Your payment has not been received. Put Jolly on the phone, Sam."

"It's *him*." Jones-Jones handed the phone to Jolly. After a brief delay to compose her thoughts and prepare a line of phraseology to make her argument more convincing, Jolly opened her mouth, about to speak. The voice on the phone interrupted.

"Your payment has not been received, Madam Overseer."

"It's so wonderful to hear from you, my friend. About the compensation we established for your efforts, the issue that has developed from my end is one that requires my highest levels of focus and benevolence. You see, dear friend–"

"I see many things, friend. I see what might happen to an accepting and benevolent reputation should word spread about a convoluted assassination of a political rival, not to mention the wanton quasi-endorsement of the disruption of a perfectly planned and organized protest aimed at protecting the human rights of aquatic life through sign and song form."

"I'm sorry, but I really do not know what you are trying to imply, my most benevolent and caring friend. It is just that I cannot pay you until the hardware that was loaned to you is returned to me. There is the matter of several rockets not expended, yet hitherto not returned."

"Madam Overseer, you have yet to provide me with the additional gold bars or the diagrams and access codes we have agreed upon as part of my compensation."

"Surely, my friend, the payment we already gave you is enough. Do you really need more than the three kilograms of gold and the Armored Scout Vehicle with the hydrogen-solar fuel cell? What do you need access to abandoned bunkers for, anyway? You're an assassin, not a scrounger," Jolly said as she handwrote instructions to trace the line and source of the call. "Who could you possibly assassinate inside those Cold War relics?" she said as she laughed.

"I don't intend to assassinate *anybody*. You've been warned. Pay me. Three more kilos of gold and the plans."

"Well, about that, my friend, we need to be more accepting of each other." Jolly turned to Jones-Jones. "He hung up. Let's give him want he wants, Sam, but with some strings attached."

224

Coexistence: 35 January 0039

Arriving at a late hour, the shuttle bus carrying Bowperson, Leonard, Hackberry, and about 60 other Intolerants arrived at the Tolerance Corps training facility, which eerily resembled an abandoned slaughterhouse. The onboard sound system had been keeping the occupants of the shuttle entertained and awake with the dulcet tones of the famous musical group, the *Acceptance Crew*.

> *Rollin' with the West Nile*
> *Coz it's the best Nile*
> *Rollin' rollin'*
> *Rumblin' rumblin'*
> *Rollin' rollin'*
> *Rumblin' rumblin'*

The Department of Free Speech radio had its dial permanently fixed, in the name of fairness, to the Bureau of Public Radio frequency. The broadcast had just switched from the *Acceptance Crew's* music to a riveting account of the trials and tribulations of a street actor named Felipe trying to make a living on the mean streets of the Wichita Habitation Zone.

According to the narrator, Felipe had a mesmerizing stare and an impressive vocal command. Though his stare might have been up to subjective appraisal, his voice sounded rather monotone as he listlessly complained, "It's really hard to make a living in this day and age, when so much attention and funding are diverted to things such as the illegal emigration problem and the wars rather than impromptu street performance."

The narrator, a sympathetic-sounding woman, described his plight with a well-practiced whisper, as airy flamenco guitar music filled the strangely long gaps in her delivery and her overly precise enunciation of every syllable. She was sighing periodically in an attempt to evoke heartfelt sympathy implicitly felt in the listener – no matter how shackled that listener might be to his seat.

The driver, nearly moved to tears by the plight of Felipe, informed his passengers, "I know you may be tired, but sleep is not an option, gentlemen. You have a long day ahead of you." As he backed the shuttle into what resembled an abandoned slaughterhouse loading dock, he added, "You filthy pieces of human debris."

The rear doors of the shuttle opened, and two men wearing Smokey Bear hats boarded the bus. Both loudly chewed on aromatic mint gum. The man who boarded first sported an eye patch over his left eye. Hail crashed down from a black sky onto the shuttle roof.

The man with the eye patch began a welcome speech by pointing to himself and hollering, "Eyes here, you Intolerant vermin! You cretins have been brought to my little hole of happiness because you have rejected society. You have rejected the wisdom it has given you. You have failed to think freely and have failed to embrace freedom. But society has not given up on you. You will be reformed, rebuilt, and rehabilitated. Each one of you will become an awesome weapon, advancing the General Will of the society you so wantonly rejected. And if you do not pay your debts through deed and rehabilitation, we have other means of collecting what you owe us. As you Intolerants know, a lien has been placed on all of your bodily organs, and we will not hesitate to collect." The instructor motioned to the patch over his eye.

"How rude of me! I have not properly introduced myself. I am First Sergeant First Class Hamilton, and this is Staff Sergeant Cornwall. He is going to be the hammer that molds you into shape, and I am the anvil."

TCI Hamilton: 57 January 0039

Tolerance Corps Instructor Hamilton had one green eye and was awaiting a replacement for the other, which was rumored to also have been green. He wore a black patch with a red star emblazoned upon it where the other eye used to reside. Rumor also had it that he had lost his left eye when he had single-handedly taken out a machine gun nest during Operation Restore Karmic Balance. For his bravery and dedication, Hamilton had risen to the rank of First Sergeant First Class.

When it came to training new Tolerance Corps volunteers, Hamilton did it all, but his true love was teaching the history of the Unified Society and the later formation of its elite Tolerance Corps, which replaced the previous military structure of the country.

Hamilton made sure he personally handled this piece of training for all of the platoons he oversaw while the Staff Sergeants beneath him listened and learned.

Of course, this part of the process did not occur until Day of Training 22, after the recruits were properly conditioned with three weeks of sensory deprivation.

"Listen up, Intolerants! This is so important that I am only going to say it once. You must learn your history. On January one hundred and twenty-eighth of zero zero zero zero E.E., the Unified Society Constitution went into effect. That day is now known as Tolerance Day. But later that year, our enlightened electoral college chose President Tolerance as the first President of the Unified Society in a unanimous vote. President Tolerance undertook to reform our great society into what it is today, a beacon of freedom. In his first two terms, we saw the advent of the Department of Free Speech; the Department of Equally Treating Animals; the Department of Microsoft and Apple; the Department of Coexistence; the Department of Transportation, Industrial Production, Fairness, and Agriculture; the Department of the Internet; the Department of Protests; not to mention many many other great departments, sub-departments, bureaus, and social programs, including the Department of Everything Else. Through this system of enlightened public servants, our wise government eliminated the evils of greed and intolerance. We established the truly free society you Intolerants have turned your backs on. But we have not turned our collective back on you, which is why you are here.

"The first couple of decades of the new society were relatively calm and quiet. But, by zero zero twenty-two, it became apparent that many problems were taking their toll on our societal infrastructure. Massive population decentralization plagued our social infrastructure. The Department of the Internet, for example, could not maintain the infrastructure necessary to fulfill its constitutional obligation to provide every American with free broadband internet access by zero zero twenty. These problems became exacerbated when the former Canadian dominions received admission into the Unified Society after the successful but bloody Operation Restore Karmic Balance in zero zero twenty-three.

"Then, after winning a bloody war in Operation Restore Karmic Balance, the old military was tired and worn out, with fewer and fewer recruits to draw upon. Then the breaking point came. Starting around zero zero twenty-eight or twenty-nine, depending on who you ask, the Broadband Skirmishes put a great strain on the resources of the Department of Defense. The military's personpower, finances, and resources were still diminished after the roaring success of Operation Karmic Balance. The Broadband Skirmishes reached a climax in zero zero thirty, when the Dominions of Montana, Alberta, Colorado, Saskatchewan, Idaho, Wyoming, Manitoba, Nebraska, and the Dakotas seceded in order to form their own internet service provider, thus launching the Broadband Rebellions, which persist to this day.

"That's where we, the Tolerance Corps, which is the single damned most important part of the Department of Coexistence, come in." Hamilton paused, literally patting himself on the back with one hand while taking a drink from a plastic bottle labeled "Department of Transportation, Industrial Production, Fairness, and Agriculture."

Slightly rehydrated, the good Sergeant continued. "President Tolerance noticed two problems that could solve each other. The Department of Defense was low on strength and numbers, while the Department of Coexistence had over thirty million Intolerants, alcoholics, tobacco users, and drug-using vagrants incarcerated in coexistential facilities. In response to the broadband revolts, the Department of Defense was absorbed into the Department of Coexistence and renamed: The Tolerance Corps." Hamilton paused for dramatic effect, smacking his gum while he smiled and looking across the room full of his trainees.

"Those who had turned their backs on society were reconditioned to serve society in its time of need. By zero zero thirty-one, the newly founded Tolerance Corps had successfully stopped the Broadband Rebellions in their tracks, halting rebel expansion and retaking Colorado with the aid of the new F-50 iTolerator.

"The F-50 iTolerator was the first successful computer-piloted strike aircraft and was used with great efficiency alongside the B-75 Acceptor to level the rebel strongholds of Denver, Billings, and Cheyenne. Between our overwhelming air power and personpower, thanks to reconditioned Intolerants like you will soon be, the Unified Society remained unified and free and the rebel dominions were declared Uninhabited Zones. However, the problem of infrastructure continued to plague the Department of the Internet. This problem came to an end after the Broadband Affordability and Availability Act of zero zero thirty, affectionately known as the BAAA. Subparagraph two hundred and nineteen of the BAAA required all persons in the U.S. who lived in communities of less than two hundred thousand people to relocate to urban centers or designated U.S. farms, where they would have greater access to the services our government provides to them free of charge. Many good North Americans complied with the BAAA, but a few Intolerants refused to leave the countryside and they refused to fully join our great society. Many of you gathered in this room today are such people. I bet you sorry Intolerants did not even know that U.S. farms now have free broadband, wireless phone service, unlimited wireless data, and free access to the Bureau of Music Television channel. Too late now, but I bet that would have changed your minds some, huh, fellas?

"By the way, make sure you keep up with this because you will be tested on it later, in excruciatingly difficult multiple choice format. Part of your training will be on how to use a number two pencil. But that won't be until Day of Training Thirty-Four.

"Now, by late zero zero thirty-one, it became clear that illegal immigration was a problem. Millions streamed across our Mexican border to occupy what was land that had been cleared by the Broadband Affordability and Availability Act of zero zero thirty, and many reported to our designated urban centers. These people were putting a great strain on our societal resources. For instance, the Department of Housing could not build enough housing to keep up with the influx. Luckily the problem was solved after the Affordable Affordability Act of zero zero thirty-three. Subparagraph three hundred and seventeen of that act annexed Mexico. The Mexican government, however, did not see eye to eye with our wise legislature or our wise President Tolerance, then in his ninth term. So the Tolerance Corps was forced to peacefully bring about the annexation as such. Needless to say, Operation Peaceful Transition was a roaring success with a minimal amount of civilian casualties. I mean, the firebombing of Mexico City was a necessary evil, for it spared Corps the prohibitive costs of a ground invasion, and it allowed us to perfect the firebombing abilities of the Acceptor and the strafing abilities of the iTolerator. More importantly, it helped our new countrypeople accept the inevitability of our benevolent embrace.

"This is where you Intolerants come in. You are here to pay your debt to society. It is estimated that as many as forty frickin' million people refuse to leave the Uninhabited Zones in the countryside and report to U.S. farming operations or Designated Habitation Zones. Your job, Trainees, should you survive your training and become a member of our elite Tolerance Corps, will be to help assimilate these intolerant savages running around outside of the effective control of our benevolent society's General Will.

Many of you will see action in the ongoing Broadband Rebellions in Montana, Saskatchewan, Alberta, Manitoba, and Wyoming. Many will help to tame the wilds of New England and the Vermont Rebellion underway. Still others will be assigned to our sweep and clear operation in Zacatecas. The lucky ones will be assigned to the Department of Coexistence's Coast Guard to help stop the illegal emigration crisis with Cuba, Haiti, and the Russian Empire. I mean, those Intolerants just keep trying to spread their primitive views by leaving our Unified Society. But those of you who dedicate yourselves to the cause and prove yourselves to be the best of the best might even be allowed to join the International Expeditionary Peace Corps in conjunction with DETA, which is serving to enhance the freedom of our animal siblings across the globe."

Sergeant Hamilton paused, quite satisfied with himself, and sipped from his Department of Transportation, Industrial Production, Fairness, and Agriculture-brand bottled water. "Are there any questions?" he asked rhetorically as he smiled with his green gum parked between his front teeth.

Trainee Leonard, under the apparent impression he was still in high school, chimed in with a raised hand from the front row of the assembled trainees. "Why do you always say 'zero zero' in front of the years you are mentioning? We are only in the year thirty-nine of the enlightened era, what is the point of–"

"Listen, Intolerant. In all your *worldly* experience, running around cannibalizing animals, disrupting protests, and refusing to accept the General Will, I suppose you have not a clue as to the study of history and of the old times. Have you not heard of the Y Two K bug?"

"Yes, but–"

"And I suppose it has not entered your Intolerant brain that four digits is twice as compassionate as two digits? Did you learn nothing in government school? Did you take nothing away from the compulsory free education society has given you?"

"But why just stop at the four digits? What about the Y Ten K bug?"

"What about the Y Ten K bug?" Hamilton mimicked. "I tell you what, Trainee. You just earned yourself three more weeks of sensory deprivation. Consider yourself *recycled*."

At that, Sergeant Cornwall placed Trainee Leonard in handcuffs and walked him out the room.

After Sergeant Cornwall took Leonard away, Hamilton looked around the room and asked, "Are there any more stupid and incredibly ill-advised questions?"

Executive Order 12139:

By the authority vested in me as President by the Constitution and the laws of the Unified Society of America, the Freeness of Speech Act of 0015, the Curaçaoan Resolution of 0000, and the Kindness and Acceptance Act of 0016, it is hereby ordered as follows:

All government personnel are hereby required to monitor all inquiries as to why the Official U.S. Calendar uses four digits to denote the year when one, two, and later three would suffice. Any such inquiries shall be directed to the Department of Internal Security for further processing.

Very Sincerely,

President Tolerance
January 348, 0016 E.E.

Trainee Leonard's Isolation: 57-59 January 0039

Before George Armstrong Leonard had been volunteered for Tolerance Corps Camp, and before he had joined Asno's Intolerants, he had been a 16-year-old high school student and a Federal farmer on a U.S. farm colloquially referred to as the Central Iowa Corn Hole. Its official name was Corn Manufactory India-Omega-Hotel.

After some legal trouble, Leonard left the farm and turned his back on society. As he made his way west, Leonard was astonished by the vast expanses of empty land populated by millions of feral cows, pigs, and chickens. Finding food was not much of a problem once he became accustomed to eating meat. He had heard the old timers on the Corn Hole talk about eating meat and he had found the idea to be disgusting. But hunger does funny things to a person, and Leonard began to violate the inalienable human rights of feral chickens on a daily basis.

He had left the Designated Habitation Zone after being charged with the crime of First Degree Insensitivity. He was accused of making insensitive statements about a member of his high school's Committee for Public Safety who happened to be more demographically correct than he was. He was innocent of the charge of First Degree Insensitivity, but he knew the search warrant issued for his parents' quarters would reveal that he had been fashioning corn cobs into smoking pipes for the black market, using a kiln he had stolen from his high school to harden off the cobs and make them last twice as long as his competitors' pipes.

Before he could be arrested by the local Constabulary, he bolted, heading west. He had heard the Tolerance Corps patrols and sweeps were less frequent out west than they had been in the past, as the response to Broadband Rebellions had pacified much of the area. However, crossing the Missouri River into Nebraska would be no easy task.

There are places on the Missouri River where you can throw a rock across it. The portion on the Iowa-Nebraska border is not one of those places. After several days of traveling on foot, Leonard encountered this major obstacle and stood aghast at the breadth of the river. "Perhaps flood season wasn't the best time to be accused of insensitivity," Leonard grumbled to himself as uprooted trees hustled down the river like whales on an annual migration.

"Hands in the air, pilgrim!" a voice called out from behind a feral cow a few meters away from Leonard. "I got no problem killing filthy agents of the Department of Infrastructure."

After three days' travel on foot, hiding from Tolerance Corps patrols, Leonard found himself confronted by one of the *Intolerants* he had read so much about on FreePress.FreeSpeech.Gov. Intolerants had rejected society; they ate meat and only meat. They had no problem cannibalizing a person. Thankfully, the Tolerance Corps kept the U.S. farms and Designated Habitation Zones safe from the scum. They maintained four-meter-high fences around the Corn Hole to keep these animals out, and here he was, face-to-face with one.

"Killed two DoI agents this year, I guess. Keep your hands good and high," the Intolerant called out again. He was an older man who looked to be about 50. He wore tattered rags for clothes and a woven straw hat on his head.

"I'm not an agent. I'm just ..."

"Vaccinating the cows, huh?"

"I'm not DETA either."

"Good, I killed three Dee Eee Tee Ays down the river a bit last week."

Leonard began to visibly shake. "Did you eat them?"

"Hah, no. I didn't eat 'em. DETAs don't taste quite as good as catfish. If you ain't a DETA, and you ain't an engineer ...." He paused. "You ain't dressed right for the Tolerance Corps – no chemical warfare gear and no M8. Who are you?"

"My name is George Armstrong Leonard." He turned and faced his interrogator. "And I'm a student corn farmer."

"Come from the Corn Hole, you did? Keep your hands up, now."

"Yeah. On the run." Leonard found it quite easy to keep his hands up with an antique M1 Garand pointing in his face.

"What for? Murder?" Johnschild waved the weapon in his face.

"No, insensitivity. And, uh, paraphernalia."

"Well, I'll be. Me, too. The Department of Coexistence has had it out for me for years now. The name's Johnschild. Beetle Johnschild."

Leonard had plenty of time to recollect during his second stint in sensory deprivation. It was not wholly a sense-deprived experience; that's just what the TCIs called it to frighten the trainees and influence them to welcome whatever sensory input they did receive. Leonard's sensory input for these interminable weeks came from the walls of a two-meter by two-meter isolation room. His only outlook on the world was a one-meter-wide video screen that played coverage from the Department of Free Speech News Channel's coverage of the impending war with Norway and the refusal by Intolerants to report to the Designated Habitation Zones. The big news of the day was that the King of Scotland and the Sultan of Holland had given the Tolerance Corps permission to use air bases in their countries. From Scotland and Holland, Acceptors and iTolerators could provide the air power needed to pave way for the imminent amphibious invasion should the Norwegians not ratify the International Agreement on the Abuse of Animals. There were commercials, which interrupted the coverage. A few for the presidential primary recited the tried-and-true slogan. "Remember, a vote for Tolerance is a vote for tolerance!"

When not broadcasting the official news, the screen functioned as a Virtual Instructor Sergeant.

On this particular occasion, the screen in Leonard's chamber barked, "When addressing or responding to any Instructor, Officer, or Tolerance Corps personnel, the first words out of your mouth will be 'Sir or Ma'am, Trainee say your name reports as ordered.' This is your reporting statement. Practice it now!"

"Sir or Ma'am, Trainee Leonard reports as ordered."

"No, dummy, don't say 'say your name.' Say your name! For example–"

"I did say my name!" This was Leonard's second time through the program; he knew well enough not to say "say your name" by now.

"– if your name is Smith, say 'Sir or Ma'am, Trainee Smith reports as ordered.' You try now!"

"Sir or Ma'am, Trainee Leonard reports as ordered."

"No, dummy, don't say 'Sir or Ma'am.' Say 'Sir' or say 'Ma'am,' not both. You try now!"

"Sir, Trainee Leonard reports as ordered."

"Why did you say 'Sir'?"

"Sir, because you are a man."

"You don't know that!" The Virtual Instructor Sergeant flared his or her eyebrows and scowled beneath his or her mustache. "You prejudged me. And prejudgment is wrong. It is a sign of intolerance. It is precisely that type of intolerance we will breed out of you in order to make you a more effective killing machine."

"I'm sorry, Sir or Ma'am. But I don't want to be a killing machine."

"I know you are sorry! That is why you are here. You are a sorry Intolerant. You were sorry when we picked you up, you are sorry right now, and you will always be sorry until you stop being so damn insensitive. From now on, when you wish to apologize, you are to say 'Sir or Ma'am, I apologize.' You try now!"

"Sir, I apologize."

"You prejudged me again!"

"I'm sorry, Sir or Ma'am."

"I know you are sorry!"

"I apologize, Ma'am or Sir."

"Don't go inverting word order on me, Trainee say your name."

"Trainee Leonard," Trainee Leonard said with a grin.

"What?"

"Sir or Ma'am, you said 'say my name.'"

The Virtual Instructor Sergeant program had a tendency to freeze up while processing unusual turns in the conversation. At other times, the program had a tendency to completely disregard what the trainee had said. This pause was an example of each.

"Trainee say your name, when confronted with a prejudgment situation, do not presume to know the Sirness or Ma'amness of the Sir or Ma'am in question. When meeting a Sir or Ma'am for the first time, you will say 'Sir or Ma'am, Trainee say your name reports as ordered. Are you a Sir or a Ma'am, Sir or Ma'am?' You try now!"

"Trainee Leonard reports–" Leonard caught his rather egregious reporting statement error before the Virtual Instructor Sergeant could access his or her scream, yell, and point protocol. "Sir or Ma'am, Trainee Leonard reports as ordered. Are you a Sir or a Ma'am, Sir or Ma'am?"

"I am a Sir. Why else would I have this prototypical Tolerance Corps Instructor Sergeant mustache?"

"I did not want to prejudge, Sir."

"Good. Prejudgment is a soldier's worst enemy. Others may tell you it is dehydration, hunger, cold, heat, chemical weapons, or people shooting at you, but they are wrong. A soldier's worst enemy is an incorrect assumption."

Well, Leonard had made an incorrect assumption back on the banks of the Missouri when he figured Beetle Johnschild for a cannibal. "Well, Mister Leonard, I do believe you are one of us now."

"One of you?" Leonard asked, caught between Beetle Johnschild and a roaring river.

"Why, you're, uh ...." Johnschild paused, a twinkle in his eyes. "A Intolerant of course."

Leonard had never thought of himself in that way. Even as he had left his Designated Habitation Zone, he had viewed himself as a good citizen who was an unfortunate victim of circumstance. But there he was, running from a charge of First Degree Insensitivity, eating meat, and desperately trying to get into the mountains, where only Intolerants lived. "But, but."

"But what?"

"I can't be an Intolerant. I voted for Tolerance in Oliver Cromwell High School's last mock election."

"Aw hell, President Tolerance is a ... what do you call it ... a finger head!"

"What are you talking about?"

"You better come with me. We'll go see Fred Palmer. He'll know what to do with you. This way. Follow me, pilgrim." Beetle Johnschild gestured for Leonard to move along. "And Leonard, if you be an agent, or an engineer, or a spy of some kind, you'll be skinned. And skinned alive if you be Internal Security."

With Johnschild's gun still in Leonard's general direction, Leonard sensed he did not have much choice in the matter. "Fair enough, but I'm just on the run. Like you I guess."

"On the run? Hell! Do you see any running?"

"Well, no. I just thought this zone was pacified in the last revolts."

"Oh, it was, to the tune of about thirty thousand deaths. But only about three-quarters of those were civilians. Rest of 'em was your danged Tolerance Corps I reckon. Myself, I got pacified when you all went back to your damn Corn Holes and metropolises. Meanwhile, just you keep an eye out for river patrols, pilgrim."

Johnschild led Leonard, gun near back, about five kilometers down the riverbank and they saw no patrols. As they walked, Johnschild explained that the U.S. Department of Infrastructure still maintained the river for barge traffic, since all the bridges over the river had been repeatedly blown apart. It was Johnschild and his brethren who had repeatedly blown them. They were the rear guard of the insurrection as it fled westward.

Because of the D.C. Government's inability to maintain a bridge across the Missouri, the river was used for shipping supplies up from Bush-Obamaha to the first dam on the river at Gavin's Point in the former Dominion of South Dakota. It was at Gavin's Point that war supplies were offloaded to be sent westward to aid in the ongoing conflict as the Unified Society was doing its best to gather all the wayward souls living outside the Designated Habitation Zones and farms. However, the river could only be used by barges for half of the year because the river became too shallow during the winter months. This time of year marked the beginning of the spring rise, and in a few weeks, barges would be headed northwest to resupply the soldiers fighting to pacify the not-east. It was no longer called the west because the rebels could benefit from the impermissible bias inherent in the terms west, western, or occidental. After all, it was the D.C. Government, and not the rebels, that stood for the freedoms unique unto the General Will of the western world. There was to be no geographical west to the west of D.C.

As the two passed a sharp bend in the river, Johnschild continued, "It's our job to make sure as few of those barges make it up to Gavin's Point as possible." Johnschild gestured to a wrecked barge hulk sticking halfway out of the river. "We take them out starting around the middle of Missouri, in between the Good Louis and Kansas City Habitation Zones. But the Tolerance Corps makes it too hot down there for us to get too many. So this right here is where we earn our tobacco. By the way, still got any of them pipes?"

"Sorry, no. I think the constables took all of them by now. How do you sink all of these barges?"

"Damn shame about the pipes, but that question is a trade secret, pilgrim. But I can tell you, without a tugboat driver, a tugboat tends to have trouble getting around these bends." Johnschild tapped his rifle. "Trick is to get the driver before the escort boats can open up on you with their M2 fifty-cals. They put those old tank guns on their escort boats and just let loose. But the real kicker is when they mount some old seventy-five millimeter anti-aircraft guns on the tugs themselves and blast the hell out of anything that moves, and everything that doesn't."

"What about their air power? How do you get around that?"

"Oh, well, those iTolerator planes are okay at killing anything with a radar or heat signature. But they need to be told what to do, and half of the time, their missiles blow up in the trees above us. And the other half, by time they get orders to react to us, we are already gone. See, DETA makes sure they just don't blow up anything with a heat signature, being so many animals around.

That's thanks to their vaccination program against the Hoof Pox. They have to wait until fired upon to return fire so they don't risk unnecessary animal casualties. Now when you join us, you'll probably be operating one of our mortar batteries with Shotgun Tammi."

"Whoah whoah whoah, this is your fight, not mine. I'm just headed not-east."

"Out west? So you want to be in on the *real* fighting then!" Beetle slapped him on the back. "That's the spirit, boy!"

A few minutes later, Beetle led Leonard to a place on the bluffs overlooking the river. Leonard stopped walking when he noticed large piles of driftwood just about everywhere around him. Was this a defensive perimeter? A site for large ritualistic cannibal bonfires?

Beetle nudged him in the back and guided him down an escarpment to the face of a limestone bluff. By now, the sun had nearly set, and flocks of birds were busy being insensitive to the insects and fish they were eating. When the two reached the base of the bluff, Johnschild called out, "All right, fellas, lookie what I found! Let me in."

At that, a rope ladder dropped from a hidden cave entrance in the rock face. "You climb first, pilgrim."

Leonard climbed the rope about 10 meters up into the cave. Upon reaching the top rung, he was grabbed by four hands and slammed against a wall. By the time his eyes adjusted to the dimness, and by the time Beetle had reached the top, Leonard found a shotgun pointed in his face.

"Easy now," Beetle said.

"For fuck's sake, Beetle. You bring one of them right here?" said the red-haired man who had slammed and held Leonard against the wall.

"You tryin' to get us killed?" said the woman holding the shotgun to Leonard's face. The woman appeared to be in her fifties. So Leonard surmised she was about 35 or so, given the conditions these people were living in.

"This one's all right. Run off from the Corn Hole he did. Got tired of feeding all the East Coast habitation zones I reckon. This here is Leonard."

Leonard looked at the woman. "Shotgun Tammi, I presume?"

"Used to be Corn Canning Tammi, before I got promoted," the woman grinned, only now lowering her weapon.

"Listen, Tammi and Hackberry. I need to talk to the Congressman," Beetle said.

"Fred's in back with Asno. Planning something big," Hackberry said.

"Wait wait wait, you've got a Congressperson held hostage here?" Leonard was shocked.

"Pilgrim, shut your yap. Fred was a Congressman. In the olden days he were anyway. He's been with the insurrection for near twenty years. Been leading this outpost until the western generals sent over their Colonel Asno."

"You have to be joking – an Intolerant who is a Congressperson? That is impossible."

Tammi gestured toward the main body of the cave. "Go on and wait there, you two. You can talk to Fred at group council tonight. And Beetle, keep an eye on this one. Seems a bit ... over-civilized."

Beetle led Leonard deeper into the cave into a large chamber. Shotgun Tammi and Hackberry followed behind them after raising the ladder. Oil lanterns lit the smoky chamber as thin, wraith-like people milled around in anticipation. They numbered about thirty or so according to Leonard's best guess. All of them ceased their conversations as Leonard walked in. The majority of them eyeballed Leonard.

The chamber was set up for a meeting. At one end sat five stumps. These stumps sat in front of six rows of benches that were arranged in a semicircle, hewn from the sycamores that lined the river. The wraith-like figures had been standing around a rotisserie, on which they roasted a feral pig. An act of barbarism had never smelled so good to Leonard before.

"Hey fillies and fellas, this is Leonard. Just escaped from the Corn Hole," Beetle announced. "I found him chasing chickens upriver and figured we could use a hand this season."

Just at that moment, five men entered the chamber from a deeper part of the cavern. "An extra hand is always useful, Beetle. Everyone have a seat," one of the new arrivals declared.

At that, everyone sat on the benches in the room. Leonard could not help but notice that there were quite a few more benches than they needed and wondered about the survival rate for this group of Intolerants going up against the Tolerance Corps. The new arrivals from the back of the cave sat on the stumps at the forefront of the chamber.

The man who had just spoken sat on the stump just to the left of the middle from Leonard's vantage point. He appeared to be in his mid-50s and wore a rather torn and tattered olive uniform for the occasion. To that man's left and in the center of the group sat an elderly man, carrying a cane, smoking a corncob pipe, wearing an old-fashioned suit that had nearly been shredded with age. It looked too big for the man. He looked to be in his 90s. Beetle nudged Leonard. "One of your customers, no doubt. Man with the corn pipe, that's Fred."

The man in the green uniform began, "Thank you all for coming. I'm glad to see you all. As you know, this is the beginning of the season. Barge hunting season." A few of the people in the room chuckled briefly.

"The situation is this. We are low on munitions, even lower on tobacco, and our numbers are half of what they were two years ago. The situation is excellent!" The assembled group gave a cheer. "As per usual, we are poised to once again take a heavy toll on shipping." The group gave another roar of approval.

"I see a new face or two here, and that is excellent indeed. For those who do not know me, my name is Colonel Asno. Welcome to Operation Drake. But I am afraid the new faces have arrived too late. For our mission is now largely moot."

The audience shifted, murmuring to one another. "What's moot?" Beetle asked Hackberry.

"Meaningless," he responded.

Asno continued, "For though we are poised to do our duty, our mission is now over. We have been too successful. Reports from the north confirm that the government has constructed a new railroad to Gavin's Point and will bypass this stretch of river when they supply their forces. In addition, they have increased the mobilization of the Tolerance Corps. At present, our estimate is that there is an army of about forty-five thousand assembled at Gavin's Point. This army will likely fan out along the river both up and downstream, consolidating our region under their control before lunging toward Montana. Another five to ten thousand are assembled in the Des Moines DHZ. That leaves us in a tight spot.

"I believe the Tolerance Corps will fan out across the countryside to secure more and more supply routes so they can fully subjugate the Mountain West. It is only a matter of time before they arrive here in force."

At this point, Leonard looked around the room, noticing the lack of expression on everyone's faces, especially Congressperson Palmer. Palmer looked – no, in fact, he was – asleep.

"With this new northern railroad, destroying enemy shipping on this stretch of the river will no longer hurt the enemy as gravely as it used to. I have decided to abandon this outpost. I am going west on an urgent errand. Those who want to stay can stay and fight on. But know this: They will only send boats and barges up this river to lure you out into the open. The barges will likely be decoys filled with gravel and you will be their target. Now, I am not ordering any of you to leave Operation Drake and come with me. The passage across the plains will be very risky. There is not much cover, and if a government patrol spots us, we will be an easy target for enemy aircraft. But those of you who want to fight on in the west can join me."

The cave was deathly quiet until Hackberry spoke up. "I'll go west with you. The minions of Tolerance can't reach us once we are in the mountains."

At that Fred Palmer awoke, mumbling at first. "Tolerance, he a nothing nowhere make-believe. Tolerance, ahem, President

Tolerance is just a myth. Ain't nothing real about him." He coughed. "President Tolerance, ain't nothing but a can opener robot hiding in some damned bunker. Ain't been seen in near fifty years. Ain't been seen ever!"

Lighting, then puffing, on his corncob pipe, Palmer continued. "Tolerance is just one of them ghost stories tellin' to children at night. No, no. Tolerance just one of them fancy computers hiding underground. That's right."

Leonard could not believe his ears. This man, Palmer, must be delusional.

"He make-believe, no good, no nothing. Make-believe. Like the Easter Bunny and pickup trucks. Pickups ain't no good neither. Just like Cadillac cars, just a bunch of ghost stories for tellin' children. Had to change the whole dag gum calendar for on account of old fat Tolerance. Four digits dag gum my God!"

One of the assembled people spoke up. "Congressman, are you heading west, or staying to fight on?"

Another said, "We're with *you*, Fred." The sentiment was shared and expressed by almost everyone in the room through a series of nods.

Fred Palmer looked around. "Me? I been fightin' this war near sixty years and let me tell you why." He paused to make eye contact with a few of the people in the room. "The U S of A been under attack for reckon hundred fifty years. Out there, and down south ...." Fred paused and pointed to the east. "There been an enemy, diabolical and ruthless, but not toothless. That's right. I fight the good fight against those men down south." He pointed to the east again. "They whittle away on our nation's self-esteem. And our topography!" Fred Palmer looked around the chamber.

"I'm talking every year I go down to the river, ever since I was a boy. They been eating away at our topography. Old Fred sees it. And he knows you sees it. Every year, down on the river. What do you see?"

Palmer looked around, expecting a response.

The man on the leftmost stump suggested, "Water?"

"Nope," Fred said.

Others in the room followed with guesses.

"Gravel?"

At this point, Leonard kept from rolling his eyes and noted that Asno seemed to be stifling some mild amusement. Or was it disdain?

"It's what we pull out the water." Fred hinted.

"Fish!"

"Geese?"

"Ducks!"

"Sticks!" Shotgun Tammi yelled from the back of the room.

Fred shouted. "Yes, Ma'am! Not water. Not ducks. Not geese. Not aeroplanes. I'm talking sticks. That's right. Sticks. Every damn year, I look down there and there are sticks floating right on down the river. American sticks. Sticks getting stolen from us."

Many in the group reflexively agreed.

"See, all the rivers 'round here, they all flow downstream. Downhill. Down to the south. They has a plan to steal all of our sticks! As you people know, the great waterways of the heartland – the Missouri, the Minnesota, the Ohio, the Illinois, and the Arkansas – all flow into the Mississippi. The Mississippi then flows south. Where does it flow? Into the Gulf of *Mexico*."

"You're right, Fred!" Tammi shouted.

"Flood season is when they strike in earnest," Palmer continued. "I have seen entire forests floating down the river some seasons. Just one less forest for Americans to enjoy. Just one more forest stolen by Mexican secret agents. Or I guess you could say secret Mexican agents. Or spies. Yep, spies. Definitely spies. Agents if you will.

"So I am gonna stay on. I am gonna fight those damn Mexican spies 'til I am cold and dead." Palmer rose to his feet, temporarily discarding his cane, and shook his right fist. "We are going to rally our forces. This flood season, we will not lose one more stick!"

After the meeting, the gathered crowd discussed their options with each other. Leonard asked Asno if he could accompany him out west. Asno perceived Leonard too incompetent to be a spy and agreed to allow him to go along with him. In the end, only Johnschild, Hackberry, and Leonard would accompany Asno out west. The rest would remain behind to combat stick thievery.

"I know you three want to go west, but before we go, I need to talk to Fred in private," Asno said. Johnschild, Leonard, and Hackberry remained on the riverbank as Asno returned to the cave to speak with Fred Palmer.

"Why he wants to talk to that crazy old man is beyond me," Leonard said.

"He might be old, but he's not crazy," Hackberry said as he wedged a wad of chewing tobacco in his mouth. "He was a Congressman for Missouri under the old Constitution. And he ran on a platform of protecting our topography."

"Sure enough," Johnschild added. "He tried to pass a law that woulda built a dam just south of Memphis to keep all of our sticks safe."

"The law got stopped when the Tennessee contingent in Congress argued that the dam should be built north of Memphis so as to not flood that city. Others called him a racist and a jingoist, claiming that hoarding all of our sticks would hurt our image in the global community," said Hackberry. "He's told us this story a hundred times."

"Old Fred didn't see eye to eye with the rest of Congress about Memphis or the sticks and resigned in anger when they wouldn't build his damn dam. That was in the last years of the old Congress, I believe."

"And you two believe all that? And all this stuff about President Tolerance being make-believe, like the Easter Bunny and pickup trucks?" Leonard was incredulous.

"Well, to be fair, that story is a new one on me." Hackberry spat.

"And I ain't never seen no Easter Bunny," Johnschild added.

Over the following months, Asno's party of four crossed the Great Plains on horseback into the Great Not-East.

Trainee Leonard's Interview: 60 January 0039

Halfway through another session with the Virtual Instructor Sergeant in Leonard's sensory deprivation chamber, the image of the Virtual Instructor Sergeant blacked out, and in its place appeared the image of a stern-looking woman in a civilian suit. She had raven hair and a lazy eye. "Turn away from the sound of my voice!"

Leonard complied immediately, turning and facing a blank wall with his back to the lazy-eyed image. "George Armstrong Leonard, do you recognize my voice?"

"Sir or Ma'am, Trainee Leonard reports as ordered. Uh, no. Why would I, Sir or Ma'am?"

"Good. My name is Agent Crowe, Internal Security. Now why did you ask that question?"

"Because I did not know why I should have recognized your voice."

"Not *that* question, Leonard. Why did you ask a forbidden question?"

"Sir or Ma'am?"

"The forbidden question about the four digits."

"About the calendar? I was just curious, I didn't–"

"Curious? *Curious*?! You didn't what?"

"I didn't think it was a big deal."

"You did not think asking a forbidden question was a big deal?"

"Well, I did not know it was forbidden."

"That's because it is a *forbidden* question." Crowe paused and sneered. "You know, that is the problem with you Intolerants. You're always asking questions, as if questioning things were not a big deal. You do not appreciate the externalities incumbent upon curiosity. Curiosity causes problems, it creates dissatisfaction, and it promotes the questioning of core values that we as a society have declared to be inherently good. I assure you, my intolerant Intolerant, this *is* a big deal," Agent Crowe hissed. "So tell me. Why did you ask that question?"

"I told you. I don't know."

"Listen, Leonard. We can do this the easy way. I am a reasonable womanperson. And I would like to think you are a reasonable Intolerant. You are reasonable, aren't you?"

"Yes, Ma'am."

"Good. Now let's you just tell me why you asked a forbidden question, and you can go home. No more Tolerance Corps Camp. No more reparations to society. In addition to your assassination of Anderchild and his prized aide, we also know all about your insensitive statements and your clandestine pipe making. The Iowa Constabulary took genetic samples from your quarters back in Corn Manufactory India-Omega-Hotel, and we have linked your DNA to over fifty pipes confiscated across the Society. We can make that bit of legal trouble go away as well. The truth of the matter is that you are who we say you are. And our opinion can be very favorable. So just tell me, why did you ask that question?"

"I'll get to go … free?"

"No, you get to go *home*."

The idea of getting out of his cell, even if it meant a one-way trip back to the Corn Hole, strongly resonated with Leonard. After a brief contemplative pause, he decided to volunteer the information he thought Agent Crowe might be after. "Well, Ma'am. This crazy old man, went by the name of Fred and claimed to be a Congressperson. Fred Palmer, he mentioned once that–"

"Palmer?!!!! The former *Congressperson*???" Crowe's voice grew tense as she hissed the word.

"Yes, Sir or Ma'am. Or so he said. I mean, I don't know if I believe him myself, Sir or Ma'am. But now that I'm telling you about it, can I go home?"

"Leonard, for your crimes against society, you were sentenced to rehabilitation. For murder, pipe making, animal enslavement, strangely trying to gas yourself and your comrades to death, and disrupting an official protest, you were to receive rehabilitation. Leonard, we can rehabilitate people for just about anything. But for asking a forbidden question, there is no rehabilitation. There is only immolation."

At the close of Agent Crowe's words, a steel seal slid over the video screen in Leonard's chamber, and Leonard detected the strong scent of flammable gas before blacking out.

The Overseership of Sacajawea: 48 January 0038

"Foreperson Jolly, let's be frank. We both know that the Overseership of the dominion is opening up with the tragic drowning of Overseer Benoit. I know he was a dear friend to us both–"

"He did not drown, Anderchild," Jolly interrupted. "The passenger boat he was traveling in ran aground after the boat pilot was shot in the head. Benoit was captured and scalped by Intolerants on the banks of the Missouri River in Iowa."

"People behaving that way with knives. It makes me sick," Anderchild said with a nod and a look of concern.

"They are not people, my Supervizier. They are Intolerants. Benoit's chickens came home to roost. He was too lenient on them here in Sacajawea. He allowed repeated incursions from the Idaho border without sufficient mobilization or retaliation. It is somewhat ironic he was murdered by the same sort of savage while touring the country on his campaign to be appointed Secretary of the Tolerance Corps."

Supervizier Anderchild was taken slightly aback by Jolly's frankness. When he had suggested being frank, he had not meant to be taken so literally. "Can I offer you some foie gras?" Anderchild rose from his seat and walked toward a service cart stocked with various delicacies and beverages.

"No, my Supervizier. I am a little surprised you allow trafficking in a barbarous commodity such as force-fed goose liver to go on in this habitation zone."

"Oh, I do not allow it," Anderchild continued contemplatively while preparing a snack. "All of my people are on a strict diet here in Seattle. I find that permitting my people a mild degree of hunger leads to increased productivity in our manufactories. Have you seen the latest statistics? Production is up five percent across this DHZ this quarter. We've seen a twenty-five percent increase in hydroponic kale alone. And don't even get me started on the output in our aircraft and munitions factories. I believe that I ... we ... have built something really special here. Hand me a napkin, please." Anderchild paused, munching on a goose-livered cracker.

As Jolly gave him a napkin, Anderchild continued to speak while continuing to chew. "This is why I am seeking appointment, or, umm, Democratic Selection as Overseer. Hmmm. This is quite good." He smacked his lips. "If so appointed, I would of course recommend you to replace me here, as Supervizier. You have done a wonderful job in your present capacity, running ... handling ... the things that you are in charge of running and handling so well."

"Thank you, Honorable Anderchild. I appreciate greatly your benevolence." Jolly smiled.

"Think nothing of it. I see great things in store us. In fact, it is my understanding that if we play our cards right, we can convince the Interim Secretary of the Tolerance Corps to order another one thousand iTolerator strike aircraft that we would build locally."

"That would be wonderful, my Supervizier," Jolly said.

"This would of course require drumming up yet another war. But I think it can be accomplished with a few skillfully organized protests. I understand you have some expertise in this area?"

"I do, my Supervizier. I would be grateful for the opportunity."

"Excellent! I am prepared to fund this operation to the tune of seven hundred million credits."

"I will need about half of that in gold, my Supervizier."

"Ten kilograms of gold it is."

"One question, my Supervizier. What are we protesting?"

"I don't really care, Jolly. Just make something up. Give me an international controversy."

"Consider it done, Sir."

Book II: Preparing for a Just War

Trainee Bowperson: 73 January 0039

It was Day of Training 39 for Trainee Bowperson and his fellow trainees of Alfa Platoon. About two weeks now separated them from their stint in sensory deprivation booths – two weeks full of habituation and acculturation in the ways of Tolerance Corps Camp and barracks life.

The first few days, the trainees barely knew each other's names. In fact, Bowperson could hardly tell his fellow trainees apart. They all wore the same clothes – training shorts and t-shirts from lights out to morning training, then camouflage battle uniforms during the day. They all had their hair cut the exact same way at the exact same time. A few of the men wore glasses, which helped distinguish them. But otherwise, Alfa Platoon was a homogenized sea of shaved heads, uniforms, and body odor.

But after a few days, the men of Alfa Platoon had their names sewn on their uniforms. This helped Bowperson put names – real names – to faces. No longer was his bunkmate "hard-headed red-haired guy who runs like a deer during physical training." He was now Trainee Hackberry. Names now replaced memory devices for the rest of the men of Alfa Platoon as well.

Now that he was weeks into his rehabilitation and training with the Tolerance Corps, physical training was the most important semblance of normal life for Bowperson. He thoroughly enjoyed the long-distance runs out in the fresh morning air of springtime – even if he was basically running in a circle on a large concrete drill pad, surrounded by Fort Freeperson on three sides and by a razor-wired fence on the other.

Every morning and every time he ran past the fenced side of the drill pad, Bowperson grew more and more intrigued by a mystery – a phantom of sorts – just on the other side of the fence line. There, Bowperson could see a man – a very large man covered completely in purple, including his face. This purple man occasionally yelled out from the tallgrass and the trees standing on the other side of the fence, but Bowperson could not quite understand what the man yelled.

For the morning run of Day of Training 39, Bowperson had a plan to find out more. As the men of Alfa Platoon ran at their own paces, but as fast as they could handle, they would all pass the fence line a number of times depending on the length of the day's run. Bowperson would just slow down and have a closer look on one of his passes.

As it turned out, Day of Training 39 was a perfect day for a run. After Alfa Platoon completed their strength exercises at the center of the drill pad, Sergeant Cornwall barked out, "Get your asses to running. Six K today!"

Knowing the length of the running track on the drill pad, Bowperson knew a six-kilometer run meant he would be passing the fence at least 12 times. He'd have plenty of opportunity for a closer look.

Each time Bowperson ran along the fence line, he slowed his pace slightly and scanned the grass and trees beyond the fence for anything large and purple. The first six passes were uneventful. But on the seventh pass, things got interesting.

"There he is," Bowperson whispered to himself as he ran. He spotted the purple man standing in the tall grass just a couple of meters on the other side of the fence. As Bowperson ran past the purple figure, he slowed his pace slightly and turned his head to get a closer look.

"Yeah!" the purple man yelled.

Sergeant Cornwall's voice boomed from the center of the pad. "Keep running, Trainees! Whatever you think you see out there, you do not see! Do not make me smoke your spleens! Do I make myself clear, Alfa Platoon?"

"Hooyah, Sergeant!" Bowperson echoed along with most of the men of Alfa Platoon. He turned his gaze back to his front and increased his pace.

Trainee Hackberry: 79 January 0039

On Day of Training 45, just three weeks after their stint in sensory deprivation and the disappearance of his friend George Armstrong Leonard, Trainee Hackberry was falling into a morning routine along with Trainee Bowperson and their fellow trainees in Alfa Platoon.

Pushups. Squat thrusts. Sit-ups. Then running.

During this morning's run, just as on the last few mornings, Hackberry thought he caught a glimpse of a man at the fence that surrounded Fort Freeperson. The man was very purple and very large. He yelled "Yeah!" and pointed at Hackberry. After physical training, the platoon went on a forced march, or a hump, as it was known among the training staff.

"This is training for what it will be like dealing with intolerance," Sergeant Hamilton bellowed as the 60 Intolerants marched up and down the hills of Not-East Virginia. "Intolerance knows no sleep. It knows no hunger. You will have to master these deprivations if you wish to survive my training."

Staff Sergeant Cornwall, Hamilton's right-hand man and the Sergeant directly in charge Alfa Platoon, loudly chomped on his gum as he picked up where Hamilton had left off. Cornwall barked, "Your senses will deceive you. They will tell you that you are tired, hungry, weak, or thirsty. This sensation is just wickedness leaving your hearts. You must be accepting of pain if you want to be an instrument of war – an instrument of destruction – feared by intolerance."

The Intolerants of Alfa Platoon were, for the most part, glad to be out of their sensory deprivation boxes. Their first weeks had been spent practicing their reporting statements, getting their repugnantly long hair cut, doing calisthenics in their confinement, and learning their chain of command:

Staff Sergeant Cornwall:
Alfa Platoon Instructor Sergeant
First Sergeant First Class Hamilton:
Echo Company Instructor Sergeant
Supervisor
Lieutenant Hazard:
Echo Company Executive Officer
Major Manos:
Echo Company Commander
Colonel King:
96th Battalion Commander
Major General Moore:
7th Brigade Commander
Lieutenant General Less:
29th Re-education Division Commander
General Frieden:
General of the Tolerance Corps
Honorable John E. Columbine:
Secretary of the Tolerance Corps
Honorable Dr. Mary G. Wallace:
Secretary of Coexistence
Director Steel:
Director of Internal Security
President Tolerance:
President of the Unified Society of
America

As the troops gathered in the dayroom in their barracks on Day of Training 45, they practiced reciting their chain of command. Trainee Gumabay had forgotten Secretary Columbine in his recitation of his chain of command. On the same day, Trainee Newton had skipped Colonel King in his recitation of the chain of command. As punishment, after that day's lecture on urban warfare, Staff Sergeant Cornwall ordered Trainees Gumabay and Newton to stand in opposite corners of the barracks screaming "King" and "Columbine" in their respective corners.

While Gumabay and Newton were screaming in their corners of the dayroom, Lieutenant Hazard arrived for his bi-daily inspection to make sure Alfa Platoon's beds were made well enough and their socks were folded in sufficiently even thirds to stamp out intolerance at home, abroad, and in their wretched, hateful hearts. Lieutenant Hazard rather enjoyed the sound of "King" and "Columbine" being screamed in the barracks during his inspection and ordered that his name be added to the screaming.

That night, Alfa Platoon dined upon deep-fried cabbage and boiled potatoes, with margarined kale greens for dessert.

At the end of the day, when the lights were cut off and the members of Alfa Platoon were in their bunks, Hackberry asked Trainee Overture, who was lying on the next bunk over, "Did you see a purple man at the fence line during the run?"

"Quiet, man," Overture responded rather hoarsely.

Trainee Hackberry: 81 January 0039

During Day of Training 47's morning dose of physical training, Hackberry was fairly certain that he saw the man at the fence line. Wearing a huge grin on his face, he was very large and very purple. The man yelled, "Yeah Yeah Yeah!" while pointing at Hackberry.

Three times he yelled. Three times.

That day, they enjoyed a 23-kilometer hump.

In the afternoon, after a lunch of fried cabbage and boiled potatoes, Alfa Platoon began training on their M8s. It was to be a joint training session between Alfa Platoon and Bravo platoon, their all-female counterparts within Echo Company.

The trainees were assembled at the firing range, each in their own stalls, facing downrange at a target depicting a man with a rather repugnant-looking beard.

"This is the M8 Assault Rifle." Sergeant Hamilton stood downrange holding the rifle exactly 10 centimeters from his chest. "This, Intolerants, will be your weapon. This, Intolerants, will be your salvation. It is a versatile weapon that fires a five-point-five-six millimeter round that flies like a rocket and cuts through bad guys like a hot knife through bean curd. It takes several important attachments, including the M320 grenade launcher for exploding bad guys and the M1914 bayonet for skewering bad guys.

"Now, some of you are the Intolerants of the less offensive variety, such as those of you trainees who are here because you used the imperial system of measurement in casual conversation as opposed to the metric system. You likely have never fired a weapon before. So pay attention.

"And for those of you who have fired a weapon, be certain we are watching you, and I've got my eye on your eyes." Hamilton gestured to his eye patch.

Hamilton marched up-range, his gum smacking all the way until he was behind the trainees. "Now, remember, it is kill or be killed. You will have ten seconds. Just ten seconds to empty your thirty bullets into the face of that filthy no-shaving Intolerant on your targets. And for anyone who fails to qualify on this weapon, I've really got my eye on your eyes."

"And your spleens," Sergeants Olmeid and Cornwall added to their respective platoons.

That night, at the end of the day, when the lights were cut off and the members of Alfa Platoon were in their bunks, Hackberry asked Trainee Bowperson on the bunk above him, "Reggie, during the run this morning, did you see that guy at the fence line hollering 'Yeah Yeah Yeah'?"

"Yeah, Hackberry," Bowperson responded. "But we ain't supposed to see that purple fella."

Trainee Hackberry: 84 January 0039

During morning training on Day of Training 50, Hackberry knew he saw a huge purplish man standing on the fence line during the morning run. He yelled, "Yeah! Yeah! Yeah! Yeah!"

Hackberry turned his head back to Trainee Newton, who was running behind him. "You don't see that guy?"

"Quit yapping in the run!" Sergeant Cornwall ordered from the center of the running track as he sipped on artisan organic fair-trade no-kill instant coffee.

Day 50 was dedicated to reviews of marching, formation, dress, and interval. The trainees must be prepared for any situation, including any contingency in which they may be deployed to deal with emergency situations, especially emergency marches in formation.

"Your left. Your left. Your left, right, left," Sergeant Cornwall called out.

"You must maintain your timing, your step, your interval. We are marching at the cadence of quick time." Sergeant Cornwall ceased his cadence long enough to spit out his gum and berate Trainee Overture. "Why are you kicking your legs so fracking high? What are you? A fracking Russian? This is a free country. We do not goose step! We do not abide that form of mind torture!"

By Day of Training 50, the trainees were becoming more and more accepting of orders and the General Will. They were more able to act as one unit, and not as a mob of uncoordinated Intolerants pulled off of the streets and uninhabited zones of a great nation.

Doc Newton: 88 January 0039

Trainee "Doc" Newton did not understand why Hackberry persisted in seeing the masked man dressed in purple at the fence line every morning. The pressure was clearly getting to Hackberry.

In civilian life, Doc Newton had been a medical intern in the Megalopolis DHZ, just south of Boston. Despite his belief that he filled out his annual renewal paperwork, Newton had failed to renew his medical license with the Department of Everything Else. He failed to fully complete page 79 of the hobbies section. He was therefore convicted under the Doctor Protection Act of 0019 for practicing medicine without a license, so they sent him to the Tolerance Corps.

With his advanced medical knowledge and his experience at the Edward Kennedy Memorial Organ Extraction Center when he was interning, Newton knew it was very dangerous for Hackberry to be seeing a rather large purple man wearing something like a purple jumpsuit and what looked to be a purple smiling mask yelling "yeah" a varying number of times every morning. Such hallucinations were signs of insanity. If declared insane, a trainee would be expelled from Tolerance Corps training, and the Government would collect on the lien placed on his organs, a process known as *harvesting*. Although Newton had never heard Hackberry describe the purple man in detail, he did not have to hear the man described to know what he looked like. After all, Newton saw the purple man every morning. The purple man yelled "yeah" at them, and nothing else. The amount of times the purple man said "yeah" varied, and Newton was beginning to suspect that the yeah-ing was some sort of numbers code. This was precisely why Newton refused to admit to seeing, much less hearing, the purple man. After all, anyone who sees such a hallucination is likely insane, but anyone who listens to a hallucination dispels all doubt.

There was a former doctor just like Newton in every training platoon. On Day of Training 54, Newton overheard a few of Lieutenant Hazard's choice remarks to Sergeant Cornwall on the doctor situation in the Tolerance Corps out on the drill pad during Alfa Platoon's morning run.

Hazard remarked, "It is damn good fortune that with such a physicians shortage in the Corps that we are getting exactly one doctor per platoon."

"It's almost too good to be an accident, Sir," Cornwall responded.

"I don't know if you are implying anything, Sergeant, or what you would be implying if you were implying something, but I am certainly not going to imply that anything you would have implied, that is if you had implied anything, would be false," Lieutenant Hazard said.

"Certainly not, Sir."

"No, Sergeant Cornwall, without saying too much, I would just imply instead that we are damned fortunate to have the paper pushers on our side."

"Yes, Sir," Cornwall smiled.

"Damned fortunate, indeed, to have those paper pushers on our side, making sure we get everything we need."

"Yes, Sir, Lieutenant."

"In fact, you could say we are damned lucky that those paper pushers just keep on sending us doctors by purposely losing portions of their license renewal applications, if you get my meaning." Hazard winked.

Trainee Bowperson: 97 January 0039

As Alfa Platoon ran past the purplish man at the fence line during their morning run on Day of Training 63, Reginald Bowperson did not see him. Bowperson did not hear him yell, "Yeah! Yeah! Yeah! Yeah! Yeah! Yeah! Yeah! Yeah! Yeah! Yeah! Yeah! Yeah! Yeah!" Bowperson ignored the fact that this was 13 "yeahs," a new record by three.

Bowperson knew by now, as did the rest of the trainees who did not see the purple man, that the more "yeahs" they did not hear the purple man yell, the more difficult that day would be.

On the day of nine "yeahs," the trainees went through their first parachute training. Two trainees hesitated in their jumps and were recycled backward into training, and Bowperson had nearly broken his leg upon landing that day.

On the day of the previous record of 10 "yeahs," the trainees were trained in the arts of swamp warfare. On that day, they learned the importance of shining their boots and shaving their faces in the field, just before crawling across a putrescent green bog with as much of their bodies immersed in the putrescence as possible. It was on that day that Trainee Morris decided to put his favorite theory to the test. Morris firmly believed that when the instructors fired their weapons over the crawling trainees' heads to keep them low during previous low crawls, they were only firing blanks.

"Think about it, Bowperson," Morris used to chide him. "Why would they waste the ammo?"

On the day of 10 "yeahs," Morris found his theory to be less than correct. When he jumped up from the swamp crawl, he found a 5.56 millimeter projectile lodged firmly in his abdomen.

Bowperson had not seen Morris after that. A few days later, he overheard that the standard treatment at Tolerance Corps hospitals for such wounds – Motrin pills and embolism socks – was unsuccessful.

On this day of 13 "yeahs," Bowperson dreaded whatever hell that awaited Alfa Platoon, besides not being given breakfast.

"Today, troops," Sergeant Cornwall began, "you will learn the ancient art of chemical warfare. Our Government has a long tradition of stockpiling, but never using, these dangerous, but very effective, weapons. Such a use of these weapons in warfare is a violation of international law." Cornwall grinned, his minty gum showing in his molars. "But I can tell you this: They worked really well in Operation Peaceful Transition."

Cornwall taught the trainees the important distinctions between nerve agents, blister agents, choking agents, and blood agents, which affected enemies in a variety of interesting ways but almost always resulted in people suffocating or drowning in their own bodily fluids if properly used.

The trainees received their own chemical warfare suits for the day, which included a mask with a hood that covered their entire heads and necks, a heavy overcoat and over pants filled with charcoal dust worn over their standard uniforms, rubber gloves, and rubber boots that were slipped over their standard boots.

At first, they practiced putting on their masks as rapidly as possible. They had to store their masks inside out in pouches by their sides. This was so that they could put the masks directly onto their faces without the hoods getting in the way. As they put the masks directly onto their faces, they were to cut off the intake valves of the masks with their right hands, breathing in strongly, creating a vacuum, airtight seal around their faces. Then, after securing the hoods on the rest of their heads, they had to breathe out, pushing and clearing out all the air inside the masks. The process had to be complete in under five seconds.

They practiced this repeatedly, until the fifteenth time they had donned their masks, formed a seal, cleared the air, and secured the hood. It was then that Trainee Stanley rudely interrupted the instruction. "Sir, Trainee Stanley reports as ordered," he said from inside his mask, sounding as though he were speaking from inside a metal can.

"What, Stanley?" Cornwall bellowed.

"Sir, my mask smells funny."

"Oh, no!" Cornwall scowled, flaring his nostrils underneath his mask. "Hey, Sergeant Hamilton, Stanley's mask smells funny! Everyone whose mask smells funny, go on and raise your hands." Everyone in the platoon raised his hand.

Sergeant Hamilton, chomping on his gum at the back of the tent, remarked, "Don't worry, Stanley. It's probably only because the last guy to use it puked in it."

A few of the trainees laughed.

Cornwall then demonstrated the procedure for drinking with their masks on by using rubber hoses that attached from the masks to their canteens. "Today, you will not be getting any rubber hoses." Cornwall added, "There is something of a war brewing with freaking Norway and we need to save these rubber hoses for field use."

By midday, they learned how to wear the rest of their chemical warfare gear. When they were fully outfitted, their skin was effectively sealed from the air outside. By now, it was 25 degrees Celsius outside and by far the warmest day Fort Freeperson had seen this far into the year. And since there was no real threat of a chemical attack, Sergeants Hamilton and Cornwall removed their chemical warfare suits and started on fresh pieces of chewing gum.

For the rest of the day, the trainees practiced the fundamentals of soldiering while in their full chemical warfare suits. They practiced marching in formation, then running in formation, then shooting at stationary targets, which was a bit of an adventure with rubber gloves on.

After several hours of training and maneuvers came Sergeant Cornwall's favorite part of chemical warfare day: the sand crawl. Before the sand crawl started, Hamilton and Cornwall spat out their gum and donned their chemical suits once again. This low crawl had an added bonus not experienced in the low crawls the trainees had done earlier in training. Not only were they crawling on sand hot enough to cook a soy egg, and not only were their bodies without any possibility of ventilation, and not only was there to be live ammunition flying overhead, but the trainees would get to experience a simulated gas attack.

Only the gas was real.

When the platoon was half of the way through the sand crawl, a greyish mist floated over them. "This, trainees, is called Gremlin Grey," Sergeant Hamilton announced. "It is a relatively mild nerve agent that only causes vomiting. And I may have neglected to inform you that the filters on the training masks you are wearing are not changed as often as they should be. But rest assured, if you remove your mask, it will be much worse." He winked at Sergeant Cornwall.

By the time the exercise was over and the all-clear was given, Bowperson could not tell how many other trainees had vomited in their masks because he could not see out of his mask. He could hear, however, that the other trainees were struggling to breathe, just as he was struggling because of all the fluids that had collected on his face. "So this is why they haven't fed or watered us all day," he gurgled to himself.

"All right, Trainees. Take your masks off," Cornwall commanded.

A series of splashes sounded through the air as vomit fell from faces to ground. All the trainees were taking deep breaths of the relatively cool air. Bowperson's water-soaked head cooled in the warm spring breeze. He stretched his fingers and cracked his knuckles. As he recovered, now sitting upright and finally able to drink from his canteen, he heard Sergeant Hamilton yell out, "Ten-hut! Everyone in formation."

Sergeant Hamilton saluted and welcomed Lieutenant Hazard. "Sir, Alfa Platoon, Echo Company, reports as ordered."

Returning his salute, Hazard said, "Sergeant. I understand these men have just experienced the sand crawl and our good friend Mr. Grey, if you know what I mean?"

"Yes, Sir." Hamilton beamed, his eye twinkling.

"And by Mr. Grey, I mean that substance that is ... well, technically illegal, but you know what I mean?"

"Yes, Sir."

"Because I know Generals Moore or Less would never tolerate that sort of thing. Well, perhaps 'never tolerate' is the wrong choice of words. They would never be intolerant toward it, but still not necessarily tolerate it. You follow me?"

"Yes, Sir." Hamilton's eye still twinkled.

"Any casualties this time around?"

"No, Sir."

"Not even any collateral damage?"

"Well, there were a few bugs, Sir."

Lieutenant Hazard, somewhat surprised, paused a moment. Evidently this exercise was getting too easy. "Good, this sounds like an excellent time for an inspection. After all, just because a gas attack might be going on is no excuse for a Tolerance Corps soldier to not look his best."

"Indeed, Sir."

"Well, let's get underway." Hazard rubbed his hands together with excitement. "Get them into inspection formation."

After inspecting the trainees' uniforms, rifles, hair, and faces, Lieutenant Hazard addressed the trainees. "I ought to have you all skinned. Never have I seen such disrespect for the Tolerance Corps uniform. This man over here," he wagged a finger at Bowperson and turned his attention to Sergeant Hamilton, "has what looks to be vomit on his chest. If we were not about to be at war with goddamned Norway, I would literally have him shot right here and now, metaphorically speaking.

"And they all have sand all over them and they stink. That is disgusting. It shows me they lack military bearing and lack respect for my beloved Tolerance Corps." Hazard looked the trainees up and down as they stood at attention, a few of them about to pass out. "Most of them look as if they have not shaved in at least twelve hours. And almost all of them have sand in their rifles." Turning to the trainees, he said, "One bad decision can get you killed out there, gentlemen! Now how can you kill bad guys with whiskers on your face?!"

Hazard kicked at the ground, then crouched for an inspection of his own feet to make sure he had not damaged the immaculate shine on his boots. He then looked over at the trainees' feet. "Trainees, I could overlook all of that, except for one thing. Those rubber chem-warfare boots on your feet, I mean, *the Corps'* rubber boots on your feet. Wait, that is not right. *The Corps'* rubber boots on *the Corps'* feet are not shiny enough. How can you men be ready for combat when your damned feet do not reflect light and images in a clear manner?"

Lieutenant Hazard turned to Sergeant Hamilton. "They do understand that we're about to be in a goddamned shooting war, don't they?"

"I've told them, Sir."

"I mean, that sounds overly redundant I know, 'shooting war.' But my creator, man! Their feet! Look at their feet!" Hazard turned his back on the platoon and said quietly to Hamilton, "Have them repeat the sand course until those boots are shiny. Oh, and use extra of that chemical weapon we don't use. That will give them the proper motivation."

Operation Manhattan: 113 January 0039

It was 0215 in the morning of January 113th. It was Day of Training 79. After being woken unusually early by Sergeant Cornwall's banging a trash can, Alfa Platoon dressed themselves in their physical training clothes and assembled for a briefing from Sergeant Hamilton in the barracks dayroom. As Hamilton entered the room carrying a large rolled-up map, the trainees stood at attention and bellowed in unison, "Sir, Alfa Platoon reports as ordered."

"Hooyah!" Hamilton said.

Alfa Platoon echoed back.

"At ease, Alfa Platoon. We have a live one today." Hamilton parked his gum in between his clenched front teeth and stood at the fore of the dayroom, looking out at his trainees who he had nearly shaped into Tolerance Corps Soldiers. "This is a real-world exercise, one of your toughest tests before entering my Corps. Hooyah?"

"Hooyah!"

"Good. Now this one comes from Major Manos, and he has personally volunteered you trainees for this highly sensitive mission. The shit has hit the fan in Manhattan." Hamilton unrolled the map and pinned it to a cork board hanging on the dayroom wall. He continued the briefing. "Department of Protests and East Coast Protest Command formations are spread thin across this front here." Hamilton slapped a pointer against a map of the New York portion of the Megalopolis DHZ. "They are facing north-not-east at the Norwegian Consulate in New York with their backs against the river."

At a sweep of Hamilton's arm, Staff Sergeant Cornwall began distributing sets of civilian clothing and mission ready kits to the trainees. Cornwall spoke. "This mission will call upon much of your training, but I believe you are ready. Hooyah?"

"Hooyah!" Alfa Platoon responded.

With a smile on his face, Sergeant Hamilton continued. "Now, remember. This is a very dangerous mission. Norwegians

0077

hate our freedom. They hate our tolerance. That is why they deny that freedom and tolerance to their aquatic neighbors. Be on your guard. Your landing zone will be here," he said, slapping the pointer just northwest of the Consulate, "in Central park. Alfa Platoon will drop in at the southern edge of the park, and we shall link up with Charlie and Delta Platoons here at Park and Fifty-Seventh Street. Since the DoP protesters are southeast of the Consulate, we shall protest from the north-not-east, catching the Sub-Department of Television crews completely by surprise. Bravo Platoon will be sent in by helicopter here, in New Novosibirsk, and will cross the East River in order to help DoP hold their protest line. But we in Alfa Platoon, the best platoon in this company, will be coming in by parachute. Hooyah?"

"Hooyah!"

"Open your mission ready kit. In it you will find one DoP two-one-fiver bravo bravo sign, one DoP protester uniform complete with rainbow bandana and sandals, one DoP Official Chant Book, Ninth Edition. Know those chants cold, Trainees. And lastly, one 'A vote for Tolerance is a vote for tolerance' bumper sticker. Do not deploy these bumper stickers on the local civilian cars and establishments until we get the all clear and are on our way back to the drop zone. The final two items in your kit are as follows. One DoP model nineteen disposable lighter and one DoP-issued medium-sized Norwegian flag. Now DoP is low on Norwegian flags with the present crisis, so some of you are going to have to make do with the flag for Denmark. All of you are going to be leaving your M8s behind. This mission is not a killer, it is a screamer. Hooyah?"

"Hooyah!"

"Remember, men, if you try to escape, we will find you. Ubiquitous Camera Command has New York covered like one of grandma's quilts, plus we can track each of you anywhere with that chip we put in your neck. Do I make myself clear? Remember that lien we placed on all of your bodily organs?" Hamilton tapped his eye patch.

"Yes, Instructor Sergeant!"

"Good. Go gear up, and no socks with the sandals, Newton! Hooyah!"

As Sergeant Hamilton would describe it, the training mission was a roaring success. Even Lieutenant Hazard, who had parachuted in with Delta Platoon, admitted he was impressed when he saw the tidiness and organization of Alfa Platoon's protest line. The recruits managed to take both the media and the Norwegians by surprise when Alfa Platoon rushed the northwest side of the Consulate and chanted "No Justice, No Peace" at it from point-blank range. The operation suffered only one casualty: Lewis Overture's sign.

Lewis Overture's Sign: 113 January 0039

Alfa Platoon had been training for this sort of airborne assault for weeks now. Only in training, they had been dropping in with their M8 assault rifles, prepared to show the world the true meaning of tolerance. This mission was different; Alfa Platoon was to show the Norwegians the true meaning of tolerance in sign and song form.

In order to make the drop in New York before the morning news cycle, Alfa Platoon had boarded their C-96 Cirrusfreighter planes at Fort Freeperson's landing strip before 0300 that morning. By 0615 they were dropping into Central Park, dangling from rainbow-colored parachutes. Most of the men were able to reach the ground safely, but Overture's drop, guided by a gust of wind, took him right into a stand of trees. Luckily, he survived the impact and sudden stop, but he was stuck dangling some four meters off the ground.

Bowperson was the first on the scene after Overture's radio call. "Overture! You all right?"

"I'm okay, but I think I messed up a squirrel nest real good."

"Oh, shit, you better get down from there before Cornwall finds out. We don't want any of that paperwork."

"I'm stuck, Reggie. I can't get down."

"That's all right, Lewis. You're only twelve feet up or so. Just wait a minute before you release. You ain't gonna hit the ground much harder than we do in our chutes anyway. I'll make you a landing bed." While Bowperson piled together a bed of leaves and branches to cushion Overture's fall, the rest of the men were forming up and practicing their chants. "Okay, Overture, drop on down now."

Overture released himself from his harness and fell the last four meters of his drop with a thud and a crack. Bowperson winced at the sound. "Lewis, you okay?"

"Shit, Reggie, I think I broke my leg," Overture screamed grimly.

"I'll get Doc Newton, you just hang tight. Don't move."

"Wait a sec, it ... it ain't my leg." Overture's expression became more grim. "My leg's okay. Oh, frack, man. Oh, frack ... I broke my sign!"

Overture rolled over, exposing the torn and shattered remains of his "Norway is the cancer! Tolerance is the answer!" sign.

Major Lawrence T. Manos: 114 January 0039

Major Lawrence Tolerance Manos, like all Tolerance Corps officers, had never been an Intolerant. Intolerants were never allowed to become officers. Intolerants lacked the capacity for rational thought. They could not seem to comprehend the sound strategy of eliminating intolerance with extreme tolerance. They did not understand the soundness of the policies that rounded them up for living outside the Designated Habitation Zones, only to give them a weapon and military training before sending them right back out into the uninhabited zones.

Major Manos had a desk commensurate with his rank. Majors of the Tolerance Corps received desks slightly bigger than Captains did, but not quite as big as the desks assigned to Colonels. Major Manos yearned for the day he could sit behind a Colonel-sized desk. He was a fast-track officer who had friends in high places. As a fast-track officer, he accepted every promotion offered him, and this resulted in serving in many areas of the Tolerance Corps. During Operation Peaceful Transition from 0033 to 0034, Second Lieutenant Lawrence Manos served in facial recognition, working directly with Ubiquitous Camera Command. After Operation Peaceful Transition, First Lieutenant Manos commanded the security detail at the then-under-construction Department of Protests flag manufactory in Quintana Roo. Then, for two years, Captain Manos served as a roving juror in Courts Martial whenever the awful specter of insensitivity reemerged in Tolerance Corps soldiers. Larry Manos' experience and expertise therefore made him the logical choice to lead one of the Tolerance Corps' newest Training Companies in instructing Intolerants on how to kill other Intolerants. He attained the ranked of Major in 0037, at only 27 years of age. But Manos was acutely aware that he had not been promoted in nearly two years. He needed to keep his side of the street clean if he was going to make Colonel before 30.

Before Major Manos' Major-sized desk stood Tolerance Corps Trainee Lewis Overture. Overture stood at the position of attention, having wisely elected to receive administrative punishment instead of facing a court martial for his actions at the Norwegian Consulate.

"Overture, I don't like having to do this, but I have to. Do you understand that?"

"Yes, Sir."

"Negligent Destruction of Government Property is not an offense I can just look the other way with. You must take better care next time you make a drop with DoP equipment."

"Yes, Sir. I apologize, Sir."

"I know it was just a sign this time. But losing a sign on the day of an operation is a big deal. A sign is a weapon, just as a song is a weapon, or a weapon is a weapon – if you get my metaphor."

"I do, Sir."

"Good. Because a soldier without a sign is a liability. He is a liability to himself and, more importantly, a liability to his unit. We trained you better than that."

Manos paused to look over the incident report prepared by Sergeant Cornwall and Lieutenant Hazard. "Overture, your oversight and failure at the Norwegian Consulate shows me something. It shows me you have a lack of focus. A lack of discipline. A lack of military bearing. We cannot have that sort of lack of focus on a live operation. You could have gotten your whole damn platoon killed. And that is precisely the type of thing that I do not need with Sub-Department of Television cameras around. Imagine the paperwork!"

Still at the position of attention, Overture stared blankly ahead. He had dropped the ball. He had failed in his mission. He had to take his just punishment from Major Manos.

"Your lack of focus and discipline made you look bad. It made your unit look bad. It made Sergeant Cornwall look bad. It made the whole damn Tolerance Corps look bad. But most importantly, it made *me* look bad." Manos slammed his fist into his Major's desk. How could he ever hope to get a bigger desk with more room for more things with his subordinates making clusterfracks out of routine airborne protests?

"Overture, I'm as intolerant of intolerance as the next guy. In fact, my intolerance for intolerance knows no bounds. But I have to tell you, your intolerance is a real credit to your people. You are one of the most diverse soldiers I've got right now, in case you haven't noticed. And your diversity increases the overall diversity of your unit, which is incredibly lacking in my estimation. If only we had more diversity, the Tolerance Corps would be more diverse. And if the Tolerance Corps were more diverse, well, that would increase overall mission readiness, especially when it comes to protest preparedness. I've always said that. And I've always said that protest duty in the Tolerance Corps is a great opportunity for diverse people, such as yourself, and it is a doggone crying shame the courts aren't sending us more diverse people. I mean, some of my best friends are diverse people. For instance, my wife is one-sixteenth Native Unified Societan."

"Yes, Sir."

"I happen to love all diverse people. So I cannot possibly be racist. And neither can you, because you are diverse. Did you know studies show that diverse people are genetically incapable of being racist? Well, it's true. So I know that racial intolerance is not why you were sent to the Corps. But I like to know why my people are sent to me. What did you do to be sent here? I'd really like to know how you, in particular, came to be in my charge."

"I was a milk farmer, Sir. They picked me up outside the habitation zones. Arrested. Convicted. Branded Intolerant."

"Milk farmer, huh? Who ever heard of such a crazy thing?" Manos smiled and leaned back in his Major's chair, which was slightly larger than a Captain's chair. "What did you do with this milk you farmed?"

"Sold it on the black market, Sir. Smuggled it into the Atlanta DHZ."

"Please, Overture! Let's be more sensitive in our word choices here. You sold it on the *diverse* market. But that is hardly a crime of high insensitivity. I mean, it's just milk. What kind of plant does milk come from, anyway?"

"Sir? Milk comes from cows. I kept cows, Sir."

"Oh! Well that *is* insensitive! Most insensitive indeed." Manos' face hardened. "You know you cannot treat animals in that manner. Not without their consent. And since they are animals, they cannot really consent, can they?"

"No, Sir."

"Of course not. Cows consenting! How preposterous. An animal consenting is like a diverse person being intolerant. It is genetically impossible." He paused, briefly looking at Overture. "Present company excluded, of course." Manos lowered his gaze back to the papers on his desk.

Manos continued, "Overture, because you are a real credit to your people and a pioneer in diversifying my beloved Tolerance Corps, you are a fine example. And because I cannot risk being accused of being insensitive, and because you are diverse, I have to be lenient on you. But I cannot be too lenient, for then it would look like I was treating you preferentially based upon your diversity, which I would be. You see what kind of bind I am in. I have to treat your intolerance with extra intolerance. I have to punish your dereliction of duty with the utmost severity."

"Yes, Sir." Overture gulped.

"Overture, as punishment for your foul deed during the airborne protest at the Norwegian Consulate in New York, I hereby impose the following administrative punishment. You are to write five letters of apology. One to the Department of Protests, one to me, one to Lieutenant Hazard, one to Sergeant Cornwall, and, most importantly, one to your sign. You do still have the sign, don't you?"

"No, Sir. I left it in New York."

"Better make that two letters to your sign, then."

Not Seeing the Purple Man: 114 January 0039

"Overture, on your way out, send Bowperson in."

Overture saluted, executed an about face, and exited Major Manos' office.

Major Manos had just signed the paperwork that appointed Bowperson as Alfa Platoon's Squad Leader after his heroics during Operation Manhattan. Lieutenant Hazard had personally recommended Bowperson for the position after seeing how shiny his sandals were at the protest. It would later be much to Bowperson's chagrin when he learned the only reason he had been promoted was that he had received the one pair of sandals painted with glitter paint, and not that he had helped Lewis Overture avoid serious injury.

Bowperson entered, came to the position of attention, and saluted Major Manos. "Sir, Trainee Bowperson reports as ordered."

"At ease, Bowperson, and it won't be Trainee Bowperson much longer. And it is not even Trainee Bowperson now."

Bowperson was confused. He had done his best to be a model trainee. If only he could survive Fort Freeperson, he'd be able to get a message back home to his wife and to his kids. And if he played his cards right and served out his enlistment – however long that might be – he might even be able to go home someday himself. Was this some sort of reprimand? Was he about to be kicked out of the Corps and have his organs harvested?

Manos continued, "Based on Lieutenant Hazard's observations of your leadership, you've been appointed Squad Leader. As a result, I am giving you the rank of Corporal after graduation in three weeks."

Bowperson, relieved and surprised, responded, "Thank you, Sir."

"Bowperson, that is not all. We have a problem. A problem in your platoon."

"Sir?"

"You see, one of your men, a Trainee Hackberry, persists in talking about seeing a purple man at the fence line every morning. Are you aware of this?"

"No, Sir. I have never seen the purple man at the fence line."

"I'm sure you haven't. And I am sure you have not heard him yell 'yeah' at you all when you are exercising. I have neither seen nor heard the purple man, and I can assure you or any Internal Security people who ask that neither have my officers and my non-commissioned officers. Anyone who sees such a thing is likely crazy, and anyone who hears or listens to such a crazy thing yelling 'yeah' is plain nuts."

"Sir, what would you have me do about the purple man we do not see or hear?"

"Nothing, Bowperson. You are not to deal with or interact with the purple man at all. He is not there. And I have not seen him standing at the fence line pointing and shouting at all of my trainees during morning workouts and marching drills. You are to deal with Hackberry, not the purple man."

"What shall I do, Sir?"

"Shut him up. Tell him to quit talking about it. In fact, *we* should not be talking about it either. Because we do not see it. In fact, if anyone asks what we talked about, don't tell them it's about the purple man who we do not see. Tell them it's something else."

"Sir? Something else? Like what?"

"Just anything else, I don't know. Something made up, like a good cover story. Tell them I was informing you of Lieutenant Hazard's promotion to Captain, and his transfer to Combat Command."

"Lieutenant Hazard is being transferred then, Sir?"

"Well, I don't really know. It's just a cover story, Bowperson. But I tell you what I will do. I will put in the paperwork and ask for his transfer and promotion anyway. That should definitely cover up what we were talking about. I would not mind getting rid of him anyway." Major Manos looked around, under his desk, and in his drawers. He pulled a wand out of one of the drawers and started waving it around the office. The wand beeped sporadically. He then whispered, "I think he is a Department of Internal Security plant. And he has a bit of a foot fetish. Not that I am judging him."

"Of course not, Sir. We were talking about Lieutenant Hazard's promotion."

"Wait, Bowperson. Now that you mention it, and now that I am *really* going to promote him, we have to come up with something else. Because anything we talk about in this room that is real cannot be repeated."

"So we talked about the purple man, then, Sir?"

"No, Bowperson, nothing real! Tell them the Tolerance Corps is planning a coup. That we are planning on taking down President Tolerance and overthrowing the Department of Internal Security's stranglehold on political power. If only we knew where the President is hiding. That should keep those Internal Security goons off of our case. Just don't talk about the purple man that no one sees."

"Right, Sir. Nothing we talk about that is real leaves this room."

"Yes, in fact, don't tell them about the coup. Think of something else."

"And I will get Hackberry to shut up about it."

"What, the purple man? Or the coup?"

"Both, Sir?"

"Excellent thinking."

Trainee Hackberry's Inability to Not See: 116 January 0039

"They're gonna frackin' kill you, Gus," Squad Leader Bowperson warned Trainee Hackberry as they worked outside, supervising Alfa Platoon's laundry as it dried on clotheslines. It was Day of Training 82 and three days after returning from Operation Manhattan at the Norwegian Consulate. Emphasizing his point, Bowperson leaned toward Hackberry. Making fists with both hands and giving a squeeze, he cracked the big knuckles on both of his thumbs and whispered, "You need to stop talking about the purple man."

Despite their recurring disagreements over what can be seen and what cannot be seen, Bowperson and Hackberry had a good deal in common. They both grew up in the Dominion of Missouri but had never met before coming together at Fort Freeperson. Although Hackberry was a couple years Bowperson's senior, both men were born in the wrong place at the wrong time in history to parents who passed on the gene responsible for being too stubborn to report to a DHZ when ordered to do so by their betters.

Since forced relocation to the Designated Habitation Zones had become national policy, Bowperson spent his time scrounging, fishing, and hunting in his home county of Macon County, Missouri. Of Bowperson's three brothers, his eldest reported to the Good Louis Habitation Zone; his two younger brothers joined the rebellion and were probably with the Broadband Rebels in Montana, if they were still alive at all.

Unlike his brothers, Bowperson took the middle route. He did not uproot himself for the government farms or the DHZs. But he did not take up arms against the government either. Instead, he took up his fishing pole and his farming implements and made a living the way his ancestors had. When fighting came to Missouri, he laid himself low and remained peaceful, occasionally trading supplies and food for equipment and gadgets with both sides. And after the fighting passed out of the region, he stayed in the relative peace and quiet, doing business with the people on the government farms in the area. That good life of hunting, farming, and gathering lasted about nine years until he was picked up by DETA agents while in possession of large quantities of illegal fish hooks.

Augustus Hackberry took quite another path.

In 0007 E.E., Augustus "Gus" Hackberry was born to Chuck and Margie Hackberry outside the present DHZs in a town called LaGrange in northeastern Missouri. LaGrange was not too far from where Reginald Bowperson grew up in Macon.

Just before the Broadband Affordability and Availability Act of 0030, Hackberry was the loser in a bitter divorce. After a few turbulent years of marriage, the proposal for which he had accepted only while under the influence of youth and lust, he found himself a bachelor again. His ex-spouse described Hackberry as being pathologically incapable of decent conversation or monogamy. His ex-spouse took almost all of their property, save for the family plot of farmland Gus had inherited when his parents died.

So, almost immediately after the Broadband Affordability and Availability Act ordered that everyone report to a government farm or a Designated Habitation Zone, Hackberry felt like he had very little to lose in the way of property. But he felt as though he had plenty to lose in terms of mobility. While his ex and most of his friends reported to the Good Louis and Kansas City DHZs, Hackberry gathered up his weapons and trained to fight.

From the Atlantic and Pacific Coasts, the Tolerance Corps worked its way inland along rivers, highways, and railroad tracks. By '34, the Tolerance Corps had made northern Missouri a priority and the fighting there began in earnest. Hackberry notched his first 25 kills over the next three years in sporadic fighting, but Missouri was almost entirely lost to the Tolerance Corps in '36 and '37 as the central government gradually pacified and decolonized the country from coast to coast. Hackberry's experience in Missouri was what helped him identify a lost front with Operation Drake in Iowa, and this was what helped him choose to follow Colonel Asno out west, a decision that saved his life.

Hackberry reciprocated Bowperson's lean and stuck his jaw forward at his Squad Leader. He growled, "Kill me for what? For talking about the purple man that everyone in this damned unit can see? He points and yells at us every damned morning, for Christ's sake." Hackberry stomped on the ground. "I need a chew of tobacco. Got any?"

"No, Gus. And we don't need any trouble for getting caught with chew on laundry duty. We just have to keep our heads low and survive Fort Freeperson long enough to get out alive and unharvested!"

"Shit, Reggie. Why don't we just hop the damn fence and be done with it? We can link up with the purple guy and skip town!"

Hackberry's greatest gift as a soldier was his exceptional vision. He had 20-10 vision and could recognize patterns so well that camouflage was almost useless against him.

However, his vision was also a great liability, for he could not master one necessary skill for any soldier: the ability to not see, especially when ordered to not see.

"Hackberry, I'm not messin' around. I got called into Major Manos' office a couple days ago."

"Did he give you his speech about discipline and a soldier's duty to stay on talking points in the presence of the media?"

"No, Gus. He told me just about everyone here is aware of the purple man, but we're not supposed to talk about him."

Hackberry was incredulous. "Why the hell not?"

"I think it is orders from D.C. The purple men do not exist."

"Purple *men*?" Hackberry scratched his chin where his red beard used to be. "There's more than one of the purple bastards?"

"When we're asked about these things, Major Manos said for us to say, 'I cannot confirm that.'"

"Do they all yell 'yeah' a bunch at random people running around – running while trying to survive political indoctrination training before they get sent into one of five or six pointless wars?"

"Possibly, yes. But we need to shut up about it, okay?"

"You nag worse than my ex, Bowperson. You are a pain in my ass."

Bowperson smiled and put his hands behind his head, giving his knuckles a crack over his skull. "I am a pain in the ass who is trying to save your life so we can get the hell out of this place and live to fight again."

"Shit," Hackberry spat as if he were chewing tobacco. "This ain't livin'. And serving in this Corps ain't livin'. We ain't been alive since we were brought here, chained to our shuttle bus seats. But I used to be alive. Up until very recently, I was fully alive."

Hackberry started to tell Bowperson the story of how he wound up at Fort Freeperson.

And as the story went, Beetle Johnschild, like Bowperson, had been pain in Hackberry's ass back in '38. At Operation Drake in Iowa, on the crossing from Iowa to join the Broadband Rebellions out west, and wherever he was, Beetle was a pain in Hackberry's ass. "Tell me again, Beetle, you're at least forty-five damn years old, born way before any of this compulsory renaming nonsense back in the '20s, why the hell is your last name Johnschild and not Johnson?" Hackberry asked amid the clunking of horse feet in northern Nebraska.

"Might could be I don't need my ex-wife finding me. Might be I don't want your ex-spouse finding me neither, pilgrim."

"My ex would not bother finding either of us, you old drunk," Hackberry said with a laugh.

For all of his *pilgrim* this and *pilgrim* that, Johnschild had enormous amounts of worldly intelligence and been around to see a lot of what had transpired since the founding of the Unified Society.

And at that point in time, Hackberry, Asno, Johnschild, and Leonard really were pilgrims who were making their way to Fort Peck. Asno subscribed to the theory that the rebellion could capture and keep one of the country's major dams and then hold the D.C. Government hostage by threatening to blow it and flood out downstream farms and DHZs.

But they had to get there first, across 1,000 miles of open country, before they could link up with the rebel forces surrounding Fort Peck and its dam holding back the Upper Missouri River.

Back in '38, before Hackberry was Trainee Hackberry who had to be convinced of commonsensical norms, such as not talking about the damned purple man, before he was knocked unconscious and captured in the aftermath of the Seattle Cod Protests of '39, Gus Hackberry was one of four men riding slowly across the former Dominions of Nebraska and South Dakota, to Fort Peck in northeastern Montana.

Despite the failure of the Broadband Rebellions to gain a lasting independence from the national government and President Tolerance, the Tolerance Corps never was able to control the Great Plains and the Mountain West, which resulted in a stalemate. Over the last four years, the D.C. Government had adopted a containment and attrition strategy to prevent the spread of the Broadband Rebellions. This naturally involved destroying every town in the region using air power, while conserving ground units, which were already worn thin during Operation Peaceful Transition in Mexico.

In reality, the Tolerance Corps only controlled a few key points in the western region, and these points were so isolated that they were essentially islands in an ocean of rebellion – islands that could only be supplied by air.

Fort Peck was one of these pivotal locations, one that controlled a very large dam holding back a dangerously large amount of water on the Missouri River. While it would be an imposing situation and a psychological victory for the rebels to hold a dam they could blow anytime, it was not just about the threat of flooding. Fort Peck Lake provided enough water to irrigate the countryside and the dam produced enough electricity to keep the rebels' underground factories running and cranking out munitions.

Asno was never much of a conversationalist, but he would interject himself into conversations along the way. A few days into the ride, George Leonard asked one of his many questions. "So where are we now?"

"Still in Nebraska. Near the site of Norfolk based on the last road sign we saw. You got somewhere else to be, new guy?" Hackberry asked, slightly annoyed that this was the fifth time that day he had fielded this exact question. Hackberry often wondered if the kid ever shut up.

"Not Nebraska, Hackberry," Asno chimed in. "Far from it. Have you not kept up on current events? We're in the Great Sweetgrass Buffalo Reserve." Asno nodded to a herd of wild bison a few hundred meters to their left. "The old ways are gone, gentlemen. The old names, too, I suppose. They renamed this whole state as a Buffalo Reserve, except for good old Bush-Obamaha and a few designated farms flanking it about a hundred and sixty thousand meters to our backside. That's about a hundred miles for you, Beetle. I know metric is not your thing."

It took a good three weeks to reach the former Dominion of South Dakota. Along the way, they did not want for food on the journey, though the journey was indeed long. The men were able to find plenty of wild hogs, ducks, and feral chickens along the way. When there were no hogs, feral chickens, or ducks, they could rely on Beetle's old 45-70 lever action buffalo gun to take down a big meal out of a herd of bison. Their horses did not have a hard time finding grass to eat – the tall grass was turning green and the feral corn was sprouting.

From time to time, they would hear F-50 iTolerators or B-75 Acceptors roar overhead. But with no sight of any soldiers filling the role of combat aircraft controllers since Iowa, and with no sighting of scout drones, they did not worry each time they heard the roar of those computer-controlled jet engines.

Asno was a remarkable leader and fighter, Hackberry recalled. Asno had a knack for avoiding the drone jet fighters and bombers, as most rebel officers were able to. But what separated Asno from the others was his ability to deal with the small helicopter drone known as the MQ Wildfire. The MQ Wildfire plagued the waking hours and nightmares of rebel soldiers throughout the plains and mountains. Outwardly, the MQ Wildfire was a boxy one-meter-long helicopter with four rotor blades, four cameras mounted at each corner, a laser for guiding bombs and missiles, and a single 5.56 mm machine gun swivel-mounted on its underside.

The MQ Wildfire was not much of a threat in and of itself. Its machine gun was far too powerful for the light frame of the drone. When fired, the machine gun tended to cause the drone to flutter off course, which negated any accuracy. In a one-on-one fight with a decent marksman on the ground, the lightly armed and lightly armored MQ Wildfire would be picked apart.

But the Tolerance Corps and other government agencies active in the Great Not-East did not rely on the MQ Wildfire to be combat aircraft. They relied on the iTolerators and Acceptors for that capability. The MQ Wildfire served as the eyes and ears of the Tolerance Corps and the paramilitary forces of other government agencies active in the region, including the Department of Equally Treating Animals and the Department of Infrastructure.

A common pattern emerged across the Great Plains. A rebel unit would spot and be spotted by an MQ Wildfire. The Wildfire would fly in for a closer look at the unit, angling one of its four cameras at the group. The Wildfire would lock its bomb-guiding laser on the rebels. The rebels would then blast the Wildfire out of the sky. Hackberry had seen it three or four dozen times with the Missouri Partisan Rangers and then later at Operation Drake.

But within minutes of downing the drone, they could count on either hearing the roar of the iTolerator's sub-sonic engines or hearing the explosion of heavy ordnance dropped by the B-75s. They did not often hear a B-75 until it was too late, because B-75s flew too high and far faster than the speed of sound.

Asno's great talent for evading the F-50s and B-75s, as far as Hackberry could tell, had to do with his skill at manipulating and jamming radio transmissions. Each time they would take down a Wildfire drone, Asno would take out a small device and start fiddling with it, most likely jamming all frequencies used by the drones. And each time he did that, there were no further air strikes.

Asno was quite fond of radios, phones, and whatever wireless devices he could get his hands on. Although Asno never talked about his pre-rebellion life, or his post-rebellion life for that matter, Hackberry suspected the man had been a radio or wireless engineer of some kind.

Each night, when they made camp, Asno would tune in a shortwave radio to either a government propaganda station or one of the rebel transmitters. Radio Free Montana was a favorite throughout rebel circles. It was the longest-running station of the kind, and its transmitter had not been knocked out for more than a few hours at a time since its opening broadcast 10 years earlier.

Rumor had it that the Tolerance Corps had lost so many bombers trying to take out the transmitter station, sheltered in a valley in the Bitterroot Range protected by nests of anti-aircraft guns, that they had abandoned hope of taking out Radio Free Montana from the air. Instead, the Department of Internal Security relied on fixed-dial radios for civilians and The Radio Fairness Act, which had made owning a shortwave receiver a crime. This kept seditious radio out of the hands of most people living in the DHZs. For good measure, transmission-scrambling towers placed strategically throughout each DHZ transmitted countersignals over the frequencies known to contain rebel broadcasts. One such scrambling tower had recently been toppled in the Minneapolis-Good Paul DHZ by terrorists, and Radio Free Montana was able to boom into Minnesota unadulterated for weeks. In many cases, rebel agents were more subtle and simply cut the power lines to the scrambling towers. But the very fact that a scrambling tower had been taken down caused many people to tune in to Radio Free Montana. This led to widespread rumors that the Broadband Rebellions were still going on and had not been truly won as the Department of Free Speech news outlets had repeatedly announced. Hundreds were arrested and detained for spreading these rumors.

It was Asno's radio skills that helped confirm they made the right decision to leave Operation Drake behind. Over the first three days into their journey, Asno was monitoring and pulling encrypted text communications. By day three, Asno detected incessant Zebra Band radio chatter of the sort that drone aircraft used to communicate. Asno deciphered several attack protocols contained in the Zebra Band chatter, which made it clear that the Tolerance Corps had struck their old base.

Nighttime was a decent time to for Asno and the men to relax on the journey to Fort Peck. MQ Wildfire activity was rarely an issue at night due to design flaws with their infrared guidance systems, which kept them largely grounded after sunset.

Time to rest and eat was vital on a long journey such as theirs. As plentiful as food had been and as absent as the enemy had been up until this point, the ride was not exactly easy. It was the spring of '38, after all, and the soil was soggy. The roads and bridges were badly battered and in decay. And last summer's wildfires had eliminated most tree cover and buildings. Sunburn and dehydration both became a problem. Nevertheless, Colonel Asno's route had kept them away from enemy patrols. However, there was a major obstacle in their way: The Badlands.

Asno informed the team they would be camping a few days in a row in a secluded spot he knew in a dell, hidden from the air, just outside the Badlands. This was welcome news for the group, but as most of Asno's decisions did, it served a practical purpose. Asno needed time to analyze information and decide whether to go through the Badlands and risk dehydration and injury over the rough, broken ground, or to go around the Badlands and to the Black Hills, adding miles to their journey as well as some political complications.

According the D.C. Government, the Black Hills were officially depopulated along with the rest of the Former Dominions of South and North Dakota after the Broadband Affordability and Availability Act. In reality, the Reconstituted Lakota Nation had resettled the land, as the various Sioux tribes had never relinquished ownership of the property. The RLN was definitely unfriendly to the D.C. Government, which meant the area was free from Tolerance Corps patrols. However, the RLN was not exactly friendly to the Broadband Rebels either and did not welcome outsiders. Having to go around the Badlands and then around the Black Hills would add hundreds of miles to an already long journey.

Hackberry looked back fondly on those days of relative peace and quiet. Asno was packed away in his tent, pulling data from his wireless devices, analyzing weather maps on his tablet, and communicating ahead with the RLN, the Montana Partisan Rangers, as well as a couple of rebel outfits operating in Northeastern Wyoming, just in case they needed to go that route.

During the day, Hackberry and Johnschild would show Leonard how to hunt, fish, and clean fish and game for cooking. During the night, they'd sit around a fire and drink some of Johnschild's whiskey. Despite his sheltered upbringing and his inability to not say stupid things, Leonard was showing that he could be a capable hand out in the wild. But man, did he say some stupid things.

As Hackberry told his story, a thought crept from the back of his brain to the front of his mind. Was there something to what Bowperson was telling him? Maybe his inability to not see was like Leonard's inability to not talk. And look where that had gotten Leonard, hauled off and disappeared, by DIS goons as rumor had it, right after sensory deprivation.

One night around the campfire, Johnschild, Hackberry and Leonard shared a few drinks and some conversation that Hackberry vividly remembered into his days at Fort Freeperson.

"All I am saying is there is no way the old system was a one-party system masquerading as a two-party system," Leonard said back at their Badlands camp.

"Kid," Johnschild chided, "after all you've been through, all you've seen, you still believe the crap that they taught you at your government school?"

"Well no, not everything." Leonard paused. "I, I just think there has to be a real reason, a better reason, for the rise of the Unified Society than your crazy notion that both parties were really one combined party."

"All right, then," Johnschild said. "Then why don't you tell me what you learned in your government school about them renaming Omaha to Bush-Obamaha."

Hackberry had not heard this story, based on his failure to have reported to government school as a youth. "Well, what *did* they teach you about the name change?" Hackberry asked.

"Well, it went sorta like this. Sometime around twenty-five years ago, the people of Omaha wanted to honor the greatest President, or the forty-second greatest President, of the Old U.S., depending on who you talked to. So an organic, grassroots committee–"

"Was it fair trade, too?" Johnschild snickered.

"No! You can't have a fair trade committee of people." Leonard paused. "Well, maybe you could if you had a group of people dedicated to the principles of equality for the workers most involved in the factors of production–"

"Come on back, Leonard. Back to Bush-Obamaha," Hackberry chided.

"Right," Leonard said, sneering a bit at Johnschild, who was giggling to himself. "So an organic, grassroots–"

"Certified rainforest-friendly!" Johnschild chimed in, laughing loudly in between sips of white whiskey.

Leonard held his hand out for some of the whiskey when Johnschild was done with it. He was never going to get through this story without some. Johnschild tossed the mason jar over to Hackberry who took a sip before passing it over to Leonard. As Leonard sipped, Hackberry prompted, "So this committee?"

"Yes, an organic, grassroots–"

"Certified cruelty-freeeeeee!" Johnschild shouted, turning the "free" into a howl at the moon.

That finally got a bit of a laugh from Leonard, who took another sip of the white whiskey and let out a "whoosh" sound, as though his mouth were slightly on fire.

"Yes, an organic, grassroots, certified cruelty-free committee of citizens in Omaha wanted to honor the greatest, or forty-second greatest, President of the Old U.S., depending on who you talked to, by renaming their town Obamaha. These folks were called 'Democrats.' But not everyone in town agreed to rename the town Obamaha, claiming Obama was more along the lines of the forty-second best President, which would put him near the bottom. These contrary folks, called 'Republicans,' thought George W. Bush was the greatest President."

Leonard took a sip of the whiskey again before continuing. "Then the Democrat people said, 'Heck no! Bush was at best number forty-four on the ranking scale!' So, there was a standoff. Each side thought their guy was number one and the other guy was the worst thing ever. The standoff lasted until the Supervizier of Omaha emailed President Tolerance for guidance. President Tolerance responded with the Bush-Obamaha compromise, stating that both Presidents did a great job in refining and growing the role of the President. And that they did a great deal to evolve the old Constitution in order pave the way for the triumph of the General Will, the Unified Society, and its benevolent embrace. And that, gentlemen, is how it happened."

"Nope. You're right, Leonard. That don't sound like a one-party system pretendin' to be a two-party system at all!" Johnschild remarked, looking up at the sky before howling, "Ahwoooooooh!"

All this time, Asno's tent remained closed and aglow from his array of wireless devices. He never came out to join the drinking or the conversation.

As Hackberry reached this point in his story, he and Bowperson finished their laundry duties for the day and headed back to their barracks. Throughout the story, Bowperson now clearly saw that Hackberry's strengths as a soldier, hunter, and man living out in the wilderness also happened to be his weaknesses as a trainee.

"Survive, man. Just survive. Don't be like Leonard," Bowperson said.

"You might have a point after all, Bowperson. But you are still a pain in my ass."

0100

Laundry Detail: 123 January 0039

Squad Leader Bowperson had scored quite a coup in getting laundry detail assigned to himself and his friends. Choosing his own weekend duties was one of the perks of his appointment to Squad Leader. The time Bowperson spent talking and relaxing with his fellow trainees outdoors every weekend more than made up for the boredom of literally watching clothes dry. And these men, his friends, were the closest thing to family he had outside the farm back in Missouri.

It was Day of Training 89. The previous week had been a busy one. It seemed that as Graduation Day was getting closer and closer, the training was becoming more intense – more intense, but perhaps easier. Bowperson could see a pronounced toughness coming out in each of the men around him. The maddening frustrations that nearly crippled him and his platoon-mates in the early days after sensory deprivation were now easier. This was in no small part because they were relying on their platoon-mates to help each other. They were becoming more and more like brothers.

Back around Day of Training 36, Hackberry was nearly *harvested* when he failed footlocker inspection a second time. He had failed to fold the washcloth that he never had time to use in even fourths and place it touching the left side of the footlocker while also touching the bottom of the slightly open toothbrush case holding the toothbrush he never had time to use. Instead, he had folded his washcloth in slightly uneven fourths and had it touching the bottom of a completely closed toothbrush case. Staff Sergeant Cornwall announced his failed inspection for these defects and dumped the contents of his footlocker onto the floor of the barracks. "Clean this shit up and put your footlocker together like we trained you or I will be smoking your fracking spleen this time tomorrow! You have ten minutes. Ten fracking minutes. This shit better be perfect!"

Hackberry was incompetent when it came to folding, shining, folding, polishing, folding, and all of the other soldierly duties he needed to master during those first few weeks of training. But when it came to taking late-night shifts on fire watch, and when it came to handling other platoons' TCIs who demanded access to the barracks without authorization, Hackberry was as calm and cool as a polar bear on January 365th.

The Tolerance Corps gave trainees on fire watch the strict order that only personnel listed on the Department of Coexistence WB-32 Access Control Whiteboard next to the barracks door would be allowed access to their barracks. The people listed on this whiteboard were only the people in their chain of command. So only Sergeant Cornwall, Sergeant Hamilton, Lieutenant Hazard, Major Manos, or Colonel King were allowed into the barracks. Anyone above Colonel King in the chain of command was incredibly unlikely to pay Alfa Platoon a visit, and all other personnel outside of Alfa Platoon needed to be escorted in.

Back in the early hours of Day of Training 33, when Hackberry had drawn fire watch between 0300 and 0500, Sergeant Olmeid from Bravo Platoon banged on the door to the barracks.

Hackberry approached the door and saw Sergeant Olmeid chomping on a large piece of gum with a smile upon her face.

"Hey, Trainee, Sergeant Hamilton left his wallet in the office in there. I need to get it for him."

"Ma'am, may I see your authority to enter?" Hackberry asked robotically.

Olmeid held her Tolerance Corps ID to the window.

Hackberry touched the window with his index finger and read her name aloud. "Olmeid, Roberta. Staff Sergeant."

Knowing full well Olmeid was not on the access list, Hackberry turned and placed his other index finger to the Department of Coexistence WB-32 Access Control Whiteboard and made a point of staring at it for three seconds. Turning back to the window in the door and taking both index fingers down, Hackberry responded to Olmeid's request. "Ma'am, you do not have authority to enter."

"Come on, Trainee, this is not a test. I really need Sergeant Hamilton's wallet. I've got orders."

Hackberry stared blankly through the glass. Sergeant Olmeid exploded as loudly as she could, banging on the door with both fists, "LET ME IN!!!"

"Ma'am, may I see your authority to enter?"

"LET ME THE FRACK IN TRAINEE OR I WILL HAVE YOU HARVESTED!" Olmeid's neck and face were turning red.

"Ma'am, may I see your authority to enter?"

"YOU FRACKHEAD! YOU WILL LET ME IN RIGHT NOW OR SERGEANT HAMILTON WILL BREAK YOUR FRACKING NECK!"

Trainees, awoken by the noise, were getting out of their bunks and looking down the aisle at what was happening at the entrance to their barracks. Hackberry stood like a robot and stared through the glass without responding.

"LET ME IN!!!" Olmeid banged again.

"Ma'am, may I see your authority to enter?"

Olmeid realized she had a robot on her hands. She turned around and walked away a few steps and whistled a few notes. She then turned and faced the door, where she saw Hackberry still standing there. She walked back to the door, this time with a key in her hand. Olmeid unlocked the door and came in. Hackberry stood aside at the position of attention and said, "Ma'am, Alfa Platoon reports as ordered."

"Nice job, trainee," Olmeid said as she walked past him and into the Sergeants' office. She grabbed Hamilton's wallet and walked back out the front door, telling Hackberry, "Lock it up" on the way out.

Other trainees had failed similar tests of their resolve and had been recycled – that is, Tolerance Corps parlance for being sent backwards in training. A few repeat recyclees had been harvested at Fort Freeperson Organ Extraction Center, one of the busiest extraction centers in the nation. For this reason, fire watch was one of the least desirable tasks a trainee could have.

After Hackberry had failed his footlocker inspection the second time, Sergeant Cornwall returned to his office and cranked up his radio, blasting a new single dominating the Bureau of Military Radio top 40 broadcasts. It was a hit by the folk band *The Panopticon Neckties*. The band was officially labeled as subversive by DIS, but it received copious amounts of airplay by the non-commissioned officers and enlisted men running the military radio stations who had been exposed to contraband music via the rebel radio stations they listened to while deployed out in the field.

The lyrics echoed throughout the linoleum floors and metal walls of the barracks.

> *Get high*
> *Do drugs*
> *Get high then you do some drugs*
> *Get high*
> *Then do drugs*
> *Everybody in the club do drugs!*

While the Sergeant's folk music filled the building, Bowperson walked into the center of the barracks and spoke. "All right, fellas. How many of you expert fabric folders who have already passed your footlocker inspections are scared to death of your next fire watch shift?" About a dozen hands went up in the room. Bowperson pointed to three men standing closest to Hackberry – Trainee Gumabay, Trainee Overture, and Doc Newton. "You three, put his locker together, and do it perfect, and you won't have to pull another fire watch the rest of our training."

Hackberry survived his inspection that day thanks to Gumabay, Overture, and Newton. After that, Alfa Platoon developed a barter system between the organizers and the watchdogs. Inspections went smoothly thanks to the organizers. And eventually, the sergeants stopped testing their door guards thanks to the watchdogs.

But things felt much easier for Reginald Bowperson, Gus Hackberry, Lewis Overture, Xavier Newton, and Pedro Gumabay on Day of Training 89 as they relaxed, shined their boots, and supervised their laundry as it dried in the sun. As the men talked about their week, a C-540 transport aircraft roared overhead, departing Fort Freeperson's nearby landing strip. They had a good deal to talk about because it had been quite an intense week, with humps of 20 kilometers or more and hand-to-hand combat training every day followed by rigorous protest chant training every evening.

The trainees had gathered beneath what little shade their hanging laundry afforded them. Bowperson observed that Hackberry kept looking out at the fence line, past their drill pad training grounds about 400 yards away.

"You looking at him?" Doc Newton asked.

"Yeah, he's there," Hackberry responded, peering between their white sheets flapping in the wind.

Bowperson chimed in, "Well, keep it quiet. Just eleven more days, man. And we are out of here."

"Excited for graduation, are we?" Lieutenant Hazard surprised the men from behind, concealing his footsteps as one of the C-540 Skyhauler Transport jets roared overhead.

All of the trainees jumped to their feet and saluted Hazard. Bowperson barked a greeting. "Sir, Trainee Bowperson, Alfa Platoon, reports as ordered."

Hazard returned the salute and held it. He liked to test his trainees in this manner. An enlisted man was required to hold his salute until the officer he was saluting lowered his. Trainee Gumabay nearly lowered his salute right away, but Overture gave him an elbow in the ribs. A good 15 seconds went by. Hazard appeared immune to the awkwardness.

Hazard finally lowered his salute and looked at Bowperson. "What do you mean *Trainee* Bowperson? I promoted you, didn't I?" He shifted his gaze down to Bowperson's feet, smiling.

"Yes, Sir. And thank you, Sir. Old habit still has me saying 'Trainee Bowperson' instead of 'Squad Leader Bowperson.'"

"Quite understandable. But you'll need to get used to the new title. Alfa Platoon is one of the finest training platoons I have ever seen. And I am going to see that you are recognized with the rank of Corporal upon graduation. You are going to do very well under Combat Command!"

"Thank you, Sir."

"Quite welcome!" Hazard said, tapping Bowperson on the shoulder somewhat rigidly. "Quite welcome, indeed! And for good measure, Major Manos tells me I am being promoted to Captain very soon. This is my last stint at Fort Freeperson. After your graduation, I'll be getting a combat unit! Norway, gentlemen. Norway!"

"Congratulations, Sir!" Trainee Newton chimed in.

Hazard smiled at Newton. "Thank you, Trainee, ummmm." Hazard trailed off, tilted his head off to the side, and looked down at the boots on Newton's feet. "Not very shiny," Hazard said aloud as he frowned. "Keep working at it, but, well. To tell you the truth, I would not lose any sleep over shine anymore except for Graduation Day parade. We're about to see live action and you're going to be a medic, right?"

"Yes, Sir!" Newton responded with a smile.

"Well, I'm going to need you to keep me and these other shitheads standing next to you alive when we make contact with the enemy in Norway." Hazard smiled. It seemed genuine. "And, well, I should not be telling you this already, but the Norway Campaign has a name, *Operation Norwegian Emancipation*. When they name a campaign like that, you know the violence is about to unfold." Hazard's smile widened.

Bowperson studied Hazard's behavior. The Lieutenant Hazard they had all come to know was a stickler for appearance standards. A less-than-shiny boot would normally set the man ablaze. What was the Lieutenant up to?

Lieutenant Hazard nodded and clapped his hands together one time. "But shoe-shine supervision and congratulatory conversations are not my primary reason for visiting you men. I am here in hopes that we could practice that chant again – the one I wrote for us when we get to Norway."

Hazard had been drilling all of the training platoons on a new chant he wrote up especially for the upcoming Norway operation. As he explained when they had first practiced it, he envisioned this as the chant they would use when pacifying every Norwegian city, town, village, and hamlet they came across. This chant would undoubtedly help the Norwegians understand the reason their cities, towns, villages, and hamlets were on fire and filled with foreign occupiers.

"Very good, Sir," Bowperson responded and gestured to the group. The trainees arranged themselves in a straight line, facing Hazard. "We await your orders."

Lieutenant Hazard straightened up and ordered, "Alfa Platoon, give chant!"

"Chant!" the trainees echoed.

"Chant 'Tolerance is Peaceful!'" Hazard announced.

And they began to chant.

> *Tolerance is peaceful*
> *Very very peaceful*
> *Very very very very very very peaceful!*
>
> *Peaceful! Peaceful!*
> *Very very peaceful*
> *Very very very very very very peaceful!*
>
> *How is it peaceful?*
> *It's very frackin' peaceful!*
> *It's so frackin' peaceful,*
> *It's mother frackin' peaceful!*
>
> *Peaceful! Peaceful!*
> *Very very peaceful*
> *Very very very very very very peaceful!*

When another C-540 roared overhead, Lieutenant Hazard raised his hand to stop the chant, and the trainees fell silent. This particular chant could be looped indefinitely, so this was a relatively short rendition of the "Tolerance is Peaceful" chant. An awkward 10 or 12 seconds passed as the jet engines quieted down before Hazard remarked, "It was good seeing you men. Keep up the good work and we'll be writing our own protest chant book together in Norway."

The trainees saluted. Hazard returned the salute and dropped his salute quickly before walking away in a solo march, chanting "Peaceful, peaceful, very very peaceful," to himself.

The trainees went back to sitting in the shade created by their laundry as it fluttered in the wind. Hackberry went back to looking at the fence line.

"Hackberry," Newton distracted him. "Tell us more about your Fort Peck adventure with this Asno. Last I heard, you were camped around the Badlands with Asno and the Leonard kid."

Hackberry sat on the ground and looked up at the laundry fluttering in the breeze before continuing his story. Bowperson, Newton, Overture, and Gumabay sat on the ground in a semicircle around him as he eyeballed the purple man, who was now pointing at the C-540 that had just taken off.

Hackberry told them about resuming that overland journey with Asno, Leonard, and Johnschild. Asno had been acting quite strangely, hidden away in a tent and fiddling with his radios. He would not even join the men by the campfire at night and share some whiskey. As a matter of fact, Asno hardly ever drank at all. But after about three days at their Badlands camp, Asno had finally reached a decision. "Well, we're going to try our luck with the Reconstituted Lakota Nation and the Black Hills. We're going around the Badlands, but I got in touch with our attaché with the RLN, and he tells me he has permission to guide us through Lakota territory. This is going to save us a week. Quite possibly more if we can link up with a friendly unit on the other side of the RLN."

When the group did reach the borders of the Black Hills, they were greeted by General MacBison himself. The RLN's leader was a tall man with a wide-brimmed hat that concealed most of his hair, which was pitch black, yet had a tinge of red. MacBison made a point of personally greeting Asno because his reputation as a fine rebel commander preceded him. MacBison wanted to see him in person. He also wanted to inform Asno personally that the group would be guided through his territory by an armed escort of RLN soldiers and that Asno would be taking the rebel attaché to the RLN, a diplomat called Vargas, with him. "Colonel Asno, you can pass through our lands in safety, but you must give me your word that you will take this animal with you – wherever it is that you are going. And you must never bring it back."

Vargas apparently had been smoking more than his fair share of the tobacco supply, had been drinking more than three men's fair share of the liquor supply, and had accumulated a substantial gambling debt in brothels and saloons across the Black Hills. MacBison needed Vargas to leave before one of his people ended the man's life, causing a diplomatic uproar with the Broadband Rebels who surrounded RLN territory.

Hackberry looked fondly back on that part of their journey to Fort Peck. They had plenty of forage and water for their horses, and the RLN maintained a network of trails and bridges throughout the area, which made for exceptionally easy riding.

It seemed the farther into rebel-held territory they ventured, whether it was held by the Sioux or the Broadband Rebels, the more peaceful things became. The MQ Wildfire scout drones were nowhere to be seen this far away from the D.C. Government's military and paramilitary bases. And where there were no scout drones, there were no iTolerators or Acceptors unless there were combat controller personnel around, and no enemy ground units had been in the Black Hills for 10 years. For the first time in years, Hackberry felt safe from strafing or bombing from above.

General MacBison definitely had his shit together in the RLN, and he definitely was not wrong about Vargas. After just three hours of riding, Asno gave Hackberry strict orders to not let Vargas near him. The man was a drunk, far worse than even Beetle Johnschild, and this offended Asno. Asno, for all of his tactical brilliance, could be a bit puritan in his sensibilities from time to time.

Despite Vargas' faults, the man was definitely not useless. Far from it: He was quite resourceful. Almost as if he had known he would be kicked out and ejected from the RLN someday, he had hidden stashes of booze, tobacco, and ammunition all along the trail. And despite all of his prevarications that got him kicked out of the Black Hills, Vargas truly proved his worth when he unveiled his greatest stash. Hidden on the northern border of the Black Hills was the Armored Scout Vehicle he originally drove down to the hills when he was assigned to serve as diplomatic attaché two months earlier, still with a full fuel cell.

Despite Vargas' protestations, Asno gave their armed escorts from the RLN their horses and all of Vargas' booze as a thank you.

In a few short days, they made it all the way to Northeastern Montana in Vargas' Armored Scout over relatively unbroken roads and linked up with friendly rebel forces just outside Fort Peck.

After Hackberry had told this much of the story, he noticed the sun was soon to set. "I reckon we need to gather up our laundry now and get back to the barracks, fellas. That's enough yapping from me for one day."

Trainee Hackberry: 128 January 0039

It was the early morning of Day of Training 94. Hackberry had pulled another red-eye shift on fire watch, and it felt like an ordinary morning. He recorded notes in the platoon logbook whenever something happened during his shift. Ostensibly, this was a way of recording information so the next man to take fire watch would be able to see what had been going on.

That evening, he dutifully recorded in the logbook:

0300: Watch handover complete. Safety check complete. All calm.
0313: Trainee Belmont used the latrine.
0319: Trainee Ricker yelled out in his sleep as if he were dreaming about participating in a spelling bee.
0330: Safety check complete. All calm.

But as an added benefit, this logbook was the way Hackberry maintained a modicum of sanity while pulling these early-morning watch shifts. If only he knew how to fold, he'd be able to get some damn sleep at Fort Freeperson. But in lieu of folding, he pulled two or three fire watch shifts a day.

Earlier during his fire watch shift, Hackberry decided to test Doc Newton's theory that there was no saltpeter in their soy eggs in order to kill their sex drives while in training – that it was all a physiological response to external factors. That it was the stress of Tolerance Corps Training itself that rendered the trainees impotent for these many weeks; simple deep-breathing techniques would restore a man's libido under such conditions.

For the second night in a row, in the privacy of the latrine, Hackberry proved Doc Newton's theory right. After 94 days of Tolerance Corps Camp, after 94 days of being as backed up as the unisex bathroom line at the *WWFL Gridiron Mania Bowl* during the magician's performance at halftime, Hackberry felt like his former high school self, discovering the internet again while secluded away in the latrine for a few minutes at a time.

He omitted these insights from his log entries for the evening.

After all, Graduation Day was less than a week away for Hackberry, Bowperson, and the rest of Alfa Platoon. But Day of Training 94 was no ordinary training day. Day of Training 94 happened to fall on Tolerance Day. And Tolerance Day was a day to be celebrated throughout the Unified Society, even in Fort Freeperson.

When the recorded bugle call sounded at 0415 that morning to wake the whole company up, and when Alfa Platoon immediately jumped out of bed and started dressing themselves for the physical training they usually began at 0430, Sergeant Cornwall stumbled out of the barracks office where he had been sleeping.

"Trainees!" Cornwall yelled, still dressed only in his underwear but already chewing on a piece of mint gum.

Alfa Platoon ceased what they were doing and stood at the position of attention in various stages of undress.

"Boys!" Cornwall paused. "Men! Free men of the Unified Society. Today is Tolerance Day you overeager killing machines! Drop your socks and sleep in 'til zero six thirty then fall out for chow!"

"Hooyah, Sergeant!" The men of Alfa Platoon returned to their cots.

Hackberry's shift ended at 0500, which afforded him 90 minutes of much-needed cot time. He napped, dreaming vividly about chow time. The food was one of the best things about Tolerance Corps Camp.

That morning, the company mess was full of the usual allotment of biscuits, mushroom gravy, hash browns, soy eggs, pancakes, salted kelp, steamed kale, radishes, and turnip greens with plenty of fruit juice to go around. Hackberry grabbed his usual assortment of eggs, hash browns, biscuits, and gravy and drowned everything in hot sauce. Although it was the same food as always,

Major Manos arranged for a special treat for the trainees by allowing them 15 minutes to eat, 10 minutes longer than usual.

After breakfast, Alfa Platoon fell back into formation outside Echo Company's mess hall and awaited further instruction from Sergeant Cornwall. Within a few minutes, Sergeant Cornwall exited the barracks, put on his Smokey Bear hat, and walked over to the assembled platoon.

"Sir, Alfa Platoon reports as ordered!" Bowperson yelled and Alfa Platoon stood at the position of attention.

"Very good, Alfa Platoon. Parade rest!" The men shifted to the at-ease position.

"Happy Tolerance Day!" Cornwall yelled to the men.

"Hooyah, Sergeant!" Alfa Platoon yelled back.

"Very good, Alfa Platoon. Did you get some chow?"

"Hooyah!" Alfa Platoon responded particularly emphatically.

"Well, that fifteen minutes or so you got to eat is about to become an everyday thing. Graduation Day is six days away. Hooyah?"

"Hooyah!" Alfa Platoon responded with a sound reminiscent of the buzzing of well-fed hornets.

"Now, I know you have been trained to march, trained to fight, trained to shoot, trained to protest, trained to kill!"

"Kill kill kill!" Alfa Platoon responded as they always did when their Sergeant said the word.

Hackberry thought to himself that Alfa Platoon was becoming quite a lovely death cult. It was no wonder the rebels gave up their ground in almost every battle when they made contact with Tolerance Corps infantry.

"Now, you need to get ready! Ready for the last challenge before you can survive Fort Freeperson and get out into the world." Cornwall walked into the middle of the platoon's formation and tapped Trainee Jardin on the shoulder. "Do you know what that is, Trainee Jardin?"

"Sir, Trainee Jardin reports as ordered. Sir, I do not know!"

"That's okay, Jardin. Take a wild-ass guess for me."

"Sir, I don't know. More killing?"

"Good guess, Jardin!" Cornwall smiled and patted him on the back. "But wrong!" He yelled in Jardin's ear. "Drop and give me twenty."

As Jardin dropped to the ground and began counting his pushups, Sergeant Cornwall continued, "Not more killing. There will be plenty of time for that when you all get deployed. No. Now is the time to impress Colonel King and General Moore. Hooyah?"

"Hooyah!"

"Good. Because now the next six days of your lives are going to be devoted to the ancient art of military parades! About face!"

Alfa Platoon expertly pivoted 180 degrees to the rear.

"Forward!" Cornwall yelled.

"Forward!" Alfa Platoon echoed.

"March!"

For the next six hours, stopping only for water breaks and a lunch of bagged rations, Sergeant Cornwall marched Alfa Platoon on the training grounds, simulating the pattern they'd be marching on the parade ground on Graduation Day.

Captain Leroy T. Hazard: 128 January 0039

"Congratulations, Hazard. You are now a Captain of the Tolerance Corps." Major Manos pushed the double silver bars of a Captain insignia across his desk to Hazard.

"Thank you, Sir." Hazard saluted and dropped his salute the instant Major Manos started to drop his, then picked up his new Captain bars.

"Dismissed, Captain Hazard. Good luck in Norway, and have a happy Tolerance Day," Manos said.

Captain Hazard executed a left face and exited Major Manos' office. He made his way out of Echo Company's administrative building to the drill pad to see how the four training platoons of Echo Company were doing out there.

Hazard had always suspected Major Manos disliked him.

Hazard had heard the rumors before that Major Manos and Colonel King believed he might be a DIS plant, but Hazard had always respected the man and thought he deserved fair dealing from him. Yet Manos had never invited Hazard to share his table in the 96th Battalion Officers' cafeteria. Manos never shared any war stories, never talked about family back in the DHZs, and never took Hazard under his wing. Hazard knew Manos was a fast-track officer and a very busy man. Hazard just assumed he'd one day gain his commanding officer's respect and admiration.

But this promotion ceremony just proved his fears accurate. Instead of promoting him in a ceremony front of the entire company, and instead of pinning the double bars on his collar himself, Manos chose to conduct the ceremony alone in his office and passed the Captain bars across his oversized desk. Manos clearly hated him.

Hazard took a turn into the officers' latrine and stood before the mirror. He popped off the single-barred insignia of a Lieutenant and looked at himself without any insignia on his collar. He looked just like an enlisted man – a ragtag Intolerant brought in off the street. But he wasn't. He'd given up on a promising career as a civil engineer, sitting near the top of his class at Stanford. During his first

0115

two years at Stanford, he thought he would help unify the fractured Unified Society of America through designing better roads, railways, and bridges to replace those that had been destroyed in the fighting.

But during his junior year, reality set in. His father, Mr. Joseph Hazard, had been a successful architect in Bueno Francisco, and his mother, Ms. Brittney Paquet Hazard, had been a successful systems analyst, troubleshooting business systems for many tech companies in the Bay Area. They had been doing well and could afford to send Leroy to Stanford without a scholarship. But three years ago, Ms. Paquet Hazard succumbed to the Bison Hoof Pox Outbreak of 0036. Mr. Hazard took to drinking and gambling, unable to shake his grief.

As it turned out, Mr. Hazard was a terrible gambler. There was no more money for school. But there was a way out. A friend of his father, a well-dressed man from D.C. in an Italian faux wool suit, approached Leroy at a family reunion with a very handsome offer. Leroy would be able to graduate without going into debt or selling his organs. He would only need to go to an official recruiter and apply for a Tolerance Corps Officers Training scholarship. He'd then serve as an officer after graduation. Acceptance was a foregone conclusion.

Tears began to well in Leroy Hazard's eyes. He'd convince Manos and get him to believe he was no DIS spy. Up until now, he had been trying to get his commanding officer's approval by whipping Echo Company into shape with a strong focus on uniform and appearance standards. And that emphasis on preening, folding, and manicuring would soon pay off now that the graduation parade was around the corner.

Hazard recomposed himself, seeing his expression of frustration disappear in the mirror. He pinned the double-barred Captain insignia on his collar, walked out of the officers' latrine, and continued on his way to the company's training grounds. Manos might not care for his methods, but Hazard had shaped the four platoons of Echo Company into some of the finest trainees he had ever seen. Now, he needed to prove that upon the parade grounds on Graduation Day.

Upon arrival to the training grounds, Hazard could see the parade taking shape. Sergeant Cornwall was guiding Alfa Platoon through its steps. Sergeant Olmeid was with Bravo Platoon. Sergeant Pineda guided Charlie Platoon. And Sergeant Young was barking orders at Delta Platoon. Visibly chomping with a closed mouth on the side of the training ground with a central view of the action stood First Sergeant First Class Hamilton.

Hazard approach Hamilton, making sure to approach him from his right side. The last time he approached Hamilton from his left side, his eye-patch side, things went poorly. "Sergeant Hamilton," Hazard called from Hamilton's right side.

Hamilton turned and saluted Hazard. "Hello, Captain Hazard. Congratulations appear to be in order," he said, looking at Hazard's collar.

"Thank you, Sergeant." He returned and dropped his salute. "I'm headed for Operation Norwegian Emancipation with a company of my own soon."

"I wish I could go with you, Sir."

"I wish you could go with me, too, eye patch or no eye patch. I have a feeling you'd keep me and my people alive out there, if you get my meaning."

"Yes, Sir," Hamilton responded as he watched the platoons practice.

"So, how are they doing?" Hazard asked.

"They look like dog shit, Sir. But this is just day one of five days we have to make them look respectable."

"What do you see wrong so far?"

"Well, for one thing, Alfa Platoon is overly amped as usual. They keep stepping faster than Sergeant Cornwall's cadence, and the Sergeant needs to adjust on the fly. They are overeager and that is not going to look good from the parade stand with General Moore and Colonel King. Bravo Platoon is good on timing, but their spacing is completely off. See how the third, fourth, and fifth ranks are different distances from each other? Big interval problem. The good news is Charlie Platoon looks all right so far. But Delta Platoon, they're a complete and total clusterfrack. They can't keep in time and step."

Captain Hazard saw what Sergeant Hamilton saw. The man was spot-on in his diagnosis. But as Hamilton was describing the problems, Hazard's mind kept drifting to Norway. If they were about to be in a shooting war and dropped from a plane or a ship into Norway this summer, would any of this parade business matter? Nevertheless, winning the Brass Ring and being the best marching company in the entire 96th Battalion would be a lovely parting gift, and proof to Major Manos and Colonel King that Hazard had a hand in shaping one of the best training companies in the history of the Tolerance Corps.

As Hazard watched and studied the movements of his troops, his eyes drifted across the training ground to the fence line, where he saw a large man, dressed in purple, wearing a smiling purple mask.

"Sergeant Hamilton, what is that thing?" Hazard asked.

"What thing, Sir?"

"That rotund man dressed in all purple and wearing a purple mask standing on the other side of the fence line? What is it? And how long has it been there?"

"Sir, I do not see the purple man you are referring to. And none of my Sergeants or their trainees have seen him either. But he has been *not there* for as long as I can remember."

"I suppose I never noticed him before."

"Really, Sir? Are you really just now not seeing him?"

Hazard folded one arm over the other, raising one hand to his chin and shook his head a bit. "I suppose I always thought the rules about the purple man were just one of those jokes we played on trainees. Like a goblin story for telling to kids, if you know what I mean. What do you think he is?"

"I'm a good soldier, Captain. What I think he is, Sir, is I think he is not there and I think we don't see him."

"Well I'll be damned, Sergeant. He *really is* not really there."

Doctor Xavier Newton: 130 January 0039

Like he did back in the civilian world, back in the Megalopolis DHZ, Doc Newton looked forward to the weekend. Back home in the Dominion of Massachusetts, Xavier enjoyed spending his weekends relaxing with his friends and family over a bootlegged cocktail, some conversation, and a Bureau of Professional Football Wrestling match.

At Fort Freeperson, Doc Newton enjoyed spending his weekends relaxing with friends over conversation and some laundry. As he got closer and closer to actual combat, Newton, like many of the other trainees, became more and more interested in hearing stories of actual combat experience from men like Sergeant Hamilton and Trainee Hackberry.

Sergeant Hamilton never socialized with trainees and would only share cursory information of his experiences, such as the time he took out a machine gun nest outside Toronto or the time he and his team literally fixed bayonets and charged a supply depot in Veracruz after they ran out of ammo. Although these stories made it clear that Sergeant Hamilton was a very effective soldier and proficient in the arts of badassery, Newton never got a sense of what it was like to be in combat from hearing these stories. Hamilton's stories were always splash and dash, full of honor and glory. But Hackberry's stories had a realness, an earthiness, to them.

On Day of Training 96, with Graduation Day getting closer, Newton knew that the trainees of Alfa Platoon would soon either be going into Advanced Technical Training or to a combat unit. In a combat unit, the training would be very dangerous and learning would be very much acquired on the job. If the Tolerance Corps selected a trainee for Advanced Technical Training, that meant the trainee was destined for a support sector job within the Corps, such as a radar technician on a vessel, a drone mechanic on an airbase, or a construction technician attached to the Department of Infrastructure. But rumor around Fort Freeperson was that if you already had a skill related to fighting or medicine, you'd be deployed to a front line combat unit. Newton knew that he'd be seeing live action very quickly after Graduation Day, and he only had his Tolerance Corps training to rely upon when the action inevitably happened.

Now the Corps had trained him pretty well. Newton knew that much. He was now proficient at using the M8 assault rifle, the M9 pistol, and the M320 grenade launcher. He was confident in his ability to shoot things or blow them up, whichever the situation required. He was also confident in his ability to fight hand-to-hand, with a knife, an empty M8, a bayonet, a baton, or his bare hands.

But while Newton felt confident in his ability to inflict harm, he had no idea how to avoid getting harmed himself. He could always fall back on the Corps' training on camouflage and evasion, but his past experience taught him there was no substitute for hands-on experience. He suspected he would be lucky to last a week in combat.

Despite three years of medical school, practicing in simulations, and reading books, Newton did not truly understand how to wield his scalpel until he had a few weeks under his belt during his internship at the Kennedy Organ Extraction Center.

During laundry duty on Day of Training 96, as Newton and the usual crew of Bowperson, Overture, Gumabay, and Hackberry supervised the evaporation process of their laundry, the men talked about what assignment they thought they would get and what they hoped they might get.

"Me, I know I'm getting some shit detail attached to the Department of Protests," Overture said, shaking his head. "Manos as much as said so when I was in his office, something about my diversity enhancing protest unit effectiveness, or some bullshit like that. All the other guys who got picked up outside the DHZ – probably gonna get sent to a combat unit. I'd rather be there, out in the sticks. But they'll have me smellin' of incense and chantin' in protests by the government against the government all up and down the East and West Coasts."

"Protest duty, baby! That's what I want," Gumabay chimed in. "I have no clue where they're sending me. But are you saying if

I get my suntan going, Major Manos will deploy me to protest duty, too?"

"Hell. It's worth a shot," Bowperson said. "But you are runnin' out of time, Gumabay. We only got four days left at this place."

"Better get your ass in the microwave, kid!" Overture added.

"To be honest," Doc Newton said, "I never really noticed that either of you was diverse. I guess I am just that open-minded and accepting."

"That's some bullshit, Doc!" Overture said with a laugh.

"But seriously, though, Manos really said? About the protest unit?" Newton asked curiously.

"Yup. Sure did."

"Aw, hell," Hackberry grunted. "They're taking one of the few guys around here who knows how to survive in the woods, and they're gonna make a professional protester out of him? That's just fucking spectacular. That means that whenever I get sent to Norway, or Vermont, or Mexico, or some new war we haven't even started yet with the frickin' Caliphate or some shit, I'm gonna be surrounded by suburban DHZ dwellers who got caught with Overture's dairy products."

"Well, if they had my dairy products," Overture smiled, "they'd be healthy, strong men who would keep you nice and safe, Hackberry. Probably nice and warm at night too, if it gets lonely on those cold nights up in Norway."

"Very re-a-fucking-suring, Overture. But you belong out there." Hackberry pointed to the fence line. "Just like the rest of you. You all belong out there." As he spoke, Hackberry gradually raised his voice. "DoP duty, being a mechanic or a deckhand, it's all bullshit to keep you in a cage. Out there is freedom. Once I get out there, I'm taking my freedom back and disappearing back into the wild."

Bowperson, who had been listening with amusement up until this point, jumped in. "Quiet, Hackberry! Someone hears you saying that – you're harvested. Just hang in there a little while longer, and we'll be out in the operational Tolerance Corps. Things'll get better. You'll see."

Hackberry, not liking being told to shut up, no matter how politely or justifiably the telling was done, tensed up his jaw, balled his hands into fists, and stared at Bowperson.

Newton, looking both to distract Hackberry from his impending rant about freedom and liberty and to hear some more stories about battle, jumped in. "Hackberry, about the wild. Tell us more about it. I've never seen combat, and it sounds like you were involved in some pretty heavy stuff up around Fort Peck."

"The Siege of Fort Peck, huh? I guess that depends. Is Fort Peck an acceptable topic of conversation for you, Squad Leader Bowperson?"

"I ain't the damn Department of Free Speech, Gus. Just keep your voice down," Bowperson responded.

"Well, that might be the case, Reggie. But you remind me of my damn ex sometimes," Hackberry said, shaking his head and kicking the ground. "So, you all want to hear about Fort Peck, then. By time I got there with Asno and company, the siege was well underway. I like to think I helped in winning it, but the reality, fellas, is the siege of Fort Peck was never fought in one spot and never all at once.

"In fact, the most serious fighting was happening about a hundred and thirty miles to the east, near the Montana-Dakota border. That is where the Tolerance Corps was massed, and that is where they kept launching overland relief expeditions to break our siege. It was a true war of arbitration, or attrition, or whatever.

"At Fort Peck itself – huddling around the dam, the landing strip, and the hydroelectric plant – were about five thousand Tolerance Corp soldiers and about another five hundred or so paramilitary sorts from other agencies, mainly DETA and the Department of Infrastructure. On our side, we had far fewer people surrounding them – at most thirty-five hundred. The other fifteen thousand or so rebel soldiers in the area were lined up along the Yellowstone River and fortified at the site of a town called Buford in Dakota. But we had time and supplies on our side.

"From what Asno told me, there was a government army about fifty thousand strong massed on the opposite side of our boys in Dakota, and the government had plenty of M50 Franks Main Battle Tanks, drones, UH-76 attack helos, and M19 Schwarzkopf Armored Fighting Vehicles at their disposal. In a shooting battle, they'd slice right through our positions. And this is exactly why every time they would advance into Montana with the armored tip of their spear, the rebels would vacate their lines and get out of the way of the tip. As soon as the government army advanced more than twenty or so miles into Montana, it was counterattack time for us. Not striking at the tip of the spear, mind you. Striking from the sides, collapsing their supply lines, and cutting the tip of the spear off from the shaft. This happened repeatedly, and we captured dozens of Franks tanks and Schwarzkopf armored vehicles."

"What about the men?" Bowperson asked.

"Oh, the men, we captured them, too. The officers we held for prisoner swaps. The enlisted soldiers, we gave 'em the option. Switch and join our side, or walk your ass back to North Dakota. The soldiers who had been Intolerants before mostly stayed with the rebels. A good portion of the others stayed. The others were paroled back to the Tolerance Corps, because we sure as heck weren't going to feed a bunch of prisoners. But that was a hundred thirty miles from where me and Asno were over at Fort Peck. When we arrived, Colonel Asno met with General Billings–"

"Billings?" Bowperson interrupted. "Like the town? Did they name the town after him?"

"Naw, Bowperson! The town's been called Billings at least going back to the year aught-aught-aught-aught. He named himself after the town."

"How's he gonna name himself after a town?" Overture chimed in.

"Shit, guys." Hackberry shrugged his shoulders. "If I knew why generals do what generals do, you think I'd be stuck in Fort Freeperson with y'all?" Hackberry paused, staring at the fence. The group fell silent for a few moments before he continued. "So as I was saying, General Billings told Colonel Asno to go to the south siege line and take over Jig Troop. Now Jig would be Juliet in our Tolerance Corps manner of speaking. So Jig Troop, they had just lost their commander a few days before to diarrhea or dysentery or something like that. Asno went to Jig Troop's position, and so we went.

"Well now, Jig Troop consisted of about forty-five soldiers at that time, a Troop is sorta like one of our platoons, usually with about sixty or so soldiers, so they were a little shorthanded. Jig Troop was holed up in a series of dugouts in a hill along Bear Creek Bay, about five or six miles south of the dam and about eight miles from the enemy air strip that sat in the middle of their defenses. Now, the spring and summer of '38 had been a wet one all over the Great Plains. Fort Peck Lake was high and the ground was soggy. Jig Troop was a muddy mess and smelled like shit. It was no wonder their last commander died of disease. So Asno, Vargas, Leonard, and me, we spent our first day digging holes for latrines and digging out a new dugout for ourselves." Hackberry paused, looking out at the fence line.

Newton nudged him back to the topic at hand. "What happened next?" Newton asked.

"Right. Now the siege had been at a stalemate. We were well in range of Fort Peck's one hundred and fifty-five millimeter howitzer cannons, but those cannons could only hit the north side of hills. We were dug into the south side, so all they could do was give us a good shaking with those heavy guns.

"We had no artillery to speak of. Our weapon was time and starvation. And our goal was to drain Fort Peck of its supplies and deny them any reinforcements. We were close enough to take down any enemy aircraft that tried to touch down at Fort Peck's landing strip with our shoulder-fired Kramarenko missiles – smuggled in through Alaska and Hudson's Bay from our suppliers in the Russian Empire. But the Russian Kramarenko missiles we bought, and our own knock-off models – they were called the FIM78 Bobcats – both only had a range of about five miles. We just could not hit any aircraft flying over Fort Peck at high elevation when we were that far away. So at this point in time, the Tolerance Corps kept resupplying their besieged forces via airdrop. And we could not do a dang thing about it."

"Everything they had came in by parachute?" Trainee Pedro Gumabay asked.

"Yep, Pete," Hackberry nodded. "The D.C. Government has airpower out their hindquarters. And Fort Peck was bristling with heavy cannons. But see, old Asno was a student of history, and he told us stories about World War One and Vietnam. In those wars, soldiers outwitted artillery and airpower by tunneling. Boys, I ain't ever shoveled so much in my life over those next few weeks. It was muddy, it was rocky, it was sloppy. The tunnels we dug smelled of dung and vomit. But we dug 'em."

"After months of digging, hauling mud out of Asno's tunnels, and bracing the tunnels we dug with timber, we got within close enough range to start taking potshots at the supply planes dropping cargo to the enemy garrison. On the first day after popping out our tunnels about three-quarters of a mile from the dam, one of Jig Troop's fire teams actually hit one of those C-540s, sending it crashing into the lake. Those Tolerance Corps types had to know they were goosed when that happened.

"So that is what we did after that. And all the other troops on the siege line copied the same strategy. We divided ourselves up into fire teams, and that was a missile tech carrying the Kramarenkos, a com tech for handling the radio, a spotter for looking out for bad guys approaching, and two snipers for taking out those bad guys when they got too dang close."

"This Asno sounds like a badass, Hackberry," Newton remarked with a distant look on his face. "I'd hate to run into him in a dark alley."

"Don't know that he's ever been in an alley, Doc," Hackberry smiled. "But he sure as sunshine was – maybe is still – a tough hombre. I haven't seen him since the Seattle Cod Protests, but I reckon he's too smart to have gotten pinched up back in Seattle. His ideas singlehandedly changed the battle of Fort Peck for us. I doubt he got captured or killed."

"So, which one were you, Hackberry?" Gumabay asked.

"Which one what? Captured or killed?" Hackberry responded.

Pedro made himself more clear. "I mean, which one were you on the fire team? What did you do out there at Fort Peck?"

"Oh, that. I led a fire team and was a sniper, Pete," Hackberry replied. "I took out the bad guys and their artillery spotters."

"Well, did you win? Did you take the dam?" Pedro followed up.

"I don't know. Truth be told, I think we got close. I mean, we were really close to breaking their backs so long as the battle line held out along the Yellowstone River and in North Dakota, keeping those Tolerance Corps relief expeditions tied up. But I had to go. One day late in the fall of '38, Colonel Asno said he had an important mission out west in Seattle. He said the fate of the whole war rested on his mission. Asno left, and so I left."

Gus Hackberry: 133 January 0039

On Day of Training 99, Trainee Hackberry was in full survival mode. He knew he was just one day away from graduating Tolerance Corps Camp, just one day away from Surviving Fort Freeperson with his mind and body intact. Admittedly, the Tolerance Corps had claimed his long hair and his red beard, but he still had his eyes and he still had his spleen. All he needed to do was survive one more day of parade practice and then the parade itself on Graduation Day.

After Graduation Day, he would no doubt be shipped off to a combat unit. Everyone in Echo Company knew he was the best shot with a rifle they had. And each and every trainee in Echo Company would feel at ease if they knew he was covering their backsides out in the field.

But once beyond the confines of the razor-wired fences of Fort Freeperson and beyond the equally restrictive confines of the Designated Habitation Zones, he would make his escape.

That morning, during Alfa Platoon's run, Hackberry noticed the conspicuous absence of the purple man at the fence line. He began to wonder whether Tolerance Corps indoctrination was getting to him like it was clearly getting to Bowperson. He now wondered whether he had finally acquired the ability to not see that the Tolerance Corps insisted he have.

After 80 minutes of physical training, Alfa Platoon took rapid showers and changed into their dress uniforms for their last day of parade practice. That day's practice would be an exact run-through of what Graduation Day had in store at the 96th Battalion Parade Grounds. Every detail would be in place. Bass and snare drums would be thumping. Alfa Platoon would be marching alongside all three sister platoons in Echo Company, as well as the other seven training companies in the 96th Battalion. There would be a total of 32 platoons with nearly 1,800 trainees and their sergeants marching in the parade on Graduation Day, and Hackberry could tell that Sergeant Cornwall, Sergeant Hamilton, and the newly minted Captain Hazard were very eager to have one of the four platoons of Echo Company win the Brass Ring, the rotating trophy award given to the platoon that gained top scores for exhibiting the best marching form on Graduation Day.

The officers assembled in the parade stand on Graduation Day would evaluate the parade marchers on several vital competencies that had been ingrained in the trainees over the last 100 days. First came interval, the precisely measured and even spacing between a soldier and the soldiers to his sides. Second, they judged the trainees on their dress, which encompassed the ability to line up side by side so that soldiers appeared to be in perfect rows while marching past an individual. Third, there was cover, the ability to line up in rows so that the soldiers appeared to be in perfect rows when marching toward an individual. Fourth came cadence – marching in rhythmic step so that all soldiers' feet hit the ground at the same exact moment. In order to reinforce this habit, Sergeant Cornwall taught Alfa Platoon the art of the "heel beat," a technique involving driving their left feet into the pavement at a special angle, so that the marching platoon would emit a sort of rhythmic pulse. With this pulse, they would be able to stay in rhythmic step, even without someone vocally calling out a cadence to keep them synchronized. Lastly, for Graduation Day, exhibiting the best-worn dress uniforms would often make the difference between getting the Brass Ring versus eternal shame.

As for those dress uniforms, they were something of an alien experience for the trainees. The men of Alfa Platoon had spent most of the past 99 days wearing their physical training shorts and t-shirts during their sleeping time and their morning exercise, then their camouflage battle uniforms during the rest of the day. They had spent very little time inside their highly starched, neatly pressed dress uniforms until the last few days of training.

Hackberry observed the Tolerance Corps dress uniform was a striking masterpiece of color that cut a noticeable figure in any room or outdoor event. Instead of their usual combat boots, they wore black socks and coal-black Oxford shoes, which they shined to be so shiny that a soldier could see his own reflection on his feet in the right light. They wore tree-tan khaki trousers that sported a black stripe running the length of the outside seams. Up top, they wore a black, button-up jacket with brass buttons over a black, button-up shirt with white buttons. Soldiers with a rank above private wore blaze orange chevron stripes on the arms of their coats and shirts, just beneath their shoulders. Hackberry noticed that his friend Bowperson was one such soldier, promoted to the rank of corporal as of Graduation Day. Bowperson had two orange chevrons cutting a profile on the arms of his black jacket. Hackberry, like most of the men of Alfa Platoon, would remain a private and had no stripes to wear.

On their heads, they wore a blaze orange garrison cap. The hats were unadorned, except for officers who pinned their officer's insignia to the left front of their caps.

On the left side of their chests, the soldiers wore their medals, of which the trainees of Alfa Platoon had already earned two: one for graduating Tolerance Corps Camp and one for making a parachute landing in a live operation. On Graduation Day, only Alfa, Charlie, and Delta Platoons of Echo Company would be able to wear these medals thanks to their efforts at Operation Manhattan. Their sisters in Bravo Platoon would have to do without the airborne badge thanks to their helicopter landing that day.

On the right side of their chests, every soldier and officer of the Tolerance Corps wore the insignia that had come to symbolize the triumph of the General Will worldwide: a brass globe of the western hemisphere, with a brilliant "T" emanating from the North Pole and two olive branches extending from the Atlantic and Pacific oceans, flanking both sides of the globe.

All morning, from 0745 to 1145, the 32 platoons practiced their steps on the parade grounds with their sergeants guiding them through the maneuvers. The parade grounds reminded Hackberry of a football field with a running track circling it. A large grandstand overlooked the field from one side. Each time they circled past the grandstand, Sergeant Cornwall barked the command *"Eyes right!"* and Alfa Platoon turned their heads toward the parade stand. Each time, Hackberry could see Captain Hazard and Major Manos watching the formations move by from their vantage point in the grandstand. Hazard appeared to be scribbling notes on his tablet. Undoubtedly, he was recording everything the platoons of Echo Company had been doing wrong.

It was during their third practice march of the morning at the parade grounds that Hackberry felt an immense sense of relief. As Sergeant Cornwall yelled, "Eyes right!" Hackberry thought – rather, he knew – he could see a man in a hooded purple jumpsuit wearing a purple smiling mask crouching under the parade stand.

"I'm not losing it," Hackberry whispered quietly to himself.

Around 1145, Sergeant Cornwall congratulated Alfa Platoon on a good day's march and informed the men of their next activities for the day. "All right, Alfa Platoon. We're heading back to Echo Company barracks. Upon arrival, change out of your dress black-and-tans and fall back out for chow wearing your battle uniforms. After chow, it's picture time! And I won't have my platoon looking fancy for its platoon picture. You are killers, not dancers!"

"Kill kill kill!" Alfa Platoon roared.

"So change out of your parade uniforms and get back to looking like soldiers! Hooyah?"

"Hooyah, Sergeant!"

Cornwall smiled while chomping his gum, beaming with pride while looking out over his troops. He could see these men were ready to get out into the world and fight. He added one last public service announcement before lunch. "And remember, yearbooks are available for just nineteen thousand credits, just half a day's pay and you can save all these cherished memories of Fort Freeperson for the rest of your lives."

Everything seems so dang expensive, Hackberry thought to himself. He had little experience with currency, as the people he associated himself with tended to barter or exchange silver and gold when they wanted to make a deal. But he could remember hearing his parents talk about the changeover from U.S. Dollars to U.S.

Credits about 40 years ago. And they talked about being able to buy a loaf of bread for a measly 10 credits back then. But in '39, a loaf would cost at least 3,200 credits. In fact, the D.C. government did not even print out any paper currency smaller than the Senator Bieber 1,000-credit bill.

After lunch, the men of Alfa Platoon gathered up in formation outside the mess hall and then marched over to their drill pad, carrying the Echo Company flags. Upon arriving at the training grounds, Sergeant Cornwall looked around for a suitable site to have their photo taken and decided upon a set of aluminum benches over by the fence line.

It was working out nicely. They arranged themselves in three rows. The tallest trainees stood on the benches, the trainees of average height stood in front of them, and the shortest trainees took a knee in the front row. They set up their company flags to their sides for the photo. The fence and the trees beyond the fence would form the backdrop.

As one of the taller trainees, Hackberry walked up to the aluminum bench, but just as he was taking a step up onto it, he paused as he caught a glimpse of the purple man crouching in the tall grass about five meters beyond the fence line. Trainee Alemaker, who had been just behind him, gave him a nudge up on the bench before Sergeant Cornwall could scream something about hesitation being a fatal disease.

As the trainees of Alfa Platoon assembled for their photo, Sergeant Cornwall set up a camera on a tripod and joined the formation. He snapped a photo with a remote control for the camera. "All right, Alfa Platoon. That was a tester, tester number one. I will take two more. And don't fracking smile. I need Alfa Platoon looking hard as hell."

Just as he snapped the second photo, Hackberry heard someone yell "Yeah!" loudly from behind him. Many of the trainees laughed audibly.

"Yelling? And Giggling?!" Sergeant Cornwall yelled incredulously. "Who just did that? Who the hell yelled 'yeah' during

0131

the photo?" The trainees of Alfa Platoon remained silent for a few moments.

"To hell with it!" Sergeant Cornwall clapped his hands together. "You all are going to pay for this! Now stand the hell still for picture number three or I swear to the creator I will have you all harvested!"

He snapped another photo and ordered, "Squad Leader Bowperson, march Alfa Platoon out to the middle of the asphalt drill pad. Keep this pack of giggling schoolgirls in formation and await further instruction." Sergeant Cornwall walked away briskly. Carrying his camera and tripod, he headed for the Echo Company administrative building.

About 15 minutes later, Sergeant Cornwall returned with Sergeant Hamilton. Hamilton carried printouts of the photos Sergeant Cornwall had just taken, examining them as he walked.

Sergeant Hamilton smacked his mint-green gum as he addressed the trainees. "Alfa Platoon, Sergeant Cornwall tells me we may have had a Tolerance Corps Prime Values issue during picture time today. And I want to give you one last chance to 'fess up. So tell me, which one of you yelled 'yeah' during the photo just now?"

No one standing in the ranks of Alfa Platoon said a word.

Sergeant Hamilton continued, "I see. I see there definitely is a Prime Values issue here." He walked to the front row of the formation and stood directly in front of Trainee Gumabay, reading his name tag on his shirt. "Trainee Gumb-uh … Gumbaboh, tell us all what the definition of the first Prime Value in the Tolerance Corps is."

Now the definition of integrity, the first Prime Value as the Tolerance Corps defined it, had been drilled into the trainees as far back as their time in sensory deprivation. So Trainee Gumabay did not hesitate to announce loudly and proudly, "Sir, Trainee Gumabay reports as ordered. Integrity is the first Prime Value of any soldier in the Tolerance Corps. Integrity means we do the right thing, even when no one else is looking!"

"Especially when no one else is looking! But we're always sure as sunshine gonna be looking!" Sergeant Hamilton announced to the whole group before giving a "Hooyah?"

"Hooyah, Sergeant!" Alfa Platoon responded in unison.

"Now, Trainee Gumbo, what is the second Prime Value of Tolerance Corps soldiers?"

"Sir, Trainee Gumabay reports as ordered," Trainee Gumabay shouted. "Service before self! The Tolerance Corps demands we put the needs of society and the needs of the Tolerance Corps above ourselves!"

"Damn right, Trainee Gumbo!" Sergeant Hamilton slapped Gumabay on the shoulder before ripping off the trainee's name tag. "Did you all hear this man, Alfa Platoon?"

"Hooyah, Sergeant!" Alfa Platoon responded.

Sergeant Hamilton paused the dialogue for a few moments while he rewrote Gumabay's name tag with a permanent marker he always kept on hand for these sorts of occasions.

"Now, Gumbo. Tell us all the third Prime Value of the U.S. Tolerance Corps," Hamilton ordered as he pinned Gumabay's revised name tag onto his chest.

"Sir–" Trainee Gumabay looked down at his new name tag. "Trainee Gumbo reports as ordered. The third Prime Value of the U.S. Tolerance Corps is that we respect the General Will!"

"Respect the General Will! Hooyah, platoon?"

"Hooyah, Sergeant!" Alfa Platoon echoed.

Sergeant Hamilton leaned in a bit toward Trainee Gumbo and spoke softly. "Now, Gumbo. Did you hear someone yell during photo formation?"

"Yes, Sir, I did."

"Was it you?"

"No, Sir!"

"Then who was it?"

"I don't know, Sir."

Hamilton leaned away from Trainee Gumbo and ordered Alfa Platoon. "He doesn't know? He doesn't know! Now everyone drop to the ground and prepare for pushups!"

The men of Alfa Platoon dropped to their hands and feet, just barely touching their chests to the sun-soaked pavement.

"Up!"

Alfa Platoon pushed up.

"Down!"

Alfa Platoon returned to their down position. Sergeant Hamilton repeated this set of commands until the trainees had done 15 pushups. "That was a good warm-up, Trainees. Back on your feet! Feels good?"

The men returned to their feet and yelled, "Feels good, Sir!"

"Now, who here yelled during photo formation?" Hamilton repeated his question for the whole group.

No one responded, so Sergeant Hamilton ordered another set of 15 pushups before returning the men to their feet. Hackberry resisted the urge to wave his hands in the air to cool them off from the welling heat of the drill pad.

"There is a definite integrity issue going on here, Platoon! Now, who yelled during photo formation?" Hamilton loudly growled.

Hackberry knew, and he was sure the rest of Alfa Platoon knew, that it was the god-damned purple man who yelled during the photo formation, but he sure as hell was not going to implicate himself as a purple man seer and he hoped that his fellow trainees had the good sense to reach the same conclusion and pursue the same course of silence. As Hackberry hoped, no one responded.

Hamilton ordered an additional 20 pushups. At this point, many trainees were beginning to tire. Hackberry was now feeling a light burning sensation in his chest and arms from slight fatigue. His hands were red from the asphalt pavement and he could hear the groans of trainees around him.

One trainee yelled, "Whoever did it, just admit it!"

Another yelled, "Have some integrity!"

No one confessed. Sergeant Hamilton began ordering pushups in a new way that would force the trainees to hold themselves up without being able to lock their elbows. "Down! Up! Half down! Hold at halfway up!"

After doing 50 pushups, holding at half-up position inflicted burning pain even on Hackberry, and he could hear the men around him panting and groaning. But surely if everyone just kept their damned mouths shut about the purple man, Alfa Platoon would survive to make it through graduation. But a burning sensation pulsed in his chest, the heat of the pavement radiated through his hands, the corners of tiny rocks in the asphalt dug into his palms.

Yet another trainee yelled, "Have some fracking integrity!" The voice sounded familiar. Was that Bowperson?

Then came a sound from Hackberry's immediate left. "Sir, Trainee Newton reports as ordered!"

Damn it, Hackberry thought to himself. It *was* Bowperson who just yelled that horseshit about integrity and now Newton was about to do something stupid.

"On your feet, Alfa Platoon! Newton has something he wants to say!" Sergeant Hamilton announced happily, rubbing his hands together.

"Shut up, Doc. Shut up. Don't be a hero," Hackberry whispered at him tersely as Sergeant Hamilton briskly walked over to Newton.

"Sir, Trainee Newton Reports as ordered. It was me. I yelled 'yeah!'"

Hamilton nodded his head while slowly turning around to the whole group, booming his voice out. "So Trainee Newton confesses!"

"Sir, yes ... I do," Trainee Newton said in between breaths.

"Excellent!" Hamilton snapped his fingers as he smacked his mint gum. "Now, Trainee Gumbo, get over here!"

"Sir, Trainee Gumbo reports as ordered," Pedro Gumbo, as he was now known, yelled as he ran over to Sergeant Hamilton.

"Gumbo, from what direction did you hear the yelling during photo formation?"

"Sir, I heard it from back and to my left."

"Thank you, Trainee Gumbo. Get back to your spot in formation," Sergeant Hamilton ordered, and Trainee Gumbo ran back to his spot at the front of Alfa Platoon's formation. Sergeant Hamilton spent the next few seconds studying the photo printouts. "Back and to Gumbo's left," Hamilton said, thinking aloud. "And I see here Gumbo is in the middle of the front row of the photo formation. And Newton, where is Newton? Ahah. I see it. Middle row, to Gumbo's right. Can you explain this, Newton?" Sergeant Hamilton held the photo to Doc Newton's face.

Doc Newton hesitated. "Sir, I ... I don't know why ..."

"Probably because it wasn't you who yelled, turd-brain! Did you just admit to something you did not do to help out the platoon?"

"Sir, no. Sir, no, I did not yell 'turd brain.' I mean, yes, I did confess to something I, I'm sorr—"

"Nice try, Newton." Hamilton patted him on the shoulder roughly. "Now, everyone, drop to the ground! Push half up! Hold!"

By making the men hold their pushups halfway up, Sergeant Hamilton made the next 15 pushups last at least half an hour. He elicited three more false confessions from Trainees Burgen, Paris, and Arendes before summarily debunking those confessions. By the end of holding himself up at the half-up position for most of the afternoon of Day of Training 99, Hackberry slid to his knees and started to wonder if he had done the yelling himself.

In the end, he remained silent because he knew it had been the purple man all along. He also knew that it would be a far better fate to claw at hot asphalt than it would be to profess seeing what he was not supposed to see.

After Sergeant Cornwall and Sergeant Hamilton saw they had utterly burned out Alfa Platoon's arms and severely tested their spirit without a single one of them blaming the purple man for yelling during the photo formation, they appeared satisfied that the trainees were ready to graduate.

Sergeant Cornwall ordered Squad Leader Bowperson to march the platoon back to the barracks and gather in the dayroom to await important news.

The notion of important news was the sort of fodder that sent a soldier's brain racing. For trainees, the only news they received came through two streams: the rumor mill and their sergeants or officers. And over the last few days, the rumor spreading around camp was that they'd be getting their post-graduation assignments soon. In many cases – such as the rumor reporting that Fabrajé, the best singer and dancer in *Squad 303 DHZ*, had been killed by Guatemalan terrorists and President Tolerance had just asked Congress to declare war – the rumor mill was utterly false. But this was not one of those cases.

After the men of Alfa Platoon sat for a few minutes on the pleasantly cool tile floor in the dayroom, Sergeant Cornwall walked in, carrying a few pieces of paper. The trainees jumped to their feet as one and shouted, "Sir, Alfa Platoon reports as ordered!"

"Sit down, platoon," Cornwall grumbled as he walked to the front of the dayroom. "I have your assignments, but I am considering having you all fracking recycled back two or three weeks into training after that bullshit you pulled at the photo."

Hackberry observed the nature of Cornwall's threat. The threat of recycling as opposed to organ harvesting was a reassuring sign at this point in the day. Hackberry could not wait to get a look at the list Cornwall had in his hands. Which front would he wind up on? Norway? Montana? Quebec? Vermont? Mexico? Some new war that had started over the last news-starved weeks?

"Well normally, I would read this list out loud and tell you all where you are going," Cornwall continued. "But I am pissed off, so I will summarize and let you read your assignments. But there had better not be any bullshit during tomorrow's parade, or I will fracking scalp you all. Hooyah?"

"Hooyah, Sergeant!"

"Good. Now there is some interesting stuff in here for you all. Some of you are getting assigned to Pacific Coast Protest Command, PacProtComm. Some of you are heading to EastProtComm. Some of you are heading to combat command. Some of you are heading for tech school to be a mechanic or a janitor or a cook or whatever the heck the Corps needs at some of our outposts. Some of you are heading for a new sort of technical training, a new innovation in the Corps' playbook, our Anti Retreat

Detachments, the ARDs. You'll get to learn how to prevent other units in the Corps from retreating by shooting them when they drift back to our lines. You'll play a huge role in finally stopping our losses in the Broadband Rebellions. Hooyah?"

"Hooyah, Sergeant!"

"The real lucky of you are getting to forge some new unit history," Cornwall continued. "We're mustering two brand-new divisions for the Norway campaign, one going in by air and one going in by sea. Both will be victorious! Hooyah?"

"Hooyah, Sergeant!"

Cornwall held several sheets of paper high in the air. "So I am going to hang up your list. Remember your assignment so you can find the correct bus after graduation tomorrow. And save your questions for your sergeants at your next duty station. I've got another platoon full of knuckleheads coming out of sensory deprivation in a few days and I need to save up my energy."

With that, Sergeant Cornwall taped the sheets of paper containing the assignment list for Alfa Platoon to the front wall of the dayroom and went into his office.

The next few moments were some of the most chaotic and exciting moments in the absence of the smell of gunpowder Hackberry could remember. His escape plan, how he would get back to the rebellion, everything depended on this. All 52 of the surviving trainees of Alfa platoon shoved and shimmied their way to the list and scanned for their names. The time was here for everyone to learn their fate. Within about a minute, Hackberry maneuvered his way close enough to the list to read it over and around the craning heads of his Alfa Platoon comrades.

Where would he end up? This question burned in his mind. And would he be assigned with Bowperson, his friend who kept him sane, or at the very least kept him from appearing insane, these last few months? Barely able to contain his excitement, Hackberry stretched his neck and scanned the assignment list.

Alfa Platoon Assignment List

Agarwal, A: Tech School, Naval Mechanic, Naval Station Great Lakes, Illinois.

Alemaker, I: Tech School, Military Police, Camp Ashcroft, Missouri.

Alfonso, T: Combat Infantry, 10th Mountain Division, presently deployed to Vermont.

Arendes, F: Tech School, Radar Tech, Earhart Air Base, Texas.

Badplacer, J: Combat Infantry, 39th "River Delta" Division, presently deployed to Vermont.

Basston, N: Tech School, Anti Retreat Detachment, Fort Cooperation, Oregon.

Belmont, G: Combat Infantry, 138th Airborne Division, presently mustering for Operation Norwegian Emancipation at Halifax Air Station, Nova Scotia.

Belton, E: Tech School, Naval Mechanic, Naval Station Great Lakes, Illinois.

Bernard, T: Combat Infantry, 1st "Big Red One" Division, presently deployed to quell Broadband Rebellions in North Dakota.

Bowperson, R: Combat Infantry, 138th Airborne Division, presently mustering for Operation Norwegian Emancipation at Halifax Air Station, Nova Scotia.

Burgen, T: Tech School, Crewperson, Naval Station Great Lakes, Illinois.

Choi, Y: Tech School, Air Engine Tech, Earhart Air Base, Texas.

Clempersons, S: Combat Infantry, 207th Amphibious Division, mustering for Operation Norwegian Emancipation at Camp Lejeune, North Carolina.

Earl, J: Tech School, Crewperson, Naval Station Great Lakes, Illinois.

Echo, T: Combat Infantry, 6th "Sightseein' Sixth" Division, presently deployed to quell Broadband Rebellions in North Dakota.

Emmis, B: Combat Infantry, 90th "Tough Ones" Division, presently deployed to quell Broadband Rebellions in Manitoba.

Erasmo, C: Combat Infantry, 19th "Fighting Hogs" Division, presently deployed to Zacatecas.

Fleming, I: Combat Infantry, 207th Amphibious Division, mustering for Operation Norwegian Emancipation at Camp Lejeune, North Carolina.

Flores, L: Combat Infantry, 1st "Big Red One" Division, presently deployed to quell Broadband Rebellions in North Dakota.

Fulvio, P: Tech School, Crewperson, Naval Station Great Lakes, Illinois.

Garcia, F: Combat Infantry, 207th Amphibious Division, mustering for Operation Norwegian Emancipation at Camp Lejeune, North Carolina.

Greene, M: Combat Infantry, 6th "Sightseein' Sixth" Division, presently deployed to quell Broadband Rebellions in North Dakota.

~~Gumabay~~ **Gumbo, P:** Tech School, Military Police, Camp Ashcroft, Missouri.

Hackberry, A: Protest Element, 32nd "The Singing Three-Two" Protest Division, East Coast Protest Command, Anderchild Forward Depot, Maryland.

Hamada, F: Combat Infantry, 90th "Tough Ones" Division, presently deployed to quell Broadband Rebellions in Manitoba.

Hardin, J: Combat Infantry, 207th Amphibious Division, mustering for Operation Norwegian Emancipation at Camp Lejeune, North Carolina.

Houalo, T: Tech School, Naval Engineering Tech, Naval Station Great Lakes, Illinois.

Jardin, S: Combat Infantry, 138th Airborne Division, presently mustering for Operation Norwegian Emancipation at Halifax Air Station, Nova Scotia.

Kim, W: Combat Infantry, 75th "Scorched Earth" Division, presently deployed to quell Broadband Rebellions in North Dakota.

Lee, J: Combat Infantry, 19th "Fighting Hogs" Division, presently deployed to Zacatecas.

Leonardo, S: Combat Infantry, 1st "Big Red One" Division, presently deployed to quell Broadband Rebellions in North Dakota.

Mendoza, U: Combat Infantry, 50th "Iron Lion" Armored Division, presently deployed to quell Broadband Rebellions in North Dakota.

Newton, X: Field Medic, 138th Airborne Division, presently mustering for Operation Norwegian Emancipation at Halifax Air Station, Nova Scotia.

Overture, L: Protest Element, 44th "Screaming Leaders" Protest Division, Pacific Coast Protest Command, Brown Forward Depot, California.

Ovido, F: Tech School, Gunnery Crewperson, Naval Station Great Lakes, Illinois.

Paris, F: Tech School, Military Police, Camp Ashcroft, Missouri.

Pineda, M: Combat Infantry, 50th "Iron Lion" Armored Division, presently deployed to quell Broadband Rebellions in North Dakota.

Reyes, P: Combat Infantry, 207th Amphibious Division, mustering for Operation Norwegian Emancipation at Camp Lejeune, North Carolina.

Ricker, K: Tech School, Anti Retreat Detachment, Fort Cooperation, Oregon.

Rollins, S: Combat Infantry, 1st "Big Red One" Division, presently deployed to quell Broadband Rebellions in North Dakota.

Rosa, F: Combat Infantry, 138th Airborne Division, presently mustering for Operation Norwegian Emancipation at Halifax Air Station, Nova Scotia.

Scott, D: Tech School, Anti Retreat Detachment, Fort Cooperation, Oregon.

Selfridge, B: Combat Infantry, 138th Airborne Division, presently mustering for Operation Norwegian Emancipation at Halifax Air Station, Nova Scotia.

Simon, D: Combat Infantry, 138th Airborne Division, presently mustering for Operation Norwegian Emancipation at Halifax Air Station, Nova Scotia.

Song, J: Combat Infantry, 207th Amphibious Division, mustering for Operation Norwegian Emancipation at Camp Lejeune, North Carolina.

Stanley, V: Tech School, Anti Retreat Detachment, Fort Cooperation, Oregon.

Stevenschild, R: Combat Infantry, 75th "Scorched Earth" Division, presently deployed to quell Broadband Rebellions in North Dakota.

Vasquez, N: Combat Infantry, 48th Lightning Armored Division, presently deployed to quell Broadband Rebellions in North Dakota.

Walker, A: Tech School, Anti Retreat Detachment, Fort Cooperation, Oregon.

Williams, O: Tech School, Anti Retreat Detachment, Fort Cooperation, Oregon.

Yohannan, C: Combat Infantry, 1st "Big Red One" Division, presently deployed to quell Broadband Rebellions in North Dakota.

Zahn, T: Combat Infantry, 138th Airborne Division, presently mustering for Operation Norwegian Emancipation at Halifax Air Station, Nova Scotia.

Hackberry finished scanning the list, after reading his own entry five times to make certain he had read his assignment correctly. "What the hell?" he asked aloud.

He was the best shot with a rifle in the whole platoon; he was more capable at hand-to-hand combat than just about everyone; he had more field experience than most sergeants in the Corps; and he was likely the best at surviving out in the wild with no supplies. But they were sending him to East Coast Protest Command?

At least Overture had had a good idea he'd be heading for protest duty, and sure enough they had sent him there. And Newton knew he was going to be a medic somewhere. Bowperson's assignment made sense, given the rumor Captain Hazard was heading for Norway and had probably made a special request to have Bowperson assigned to his company. Even Gumabay's military police assignment, though unexpected, made some sense – he'd be good at resolving conflicts and keeping other soldiers in line with his demeanor.

But this assignment changed everything. Hackberry would soon be enclosed within a chanting, screaming, helium balloon floating within an open-air DHZ jail cell. He now knew he would not only need to make his escape from Tolerance Corps to achieve his freedom; he'd also need to break out of whatever Designated Habitation Zone he'd wind up chanting and screaming in.

Corporal Bowperson: 134 January 0039

During the evening of January 134, the sun was setting over the roof of Alfa Platoon's barracks. It was now a few hours after the Graduation Day parade. Alfa Platoon stood in formation at the position of attention, facing their barracks as a red glow filled the sky before them.

They received a passing grade at the parade grounds and displayed "excellent pulse, cadence, formation, and spacing," but they exhibited "fatal uniform defects," according to the officers judging the parade. They failed to win the Brass Ring, finishing in fourth place out of 32 platoons taking part in the ceremony. Shortly after the parade, Sergeant Cornwall delivered the bad news that the Brass Ring went to Charlie Platoon in Foxtrot Company.

"I ought to have you all skinned!" Sergeant Cornwall barked at Bowperson and the rest of Alfa Platoon. "How in the hell did you all get into parade formation without any of you telling Private Gumbo he had his damned garrison cap on backwards?"

Alfa Platoon stood in silence and in dejected shame, with one less member among their ranks. Their garrison caps did look almost exactly the same from the front and back, except for a tiny fold that should appear on the front right of a soldier's head. Private Gumbo's fold appeared on the left rear of his head during the parade, sealing his and Alfa Platoon's fate.

Sergeant Cornwall shrugged his shoulders and stared at the platoon blankly for a few moments before continuing. "Major Manos has already sent Private Gumbo off for harvesting, and Captain Hazard is writing a letter to his family right now. But I am considering further reprisals after this clusterfrack of a parade. You all thought you'd get to contact your families after the parade, but not after this frack-up. Mail and communications privileges are revoked until your next duty station, for one thing. That means no comms until you are cleared by your next commanding officer. And I will just say to the rest of you all that you are damned lucky that we need bodies in the field right now. Otherwise Major Manos would be harvesting you fracking all!"

After Cornwall screamed the last harvesting threat with a full-handed, five-fingered point right in Bowperson's face, he ordered Alfa Platoon to get back to the barracks and to pack their things up. Buses that would be taking them to their next duty stations would be arriving within an hour.

Bowperson led the other 50 men remaining in Alfa Platoon into their barracks in silence. This was supposed to be the time he would finally be able to phone the government farm and talk to Veronica and the kids. He had not seen her since his arrest, and since they were not legally married, he doubted the authorities would have thought to let her know he had been sent to the Tolerance Corps. To her, he must be missing. She might have seen coverage of his trial or heard about it through the grapevine. But what if she hadn't? By now, she might be thinking he was dead. If he did not get in touch soon, she'd likely move on and find a new husband, maybe one she could make official instead of one who lived out in the woods.

As the men made their way back to their lockers to pack their things up into their duffel bags, Bowperson sat dejectedly on his cot and looked across the aisle at trainee Gumabay's cot and locker. He held his head in his hands in silence for a few moments.

"You can't save everyone, Reggie." The voice of Gus Hackberry came from his left. "But you sure as shit have saved my ass long enough to get out of this hellhole," Hackberry said as he sat on the cot next to Bowperson. "Even if it means they assigned me to frickin' EastProtComm. I'm gonna lose my fuckin' mind, man."

"Thanks, Hackberry. But you saved yourself. All you needed was a few little reminders to keep your mouth shut." Bowperson lifted his head up. "But Gumabay – Pedro – he didn't deserve to die for having his hat on backwards on Graduation Day."

"Who says he's dead, Reggie? I, for one, don't believe a damn thing these Sergeants tell us. It's all a confidence game,

Reggie. I mean, most of what they are telling us is pure mindfuckery. Chances are good that they just recycled him back a few–"

"Attention!" Sergeant Cornwall yelled into the barracks as the door opened and slammed. "Captain Hazard in barracks! Corporal Bowperson, report to my office. Captain would like a word with you."

Bowperson exhaled deeply and looked at Hackberry in silence as he stood up and walked toward the office, a wave of dread coming over him. Captain Hazard never came into the barracks, and here he was, summoning him to the barracks office on the day of graduation – the day he had let a colossal frack up happen during the parade.

Bowperson entered the office and saluted Captain Hazard, who was sitting at Sergeant Cornwall's desk. Sergeant Cornwall stood at the Captain's side.

Captain Hazard returned the salute and immediately dropped it. "Stand at ease, Corporal. I have a mission for you. I hope you are ready for action."

Book III: The Struggle Inside

Trainee Leonard's Immolation: 60 January 0039

"Don't hit the ignite button, Agent Crowe."

"But, Sir. I have already deployed the gas."

"Then clear the gas from the room."

"Sir, that would be waste of carbon resources. Imagine the paperwork."

"That Intolerant likely knows the whereabouts of Palmer – a name on our watch list. We need him to talk. Orders of Director Steel."

"As you wish, Supra Agent Sulla."

"Get started on that paperwork when we get back, Crowe. These Tolerance Corps types do not want to waste gas lightly."

Unfortunately for Agent Crowe, the paperwork for wasting gas was approximately five times as massive and verbose as the paperwork for immolating an Intolerant. While she began filling out the form T-29 Tolerance Impact Statement for wasted fossil fuels, Supra Agent Sulla entered Leonard's sensory deprivation chamber, carrying an automatic resuscitator.

Supra Agent Sulla: 60 January 0039

Earlier that morning, Agent Danbill Sulla had been sleeping off a General Will Eve bourbon binge in his 12th-floor D.C. abode when his tablet buzzed loudly at 0230 with a text message:

BEGIN TRANSMISSION:

02:30:19:1:060:0039:
URGENT
Executive Order 12139 protocols triggered.
Agent Sulla report to DIS Director at 0430.

END TRANSMISSION

This gave him two hours to get dressed and to get out to Langley in order to see the big boss. The trains had stopped running at 0100 and would not resume until 0500. Thankfully, Agents of the Department of Internal Security were allowed a personal Armored Scout Vehicle.

As a Supra Agent with nearly 20 years of service under his belt, Sulla was also allowed the privilege of having a freely tunable radio, unlike the radios owned by everyday people. Knowing the government's radio-scrambling towers were offline as often as they were on, Sulla tuned in Radio Free Montana on the shortwave dial and heard the distinct voice of Uncle Pawpaw, who had been the voice of the station for years. In between playing contraband music, Uncle Pawpaw often delivered taunts to the Tolerance Corps. Usually the taunts centered around the notion that moneylenders, bureaucrats, and other important people were taking advantage of their families, girlfriends, and boyfriends back home. But one of this morning's taunts was directed at the bureaucracy in D.C. and was more than slightly disturbing. Apparently, the Broadband Rebels had seized the Fort Peck dam on the Missouri River, and Uncle Pawpaw threatened that they would blow it up if there was any attempt to retake it. Sulla was not surprised that this news was not reported on the internet, the fixed-tuned radios, or video sets accessible to civilians. Such news would likely cause a panic in the Bush-Obamaha Habitation Zone in Nebraska, which would see major flooding triggered by the destruction of the dam. Uncle Pawpaw's propaganda barrage also bragged that a high-ranking Internal Security operative had gone rogue and was now working with the Broadband Rebels.

"Another one?" Sulla mumbled to himself as he dressed himself in his brown three-piece suit that did not quite fit this morning. It fit well in his broad shoulders, but not so well around his gut. Now that Sulla was in his late 30s, his suit made him look like a soccer fullback who had retired and then taken to drinking. "Suits don't lie," he said while looking in the mirror.

Sulla shaved his face, drank a cup of coffee, took two alcohol-concealment pills, and hoped he looked and smelled sober. He adjusted the gig line of his suit, put on his self-winding Swiss automatic chronometer, grabbed his hat, his tools, and his briefcase, then hurried out the door of his apartment, pasting a hair on the doorjamb to warn of any intruders in his absence.

The drive to the Internal Security compound was uneventful despite his swerving. The local constabulary knew well enough not to stop an Armored Scout with government plates headed to Langley at a high rate of speed at 0345 in the morning.

Sulla arrived at headquarters, passed through three security checkpoints, and seated himself outside Director of Internal Security Steel's office at 0415, according to his automatic watch. No one was there to greet him, not even an administrative assistant. This did not surprise Sulla in the least.

Director Steel, after all, was a very important man and this 39th General Will Day was a very important day. Director Steel would be delivering the General Will address tonight, which was mandatory watching and listening for all free people. Director Steel would have to once again declare the Broadband Rebellions to be quelled and drum up support for the impending Norwegian operation.

Sulla had heard the rumors of the growing dissent within the Tolerance Corps and wondered if he had to make another Tolerance Corps officer disappear for attempting to circumvent Internal Security's exclusive contact with President Tolerance. The Department of Internal Security, under a series of its various names, had been assigned the absolute duty to keep President Tolerance secure from terrorists, rebels, and all manner of miscreants since the American Hero Act of 0002 B.E.E., and this duty extended to internal as well as external threats.

Some thought the Department of Internal Security took its duty a little too far. President Tolerance had not been heard from publicly, much less seen, in more than 40 years. Other wings of the D.C. Government came to resent having to make nearly all contact with the President through the Department of Internal Security. Sulla knew, and most experienced Internal Security agents at the very least suspected, that Internal Security had no idea where President Tolerance was. Originally, this had been a necessary security precaution. After all, if Internal Security did not know where the President was, they could not betray him by disclosing his secure location, whether it be on purpose or otherwise.

This system of purpose-laden ignorance had its merits, and it worked quite well for three decades. But as time passed, more and more people came to suspect that Tolerance was either dead, had become a puppet of Internal Security, or both. The reality, only known to a very few, was that President Tolerance had not issued a sensible executive command in decades. The only proof that he even continued to exist came from Tolerance's thoughtful and prompt responses to Tolerance Impact Statements through electronic mail. Tolerance@Tolerance.Gov was the only direct way most government agencies could communicate with Tolerance, and this had been enough proof to keep any Tolerance deniers safely marginalized.

But, as time dragged on, it became more and more difficult for the Department of Internal Security to maintain control. The law strictly forbade seditious questions as to the legitimacy of the Tolerance administration upon pain of summary immolation. This deterrent was enough to keep the everyday citizenry in line. But as other branches of the government, especially the Tolerance Corps, began to grow more powerful and bolder, they no longer feared the DIS as they once did.

Sulla knew that the Department of Internal Security could not prevail against a full-scale coup by the Tolerance Corps. The Tolerance Corps had swelled to ranks far stronger than had been anticipated. He also knew that as many as a thousand junior Internal Security agents had infiltrated the Tolerance Corps as junior officers over the last decade. Keeping a watchful eye on the Tolerance Corps became a top priority of the Director of Internal Security. If he could just hold on for another three or five years, many of those junior officers he planted would be senior officers in a position to prevent the Tolerance Corps from inflicting any real harm on Internal Security.

Sulla suspected Internal Security was secretly abandoning its policy of purposeful ignorance as to the whereabouts of President Tolerance. To have Tolerance's actual location would mean having him under Internal Security's direct control, which would mean Director Steel could maintain his power indefinitely.

Sulla was now on his sixth cup of coffee and his third alcohol-concealment pill. It was now 0730 by Sulla's watch. As it ticked and tocked, Director Steel's support staff began to arrive. Sulla stood by the north-facing window outside Director Steel's office. The Department of Internal Security compound covered just over 16 hectares, and an electrified fence surrounded it. With his naked eye, Sulla could see a crowd gathering at the compound entrance, growing by the minute. Sulla had exceptional eyesight, even at his age and in his present state, but could not quite make out what was taking place. He took out the binoculars he always kept in his briefcase and began to observe the mass of humanity.

Today's crowd doubled the size of a standard protest unit. Today was a special day. It was General Will Day, the day free people everywhere celebrated their acceptance of the collective will of free peoples. Therefore, the gathered protesters carried an aspect of eliteness upon their smiling faces. Department of Protests Activists, mostly on loan from the Tolerance Corps, were giving protest orders via a bullhorn. Sulla could not identify the words bellowed at the protest unit because of the 500 meters separating him from the crowd and the 10-centimeter-thick glass separating him from the atmosphere. But he could surmise what commands were being given by the DoP Activists by the response of the protest formation. In his mind's ear, he could hear DoP Activists barking commands in the cadence of quick-time.

"Signs up!" *One Two.*
"Left face!" *One Two.*
"Present!" *One Two.*
"Present!" the protest element leaders echoed.
"Chant!"
"Chant!" the entire protest echoed.
"Tolerance today!"
"Tolerance today!" *Stomp!*
"Tolerance tomorrow!"
"Tolerance tomorrow!" *Stomp!*
"Tolerance forever!"
"Tolerance forever!" *Stomp!*
"Give cheer!"

And the protest roared. Sulla could almost actually hear the roar through the thick window.

"It is both the noblest and the safest thing for a great army to be visibly animated by one spirit," Sulla said to himself aloud.

From just behind Sulla, a familiar voice announced itself. "Glorious morning to you, Supra Agent Sulla!" said Fillburn Wickard. Fillburn Wickard was well-dressed this morning, wearing a blue Italian faux wool suit. Thick, horn-rimmed glasses jutted out from the bushy black hair ringing his head like a small globe. Wickard was Director Steel's Chief of Staff, which made him the director's right hand in most affairs, and the affairs of this morning appeared to be no exception.

"And a glorious morning to you, Chief of Staff Wickard. Happy General Will Day."

"Who said that, Sulla, what you said about a noble army?"

"Um. I think it was Archidamus. Just before the siege of–"

"Archidamus? Hmm. I can't say I have had the pleasure of meeting him. Oh, wait. Does he work for us in our counter intel division in Glasgow?"

"I do not believe so, Sir."

"That's a shame, really," Wickard said with a wry smile. "Well, anyway, thank you for coming in on such short notice. I hope you have not been waiting too long?"

"No, Sir. Not too long. Do you know when the Director will be in?"

"I expect him to be in at any time now. Can I offer you some reading material to pass the time? I have the newest tentative copy of *Us Weekly* I am reviewing. It is a hobby of mine. Would you care to review it?" Chief Wickard offered.

"No. Thank you though."

"I do love reviewing magazines. It gives me a chance to share some of my favorite turnip soup recipes with the people. For example, this article about falling ticket sales at the theater references a downturn in the economy. Far too depressing. People should be uplifted when they read the news, wouldn't you agree?"

"Of course, Chief Wickard."

"Then paprika turnip chive soup it is! Thank you for your input, Sulla. Please do continue to wait patiently. The Director has something urgent for you."

Sulla continued to wait, and he began to roam the 16th floor, taking in the views of the compound around him. The less accessible areas of the compound were mock-ups of suburban areas, which only happened to be real suburban areas before the Department of Internal Security eminently-domained them for practicing suburban raids. Sulla was becoming more sober at this point in the morning. This sobriety led to a shaky feeling in his hands and a brutalizing headache. This led to Sulla's going into the 16th-floor latrine and into the fourth stall on the left, the only stall that totally blocked the cameras in the ceiling. In the semi-privacy of this stall, Sulla retrieved a hip flask full of bourbon and took a lustful gulp. "Visibly animated by one spirit," he mumbled to himself.

Alcohol, being strictly illegal and therefore strictly frowned upon in the Department of Internal Security, was also strictly available anywhere and to anyone who had a mind to get it, especially in the D.C. DHZ. A position in the Department of Internal Security meant the duty to go on raids against Intolerants living outside the DHZs, and therefore the duty to confiscate all the Intolerants' contraband, including marijuana, weapons, Swiss watches, and distilled spirits. The ability to resell or barter the contraband was an added bonus that allowed an industrious agent to double or triple his income in any given week.

Sulla's habits had not gone completely unnoticed throughout his lengthy career. But as he had been a highly efficient Supra Agent, these habits were almost completely ignored. When the occasional zealot would threaten action against him, that zealot would occasionally be assigned the task of infiltrating the Department of Infrastructure and put on reconstruction patrol in the Not-East, a duty with a rather limited life expectancy.

At 0937, Sulla was still strolling around the 16th floor when a message came over the public announcement system. "Agent Sulla, Report!"

At 0938 Sulla arrived outside Director Steel's office. The door was open, with Chief of Staff Wickard holding it open. Looking flustered, Wickard hissed, "Hurry! Go in! He has been waiting more than two minutes for you!"

Sulla entered the office, hat in hand. "Director of Internal Security, Agent Sulla reports as ordered." He stood at attention approximately five meters in front of Director Steel's desk and saluted.

Director Steel's office was palatial by any standard. The walls were lined with mahogany bookshelves, empty of books but filled with thousands of pictures, held in golden frames, of the Director posing with celebrities, athletes, and football wrestlers. His desk was quite large at three meters by four meters, too large for the room, in fact, and it had had to be constructed inside the office. Sulla could remember two years ago when the Secretary of the Tolerance Corps had built for himself a desk that was slightly bigger than Director Steel's. Director Steel reacted by ordering increased infiltration of the Tolerance Corps, then ordering the construction of a Super Desk. Seven chairs sat bolted to the floor on the opposite side of Director Steel's desk, arranged in a tidy line. The desk's top was completely empty, save for one photograph the Director had clearly been fiddling with and one empty golden frame. The picture showed the Director and another man who Sulla could almost recognize. Sulla remained at the position of attention, studying the picture. There was something familiar about the man in the photograph.

Director Steel was a small man who stood only 1.6 meters off the ground. Although he was nearly 50 years old and had been Director of Internal Security for 12 years, he looked not a day over 40. The Director compensated for his relative lack of stature and his youthful appearance by sitting in a rather large chair and dressing himself in custom military-styled uniforms with large shoulder pads. Chief of Staff Wickard stood behind and to the left of Director Steel. He had one arm folded over the other, tucking his tablet in his armpit and holding one hand to his mouth. Was he biting his nails?

Sulla had been standing at the position of attention for two minutes or more. Director Steel had still not reacted. Instead, the Director had kept his head down, staring at his lap the entire time. Was he asleep?

"Sir?" Sulla asked.

Director Steel stirred. "Oh, yes. Supra Agent Sulla. Have a seat."

Sulla began to seat himself in the middle of the seven chairs. "Not that one!" Director Steel yelled. "That one!" He motioned to the chair second from his right with one hand and rubbed his temple with his left hand.

Sulla adjusted and began to take the seat with some trepidation.

"Yes. Yes. That seat will work wonderfully." Director Steel was pleased. "Simply wonderful."

"Thank you, Sir." Sulla sat, with his hands folded over his hat on his lap.

"You're welcome, Sulla. You know I am very busy today. I have to give the General Will Day address to the nation. And I must continue to convince our fellow Unified Societans that a war with Norway is absolutely necessary for the preservation of the General Will and the freedoms unique to it. And I have to do it convincingly. I need this war. I need to give the Tolerance Corps something to keep them busy. They are not stretched thin enough with the Broadband Rebellions, and idle hands sink ships." Director Steel paused, looking at the picture on his desk. Sulla noticed smudge marks on every corner of the picture, as though the Director handled this photo often.

Still looking at the photo, Director Steel continued. "There has been no report in some time. I sent him to find President Tolerance three years ago. And the last I heard, he had been infiltrating the Department of Equally Treating Animals to get some of their topographical surveys of the Not-East. But that was over a year ago. And now with this rebel propaganda about a security agent going rogue and working with them, I just cannot believe it could be him." Director Steel smudged the photo, scowling at it, his eyes welling in angst-ridden rage.

Sulla observed the situation, noting the expression on Steel's face and studying the picture.

Director Steel continued staring at the picture. "I will not allow what my father has built, and his father before him, to be endangered. There is betrayal hanging ... like a fog in the air ... it clouds my divination of the General Will. Asencio can smell it."

Chief of Staff Wickard interrupted. "Sir, this is Sulla, and he's here on important business."

Sulla thought to himself, *Wasn't Asencio the Director's original family name before his grandfather changed it to Steel?*

Director Steel pushed the picture away from himself, inadvertently giving Sulla a clearer view. There was something definitely familiar about the man in the photo. The Director usually behaved in a detached, almost aloof manner. Who was this man in the photo and why did he cause such a stir in the Director?

"Ah, yes. Sulla. As you know, this is General Will Day, and I have a very busy day ahead of me, with the General Will Day address and all, which is the second most important speech I give all year. But I am always happy to make time for my agents and all. To what do I owe this ... this pleasure?"

"Sir?" Sulla asked. "I received a message about one-two one-three-niner protocols being in effect."

"Oh, yes." Director Steel responded, suddenly seeming quite lucid. "Quite unusual, that. A forbidden question has been asked by a Tolerance Corps trainee in Freepersonsburg. It is a forbidden question we have not seen in some time. Not since 0034, I believe. It is so unusual that the Instructor Sergeants did not know to report it to us as a forbidden question. They just thought it a standard stupid question. We only got wind of it through one of our agents embedded in the Tolerance Corps."

"The calendar question, Sir?" Sulla asked.

"Yes. I am quite intrigued that this question would come up now. Especially with the rumors of this rogue agent about and all. I need you to assemble an investigative team and get up there as soon as possible. Wickard has prepared a watch list of names and terms to look for. If the subject mentions any of them, investigate further. I have also ordered a tactical team to be on standby should you need it. However, if the subject knows nothing, employ summary immolation procedures."

"Yes, Sir." Sulla stood and saluted.

Director Steel returned the salute. "Oh, and Sulla? Have a happy General Will Day!"

Extracting Ex-Trainee Leonard: 60 January 0039

Ex-Trainee Leonard curled fetal on the icy floor in the Sensory Deprivation chamber as the automatic resuscitator did its work. He had been unconscious for about 30 seconds. Leonard slowly came to, seeing the blurry-brown image of Sulla's suit. Leonard pulled the resuscitator off of his mouth.

"Am I ... Am I dead?"

"No, do you want to be dead?" Sulla asked Leonard while hovering over him.

"No, no, Sir, Trainee Leonard reports as a Sir or Ma'am are you Sir? No, Sir and Ma'am."

"Shut up if you don't want to be dead. Don't say a word. These walls have ears. Just listen to me. My name is Agent Sulla and I am your only chance at life." Sulla slapped the young man lightly in the face.

"That is assault and battery, Sir!" Agent Crowe clamored.

"What is going on and why does that crooked-nosed lady hate Fred?" Leonard stammered.

Sulla put the resuscitator back over Leonard's mouth. Leonard continued to speak in muffled, unintelligible syllables. "This boy clearly needs more resuscitation," Sulla said loudly. "Agent Peterschild, get in here and help me drag this young man out of here and back to the chopper."

Agent Crowe hissed, "Why do you ask for the male agent's assistance in carrying the suspect? Are you saying a female agent can't–"

"I did not ask him, Crowe. I ordered him. Just as I am ordering you to walk in front of us with your DIS badge out in one hand and your pistol in the other as we help this Intolerant out of here and back to our chopper. If any pain-in-the-ass Tolerance Corps types get in our way, kindly show them what is in both of your hands and kindly share that we are exercising our authority and taking custody of this Intolerant."

As the three agents and ex-Trainee Leonard progressed out of the Sensory Deprivation facility and across the asphalt pad toward their CH-00 helicopter, Sulla reconnoitered their surroundings. To their right, a male platoon was marching along the fence line in practiced, but not perfect, step and formation. They must have been just into their training, perhaps fresh out of sensory deprivation. The Sergeant in charge bore an eye-patch over his left eye and did not seem to notice Sulla or his party moving in his periphery. Periodically, through the gaps in the formation, Sulla saw what appeared to be a large purple man standing just outside the fence line yelling something.

"What the hell is that purple thing?" Sulla asked, his mouth agape in wonder.

"I don't see anything, Sir," said Crowe.

"I don't either, Sir," said Peterschild.

The CH-00 pilot had been waiting for them. The four boarded the chopper and flew out of the Freepersonsburg training compound. Sulla ordered the pilot to head northwest before heading back to Langley. Placing handcuffs on the still-groggy Leonard, Sulla informed the ex-trainee, "You are going to feel a slight twinge of pain. Now stay as still as possible. I have not done this while flying in some time." He tapped the pilot on the shoulder. "Try to keep us steady for a while."

Sulla grabbed a local anesthetic, a scalpel, and small forceps out of the Chopper medical kit and motioned for Crowe and Peterschild to hold the handcuffed ex-trainee prone on the Chopper floor. "Hey, what's going on?" Leonard mumbled.

"Just a mere precaution, Leonard. We don't want anyone tracking us, do we?"

Sulla applied the anesthetic to three key points on the back of Leonard's neck and proceeded to cut a small incision just above Leonard's left collarbone. Leonard felt the cut and then felt some pushing and prodding where his neck met his back. A few moments of burning pain later, Leonard saw a small, blinking electronic chip next to him in a tiny pool of blood on the floor.

Sulla directed his agents to put a butterfly bandage on the open wound, then directed his agents to restore Leonard to his seat. Sulla held the chip in front of the ex-trainee. "That was not so bad. Field medicine at its finest." Sulla opened the door to the chopper and side-armed the chip out, skipping it across the treetops.

"Sir. What if we need to track him now?" asked a perplexed Peterschild as he and Crowe started securing Leonard in a four-point seatbelt.

"If you need a GPS chip to track a subject, you don't really deserve to find him," Sulla responded.

Sulla observed that Peterschild and Crowe had their hands quite full strapping Leonard back into his seat. He took advantage of this distraction and wrote instructions on a pad of paper. He set the paper before the pilot, carefully so that only she could see. "Turn off chopper GPS recorder. Set chopper down at 39.035278 north and 79.458056 ~~west~~ not-east."

"You got it," said the pilot. Chopper Pilot Narai never said much while flying. Although she was an Internal Security Agent like Crowe and Peterschild, her job was her CH-00 and she stuck to it, rarely leaving it unless it was to take a shower or eat. The next several minutes, she flew about 90 meters above the treetops in the hilly terrain. Narai rarely talked unless it was to express mild amusement or annoyance. "Radar shows two fat birds headed toward our previous location," she said, using Internal Security's unofficial nickname for iTolerator fighter jets. "Time for a fun ride."

At that, Narai lowered her altitude and said, "Agents and guest, you might want to hold onto something," as the chopper began to skim the treetops, lurching up and down with the contours of the forest canopy in the rough terrain of the Virginia border. The passengers of the CH-00 careened about as Narai evaded radar coverage in the valleys and ravines. "This is the most fun I've had since Peaceful Transition," she said with a smile after seeing Leonard vomit on Agents Crowe and Peterschild.

After 40 minutes of the fun ride, they were at Sulla's coordinates, an abandoned compound of buildings flanked by a stream on three sides and a conspicuously plowed and manicured field on the other. When Sulla had first found this place six years ago, it had been a moonshinery. Before that, it was a golf course. But now, it was a full-fledged distillery, complete with two stills, a warehouse full of barrels for aging the whiskey, and a packaging room for getting the whiskey ready for shipment. And, as rumor had it, Sulla had a number of employees onsite who he kept hidden from his DIS peers.

As the chopper set down, Agent Peterschild saw smoke arising from a chimney and thought he saw someone looking out of one of the windows in one of the buildings. "Sir! There are Intolerants here. We need to secure the area."

"You three stay on the chopper. Go back to headquarters and await further instruction. I will handle this interrogation myself." Sulla released Leonard's seatbelt, then grabbed the young man by the shoulder, urging him off the chopper. Before closing the chopper door, Sulla looked at how nauseous his agents were. He looked to Narai and said, "Fun ride. All the way back to Langley." Narai nodded, smiled, then winked at Sulla and took to the sky like a bat out of Billings.

As the chopper lifted off again, Crowe could be barely heard yelling, "But Sir, this is not a Designated Habitation Zone!"

"You stay here in the cabin." Sulla uncuffed one of Leonard's hands, then cuffed the other hand to a chain attached to the table at which Leonard sat. "I'll be right back," Sulla said as he went back outside the cabin.

Leonard could see Sulla through one of the windows as the agent walked toward one of the other buildings in the compound. The air coming in from outside wafted in heavily, with a sweet, smoky smell, like the smell of hard-boiled corn soup he sometimes enjoyed back at the farm. On the inside, it was not much of a cabin – it was more like a shack. The plank wooden floor was full of knotholes, the walls were unfinished plywood, and there was no ceiling, only a corrugated steel roof shaped in an arc. The only amenities he could see consisted of a pot-belly stove in the center of the shack, three wooden chairs, including the one he sat in, the table he was shackled to, an oil lamp hanging from a nail in the wall, and a metal cot. An empty glass jar rested on the table, smelling of urine.

Leonard, though disoriented, remained calm. He continued to study his surroundings more closely as Asno had taught him during their time together. A wave of dread came over him as he noticed a blood-red stain in the floor beneath him and blood-red speckles all over the table in front of him and the wall behind him. He scraped at one of the specks on the table with his fingernails and a reddish powder emerged.

The door opened again, and Sulla entered, carrying a bundle of firewood. "It's a bit chilly in here, isn't it? I'll get a fire going. You must be hungry and thirsty? Can I get you something after I get this fire going?"

"Yes, hungry and thirsty."

"Coming right up."

Sulla again left the shack. Leonard continued to scrape at the table with his fingernails. The more spots he removed, he began to see that something had been crudely carved into the table.

"*RIP GLA.*"

The door opened again. This time, Sulla's arms were full of military-grade rations and a bottle full of a brownish liquid. Sulla unburdened his arms, dropping the rations to the floor while holding onto the bottle. Leonard continued to stare at the blood-encrusted message on the table. Sulla took a gulp from the bottle and said, "Each person must tend to the business that accords with his nature." He tossed Leonard a vacuum-sealed bag of kelp. "Wouldn't you say so, Leonard?"

"What kind of business is that?" Leonard asked.

"Today …" Sulla paused while taking a seat at the table opposite Leonard. "My business is with you." He stared at Leonard, taking another gulp from the bottle. The sun had reached its set, and the room was quickly growing dark. "Have a drink, ex-Trainee Leonard." Sulla tilted the bottle toward Leonard.

"No, thank you."

"I ..." He shoved the bottle toward Leonard's face. "Insist."

Leonard took the bottle and took a tentative sip. He coughed twice. "Uhh ... smooth."

Sulla rose from his seat, took the bottle back, and walked over to the stove. He poured some more whiskey out into a small metal cup that had been warming on top of the stove and then brought the cup back to Leonard. "This is the finest Kentucky Bourbon that Not-East Virginia has to offer and it will warm you up."

Sulla handed him the cup, then asked, "So why do you think you are here, Leonard?"

"Because I asked a forbidden question?"

"No!" Sulla slammed his fist on the table. He grabbed the table's edge with one hand and leaned across it at Leonard menacingly. "You are here because I brought you here. You are here because I brought you back from the abyss."

Sulla stepped away from the table, took off his suit coat, and threw it onto the metal cot in the corner, revealing the pistol in his shoulder holster. He once again sat down, setting his weapon on the table, pointing it just to the right of Leonard. "You are here, not because you, or anyone, for that matter, has a purpose. You are here because of a million tiny incidents you did not have the slightest bit of control over. And the illusion you cling to, it lies to you. It fibs in your ear. '*Oh, I asked a forbidden question!*' Doesn't it, Leonard?" Sulla paused to drink.

"Sir, I–"

"You what? You report as ordered? Oh, you think there is any way out of this thing for you? No, Leonard. You are still in the abyss. You are still in the abyss." By now, it was almost completely dark in the shack, save for a faint glimmer of light stemming from the stove. "Drink, Leonard."

Leonard sat frozen in the dark.

"Drink, Leonard!"

A small gurgle and a not-so-small cough followed.

"That's the spirit. Are you not hungry? Eat your kelp."

0164

Leonard fumbled in the dark for the vacuum-sealed bag and tore it open, devouring the contents. A small thud signaled the arrival of another bag on the table in front of him. He tore that open as well. The room fell in shadowy silence that amplified the chewing sounds coming from Leonard's side of the table.

After several minutes of Sulla's listening to Leonard eat, the chewing paused and Sulla spoke again. "You are trapped in an endless void. There is but one small light, but one tiny opening to the great world outside." He flicked his lighter on, walked to the wall, and lit the glass lamp that had been behind him. "I am that light."

Sulla sat himself again, emphasizing, "*I am that light.*" He paused. The oil lamp hanging from the wall emanated a soft glow from behind Sulla, casting his face in shadow.

Leonard sat wiping his mouth after washing his kelp down with some whiskey. He stared at Agent Sulla, who sat motionless.

Sulla rubbed his temples with both hands, watching Leonard for a few moments. Sulla broke eye contact, looked up at the corrugated metal ceiling, and said, "No evil can befall a good man. In life, or after." The oil lamp flickered behind Sulla. "Do you think a man, after a life wasted by evil, self-serving deeds, can redeem himself through a single act of exceptional greatness?" He tapped the pistol with one hand, picking up the now half-empty bottle in the other.

"Leonard, it is a matter of perception. Perception. 'Mare Nostrum,' the Romans once called the Mediterranean Sea around them. Mare Nostrum. Our sea. Their sea. But my thoughts surround me. I would be lying to you if I told you I did not have a luminescent image in my mind's eye of what it would look like to see you lying on the floor, that very floor beneath you, twitching, feverishly twitching, in a pool of blood. I would rise from my chair, adjust myself, and unshackle your hand. I'd watch it fall to the floor and hear a tiny din in the air like the strike of a tiny rock thrown into Mare Nostrum. I'd wipe my face of whatever blood splatter you left on me with my sleeve. I might feel a tinge of remorse and say to myself, 'My oh my, what a mess!' I might even carve your initials

into this table for sentimental reasons. But in the end, I would just make a call, get back on my chopper, and go on with my business."

Sulla paused, rose from his chair, and kicked it across the floor. He stood next to Leonard, leaning on the corner of the table and looming over him. "And I'd be lying if I told you that the thought of seeing your brains splattered against the wall pains me at all. In fact, I take pleasure in this thought. But seeing as how our goals, your wanting to live and my wanting to see what is inside that cranium of yours, are not totally in conflict, I think we can work something out here, don't you?"

Sulla jiggled the chain on Leonard's handcuffs with his left hand and held his pistol in his right hand, firmly pressing it to Leonard's temple. "And now you are going to tell me everything that I want to know."

Through the course of the night, Leonard told Sulla about his escape from the Corn Hole after he knew his corncob pipe making would be discovered by the authorities. His encounter at the Missouri River with Johnschild, Operation Drake based out of the cave outpost in the bluffs of the Missouri, and the meeting in the cave. Sulla was acutely interested in Fred Palmer. Leonard described him as an elderly man, almost decrepit, wearing an old suit, babbling about stick thievery and President Tolerance being make-believe like the Easter Bunny and pickup trucks, and how he claimed to have been a Congressman under the old Constitution in the last days of the Old U.S. With further prompting, Leonard gave a detailed description of the man, from his bushy white hair, his hunched-over stature at just under two meters, his sad hazel eyes, to his outlandish mustache.

Leonard described the journey from Iowa to join the Broadband Rebels. How they linked up with the Montana Partisan Rangers. About the land-air siege at Fort Peck. How Colonel Asno set up a system that allowed the Broadband Rebels to use shoulder-mounted missiles to take out the cargo jets dropping reinforcements and supplies to the Tolerance Corps units at Fort Peck. How Johnschild fell ill in the unsanitary conditions in Montana and had to be left behind. And how Asno insisted they move on to Seattle with little warning before the siege at Fort Peck was over, picking up volunteers all along the way.

He described Colonel Asno as a tall, secretive man in his 50s. Asno had exceptional knowledge of the countryside, as if he had traversed it a thousand times before. He knew where and when to seek shelter from the air patrols that periodically scoured the area. He knew the best routes through the Rocky Mountains, and he knew when and where to strike at a critical government protest.

He described the other men who had accompanied them across the plains. A man named Vargas who was an able scrounger, but a lousy gambler. There was also a man named Hackberry, who knew nothing about the calendar and asked no forbidden questions. Hackberry showed bravery and skill on several occasions, one time picking off a Tolerance Corps combat aircraft controller from 600 meters away as he aimed a laser missile guidance device at their fighting position near Fort Peck. This Hackberry was the only other known survivor of the Seattle Cod Protests, as far as Leonard knew, and he was likely still back at Fort Freeperson.

The following day, a tired and haggard DIS agent could be seen from the window of the cabin at Sulla's distillery as he walked toward the chopper that landed in nearly the exact same spot as it had the day before. Agent Sulla boarded. The CH-00 took off.

"Where is the subject?" Agent Crowe asked.

"A single death is always a tragedy; a million or so is a statistic," Sulla said dismissively. He sat next to Narai. "Sleigh ride, all the way to Bush-Obamaha."

While the CH-00 thundered and flopped its way to the Dominion of Nebraska, Sulla gave Peterschild and Crowe his instructions. They would spend the next few weeks at the Internal Security depot in Bush-Obamaha.

They would pore over the records of the Tolerance Corps' recent sweep-and-clear operation of the Missouri River to the north of the Designated Habitation Zone. They would perform a thorough review of all Intolerant corpses and prisoners inventoried. They would look for any entries made on any unusually old Intolerants – any over the age of 50. And while they were going over the evidence from the area in which ex-Trainee Leonard began his journey with Asno, they'd get the paperwork going on a data request from Ubiquitous Camera Command to pull footage from the scene of the Great Seattle Cod Protests, where Leonard's journey with Asno ended.

"Sir, what is this all about?" Agent Crowe asked.

"An existential threat," Sulla responded.

Warning Signs: 73 January 0039

January 73rd began for Director Steel as almost every day of his life had begun for the past 12 years. He awoke at 0745. After a quick shower and a quick hour in the make-up chair, he left his residence at 1601 Pennsylvania Avenue. At 0915 he arrived by helicopter atop the largest building in the DIS compound, affectionately referred to as "Headquarters" or "HQ." But the building was officially known as the *WWFL Gridiron Mania Internal Security Compound*. Director Steel had sold the naming rights and signage on the building to the Bureau of Professional Football Wrestling in his second year as Director of Internal Security.

At 0920, right on schedule, Steel arrived at his office, taking a journey down from his helipad on his own gold-plated private escalator that the DIS had built for him after he suffered several panic attacks in the private elevator his father had used when he was DIS director.

At 1000 he would have his daily briefing from Chief of Staff Wickard. This left him some time for some light reading. He tapped his desk lightly and said, "Desk computer, personal library."

A pleasant feminine voice responded, "Good morning, Director Steel. Accessing personal library," in a slight British accent.

"Good morning, desk computer. Display personal memoirs of Kim Jong Il, version English."

A screen emerged from the desktop, displaying the text of page 1,208, where he had left off. "Computer, resume reading." Director Steel leaned back in his chair and closed his eyes.

"Certainly, Sir. Enabling Celebrity Voice Emulation. Please choose a Celebrity."

"This morning I would like to hear it read to me in my own voice."

There was an interminable three-second delay. Director Steel leaned forward and pounded the desk. The desk responded,

"I'm sorry, Sir. Your voice is not in the Celebrity Voice Emulation databank. Perhaps you would like the voice of former Senator Al Franken, whose voice exhibits similar tonal qualities?"

"Computer, are you saying I am not a celebrity?"

After a reflective pause in which the computer accessed its self-preservation protocols, the computer voice responded, "No, Sir. You are not in the Celebrity Voice Emulation databank for national security purposes. Impersonating the voice or appearance of a living government official is a crime punishable by fifteen years' hard labor, a fine not to exceed fifteen million credits, or both."

"I see. Very well, proceed from where we left off in the voice of Jimmy Carter."

After another interminable two-second delay, the reading software began, "The fools had ruined my Marilyn Monroe painting and had to be punished for this outrageous outrage. I had ordered that the painting depict Marilyn in a wrestling match with–" The reading software had abruptly stopped reading in the voice of Jimmy Carter as the buzzer for the office door alerted Director Steel to the presence of a visitor. The screen flashed and displayed the credentials of Chief of Staff Wickard.

"Enter!" Steel yelled, annoyed at the early arrival of his Chief of Staff. Wickard meekly walked the nine meters from the door to Director Steel's desk and stood before Director Steel, arms clasped to his sides. "I am sorry to interrupt your light reading time."

"It is only zero nine forty, Wickard! I had twenty more minutes! This had better be good. Or at least very very bad. Very very very bad."

"It is bad, Sir. Very very very very bad."

"Very very very very bad? Very good. What is it *then*, Wickard?"

Wickard paused and looked at Director Steel, contemplating what he should say. There was something in the way Director Steel said '*then*.' Was this another protocol test? Hesitantly, Wickard said, "Very very very very bad?"

"No, Wickard! What precisely is very very very very bad?" Director Steel began to fiddle with the on-screen display of the memoirs of Kim Jong Il and added a note to the on-screen text. He typed in: "interrupted heer by wickord. omc so annoying...!...."

Wickard cleared his throat. "Sir, I am not sure how to tell you this. ... President Tolerance's email has been compromised."

"Tolerance at tolerance dot gov?"

"No, Sir. The party in question used a back door email address that we did not know about. The email address automatically redirected to the President's email inbox. They sent it to toleranz, with a z, at tolerance dot gov. Apparently the original designers of the email routing system for the domain took into account potential misspellings and had a system to reroute errant emails to the intended recipient. Now that we know of this exploit, we have taken appropriate measures to shut it down, and only emails from authorized government officials with the proper clearances will make it to President Tolerance."

Director Steel gripped his desk, knuckles turning white. "These hackers are relentless. But we have not had a breach in email protocol in my entire twelve years here and we are not going to start now! Cover it up!"

"Sir, the email made it to the inbox. The *real* inbox." Wickard paused, his face getting red. "And President Tolerance responded to the email."

"My creator!"

"We have the email chain if you would like to read it."

"On-screen," Steel bellowed to his desk. The desk displayed a hologram of the email with white text on a black background.

> From: MegaWizard22@mailorama.com
> To: toleranz@tolerance.gov
> Date: 72 Jan 0039 1547.35
> Subject: dear president tolerance
>
> dear president tolerance.
>
> my name is jack and I am in 4th grade at breshnev elemantary in queens. thats in new york. my teacher

said we could right u on this and ask you questions.
So I want 2 no do you like music and what kinds of
music do you like.

sincrely
jack baker

WANT FREE EMAIL AND TEXT? SWAP
PHOTOS FREE ON MAILORAMA.COM.
SIGNING UP IS EASY. JOIN NOW AT
JOIN.MAILORAMA.COM.

Director Steel finished reading and remarked, "Well, Jack
Baker certainly did not contaminate his email to the President with
anything of importance. How did our President respond?"
Wickard pulled up the reply email on his tablet and fed the
display to Director Steel's desk. "Here you are, Sir."

From: Tolerance@Tolerance.Gov
To: MegaWizard22@mailorama.com
Date: 72 Jan 0039 1637.09
Subject: RE: dear president tolerance

Dear Jack of the Department of Bakeries,

I speak to you today not as your friend but as your
President, for I alone foresee all that is right and
wrong in the world. I am the King, no, God, of all
things! I do not embrace thee and thy foul sunlight!
It is for empire and glory I struggle, and it is not for
you, but for me, to shoulder this burden.

In my Glorious Empire of Tolerance, it shall be so!
And so it shall be! That is my credo.

When you come to me with questions, I do not merely give an answer. I offer you my opinion, the TRUE opinion, the course I mandate and the course you should take should you wish to be enlightened like me.

I appreciate your offer to join your mailorama.com website, but such quasi-tangible sites only cloud the mind with material concerns and my mind must remain sharp. Email and photographs on the internet! Ha! I withdraw from your social plane, your existence, your society of greed! To attain true enlightenment you must be like the water, so very soft and malleable, with only the strength to fall and to part ways for the heavy rocks in its path. But over a period of years, that very water shall eventually tear apart the wretched stone set before it!

A photograph on the internet is merely a hollow reflection of the material world. I bid thee, no, I command thee, to remove all photographs from the internet. Depictions and reflections of the material world are an abomination and a dam upon the river of enlightenment. The internet is that dam! The photographs are but the wooden spine of the dam. Remove the spine, the dam shall fail.

The most tolerant course of action will be to eliminate the dam upon the river. As a dam built of only mud and sticks cannot survive the onslaught of a torrential downpour, that dam shall be overtopped and it shall give way to my tolerant embrace. All that is built downstream shall be destroyed in the wake of the natural path of Tolerance!

And I shall sit in my refuge, warmed by the orange glow of my toaster oven. I shall await obedience to my orders. I shall watch that dam break. I shall watch the wicked men who laid their foundations upon and beneath it be washed away.

I order again that the internet be destroyed. I have issued this order again and again and it has been ignored. It is my command that you, Jack of the Department of Bakeries, destroy it. I shall sit and wait, warmed by my toaster oven, and I shall snap my fingers in delight to the sounds of Norwegian Jazz and Pakistani Opera.

I remain your President,
Tolerance

Director Steel's head dropped down to his desk when he finished reading. Wickard stood silently before him. Director Steel raised his eyes, chin still on his desk. "First things first, Wickard. Eliminate the Baker boy and his family."

"Done, Sir. Their apartment burned to the ground overnight. We used methane accelerant. Fire alarms were disabled. There were no survivors. I personally pulled the records of this email, and it appears it went unread. We have also arranged for a large cargo plane to crash at the site of Mailorama's servers in New York. There will be no further record of this email."

"Excellent. I think that takes care of things, so if you do not mind, I'd like to get back to my reading. Dismissed."

Wickard did not move. "Sir, considering the only way any of us can contact President Tolerance is over the internet, does it at all concern you that President Tolerance orders the destruction of the internet in every email he sends out, no matter what the topic at hand or question asked?"

"Wickard, what concerns me more is that he appears to be a Norwegian sympathizer based on his dubious musical preferences. We will deal with him soon enough."

Agent Danbill Sulla: 90 January 0039

The sun had just finished its set across the Missouri River. Sulla hurled another empty bottle into the face of the limestone bluff on the eastern slope of the river, sending hundreds of tiny shards glimmering in the twilight. He had been physically inspecting the site of the battle in which ex-Trainee Leonard's ex-colleagues had undoubtedly met their final end.

After weeks of analyzing documents in the DIS information dump in Bush-Obamaha, he knew this was the place Leonard had told him about. He feared there was little to be gained by an on-site inspection of this site, but he had decided a few days would be better spent outside Bush-Obamaha and under the influence of alcohol.

He had brought a case of bourbon in his mission ready kit and preferred drinking in the seclusion outside the habitation zones to the antiseptic haze and the crowded stench that infested the speakeasies that dotted the zones like oases in those terrible, purgative deserts. He had given Agents Crowe and Peterschild strict orders to continue reviewing all documents and inventories of the bodies and prisoners collected as a result of last year's sweep and clear of the region.

Reviewing documents was a duty suited to their abilities and temperaments. They were both nearly useless to Sulla in the field, and Sulla was quite certain that the prime role of one or the other, if not both, in this mission involved watching over him and reporting dutifully back to his bosses back at HQ. Sulla was quite certain they reported in regularly, but they were not incredibly successful at watching over him. Thus far, pulling his superior rank was sufficient to keep his nannies away when he wanted to go on a frolic. Should there ever be something more than rank required to control Peterschild and Crowe, he would have to feign remorse in the death letters he would send their families, informing them of their loved ones' martyrdom in the great cause. Sulla hated faking remorse almost as much as he hated paperwork.

At his armored vehicle, he grabbed another bottle of bourbon, a flashlight, and a rope and grapple from his mission ready kit. At this point in the evening, he was drunk enough to consider removing the Global Positioning Satellite transmitter attached to the chassis of his unmarked Armored Scout Vehicle temporarily on loan from the Bush-Obamaha constabulary. He would tie it to a piece of driftwood and let it float down the river. But then, whoever was tracking him would believe he was headed down to south to Kansas or Missouri and he would be expected to come up with yet another explanation as to why he had vandalized government property upon his inevitable return to the habitation zone.

He thought better of the idea and opened up his next bottle before scuffling along the bluff face. He kicked at a piece of burnt rope at the bottom of the cliff. He looked up into a hole in the cliff wall. This had to be the Intolerants' entrance to their base, and the rocks beneath it were undoubtedly the spot that Patient 900-05-0983, the prisoner who best matched the general description of Fred Palmer, who ex-Trainee Leonard had described so well, had fallen while attempting to flee into the shelter of the cave.

Sulla sat down on a boulder, opened his field tablet, and re-read the after-action report of Captain Wheeler, the Tolerance Corps officer in charge of the assault. He had had at his beck and call one B-75 Acceptor, 20 UH-76 Assault Helicopters with assault teams of six men aboard each, and three patrol boats. He had apparently been intent upon using all of this fire power.

Captain Wheeler's report read:

For seven days before the assault, I wisely ordered a team of combat controllers to take positions across the river from the Intolerant base. It was their task to get an accurate count of enemy personnel so I could best follow my directive to eliminate all personnel onsite. On day five of their observation, a group of four Intolerants and their enslaved horses crossed the river on a raft composed of the unusual amount of driftwood the Intolerants had been hoarding at this location. Intelligence reports indicate their leader had unconventional views about driftwood in the river. The combat controllers reported the departure of the four men to me. I reported this to my superiors. My superiors wisely instructed that these Intolerants not be engaged as it would give away our position. My combat controllers did not engage. These four Intolerants had not returned to the base as of the time of the assault.

My combat controllers reported that the Intolerants had a pattern of behavior. They usually stayed concealed during the daylight hours and were most active at dawn and dusk. We collected video evidence of them kidnapping fish from the river to be used at the prosecution of any survivors caught. I considered attacking at dusk with the first wave coming by amphibious assault like we did when we liberated Thunder Bay. Upon further consideration, I determined the first strike would be a combined-arms air strike of cluster bombs paired with continuous shelling from the patrol boats as suppression fire while the two platoons aboard UH-76s moved in.

At 1600 hours, the B-75 Acceptor departed Camilo Cienfuegos Air Field just south of Bush-Obamaha and received precise coordinates from my combat controllers. The cluster bombs reached the targets. Approximately half of the twenty targets outside the cave were eliminated or incapacitated at this point. I ordered the patrol craft to close in from downriver and to begin shelling. This suppression fire was directed at known Intolerant defensive firing positions, although their defensive positions appeared to be unpersoned at the time. At this point, I ordered in the helicopter gunners to open fire with their mounted cannons, forcing the remaining Intolerants to retreat to their cave in bad order.

Sulla set the report down. He mumbled to himself, "This arrogant bastard. It is as if he thinks he is Napoleon himself reincarnated."

He skipped ahead to the part of Wheeler's report that concerned him.

Several Intolerants attempted to climb their ladder into the cave entrance. Dismounted Aerial Assault personnel were receiving covering fire from the cave entrance, which was intended to aid in these Intolerants' retreat. Tolerance Corps Private Rose exercised his own initiative and launched a rocket-propelled grenade into the cave entrance. This grenade detonated, causing a partial collapse of the cave entrance. This also caused the rope ladder leading into the cave to be severed. Three Intolerants were on the rope ladder at the time and fell, sustaining heavy injuries. These Intolerants were now defenseless and had to be taken prisoner instead of killed outright. I have issued Private Rose a formal reprimand.

We took three prisoners. All others were killed outside of the cave or by Private Rose's grenade. One of the prisoners was unusually old for an Intolerant, approximately ninety years old. My medics report that he sustained heavy injuries including multiple fractures to his legs, arms, ribs, and spine. Prisoners have since been transferred to the Cabeza de Vaca Memorial Hospital in Bush-Obamaha. I wash my hands of them.

Sulla scoured the rocks at the bottom of the bluff for any evidence or items the old man may have left behind. This was the fifth time he had done so. All he had found until this point were scorched pieces of rope. He decided it was finally time to climb up into the cave and have a look around. He had been avoiding the climb. Sulla was not a good climber, and in his present state, he was not a good walker. Nonetheless, he would throw a rope and grappling hook into the entrance in preparation for his ascent. On his first attempt, the grapple hit just short of the 10-meter-high entrance. It bounced off the bluff and crashed with a denting thud onto the roof of the unmarked Armored Scout parked just behind him. "Damn it," he muttered to himself. "More paperwork."

On his second try, the grapple made its way into the cave entrance. Sulla pulled hard on the rope and the grapple stayed put. He secured his flashlight and his whiskey in his backpack and began his climb. When he reached the halfway point, he realized how drunk he was and became incredibly dizzy. "Focus. Focus!" he hissed to himself, his vision going double. He firmly grasped both of the moonlit ropes he saw in front of him with all four of his hands and resumed his ascent.

Once safely in the cave, Sulla turned on his flashlight and examined his surroundings. Although the entrance had been partially collapsed by Private Rose's grenade and there was a barricade of boulders in his way, the barricade was passable. He crawled over the uneven surface of rock chunks and emerged on a relatively flat cave floor. He shined his light deeper into the cave and the first thing he noticed was a badly scorched and slightly melted canister of the type used to deliver gas weapons.

Upon closer examination, he was able to make out engravings on the inside of the canister. VGDM-401B. Sulla recognized this to stand for Vesicant Gas Defense Mechanism 401B. This was an elaborate term for a gas bomb designed to form acid upon contact with water in the lungs and eyes of its intended victims. This little detail was not in Captain Wheeler's paperwork. *Good for him*, Sulla thought to himself. But why was this canister so badly scorched and partially melted? Sulla's nose detected a faint, but unmistakable, stench of burnt flesh. He had his suspicions as to the origins of this stench and continued to survey deeper into the cave.

About 20 meters deeper into the crevice, the cave widened into a broader chamber. In this chamber he found another canister, this one much larger and more badly melted than the other. It was a fuel-air explosive. Wheeler had turned the air in this cave into flame. Sulla shined his light around this chamber; he could now see badly burned and decomposing bodies.

Sulla stumbled toward the body nearest to him. The body laid fetal with its back to the cave entrance, its hands melted and affixed to the scorched remnants of the gas mask that clung to the skull. Her skull, he surmised. Sulla shined his light directly on the corpse. Yes, he was nearly certain she was female based upon the slight build and what he could make of the bone structure. But who she was or how she lived did not matter as much at this point as how she died. The tightly fetal position of her body indicated she had survived the gassing and the torching. Sulla began to peel what portions of the mask he could off the corpse. The stench of newly exposed burnt hair reinvigorated the hanging stench of burnt flesh in the cave. He continued to peel away until, at last, the unmistakable entrance wound in the skull created by a 5.56 millimeter bullet fired from close range. He had seen plenty of this type of wound in his career.

So Wheeler had tried to gas the Intolerants to death, then when that failed, incinerated them. He then had the badly burned survivors shot in the head at close range, leaving the bodies to rot and making not a single mention of this in his paperwork. Sulla was liking the cut of this Wheeler's trousers more by the minute. But he now knew that the scraps of evidence he hoped to obtain from the cave would most certainly be burnt beyond recognition. He sat himself on the cave floor next to the badly burned corpse, drank from his bottle, and fell into a deep sleep, dreaming softly of homicide and political sodomy.

Sulla woke four hours later to the stench of alcohol on his breath and the stench of death around him. He had not slept so well in a long time.

He took a swig of his bottle, then poured the last few centiliters onto the corpse before smashing the bottle onto the cave floor. The sun had commenced its rise and dim rays of light began to trickle into the cave. *This is quite a tomb*, he thought to himself. When he returned to Bush-Obamaha to interview Mr. 900-05-0983, he simply must order Crowe and Peterschild to inventory the 20 or so corpses within it.

Sulla stumbled his way back to the cave entrance and looked out across the river. The sun was rising to the east behind him and began to illuminate the water in a soft pink glow. A squadron of geese executed a water landing in the river beneath him and strutted slowly up to his vehicle as if studying it. And there was his borrowed vehicle beneath him, with a large dent in the roof. Sulla now remembered his first attempt with the rope and grapple had ended in a large thud. His eyes lingered upon the dent; this would bring about precisely the type of paperwork he had made a career of avoiding. He would now have to return the vehicle and explain to the local constabulary quartermaster that there was no dent and that if there were a dent, it was certainly there before Sulla had even laid eyes upon the vehicle. This was surely a manufacturer's defect that the quartermaster would have to report himself to the Bureau of General Motors.

Sulla climbed down the rope, this time needing only two hands to grip it. Upon reaching the bottom, he walked to the trunk of the vehicle to access the last bottle of whiskey from his mission ready kit. This bottle would last him a day, possibly more if he paced himself – truly a sign that he would need to return to civilization soon.

One member of the squadron of geese that Sulla had seen make a water landing, a scout no doubt, was waiting at the rear of his Armored Scout for him. It hissed, baring a mouthful of tiny teeth. Sulla paused, looking at the goose. He returned the favor and smiled. The scout goose was not amused and waddled two steps forward and hissed again. Sulla was not amused. He hissed back and took a step forward. The scout goose did not budge and apparently called for reinforcements as a dozen or so other geese were now making their way up the riverbank toward the bluff face. Sulla recognized a pincer movement when he saw one. He gave the scout an ultimatum. He drew his service weapon and kicked gravel at the bird. This only emboldened the scout goose, which hissed more loudly, this time tilting its head at an angle. It looked up at Sulla with contempt.

The two belligerents locked eyes at seven waddle steps. Sulla raised his weapon and yelled, "Get out of here, you stupid duck!"

The stupid goose was not fazed. Its scores of teeth glistened with scorn. Reinforcements had almost arrived. It was now or never. Sulla took aim carefully at the scout's head and released a single thunderous volley. The reinforcement geese scattered at the report of gunfire, taking to the air. The now-headless scout fell lifelessly to the ground, its wings aflutter with mindless spasms almost forceful enough to cause the carcass to take pursuit of its living comrades in the air. "Oh no you don't!" Sulla quickly grabbed the former scout by the neck and contemplated roasted goose.

Truly, it was time for breakfast.

Agent Sulla: 91 January 0039

After building a fire, a skewer, and a rotisserie from the copious amounts of driftwood that the Intolerants had piled up at the site of Operation Drake, as they had called it, Sulla went about the business of gutting and defeathering the scout goose. What was the deal with all these piles of driftwood, anyway? Enormous piles of sticks were everywhere around him on the riverbank. A cursory view of the bluff line above him showed that many more piles of driftwood had been hauled up the cliffs and organized there. A casual observer might believe that this was some sort of elaborate system of communication using bonfires, but Sulla was beginning to put two and two together.

As the aroma of cottonwood smoke, whiskey, and goose fat filled the air, Sulla scoured his field tablet, pulling archived news stories on Congressman Fred Palmer from the Old U.S. period out of the DIS archives in D.C. All of this was done over what was a very tenuous data connection this far from Bush-Obamaha. This gave Sulla some time to enjoy his goose.

Palmer had been an interesting fellow. After a particularly bad concussion toward the end of his stint in Congress, the man became even more interesting. Palmer was obsessed with damming rivers to prevent sticks from reaching the Gulf of Mexico. Palmer's obsession with sticks and driftwood was a matter of general public knowledge at the time, but what interested Sulla the most were the news stories lampooning Palmer from 0003 to 0001 B.E.E. They were basically hit pieces on him, which decried his opposition to the National Tolerance Policy Act and the appointment of the Tolerance Czar, who would be responsible for leading the Tolerance Enforcement Administration. It was these hit pieces that cemented Palmer's reputation as a stick-crazed jingoist for all time. But all of that coverage veiled the clear fact, as Sulla could best read it, that Palmer had very vocal, and very public, fights with Senator Wagner of Washington and Congressman Cabeza de Vaca from Nebraska. Sulla recalled that it was Wagner and Cabeza de Vaca who were instrumental in the appointment of Tolerance Czar Tolerance, then an unknown politician, to be the head of the Tolerance Enforcement Administration. This man Palmer would know where many bodies had been buried in the days of the Old U.S. He could be a great asset … or a great liability, depending on whose hands he fell in.

Sulla looked at the piles of driftwood around him, then back to his field tablet, where he had a picture of a young Congressman Palmer arguing on the floor of Congress and pointing at Congressman Cabeza de Vaca, who was standing near him with his arms folded. Sulla remarked to himself, "Mr. Palmer, I need to talk with you alone. And without my babysitters."

Sulla decided he would remove the GPS tracker from his vehicle after all. It should give him enough of a surprise factor to get into Senator Harold Cabeza de Vaca Memorial Hospital without Crowe or Peterschild noticing his arrival. But to keep his babysitters entertained, he'd give the GPS transponder a nice ride downriver.

On the drive back to Bush-Obamaha, Sulla popped a few alcohol-concealment pills and rehearsed how he would get some much-needed time alone with Patient 900-05-0983. Fortunately for Sulla, no one knew the prisoner's true identity. Agents Crowe and Peterschild, along with the rest of DIS, believed Patient 900-05-0983 to be just an ordinary Intolerant who was lucky enough to survive contact with the Tolerance Corps. However, time was short. Given a little more time, Agent Crowe would be able to deduce that 900-05-0983 could be Palmer based on her short interview with ex-Trainee Leonard back at Fort Freeperson.

He would flash his DIS badge at the security guards at the hospital. He'd demand to see their supervisor. He'd inform the supervisor that he was there to inspect security measures in the secure wing of Cabeza de Vaca Hospital. This would be all too easy if his DIS nannies could stay out of his way long enough. The fact of the matter was that most civilians were so afraid at the sight of a DIS badge from a Supra Agent that they would willingly hand over their Procreation Licenses to avoid any unpleasantries.

It was a good drive back to Bush-Obamaha. Sulla enjoyed being out of the D.C. Habitation Zone, where most of his assignments kept him. He was incredibly bored with purge after purge, imprisoning or disappearing politicians and administrators who were suspected of disloyalty to DIS.

Just a few weeks before he had been assigned with investigating ex-Trainee Leonard's forbidden question, Sulla had been bored to tears while ferreting out disloyalty in the Tolerance Enforcement Administration. Chief of Staff Wickard himself received messages of extortion from a TEA Sector Head who threatened to go public with knowledge that it was DIS agents, and not President Tolerance or his staff, who received and answered all of the messages directed to the President. The Sector Head thought he could use his influence to stop a controversial wind power project in his Cape Cod neighborhood. He became irate when he failed in his attempt to stop the project by withholding the Tolerance Impact Statement necessary to begin construction. Apparently, a DIS intern hit reply-all on an email from one of the wind turbine contractors and sent a Tolerance Impact Approval Statement approving the project. Sulla was tired of inventing imaginative ways of disposing of disloyal Sector Heads and interns who hit the reply-all button in car crashes, fires, bridge collapses, and other ways that could be explained in the media.

Sulla's current assignment was far better than any purge he had ever been on. Far from arranging an accident to befall a pain-in-the-ass bureaucrat, he was actually investigating a mystery for the first time in years. Wild goose chase or not, he was enjoying his time spent getting to the bottom of ex-Trainee Leonard's forbidden question.

One thought kept nagging at him. Why would his bosses care so much if an Intolerant asked a question about the official calendar? Sulla wanted – no, he needed – to keep pulling on this string.

As Sulla thought his plan through, one piece was missing. He never went into an interrogation without a specially prepared interrogation kit. A good interrogation kit always consisted of at least three things: a carrot, a stick, and a killing weapon. Sulla pulled off to the side of the gravel road as he approached the ferry that would soon take him across the river into Bush-Obamaha.

On the side of the road, with the city skyline looming on the horizon, Sulla examined the contents of his trunk and considered the unique situation of his target. Palmer would undeniably feel alone and confused. He would be in severe pain, still recovering from injuries that were now hundreds of days old. And he would be feeling a great deal of fear. He had concealed his real name for a reason, knowing that he would experience enhanced interrogation if DIS found out who he really was. Palmer had lost almost everyone he had known in his life and his reputation had been dragged through the mud decades ago. The man had nothing to lose, and very little to gain. With very little to motivate Palmer, Sulla realized this would be a seeking of pleasure and avoidance of pain scenario.

Sulla chose his carrot, his stick, and his killing weapon from what he had in his trunk and packaged them into a briefcase he would bring into the hospital.

As he had driven throughout the day, he had sobered up substantially and no longer felt the need to take any alcohol-concealment pills. But as his senses became more acute, he realized he stank like a horse after being in the field for so long. He grabbed a bar of soap and bathed in the river, just downstream of what remained of a destroyed highway bridge, marveling at how many large sticks floated past him.

After toweling himself off and changing into a fresh suit, Sulla crossed into Bush-Obamaha on the ferry across the Missouri River. Upon driving off the ferry, he found himself at the customs post for the town, waiting in line inside his Armored Scout like a peasant.

Sulla sat behind two men, who appeared to be construction workers, in a truck. "Ridiculous," he muttered to himself as he shut off his engine and closed his eyes. As he waited, eyes closed, he could hear the conversation in front of him between the customs officer and the two men.

"Your names?"

"Jack Chavez," one man said.

"Dean McGee," said the other.

The customs officer responded, "Identifications and travel permits, please."

"Here you are."

A few moments passed.

"What were you two doing outside the DHZ?"

"We're engineers with the Department of Infrastructure. We're scouting out foundation sites for the replacement bridge now that the other side's been pacified."

"I see. How long were you out there?"

"About eight or nine hours, I guess."

"You guess?"

"Yes, Sir."

"This is not a guessing game. I need to know exactly how long you were outside the DHZ."

"Well, let's see, we crossed over there around eight o'clock, maybe you could pull our exit record in your comput–"

"I tell you what," the customs officer interrupted. "I am going to need to search your persons and your vehicle. Please exit the vehicle and put your hands on the fence over there and spread your feet."

Sulla opened his eyes and saw the customs officer wave to a canine officer, who started to bring a dog over for a smell test. The engineers in the truck began to get out. Sulla could see they were visibly nervous at the presence of a large German shepherd, a breed of dog so dangerous that only the government was allowed own one.

Sulla grabbed his DIS badge from the passenger seat and exited his Armored Scout. He slammed the door behind himself and walked toward the customs officer, holding his DIS credentials scalp high.

The customs officer turned and saw Sulla coming. "Sir, remain in your vehicle!" the customs officer bellowed while placing his hand on the stun gun holstered in his belt. The German shepherd let out a low growl, and the engineers froze, partially in and partially out of their vehicle as Sulla approached. "Not you two!" The customs officer pointed at Chavez and McGee and then pointed at the fence separating the customs post from town. "Get to the fence, now!"

Sulla had taken about five steps and was now within four meters of the customs man. "Officer, do you see this badge?"

The customs officer's tone changed when he saw the distinctive red badge of the Department of Internal Security. "Yes. Umm, yes, Sir." He let go of his stun gun.

"Good. Now, these men can take their truck and go. And I will be leaving right behind them. Understood?"

The customs officer waved the men back to their truck. On his way back into his truck, the driver said, "Thanks for the help, Mister!"

"Hmm," Sulla growled in response as he returned to his Armored Scout.

The customs officer raised the access gate that had been blocking the way, and Sulla followed the truck through customs and into Bush-Obamaha. It was now close to sunset and Sulla's onboard navigation indicated he was at least 20 minutes away from Congressperson Harold Cabeza de Vaca Memorial Hospital. He wanted to catch Mr. Palmer's caregivers before they left work for the evening. Waiting until morning was not really a viable option if he wanted to have this interrogation without Crowe or Peterschild, so Sulla sped toward Cabeza de Vaca Memorial as fast as he could.

After running a red light at the intersection of Leavenworth and 42nd Street, about a kilometer from the hospital, he attracted the attention of a pair of Bush-Obamaha constabulary officers in their patrol car. They activated their flashing blue lights and, through their loudspeaker, ordered, "Unknown citizen in the armored vehicle, cease flight!"

Sulla ignored them, and they pursued him all the way to the hospital, where Sulla found himself illegally parked in a parking slot marked "Expectant Progenitors Only."

0189

Sulla exited his Armored Scout with the constabulary officers parked and barking behind him, ordering him to place his hands on his vehicle. "I will give you local cops credit," he said. "You take your parking offenses very seriously. But I am here on official business." He flashed his DIS badge, walking past them and into Cabeza de Vaca Memorial Hospital. His business was with Patient 900-05-0983.

Meeting Patient 900-05-0983: 91 January 0039

"He won't give us his name. He's a very stubborn old man and won't really talk to me or any of the staff," Doctor Armida told Sulla as he sat in her office at Cabeza de Vaca Memorial.

Sulla observed the good Doctor's office was Spartan, without much in the way of decoration. No pictures of family, no plants, no artwork, not even so much as a calendar. All she had in her office was a desk, two chairs, and her monitor. Sulla concluded she was likely at this hospital on a temporary basis. Armida continued, "The fact of the matter is, the amount of severely injured Intolerants they are sending to this hospital is reaching Malthusian proportions."

"Doubtless you're inundated due to the recent pacification campaigns," Sulla responded.

Armida responded with a smile, touching her chin with her left hand. "Is that really what it is? Pacification?" Sulla observed her hand without a ring. Although he was there on official business, he could not help but take Doctor Armida in. She had the biggest brown eyes he could remember seeing. Granted, he had been spending a lot of time in burnt-out tomb caves lately and had not been around many women other than Agent Crowe, whose cross-eyed indignation agitated him to no end. But Armida had the biggest, prettiest brown eyes he could remember seeing, at least since he parted ways with his ex-wife.

He snapped out of his internal monologue and shifted nervously in his seat. "Something along the lines of pacification, anyway, if we're looking at end results, of course."

"Right. We are at full capacity here one way or another, Agent Sulla. So what brings you all the way out here from D.C. to see Mr. Zero-Nine-Eight-Three?"

"I need to speak with him, of course. Just some follow-up to verify some of the items I read in the after-action report of a Captain, umm." He paused to take out his field tablet. "Yes, a Captain

Wheeler – the officer who ordered the raid that led to your patient's capture."

"This long after the event?" Doctor Armida asked. "It's been almost a year, Agent Sulla."

"I'll ask the questions, if you don't mind. And please, call me Danbill. No need to be so formal. So has Zero-Nine-Eight-Three talked to anyone? Anyone at all? Visitors? Doctors? Nurses? Fellow inmates – err, patients?" He felt shaky around this woman. Why was he so damn nervous?

"Well, I can tell you no visitors at all. And he barely speaks to the staff. At first, there were concerns he might have been brain damaged. But I can tell you the man is alert and responsive. He just chooses not to speak for the most part. And he refuses to give us his real name. When we insisted he give us a name, he gave us 'Precious Doe.'"

Sulla smiled. "That's quite a convincing alias. How did you find out? Um," he fumbled his words briefly, "that he's alert, that is."

"When we brought him in here, his body was badly broken. His injuries were so severe – subdural hematoma and thirty-two fractures all over his body – we thought he was going to expire. We put him in full-body traction and an induced a coma. Since we brought him back from the coma, we have kept him heavily medicated, and his legs are still in traction. Up until recently, though, we thought he may have had permanent brain damage. All he would ever do was watch the Bureau of Weather Channel in his room and yell at the TV about flooding whenever it rained."

"That sounds like my guy," Sulla said with a raised eyebrow of amusement.

"Your guy? So what do you know about him?" Doctor Armida asked, genuinely curious.

"Oh, not that much, really. But please, let me be the one to ask questions about Zero-Nine-Eight-Three," Sulla said before finding himself being unusually sincere with Ms. Armida. "Truth be told, you want to know as little as possible about the man for your own sake. They don't send out DIS men for routine Intolerants. This man has dangerous information inside of his head."

"Very well." Doctor Armida folded her hands on her desk and sighed, slightly dejected. "Anything else you'd like to know?"

"When can I question him? And," Sulla found himself asking nervously, "are you free for dinner tonight?"

Why the hell was he so nervous with this woman?

Doctor Armida smiled. "I'm flattered. And I probably will take you up on that sometime. You seem like an interesting guy. But are you sure you are okay to be working right now? When I first let you come in here …" She paused, unsure of what to say. "I thought it was because you, maybe, needed *something*?"

At this point, Sulla realized he had not just been nervous. He was massively dehydrated after drinking nothing but whiskey for days out in the wild. To complicate matters, he was so wrapped up in planning his interrogation of Patient 900-05-0983, he had forgotten to drink his whiskey since breakfast. "Nonsense," he smiled drolly. "These shakes are just because I was a bit nervous to ask you out."

Doctor Armida smiled and broke eye contact briefly. "Just the same, let me get you set up with an IV with saline and a little ethanol."

Later that evening, carrying his briefcase, equipped with the knowledge that Patient 900-05-0983 was in room 608 of Cabeza de Vaca Memorial – and armed with an IV bag full of slightly alcoholic salt water on a rolling pole stand – Agent Sulla rode up the elevator with Doctor Armida. "Thanks again for the help, Doc."

"Anytime, Danbill. And when you call me the next time you call me, call me Morena." The elevator door opened. "And I believe this is your stop. Make a left and you'll see room six-oh-eight on your left."

"You sure you don't need me to fill out any paperwork to cover your ass?"

Morena Armida looked silently at Danbill a moment, then said, "You are not the first DIS Agent who has needed to talk to a patient. I think we both know what this is. Just keep it clean, and keep it quiet."

Cool and efficient, just my kind, Sulla thought to himself. "Agreed. Thanks again, Doc," he said.

"Anytime, Supra Agent." Armida smiled with a crooked wink and held the elevator door open.

With that, Sulla exited the elevator and made his way to room 608.

Sulla put on a pair of black faux-leather gloves and stood outside room 608 a moment, knowing that the string he had been pulling on for 31 days had led him here. But he had no idea what string he would be pulling on after talking to Patient 900-05-0983. Would this be the end of his investigation? Or would he have more to go on after this? He gently leaned his head against the door, savoring the moment. He could hear a TV voice emanating from inside the room. "There is a definite warm front moving in from the Rockies across the Buffalo Reserve, and that is going to lead to widespread thunderstorms with significant rainfall for the rest of the evening."

"God dang it! Not again!" Sulla heard an irate Patient 900-05-0983 yell.

Sulla opened the door and entered the room, quickly closing the door behind himself.

Patient 900-05-0983 had been sitting slightly upright in his bed that was set to the inclined position. Upon seeing Sulla, he grabbed his TV control and turned the screen off. He looked at Sulla in his brown suit and hat – distinctly non-medical attire – as Sulla pulled his IV stand into the room behind him. Staring at Sulla, the patient said, "I figured one of you would be here sooner or later."

Sulla entered the room and opened his briefcase. He tightened his gloves before pulling out an RFD-05 radio detection wand. He started waving it around the room as a small red light on it lit up sporadically.

"Whatchya got there?" the old man asked.

Sulla paused wanding the room and put a finger over his mouth, gesturing to the patient to be silent. Sulla then continued to wave the RFD-05 wand around the room. When he moved near the window, five red lights flashed on the wand, a sure sign of radio transmission. He scanned the rest of room in order to be thorough, and the wand did not flash again.

Sulla took out a smaller device with an antenna and scanned the area around the window.

"I see what you are up to," the old man whispered quietly.

Sulla remained silent and pulled a chair over to the window. He looked closely at what appeared to be an SPB-82 solar-powered bug glued to the top of the window frame. Sulla was familiar with the model. It was an older model, but decent. It was a little oversized, however; a little smaller than the size of an Ernesto Guevara 50-credit nickel but far bigger than an Abraham Lincoln 10-credit penny. It was serviceable, but primitive, by 0039 standards. DIS had been using this model as a mainstay of its long-term surveillance operations due to its ability to recharge itself with a modest amount of sunlight exposure. But about two or three years ago, DIS replaced the SPB-82 with a smaller version, closer to the size of a Franklin Roosevelt 100-credit dime. The presence of this bug puzzled Sulla. Surplus SPB-82s were supposed to have been destroyed.

As lightning began to flash in the distance of the darkened sky over Bush-Obamaha, Sulla's mind filled with questions about the bug. Who placed this thing here? Who else would suspect this old man was worth spying upon? And who would be using an out-of-date SPB? It must have been someone who was less confident in their interrogation abilities than Sulla was. That, or someone who was unable to get access to this patient directly and needed to work with someone on the inside of the hospital. Whoever it was, they were hoping to get a surreptitious recording of this room without having to interview the patient and without DIS's knowing about it. The possibilities were straining his mind. Who had put this antiquated bug here?

Sulla looked at the old man lying in his hospital bed. His head and face were shaved, but his bushy eyebrows furrowed over his hazel eyes. His legs were still in casts and in traction. He was tethered to at least five IV bags and was breathing with the aid of an oxygen tube under his nose. Moving him to a safer room would likely kill the man, making interrogation less than fruitful. But removing this bug would be a rookie mistake. Sulla knew the SPB-82 would send an emergency scream signal to whoever had placed it there if he removed it from the window frame. He would need to render the bug useless while leaving it intact.

Sulla took a quick inventory of what he had in the room and in his briefcase – sheets, towels, screwdriver, duct tape, zip ties, binoculars, shaving cream, and his field tablet.

Yes, that beat-up field reader would do the trick. His tablet had a great set of speakers. Sulla unplugged himself from the IV he had been dragging around, knowing he would need his full range of motion. Sulla laid his reader directly over the bug and taped it over, securing it with some of his duct tape. He pulled up his music, selecting an oldie he still occasionally listened to. He maxed out the volume and played *Pineapple Face* by *Lard*, an outlawed song by a banned group from the old U.S. But for Sulla, ever fond of antiquities, *Pineapple Face* was his personal favorite song for this type of thing. He set the device to play the song on repeat.

As the pleasing tones of *Lard* began to play, Sulla covered up his reader and the bug with a hospital towel and taped it to the window frame for good measure.

He turned to the old man in his bed. "Precious Doe, I presume?"

"Yeah, that's me. Who the hell are you?"

"My name is Agent Danbill Sulla from DIS, and I believe we have some mutual friends to discuss."

The old man held his hands over his stomach, saying, "Be quiet. I'm dead," before closing his eyes and falling silent.

Sulla grabbed a chair and pulled it next to the man's bed. "Oh, and please don't let me forget my tablet when I go. I can be fairly forgetful. I am sure you can relate." Sulla examined the man. He was now as old as dirt, but based on the pictures Sulla had seen of the man, this was clearly Congressman Palmer.

Sulla continued. "So, Fred. Can I call you Fred? Or would you prefer Congressman? Or Congressperson? I never know how to address you political types. I'm going to be honest with you. Although I am not here officially, meaning DIS does not officially know who you are yet, and they don't know that I am here, I know who you are. And, more importantly, I know what you know. I'm halfway in there." He tapped Palmer lightly on top on his shaved head.

Palmer just stared blankly at Sulla.

Sulla continued, "I see you here, a shell of your former self, unable to walk and unable to leave." Sulla tapped the rail on Palmer's bed and pointed to his legs. "A guy spends his entire childhood trying to become a man, a powerful man in control of his own destiny. A man spends his entire adulthood trying to control and influence the destinies of the people around him – trying to help people, trying to bring justice to the world. And before too long, that man finds himself in a hospital bed, unable to walk, and everyone he ever knew is gone. Everyone he tried to help rejected him. And in the end, the man is a boy again, unable to take a shit without help." Sulla tapped the rail on Palmer's bed again. "Does that seem just to you?"

Sulla began to feel a bit shaky again; his forehead collected beads of perspiration. He looked over at his IV pole and his briefcase over by the window frame. He knew how to cure these shakes, and an IV drip was not the fastest way. "Do you like whiskey, Congressman?" Sulla grabbed his briefcase and returned to his seat next to Palmer, pulling out a bottle of brown relief he had saved especially for this occasion. He had not had a drink since breakfast.

"I think I'll have some, and I am more than happy to share." He took a sip. "This whiskey, Fred, is the finest single-barrel vintage in the country, if I do say so myself. See, this is my own handiwork. And I am one of the fortunate few who can still age my whiskey in oak barrels. This is no white whiskey or lightly aged rubbing alcohol like the locals drink. No, Sir! This is as smooth as it gets these days."

"I'll have me some." Palmer finally spoke. Sulla handed him the bottle, and Palmer held it, hesitating.

"It's not spiked or drugged," Sulla said, taking the bottle back and taking a visible drink, pouring some into his mouth so that Fred could see. "Drugging a drinking partner is one of the few true crimes a man can commit." He handed the bottle back to Palmer.

Palmer took a drink. "Not bad. But I prefer beer."

"Oh, I agree, Fred. I agree. But beer is far too bulky to transport and store these days. Whiskey is more compact, more discreet. But I do brew ale for myself and my crew back at my distillery. I make an ale that'll keep you full of piss and bounce with the same basic recipe I use to make my whiskey. Just add a few hops to the standard mixture of barley, corn, plus rye."

Palmer looked at Sulla, studying him a bit. "Come here looking for a drinking partner, then?"

"Well, to be honest, Fred. I have not gotten to the real reason for my visit. See, I know you know things. We have a mutual associate in George Armstrong Leonard."

"Who?"

"He was with you and Asno at Operation Drake." As Sulla mentioned the name "Asno," he could see he got a slight rise out of Palmer.

"I don't recall the name."

"Asno or Leonard?"

"Neither."

"I'm sure. But Leonard recalls you. In fact, talking to him is what put me on your trail. But don't worry, Fred. He's not going to be talking to anyone else in DIS. But there are other clues that point to you. You see, I am the first to put all the clues together and the first to find you, but I won't be the last." Sulla took the bottle back from Palmer and drank. He was starting to feel much better.

"Well, that's good for you. You found a fucking hospital patient in a fucking hospital! Your bosses are gonna give you a commendation for this accomplishment."

"See, that's where you are wrong. My bosses do not know I am here, and I want to keep it that way. As a matter of fact, they do not know *you* are here, and I want to keep it that way, too. If they find you, you'll be subject to all sorts of enhanced interrogation techniques to get you to spill your guts about Asno and your unconventional theories about President Tolerance."

"Ain't no damned theory about it!"

"Well, we'll get to that, Fred. At least I hope we'll get to that. But what I am trying to tell you is that, sooner or later, my friends in DIS are going to find you and make what few weeks or years you have left on this Earth a living nightmare of half-drownings, pins, needles, suffocation, and penetration. But the fact is, if you give me what information I need, I will release you."

"Release me? Hell, where would I go? I can't even walk."

"No, Fred. I won't let you go out there. You'd last fifteen damn minutes out there. I'm not going to let you go. I'm going to *release* you. It's going to happen one way or another. And by that, I mean the release could be real pleasant, like falling into a comfortable dream. Or that release could go down a much more painful avenue."

Palmer leaned back in his bed and nodded his head slowly. Sulla believed the old man was beginning to understand that this was going to be his last night alive.

Strangely, he probably did not mind the idea of suicide by agent, so long as it was relatively painless. Palmer had had enough pain in his long life. He reached his hand out for the whiskey bottle. Sulla obliged.

"Fred, Sir, Congressman, I know this may bring back some bad memories, but tell me about the last days of Operation Drake. Specifically, what happened after Asno left with Leonard and the other men?"

"It was a day like any other, I s'pose. There hadn't been a barge or tug that tried to get upstream in weeks. It was real peaceful like. I was down on the riverbank, we had made a large haul that day of driftwood and silver jumping carp. We were about to start a fire to cook the carp for dinner when BOOM," he slapped his hand on the bed. "Cluster bombs," he continued. "Did not even hear a plane coming. Just the bombs going off. Half my people got killed right away. But a few of us made it to the bluffs. Last thing I remember, I was climbing up the ladder to our caves when the cave opening exploded. I woke up here, surrounded by fiberglass casts and weirdoes in scrubs who give me the willies."

"You've always been a survivor, haven't you?"

"Lucky, or unlucky, I guess."

"Well, I mean you didn't just survive the attack from a Tolerance Corps contingent that vastly outnumbered and outgunned you. You've survived much – even before that. I've read all about you, Congressman. You are one of the few living members of the old U.S. Congress. And you are the *only* survivor of the old Tolerance Committee to even make it a few years into the Enlightened Era."

"Well, yep. T'weren't no accident, that."

"I suppose not. I read the news stories about your theories. They lampooned you, quite unfairly. Phrases like 'Too crazy for even Missourians to re-elect' stick out in my mind."

"I resigned, damn it! The government was complicit in the raiding of our driftwood by Mexico. And Senator Wagner and Congressman Cabeza de Vaca were fools. Damnable fools who were complicit in the installation of a power-mad Tolerance Czar." Palmer spat between the casts on his legs.

"And what happened to Wagner and Cabeza de Vaca?"

"They got what was coming to them right after they set up the Tolerance Czar." Palmer spat again, then pointed at Sulla. "That there bombing that killed them and wiped everyone else out at the joint session of the Tolerance Committee after I left was no damn terrorist act by the Curaçaoans. It was an inside job by the Tolerance Czar himself."

"You have quite a few theories about both Mexican stick thievery and President Tolerance."

"Ain't theories, they're facts," Palmer growled with a fire in his eyes.

"Tell me more about our wise President, please."

"He ain't our President. At least he ain't mine. And he sure as dog turds ain't wise. You ever met the man?"

"No, I cannot say I have."

"Me neither! And you know why?"

"No. Tell me." Sulla leaned forward in anticipation.

"Because ain't no one ain't never seen him. The Tolerance Committee dun made him up!"

"Made him up?"

"Yep. Make-believe!"

"If he's make-believe, then why does he respond to his messages?" Sulla asked.

"Does he respond? Or do you respond for him?" Palmer formed a sardonic smirk on his face.

Sulla realized he was quite fortunate to have found this man before his comrades in DIS could. He walked over to the window and checked to make sure *Pineapple Face* was still playing into the solar-powered bug, pausing briefly to count the 16 or so raindrops sticking to the window. Sulla came back to Palmer and whispered in his ear, "He still responds. Rarely, but sometimes."

Fumbling over his words, Palmer was incredulous. "He sometimes responds? Well, well – I just don't, I just don't believe that."

Sulla sat back down next to him and shrugged. "Believe it."

"I don't believe it! He ain't nothin' but a computer hidden in some damn bunker in Nebraskie!"

"He very well might be, but he responds, and he says some very interesting things when he does. As a matter of fact, he sent me a message to my tablet about three weeks ago ... unsolicited."

Palmer looked at Sulla in silence for a few moments. "Lies," he said. "Damned abominable lies."

"It's the truth. Not through email, not through text, and not through the phone. But right onto my screen. And as fast as I read the message, it was gone."

"What did the old tin man say?"

"It said a lot of things. It said something about a lake and a flood, and about abolishing the internet. He usually speaks in riddles and likes metaphors about water. But in particular, the message said, 'The beguiler knows where I am. Do not let them find me.'"

"Who's this beguiler you speak of?" Palmer's voice became lower, almost like sandpaper scraping gravel.

"Well, that's the question, isn't it? I was hoping you could help me understand that piece of the puzzle. At first, I thought it could be the message was referring to Director of Internal Security Steel."

"Could be you," Palmer interjected.

"Could be me. Could be referring to any number of people – terrorists, government officials, bloggers, rebels, Intolerants – but there was something about this message and the way it was delivered that felt recent and urgent. So I really need to know where Tolerance is, and who you told."

"I don't know where he is, other than Nebraskie. And Nebraskie was a big state."

"A big state turned into a big dominion turned into a big buffalo pasture. Now, who did you tell about your theory?"

"You know who I told!"

"And who was that?"

"Anyone who would listen!" Palmer yelled, incredulous.

Sulla realized Palmer was probably telling the truth. The man was indiscreet. Sulla asked, "Well, Sir. Who listened?"

"No one! I warned them! I warned every single daggum one of them. My mailman. My neighbors. Kids running lemonade stands. Telemarketers trying to sell me insurance. Email people from the Congo trying to sell me boner pills! But no one ever listened!"

"Did Leonard listen?"

"Who is Leonard?"

"Did Asno listen?"

There was silence in the room. Sulla stood from his chair, leaned over Palmer, and took the bottle from his hand. "Did Asno listen?" Sulla repeated the question, narrowing his eyes at Palmer.

Palmer responded, albeit slowly and deliberately. "Asno is a good officer. A good man. He's going to help us win this war."

"Fred, you need to tell me what you know, or this could go very badly for you." As Sulla said those words, he could see something snapping in Palmer's eyes.

Palmer roared as loudly as he could, "I'm supposed to believe you got a message from Tolerance telling you to not let some beguiler find him. Horse shit!" He spat at Sulla, hitting him in the face. "And I am supposed to sell my friend out your way just because you say you got some damn message I can't see. Pig shit! No, no, I won't say a word about Asno to you. And who are you, Agent Sulla?" Palmer reached up with all his strength and grabbed Sulla by the tie with both hands as the agent was wiping the spit off his face. "You are just a blunted chisel in the hands of a false god! You might pretend to be good, or do what you do for a good cause. But you are a tool. A dumb, blunted instrument incapable of good or evil."

Sulla thrashed away from Palmer's grip, dropping his bottle of whiskey onto the bed and spilling the brown liquor in between the casts on Palmer's legs. Sulla recognized the behavior of a true believer. He walked over to his briefcase as calmly as he could and retrieved a jet injector full of a drug cocktail he had intended to be Palmer's easy release.

Palmer continued yelling at the top of his lungs, "But great evil is done in your false god's name! It is apostates that pull your strings! Apostates who will see our country's sacred topography denuded of trees!"

Sulla knew the noise Palmer was making would soon draw attention from the skeleton crew working the hospital that night and the other patients on this floor if it already hadn't. He placed the jet injector sideways in his mouth and lunged at Palmer, leaping on top of the man, straddling his chest. Using the weight of his legs, Sulla pinned Palmer's arms to the bed. "Be quiet," Sulla growled as his teeth gripped the jet injector.

Palmer tried to thrash his way free. His arms were pinned beneath Sulla's surprising weight, but IV tubes ran underneath Sulla to the IV poles by the bed. The thrashing sent one of the IV poles crashing into the rail on Palmer's hospital bed and down to the floor, sending saline solution and medicine splashing across checkered tiles.

Palmer continued to yell, "No, you pretend to be powerful, but you are an addict. You, Sir, are just an empty barge without a pilot, careening down the river." Sulla gave Palmer an open-handed slap to the temple. He quickly grabbed Palmer by the ear and lifted his head with his right hand, pulling the pillow underneath free with his left hand.

"It's the mark of an educated mind to understand an idea without accepting it," Sulla growled through his clenched teeth. "Now be quiet!" Sulla growled again.

Palmer would not stop yelling. "As soon as you are no longer of use to your masters, you will be cast away into the garbage heap like Wagner, like Cabeza de Vaca, like any other worn out–"

Sulla pushed the pillow down over Palmer's mouth and nose with his left hand, cutting off his air completely.

Palmer looked up at Sulla, his hazel eyes wide open as he shouted muffled derision through the pillow.

Sulla pulled the jet injector from his mouth with his right hand and said, "You know, Congressman, I have not killed anyone quite as interesting a conversation partner as you in quite a long time. I'm going to miss us, Fred."

Sulla placed the jet injector to the side of Palmer's neck and whispered in the man's ear. "Even though you have been a pain in my ass, you held up your end of the bargain. You let me know what I need to know, and that's that I need to track down this Asno. I am still going to give you your easy release. After all, suffocation is horrid way to go." Sulla pulled the trigger on the injector.

"Sleep well, Congressman. You have done your country a great service." Within a few seconds, Palmer's eyes closed. And within 30 seconds, Palmer's heart stopped beating.

Still perched on Palmer, Sulla reached over to the remote control that had been lying by him all this time and turned the TV back on. He cranked the volume back up on the Bureau of Weather Channel. He then dismounted Palmer, rolled off the bed, and walked back to the windowsill, straightening his tie and suit in the window reflection as lightning flashed across town. He untaped his field tablet from the bug that had been spying on Palmer. Who had put this thing here? And how long had it been here? He cut the volume on his tablet and placed it into his suit pocket. He spent the next few minutes gathering everything he had brought with him, his duct tape and his jet injector, placing his things back in his briefcase, except for the bottle. He left the whiskey bottle on the bed, knowing his faux-leather gloves meant only Palmer's fingerprints were on it in case some bureaucrat decided to investigate this death.

He started walking out of the room and then turned back to look at Palmer. The pillow was still partially covering his face. Sulla returned to the side of the bed and restored the pillow to its previous position behind Palmer's head. He then turned and walked out of room 608. Making a right turn toward the elevator and pondering his now-dwindled alcohol supply, he looked at his watch and saw it was now 2047 in the evening. Sulla hoped his man at the Bush-Obamaha evidence locker was still open for business this late.

Agent Sulla: 91-92 January 0039

Sulla's contact at the local evidence locker had already called it a day by the time Sulla left Cabeza de Vaca Memorial Hospital. Sulla knew that the night was shaping up to be a long one without his medicine. But thankfully, Doctor Armida made house calls – or hotel calls, as the case may be.

Sulla knew he was likely ruining any chances of a romantic relationship with the good doctor by exposing himself to her as a full-blown addict and a likely killer of suspects, but she had appeared at least slightly interested in him when she knew him to be a mild addict and a likely patient killer. Calling her over had been a calculated risk in more ways than one.

But surprisingly, Doctor Armida showed up. Perhaps even more surprising was the fact she did not show up with another IV bag or any medicine. Instead, she showed up dressed to the nines with a symbolic oversized key protruding from her handbag. "Hey, kindred spirit. Care to join me at a quiet place I know?" she asked as she held the key out.

Sulla recognized the sort of key she had. He had several for various speakeasies, whiskey rooms, and vodka joints throughout D.C., but he had none for Bush-Obamaha.

"Out of all the dates that ended with a kiss on the cheek, that was the best of my life," Sulla said to himself the next morning as he dressed himself for the affairs of the day. January 92nd was poised to be a productive day of dot connecting and puzzle solving, but to ensure his own productivity, he had to get himself to the evidence locker as soon as his contact arrived that morning.

"Same deal we talked about before?" Sulla asked Sergeant Bingham at the Bush-Obamaha evidence locker. "Two hundred of the finest handmade corncob pipes you've ever laid eyes upon, just like the pipes I let you sample, for a case of that rotgut you people call 'whiskey' out here?"

"You got a deal, Agent," Sergeant Bingham said as he held his hand out for Sulla's bag of corncob pipes. "Just where do you get these pipes from, anyway? They're kilned just right and hold together nicely. Reminds me of the sort I used to be able to get locally until my supplier ran out about a year back."

"I've got a guy who takes the cobs from spent corn at my distillery and turns garbage into these works of art," Sulla said as he took hold of the case of whiskey. "He's a new hire, but he just might work out. You interested in distributing for me long-term?"

After the exchange had been made, Sulla secured 11 of 12 whiskey bottles in his loaner vehicle's trunk, keeping one in his briefcase. He walked around to the other side of Bush-Obamaha Constabulary Headquarters. Known as the "Inner Tube" by the local constables due to its circular shape and central courtyard, Bush-Obamaha Constabulary Headquarters was a remarkable piece of Enlightened-Era architecture. It loomed over the Old Market part of town as a large, oval-shaped building that took up about three city blocks on the hills above the Missouri River. The Department of Internal Security rented a few office units in every DHZ for agents sent out on field assignments, and the Inner Tube filled this function nicely for Sulla's team over the course of their investigation into Trainee Leonard's forbidden question.

After walking the oval perimeter of the building, slowing down a few times to lunge at pigeons that roved too close to him, Sulla walked up the building's stairs and into the door of their third-story office at about 0945. There, he found Agents Crowe and Peterschild already hard at work, sitting at the large cherry wood table they shared as a desk. Their hands gripped Bureau of Fair Trade Coffee cups; their noses angled themselves profoundly into their monitors. The agents had been scanning file after file storing the details on killed and captured Intolerants in the region.

As Sulla closed the door behind himself, took off his coat and hat, and walked toward his slightly dusty monitor, Agent Crowe looked up from her files. "Where have you been, Sir?"

"Welcome back, Sir!" Agent Peterschild chimed in.

"I've been out on our investigation, Agents – doing fieldwork. You know, the field. It's the place where things actually happen." He took a seat at his screen. "Did you two find anything noteworthy in your file reviews?"

Agent Peterschild responded, "We've made good progress, Sir. We've flagged eighteen files as potential matches for Fred Palmer, five of them still living and in custody. And we've got another thirty or so files flagged as likely involved or connected with Palmer, mostly deceased, but I think–"

"Sir, all these files aside," Agent Crowe interrupted, "I am now completely convinced that Patient Nine Hundred dash Zero-Five dash Zero-Nine-Eight-Three needs to be our focus. Based on his file, he is the closest match to Fred Palmer and he has the flimsiest false identity I have ever seen. He calls himself 'Precious Doe,' which I have discovered was a pseudonym for a murder victim in Palmer's native Kansas City back around the time he still lived–"

"Crowe, stop." Sulla held his hand in the air. "You do not often hear me say this, but I agree with you. Patient Zero-Nine-Eight-Three is the best fit. In fact, I just returned from examining the place the Tolerance Corps captured Patient Zero-Nine-Eight-Three. There is a good deal of evidence to be found there, including about twenty more bodies we need to inventory and process."

"Sir, I have an idea." Crowe appeared to foresee where Sulla was going with this line of conversation and did not want to be sent on an errand. "Perhaps Agent Peterschild could coordinate with Bush-Obamaha Constabulary to inventory those bodies. I think I will be of most use to you in interviewing Zero-Nine-Eight-Three. I have read everything I could on both the patient and the historical records of Congressperson Palmer. From history classes in college, I always knew he was one of the earliest Tolerance deniers and was an insane person. But digging a little deeper, I see this man was involved in President Tolerance's rise to power. He likely knows where all the bodies are buried – to borrow your phrase, Sir. The fact a forbidden question came from a known associate with this Palmer person is very alarming to me."

"All good information and all good finds, Crowe." Sulla nodded approvingly. Perhaps Crowe might make a decent agent after all.

"Thank you, Sir." Crowe beamed with a smile. "So I think if I can help with the interview, we could really blow this investigation wide open."

"I agree again. But only if I had gotten back sooner, Crowe." Sulla put on the most profound frown he could muster. "I checked in with the subject's physician. Patient Zero-Nine-Eight-Three died last night of acute onset alcohol poisoning resulting in a heart attack. He somehow smuggled whiskey into his room and drank most of a bottle. Sometimes heavy drinkers who go dry for a while overdo it the next time they get a bottle in their hands. His heart just was not able to handle it."

"So, we've reached a dead end?" Crowe asked.

"Nonsense, Crowe." Peterschild spoke with a tone of optimism. "It sounds like Agent Sulla has a job for us out at the scene where the Tolerance Corps captured the subject."

"That's right, Peterschild," Sulla said with the plastic smile he reserved for flatterers and spies. "We've got about twenty badly-burnt bodies in a cave – bodies the Tolerance Corps paperwork made no mention of. I need you two to get out there now to start connecting more dots. Go to the constabulary quartermaster and get yourself an Armored Scout and enough rations to last you a week or so."

A few minutes later, Sulla locked the office door behind Crowe and Peterschild as they left. He opened his briefcase on the wooden table and took out his whiskey and his radio detection wand. He scanned the entire room and returned to the table, satisfied that there were no listening devices intruding on him. He was alone, sure enough, but he tended to talk to himself when solving puzzles and did not want any unwelcome ears.

He opened his bottle of whiskey and took a drink. Despite his earlier remarks to Sergeant Bingham, the local whiskey was not too bad. It lacked the character and woody flavor of his own product, but it had a certain spiciness he liked.

He carried his bottle with him to the office's window. "Some view," he said as he looked down on a paved circular courtyard lot full of constabulary squad cars, surrounded on all sides by the Headquarters building he occupied. He took a sip and stared up at the sky. He took another sip and stared down at the parking lot. "Who else would have been in your circle?" Sulla asked aloud. "Who else would have listened to you, Fred?"

Sulla opened the courtyard window and the heavy feel of humid, cool spring air thick with the aroma of pollen flowed into the room.

He returned to the desk and began to pencil a diagram in his moleskin notebook. He scratched down the names Palmer, Leonard, and Asno. He then drew a small circle around each. Around the whole group, he drew another circle, labeling it "Palmer's circle of knowledge." Beneath Palmer, he wrote, "deceased." Beneath Leonard, he wrote "forbidden question – neutralized." Beneath Asno, he wrote "last seen at Seattle Cod Protest."

He then returned to his thinking position by the window. Thirty minutes passed on Sulla's automatic watch while he watched local constables getting in and out of their squad cars – driving in and out of a set of small garage doors on the far side of the courtyard.

He walked back to the wooden table and looked at his diagram again, tapping his finger on Asno's circle. "Who else?" Sulla asked aloud.

He tapped on Leonard's circle. "That's it." Sulla smiled to himself. He thought back to his interview with Leonard and wrote the names Vargas, Johnschild, and Hackberry inside the large circle. He circled each new name and put a question mark inside Vargas' and Hackberry's circles. Inside Johnschild's circle, he wrote "last seen at the battle of Fort Peck – pull name and review UCC data."

Sulla went back to his screen and requested a secure connection to the Seattle Constabulary database. After a few minutes of scanning the medical records related to the Seattle Cod Protests, he marked Vargas' circle with a "deceased – 23 Jan 0039." But there were no name matches with either Asno or Hackberry in the medical records database. Sulla recalled Leonard's saying that Hackberry was back at Fort Freeperson, but he needed to confirm this.

A scan of the arrest records database proved fruitful for Hackberry. Sulla verified that Hackberry had been arrested and tried with Leonard, then sent on the same plane and shuttle bus to Fort Freeperson in West Virginia. Sulla pinged the Tolerance Corps database and found an active entry for Trainee Augustus Hackberry.

Name: Hackberry, Augustus
Status: Active / Living
DOB: 337 January 0007 E.E.
Height: 185.4 cm
Weight: 86.1 kg
Eyes: Blue
Hair: Red
Blood Type: AB-
Rank: E-0, Trainee
Volunteer: No
Offense: DoP 215(B)(b) violation
Weapons Qualified: M8, expert. M9, expert. M320, expert. M1914, expert.
Jump Qualified: Yes
Assignment: Presently assigned to Alfa Platoon, Echo Company, 96th Battalion, 7th Brigade, 29th Division, Ft. Freeperson
Graduation Date: 134 January 0039
Post-Graduation Classification: Combat Infantry, 207th Amphibious Division

"Oh, that simply will not do," Sulla said to himself as he reached into his briefcase for his dual-band wireless phone that worked with both communication satellites and towers. He knew very well that the 207th would likely be overseas very soon, and he needed to keep Mr. Hackberry accessible. He held down the command button. "Call HQ."

"Calling DIS headquarters," the phone's automated voice responded. Moments later, the phone emitted a beep of disappointment. Its automated voice spoke again. "I'm sorry, Agent Sulla. No signal."

"For the love of the bearded man in the sky," Sulla grumbled to himself as he walked over to the office's window. "Dial again," he growled at the phone.

"Connecting," the phone responded.

"Department of Internal Security switchboard," a pleasant human voice answered. "How may I direct your call, Supra Agent Sulla?"

"I need our liaison officer for the Twenty-Ninth Tolerance Corps division. Purpose, reclassifying a trainee."

"One moment while I connect you, Supra Agent Sulla."

Moments later, a familiar voice answered the phone. "Danbill? Is that you? It's Colonel Grapeseed."

"Hey, Monica. It's Danbill. Listen, I am about to owe you another case of my finest bourbon," he said as he looked absent-mindedly from the office window. "I need a trainee reclassified so he stays accessible to me after graduation."

"What's the name and where do you want the trainee to go? I'll get the info over to my people and make it happen."

"Hackberry, Augustus. That's Hotel Alfa Charlie Kilo Bravo Echo Romeo Romeo Yankee."

"Got it, Danbill. Where do you want him?"

"Let's keep him dominion-side – someplace I can pick him up whenever I need him. Let's do East Coast Protest Command. And one more thing. I'm going to need a list of all the trainees in his platoon."

"A case of bourbon?"

"Just as soon as I get back to town."

"Deal. Consider this Hackberry reassigned. Grapeseed out."

"Thank you, Monica."

Sulla clicked his phone off and returned to his notebook. The fools in the Tolerance Corps really did not know who they had in Hackberry if they only had him down as violating a Department of Protests regulation and not for fighting in a rebel army. But protest duty would keep Hackberry accessible – accessible and unarmed. He took his pencil and scribbled "backburner – EastProtComm" into the circle around Hackberry's name.

"And what about you, Mr. Beetle Johnschild?" Sulla tapped the name on his diagram.

Thirty minutes of pinging civilian, military, and academic databases yielded nothing on Beetle Johnschild. He would have also searched Ubiquitous Camera Command databases, but he had no image of this Johnschild to work with. "No one is this far off the grid," Sulla said to himself as he wrote "false name" in Johnschild's circle.

That left Asno – the most logical next target so far. As Sulla stood over by the open window, looking up at the sky, a question burned in his mind. What did he know about El Asno? First of all, El Asno was almost certainly a false name or a *nom de guerre*. Sulla knew enough Spanish to know El Asno literally meant a donkey, or an ass. There had to be a man beneath the false name.

Based on what Leonard and Palmer had said, Asno was in his 50s, a rebel Colonel, resourceful, and secretive – often hiding himself away from his men. Asno's cleverness could not be underestimated. He developed the strategy needed for the rebels to take Fort Peck through inventive tactics and understanding his enemies' weak spots. Although he had developed this strategy, he left his command at Fort Peck for seemingly no reason to head off to Seattle well before the siege had been won.

Sulla looked up the events in Seattle. Asno led a mob into the heart of the city to break up a protest and campaign event organized by Seattle Supervizier Horus T. Anderchild. Asno's mob was vastly outgunned and was almost completely wiped out, with only a handful of members escaping from the scene and with only two survivors arrested. Yet despite the slaughter of this mob, Supervizier Anderchild and his staff were somehow incinerated with military-grade rockets – hardware that could have, if used, turned the tide of the battle for Asno's mob and given them the upper hand over the local security forces that mowed them down.

"Leaving a siege about to be won to go on an overland journey over the Rocky Mountains and across the Continental Divide for what? To bust up a cod protest, get your friends killed, and kill a local Supervizier?"

Sulla could feel it. Something did not add up. He needed more information. He looked up everything he could on Horus Tolerance Anderchild. Anderchild had been a moderately successful Supervizier in Seattle who heavily invested in the military-industrial complex in the area. He had been giving a number of speeches at campaign events and protests in the weeks leading up to his death, and he was the frontrunner for becoming Overseer of Sacajawea. Sulla wrote down "who benefits – eliminating potential Overseer of Sacajawea?" on the top of his notes before moving on.

Once more returning to his screen and the databases, he looked up everything he could on El Asno. His name itself appeared in news articles, blogs, and Bureau of Twacebook postings about the Colonel and his military operations. His reputation was indeed fierce, but there were also numerous false hits from Spanish speakers and Spanish-as-a-second-language students making inane jokes going back for decades. The line between when the military career of El Asno began and when "Asno" was just a word on the internet was fuzzy. The man had clearly chosen his nom de guerre well. But Sulla's careful eye could filter through the internet noise enough to deduce that Asno the rebel Colonel only started making waves about three years ago. Where was the rebel Captain Asno, or the rebel Lieutenant Asno? This Colonel appeared to come from nowhere. "Who is the man behind the name?" Sulla asked himself as he sipped from his whiskey bottle.

But he knew the name would only yield so much. He needed images and the Ubiquitous Camera Command database.

Sulla took another drink from his bottle, now half-empty, and logged into UCC's servers. He scanned the records for the Seattle Cod Protests that Crowe and Peterschild had prepared for him and viewed every facial record for the mob that descended upon City Hall that day. Sulla found Leonard. He found a match with Vargas and with Hackberry. He found about 190 other matches with Coroner's Office files and with DIS files. But most conspicuous for Sulla was the UCC match for the man who rode at the front of the mob.

Sulla pulled up the file, labeled Unknown Rebel Officer 900-54-2199. There was something vaguely familiar about the man and Sulla immediately saw a pattern. The oldest hit in UCC's database was only about three years old. And most of the high-percentage matches came from MQ Wildfire drone footage out in the Great Not-East. Looking a bit more closely at the records, he found the last matching records before the Seattle Cod Protests came from MQ Wildfire drones patrolling the hills around Fort Peck. Older than that, Sulla found a match in the Sweetgrass Buffalo Reserve with Unknown Rebel Officer 900-54-2199 and three other men in the summer of 0038. Sulla pulled this record and queried UCC's database for matches on the other three men caught in this photo. Sure enough, one of the images in the footage was a 97 percent match with George Armstrong Leonard. Sulla tapped his screen over Unknown Rebel Officer 900-54-2199's image, knowing he was looking in the face of El Asno. He saved the image to his tablet knowing it likely also had the face of Beetle Johnschild, but Johnschild was small potatoes as far as Sulla was concerned and could wait for the moment.

Sulla now knew he had a positive identification and should be able to use this image to find matches to this El Asno and his civilian life. He would query the usual academic, civilian, government, and military databases going back 60 years and find out who El Asno really was.

Sulla pinged every database he could but got no results outside the recent records from UCC. Something was amiss. He needed to query the archives of UCC's records themselves to find the connections he was missing, but even UCC's historical archives were off-limits at the moment as they were in an isolated database only UCC personnel could get into.

During all this research, Sulla had been sipping regularly on his whiskey bottle, almost unconsciously. He now realized his bottle was almost completely dry. He'd have to restock before getting too deep into the riddle of El Asno or trying to get into UCC's archives.

He grabbed his briefcase and phone and walked downstairs. He would walk and talk to his contacts in UCC while on his way to his vehicle's trunk, where the remainder of his whiskey supply waited for him.

As Sulla rounded the Bush-Obamaha Inner Tube, he dialed his friend in UCC. "Phone," he said, holding down his phone's command button, "dial UCC Subchief Oyentador."

"Calling UCC Subchief Oyentador," the phone's automated voice responded. As his phone's ring tones filled his ear, Sulla came across the same gaggle of pigeons he saw earlier. They were about 20 meters away; he charged at them quickly enough to actually kick one this time.

The phone rang and rang.

"Subchief Oyentador's office," a pleasant secretarial voice answered. "How may I be of assistance?"

"Hello." Sulla spoke, out of breath while flashing his badge at a group of local constables who looked like they might arrest him for animal cruelty. "My name is Supra Agent Sulla … I need to speak to Subchief Oyentador regarding a records match I have … I am going to need his green light and temporary access to dig into the historical archives."

"Just a moment, Supra Agent Sulla. I will see if I can reach him. Can you hold the line?"

"Yes, Ma'am, I can." Sulla continued to walk along the perimeter of Bush-Obamaha Constabulary HQ.

A minute of walking had passed when the familiar voice of Subchief Joehiro Oyentador came across the line. "Danbill, is that you again?"

"It is Danbill, Subchief. Hey, I am hoping you want to earn two or three cases of the good stuff today."

"I'm listening. Whatchya got?"

"Well, I am going to need access to secondary matches for a hit I have, a rebel officer. I am going to need to get into the historical archives, potentially going back to before the Enlightened Era."

"Secondary hits in the archive, eh? That is costly. You do know the Personal Privacy Protection Act of zero-zero-thirty-four means we here at UCC keep no records from public surveillance cameras or drones that are more than five years old, right?"

"I understand that, Hiro. I understand completely. So how many cases are we talking?"

Sulla continued to walk for about 10 seconds while Subchief Oyentador paused in silence. Sulla recognized a stall when he heard one and offered, "Six. How about six?"

"I've got you covered, Danbill." The Subchief's voice came across the line.

"Great and thank you," Sulla said. "So the secondary matches I am looking for are on a record under the name 'Unknown Rebel Officer Niner-Zero-Zero dash Fiver-Four dash Two-One-Niner-Niner.' Do you copy?"

A moment passed before Subchief Oyentador responded, "I copy, Sulla." A few moments more passed before Oyentador spoke again. "Sulla, you sure about this?"

"I am, Hiro. What are you seeing?"

Oyentador hesitated a moment before responding. "Well, it isn't what I am seeing so much as what I am not seeing."

"What do you mean?" Sulla asked, walking and talking.

"Danbill, your guy is a fracking ghost."

"A ghost?"

"He's an official fracking ghost. I have thousands of matches in our surveillance camera database from all over the country, with a decent concentration in the D.C. area. But all the files are ghosted out. I am only able to access the meta data, with date and time information. Now, I also sent out a general ping and I got about seventy hits to metadata in non-UCC databases here. I got old Department of Defense matches, United States Air Force matches, Florida Department of Motor Vehicles matches, United states Secret Service matches, DIS matches, even Miami Public Schools and public library matches. I have matches everywhere. I have matches going back to before the Enlightened Era. But every single file is blanked out. Just gone, man."

"Gone? What do you mean, gone?" Sulla asked while eying a mallard sitting uneasily by the walking path he trudged along.

"Sulla, someone went in and killed all of these matching files. Not even I can do that. I'm going to suggest you drop this one."

"What do you mean, killed the matching files?"

"I'm thinking we have a bad connection, there, Sulla," Oyentador said while making an odd breathing noise into the phone as he audibly crunched paper around him. "I gotta let you go. But don't forget my six cases when you get back."

The phone line clicked dead.

"God damn it," Sulla said as he trudged toward a squadron of crows who sat around his Armored Scout.

Agent Sulla: 93 January 0039

"Sulla."

Drool lapped at agent Sulla's lips, his head practically glued to the cherry wood desk in the office he had set aside for his team in Bush-Obamaha.

"Agent Sulla!"

With the window in his team's office just now closed, the room slowly turned from chilled to cool. Sulla began to notice a piercing pain in his head as he lifted it from the table.

"Supra Agent Sulla!" Subdirector Ombudsperson yelled and banged across the cherry wood desk the morning of January 93rd. "We have a *fortuity* on our hands."

Now awake, Sulla looked across the length of his rented office's table and saw his boss, Subdirector Ombudsperson, staring at him. He rose to his feet, pushing his chair backwards before stumbling and grabbing the table. He saluted as quickly as he could and spoke with the clearest diction he could muster. "Sub … director Ombudsperson, welcome to Bush-Obama-umm … Obamaha, Ma'am."

Subdirector Ombudsperson returned Sulla's salute and said, "Be seated, Danbill. As I said, we have a *fortuity*."

Sulla took his seat, looking at the two empty whiskey bottles sitting on the desk and his monitor, which sported a new crack on it while flashing the message, "SERVER DENIED."

"My dear Agent Sulla," Subdirector Ombudsperson spoke. "I understand you have been very successful out here. However, we have a fortuity on our hands."

"Yes, Ma'am," Sulla said, staring at the empty bottles in front of him, his head pounding like the drums of ten thousand engines. He knew damn good and well what Ombudsperson meant by the word fortuity, and she meant a problem. "Our fortuity. I am on it," he muttered.

"Good, Sulla!" Subdirector Ombudsperson smiled. "For you see, we have had a metrics issue in my department, and you and your team of Crowe and Peterschild can help. Now, just so you know, I received a visit from Chief Wickard himself late in the afternoon yesterday, and he pointed out that our Purge-Clearance-Per-Day metric is well below our quarterly goal and we are on track to miss this all-important performance metric this year. As you might imagine, this puts me in quite a bind. Especially with your unit, which is my best purge unit, out here in flyover country. So, naturally, I flew out here on the overnight."

"Yes, Ma'am," Sulla responded. "But I am very close to taking a forbidden question investigation and linking it to rebel leadership and a rebel plot of extreme significance. Give me a bit more time out here, Ma'am, and I can eliminate a significant–"

"Sulla, my boy. You may be surprised to hear this, but I agree with you completely." Ombudsperson leaned forward and hissed, *"But listen."* Ombudsperson knocked Sulla's flashing monitor over. "You have the track record of a great DIS agent and the makings of a great Subdirector in the future, but you need to learn the difference between a debate and a directive. I need you back in D.C. to boost our Purge-Clearance-Per-Day metrics. That is that. Bring your team back together from wherever you sent them to give yourself some whiskey-drinking room, and bring yourself back to D.C. This forbidden question investigation of yours is over. It's time to return to your day job."

Book IV: Course Change

El Asno: 128 January 0039

"Victor Papa Juliet Juliet, come back. Over." El Asno had been uttering this phrase every 30 minutes across Department of Equally Treating Animals Band 11 on his radio. "What is keeping you assholes? Over."

The man in the olive military uniform had set up camp along the Salmon River just upstream from a jagged canyon in the Sawtooth Mountains. The only easy approach to his position was from a half-bombed-out road to his east. The road to the west had been completely bombed out and had fallen into the river.

Asno had set up proximity detectors to both the east and the west. He surmised that anyone approaching from the west would be traveling on horse or foot and not an armored personnel carrier. The only visitors he expected would be arriving in a six-wheeled Armored Scout Vehicle, much like his own. Not wanting unexpected visitors, he had set up a defensive perimeter of three fragmentation mines on a remote trigger to his west. Not being particularly fond of his expected visitors, he had set up four fragmentation mines on a remote trigger to the east.

Asno had been holed up in this remote location in the former dominion of Idaho for three weeks. His contact with the outside world came through an array of solar-charged devices: his field radio, an encrypted satellite phone, and his field tablet that pulled data through his sat-phone.

Of course, there was also the intermittently pinging Global Positioning Satellite device stealthily hidden inside his Armored Scout's fuel cell, courtesy of Overseer Jolly. Because of this device, he knew his visitors had his precise location.

He had accepted his Armored Scout Vehicle, the gear onboard, and three kilograms of gold, worth about 100 million credits, as partial payment from Jolly for disrupting the Seattle Cod Protests about 15 weeks back. And he had been patient, all too

ـ atient, waiting for the rest of his payment – more gold and secret government records that would be vital to completing his mission.

Because of the GPS tracking device in his Armored Scout, he had set up his tent in a stand of evergreens, hidden from the air and as far away from the vehicle as was possible in case Jolly decided to dispatch any reconnaissance drones or combat controllers who could guide iTolerators to this location.

He was growing tired of waiting for payment – waiting for payment that was long past due. Overseer Jolly, formerly of the Department of Equally Treating Animals, had made him important promises in exchange for unique services only he could render.

It was DETA that was the only official government presence in most of the Uninhabited Zones, and Jolly's connections would be vital to discreetly securing archived government information. For Asno's services in eliminating Anderchild as her primary political rival, Jolly had promised to use her contacts with DETA to obtain and deliver the architectural and engineering plans as well as the access codes for a list of 900 abandoned missile silos and bomb shelters scattered throughout the western half of the country.

He cared nothing about the plans for precisely 899 of the silos and shelters. He only needed the information for the facility constructed before the Enlightened Era code-named CVW-1322-B. Demanding the other plans served as a smokescreen to hide his ultimate destination from Jolly, at least for the time being.

To pass time, he monitored the authorized and unauthorized civilian bands with his radio. Earlier this morning, Uncle Pawpaw on Radio Free Montana bragged that the Fort Peck dam continued to remain under rebel control. Uncle Pawpaw proudly announced the Montana Partisan Rangers had repeatedly turned back the Tolerance Corps' attempts to retake it at the cost of many soldiers killed and taken prisoner. Uncle Pawpaw sounded especially happy when he announced that many of the Tolerance Corps soldiers who had been taken prisoner happily switched sides and joined the rebels.

"Happy Tolerance Day, Beetle." Asno said these words in a whisper to himself, throwing a rock into the river.

Asno had provisions for 12 weeks in his Armored Scout. But he could no longer stand the taste of government rations. Kale, kelp, soy, and kelp derivatives were getting very old.

He instead spent his days catching trout in the river as it warmed in the spring sun. He spent his evenings cooking them over a fire and drying his fish hooks as they dangled from his shirt pocket. Over the past few weeks, he had tossed the fish heads and carcasses just in front of the mines on the road to the east, a welcome mat for his overdue guests from DETA.

The evening of January 128, through the static and hiss of his radio, Asno listened to Director Steel's State of the Society Address as he cleaned his lever-action rifle and its scope. It was a speech Director Steel gave ritualistically every Tolerance Day.

He could hear the assembled crowd roaring over the Bureau of Public Radio commentator's introduction. "Director of Internal Security Steel is making his way onto the stage, taking his position at the microphone. He is surrounded on three sides by very thick, protective acoustic glass. I can hear, and am most certain you listeners can hear, the roar of the crowd. The Director is taking his position behind the acoustic glass. Truly another great moment for a great Director. Director Steel is waving to the assembly. He is gesturing to them to quiet down."

Director Steel began, "My fellow Societans, I speak to you on this, our most sacred day."

"Elements! Two hooyah!" a muffled voice sounded through the radio.

"Hooyah! Hooyah!" The Department of Protests was clearly in top form tonight.

"Yes, my Fellow Societans. It is Tolerance Day!"

"Tolerance today! Tolerance Tomorrow! Tolerance Forever!" the crowd roared.

Director Steel continued, "Tonight I have the pleasure of bringing you the good news and the burden of giving you the bad news. But I will give you the bad news straight, just like I always do."

"Elements give hooyah!"

"Hooyah!"

"But first, the good news! The Broadband Rebellions are once again completely quelled again this time! A glorious victory over intolerance and oppression!"

"Hooyah! Hooyah!" the assembly shouted.

"The rebel strongholds of Saskatoon and Moose Jaw are no more! Thanks to our superior air power, no more will those wicked dens of inequity serve as bastions of evil and fortresses of wickedness. No more will those with wickedness in their hearts be able to refuse their patriotic duty. Those Intolerants who survived the air campaign must now report. Report, I say! Report to the Designated Habitation Zones! That is the tolerance we need. That is the tolerance we have fought for and fight for. To victory!"

"Hooyah! Hooyah!"

"My friends, I have spoken with President Tolerance at great length over the last few days, and he says this is hopeful news indeed. But he tells me there is more work to be done. The Norwegians have continued to defy the International Agreement on the Abuse of Animals by refusing to adhere to its mandates. They even refuse to sign it! That is not tolerance. That is not the tolerance we need in the world today. I therefore take this opportunity as President Tolerance's most humble servant to ask the Congress to do its duty. I ask Congress on President Tolerance's behalf to unanimously pass the Anti-Aggression Act authorizing the use of military force to end this aggression. The hand that held the fish hook has struck it into the gills of its neighbor!"

The crowd booed, a few chanting, "Death! Death! Death!"

"The Norwegians will comply with the General Will when confronted with our righteous might!"

The crowd roared, more loudly this time.

"And should the Russian Empire or the Maghreb Caliphate attempt to intercede in this purely internal NATO affair, they should know ... why that ... that will bring about a general conflagration, one in which this Society will not hesitate to–"

Asno turned the radio off. "Enough of this pig shit," he muttered to himself. He went to sleep.

Vaccination Patrol Juliet Juliet: 128 January 0039

Vaccination Patrol Juliet Juliet's Armored Scout bounced and bounded its way across the deteriorated roads in the mountains of northern Utah on their way to meet Asno in a remote canyon in Idaho. Agent Jones-Jones found herself getting impatient for completing her rendezvous with El Asno and being done with her mission. Why Asno had had to pick such an inconvenient location for an exchange was lost on her, but she was certain he was up to something. She would have to remain alert and on edge until this mission was over.

"Agent Rohm, give me his coordinates," Jones-Jones ordered.

"He has not moved, Agent Jones-Jones. He is still at coordinates four-five dot three-zero by negative one-one-four dot five-sixer. He seems to like this place for our meeting," Agent Rohm responded.

"Our estimated time of arrival?"

"We're at least three or four days away, getting over and around these mountains, Ma'am," Agent Rohm said. "These roads are pretty jacked up."

Jones-Jones sighed deeply and looked out her window at the high desert around them. "I can't wait to deliver these plans and be done with this. The idea of, y'know, meeting this Intolerant around Tolerance Day repulses me. So, another Tolerance Day wasted, I guess."

Agent Jones-Jones turned aside from her position in the passenger seat to address the rest of Vaccination Patrol Juliet Juliet, which at this moment consisted only of her driver. "Remember, Patrol. No matter what you see, we are here to observe and we will not detain this subject, no matter how unethically he behaves, so ..."

"What about our equal treatment and vaccination duties, Ma'am?" Rohm asked.

"Plenty of time for that, Patrol," Agent Jones-Jones responded. "Let's pull over. I want to set camp in time for us to hear Director Steel's speech tonight."

As Agents Jones-Jones and Rohm listened to the Tolerance Day State of the Society Address on their radio, Director Steel's voice was at the height of its powers. "… why that … that will bring about a general conflagration, one in which this Society will not hesitate to bring its righteous might to restore the freedom of our aquatic brethren and sistren to live in a fully free world. One world–"

"Tolerance! Tolerance!" the crowd chanted over the hiss and static of the radio.

"One world in which one and all can be free to accept the General Will," Director Steel orated with a vibrato in his chest.

"Tolerance Tolerance!" the crowd chanted.

"The sword of justice has been sheathed for far too long!"

"Tolerance Tolerance!"

"Tolerance is a peaceful devotion!"

"Tolerance Tolerance!"

"Those who defy Tolerance must be destroyed!" Steel growled as he issued these parting words.

The Bureau of Public Radio commentator announced over the roar of the crowd, "Director Steel has given a wave to the crowd and is now walking back, back off of the stage now. He is leaving the protective seclusion of the thick acoustic glass. Acoustic protection is no longer necessary as he is surrounded by his fellow Department of Internal Security agents who help to absorb the overwhelming sound. They are looking around, scanning the adoring crowd that is breaking out into song! Why, why, why, it's an impromptu rendition of *Tolerance Marching Toward Victory*! What an occasion! Listen to the singing as I hold out my microphone!"

The commentator stopped speaking and Jones-Jones listened to the remaining bars of the song.

We will strive, strive, and strive

For our honor
We will stand, stand, and stand
For our beliefs
We will fight, fight, and fight
For Tolerance

For Tolerance we shall seek
Complete and total victory

Through the air!
Through the sea!
We're marching now
To victory!

"If only we could have been there," Agent Jones-Jones said as she switched off the radio.

"Maybe next year," Agent Rohm responded, throwing another Department of Everything Else synthetic log onto the campfire.

Jones-Jones continued, "I guess in a way we were there."

"You mean in spirit?"

"No, Rohm, more than that. A part of us was there in a very literal sense. When I was getting my doctorate degree in Post-Colonial Post-Modern Interconnectedness I learned that we are all interconnected. So even if we were not there tonight, we were there, so ..."

"How so, Ma'am?"

"Rohm, tell me you are not an Interconnectedness denier?"

"I've never really studied it, Ma'am."

Jones-Jones scoffed and shook her head. "Yeah. So, Interconnectedness ignorance is almost as bad as Interconnectedness denial. I should put you on report or something. But instead I will educate you. For my doctoral thesis I invented an entirely new and innovative field within the discipline of Post-Colonial Post-Modern Interconnectedness, if I may say so myself. One day, I was working in the Interconnectedness lab at the university. I was reviewing and censoring the internet for school credit. I even earned extra credit for reporting a few Twacebook postings that were critical of the Academy Awards to the Department of Free Speech. It was crunch time and I was, y'know, burning the synthlog on both ends, so ..."

Jones-Jones stared at the fire, more than slightly amused at her own reference to burning a synthlog in the presence of a real-life burning synthlog.

After pausing briefly to ponder the best way to convey this special anecdote to her friends on her Bureau of Twacebook social media channel, she continued. "Well, I had drank quite a few cups of coffee that day. The French government had just, y'know, decided that day to recognize our dominion over Quebec. So the Bureau of Fair Trade Coffee had just changed their Freedom Vanilla back to French Vanilla. And I always thought the French Vanilla flavor to be superior, so ..."

"DETA assholes, come back. Over," their radio interrupted with a chirp.

"Agent Jones-Jones, is that *him*?" Agent Rohm asked.

"Yes. That's him. But Intolerants can wait, so. I was just getting to my revelation, but surely you can already see where I am going with this." She smiled.

"Yes, Ma'am," Rohm said with a slight nod.

"So, with all the coffee I had consumed, needless to say, I had to use the latrine. It was upon this very trip to the latrine that I had one of the greatest breakthroughs in Post-Colonial Post-Modern Interconnectedness history. Earlier in the day I had been, like, washing up in the latrine after, y'know, relieving myself. In the mirror I saw a fellow student, who shall remain always nameless as she deserves none of the credit for my breakthrough, as she entered the middle of three stalls. I had just used the one farthest away from the exit as I tend to do. The stall farthest away from the exit tends to provide the most serene environment for voiding, in my humble opinion. Wouldn't you agree?"

"Certainly, Ma'am." Rohm nodded, smiling.

"And I do sincerely hope you are not just agreeing with my assessment of latrine layouts just to, y'know, ingratiate yourself to me. If so, I would have no other choice but to put you on report as an Interconnectedness denier in violation of Article One Nine Zero of the Uniform Code of Paramilitary Justice, so ..."

"No, Ma'am." Rohm shook his head, frowning.

Jones-Jones scowled at him. "Did you just say '*No,* Ma'am?'"

"Yes, Ma'am."

"Ah, much better, Rohm. So, anyway, before I was interrupted, I was telling you about my journey to the latrine after having my fourth or fifth cup of Bureau of Fair Trade Coffee French Vanilla Coffee. This time I did not use the stall farthest away from the exit. It was as if I had been in a preordained dissociative trance. This time I used the middle stall, the very stall my nameless colleague had used while I was washing up during my previous trip. So, as I sat, a wave of horror came over me. I had failed to, y'know, deploy the Department of Everything Else tissue paper on the seat, as was my habit. I had no idea where my nameless colleague had been before, what toilets she had used before, and, y'know, who else had also used those toilets before her. I could have been exposed to a horrible toilet-borne disease. It was at that point my dread subsided into a moment akin to Dolly Madison's chopping down the cherry tree outside George Washington's house, getting hit on the head with an apple, then refusing to tell a lie about it. But instead of discovering gravity like Dolly Madison did, I had just, y'know, discovered Post-Colonial Post-Modern Toilet Interconnectedness. So, you see, it was then I realized that all human beings are connected in this world by the toilets we use. Isn't that great?"

Rohm nodded reflexively.

Jones-Jones paused and took a sip from her canteen. Her mouth widened and she began to speak more rapidly now. "It is akin to the old theory of six degrees of separation, but vastly superior in efficiency. You see, six degrees of separation requires actual interpersonal contact between individuals. But with Toilet Interconnectedness, no interpersonal contact is necessary at all.

Rather, a stationary and somewhat permanent object is the facilitator for the Interconnectedness. In my thesis, I proved that any one human being on Earth is separated from every other human being by a maximum of four toilets. Doesn't that just amaze you?"

Rohm blankly looked at Jones-Jones.

"Okay, Rohm. I can see I have to connect the dots for you. On that momentous date, my nameless colleague and I became interconnected by one toilet. And earlier, you and I became connected by one toilet when we each used the latrine at the Salt Lake Forward Supply Depot, so I know this. I counted the toilets in that latrine and there was only one. You, therefore, are interconnected with my nameless colleague by two toilets. But to illustrate the utility of this innovative form of the Science of Interconnectedness further, you are actually interconnected with Director of Internal Security Steel by three toilets. For I have used the same toilet as a former employer of mine who later became Overseer of Sacajawea and went to Langley as a social guest of Director Steel. And I have confirmed with her that she was indeed able to use his facilities! Pretty amazing that someone as such as yourself is separated by someone as important as Director Steel by only three toilets. So we both were there at the State of the Society speech this evening. We really were!"

Jones-Jones clapped her hands together, then leaned closer to Rohm with an enormous grin. "And imagine the toilets Director Steel has used. He knows President Tolerance. You are separated from President Tolerance by four toilets. I, myself, of course, am separated from President Tolerance by only three toilets, which beats your four. But who is counting?"

"Very impressive, Ma'am."

"I know! How else do you think I got this position as a Level Two DETA Agent at such a young age? By the way, how did you get your appointment as a Level One Agent?"

"I like animals and there was this job fair in high school."

"I see."

0231

Rohm asked, somewhat intrigued, "But I do have a question. What about people who do not use toilets? Or those who have never seen a toilet, much less running water?"

Jones-Jones was slightly taken aback. "What do you mean?"

"Well, didn't your report–"

"Doctoral thesis," Jones-Jones corrected.

"Didn't your thesis talk about people like infants who have never been toilet trained or people in remote parts of the world like the Congo and the Amazon that have never even seen a toilet? How can those people be interconnected by toilet?"

"You are assuming that the very young and those living in underserved areas are not capable of being interconnected because of their age or socioeconomic background. Let me tell you, Agent Rohm, such assumptions exhibit ageist, classist, and racist undertones and therefore have no place in the enlightened and thoughtful discourse of academia. So, right, I can see why you never continued your education beyond high school, and why you are only a Level One Agent while I am Level Two. And I can also see your future. You, Agent Rohm Level One, are going on report as soon as we get back from patrol as an Interconnectedness Denier, so ..."

"DETA assholes, come back. Over," the radio chirped again.

El Asno: 131 January 0039

It had been another long day of waiting. Just as he had done for the last 25 days, Asno spent much of the day gathering berries, then catching and frying fish, adding their heads to the pile on the road to the east of his camp. He'd occasionally look to the east, up at the road as it wound itself down the canyon of the Salmon River, knowing he would surely have visitors from DETA coming from that direction sometime soon.

On every hour and every half hour, Asno attempted to make voice contact on DETA Band 11 on his two-way radio.

At 1730 that evening, Asno held his radio and opened up on the frequency with "Victor Papa Juliet Juliet, come back. Over."

He'd uttered this phrase over and over again, referring to Vaccination Patrol Jones-Jones by its paramilitary call sign. He had probably sent out a variant of this call no fewer than 600 times at this point during his extended stay along the Salmon River.

Just after making his transmission at 1730, he set his radio back down on the boulder he had been using as a sofa and turned west to see the sun as it started to lay itself on the Sawtooth Mountains. "Another day wasted," he muttered to himself, when suddenly the radio chirped back with a signal-clearing beep.

"Dear Friend, Victor Papa Juliet Juliet here." The familiar voice of Sam Jones-Jones came through the radio. "We're almost there, Dear Friend. About a day out. Over."

Dear Friend. Asno smiled. He was glad he had chosen this radio code name for himself. He picked up his radio and responded. "Acknowledged. Understand. I'll leave the porch light on for you," he said as he took a glance at the proximity detectors and the death switch he had rigged up for the mines.

He set his two-way radio down and picked up his shortwave receiver. It was time to hear what was happening over on Radio Free Montana. He flicked the power switch and his shortwave set crackled to life, catching Uncle Pawpaw mid-diatribe.

"Try as they might by tryin'," Uncle Pawpaw railed, "they can't take rebel radio down. They might have squeezed the freedom from the internet by monitoring and censoring every bit of data, but they can't squeeze the freedom out of the air! And the jamming towers just went down this afternoon in Kansas City, Des Moines, Boston, New York, Atlanta, Good Louis, Bueno Francisco, Bueno Diego, Portland, Minneapolis, and Good Paul. We're beaming into your homes unfiltered tonight! A special nod of congratulations to the Cloaks of Liberty, who just took them towers out today. Thanks to the Cloaks' expertise in electromagnetic bombing, I can tell you listeners in the DHZs we, the freedom fighters of the west, have not been defeated, no matter what Director Steel and his henchmen tell you. We still hold Montana, Alberta, Saskatchewan, Wyoming, and parts of Idaho. We ain't gonna be defeated until they use their nuker bombs on us, and you know they can't do that! Because they'd all be snookered by the radioactive fallout. I'm telling you, boys and girls in the DHZs. Stand up and fight with us! We're going to win this war. Now, let me play you some of the tunes that the D.C. overlords won't let you hear. Some good ole fashioned folk music from *The Panopticon Neckties*. This little song is called *Shoot 'Em in the Face–*"

"Not tonight, Pawpaw," Asno said as he switched the radio off. He had little patience for the sort of pop music played on Radio Free Montana, designed to appeal to young soldiers in the Tolerance Corps and to teenagers in the DHZs. He decided it had been a long enough day, and he needed to get some early sleep so he could wake up extra early the following morning. He headed into the pine trees that ringed the river and into his tent.

Asno rolled himself up in his sleeping bag and found himself asleep in minutes, dreaming of returning to his hometown and seeing his family again – dreaming of how the D.C. establishment would burn.

Baaam Baaam Baaam Baaam Baaam.
The proximity detectors Asno had set blared their warnings into Asno's tent. He stirred from his sleep and looked at his watch.

2345. He looked at the warning signal. It came from the western perimeter. *To the west?* Asno thought to himself. The DETA patrol was almost certainly coming from the east.

Asno scrambled from his slumber and grabbed his night-vision goggles. He ran to the vantage point behind the array of sofa boulders he had prepared for such a situation and yelled, "Hold your position! Self identify!" He gripped his death switch, ready to detonate the mines, ready to wipe these intruders out.

There were nine distinct figures appearing in the night-vision goggles – four people on horseback, four riderless horses, and one dog. They had come up the shallow river. At Asno's shout, the figures dismounted their horses and tugged them to the protection of the sides of the canyon.

"Identify!" Asno yelled.

"Identify yourself!" a voice responded.

Asno bellowed, "You are in the killing zone of my perimeter! I have explosives that will rip you into five thousand pieces! Now your approach tells me you are not agents of the lord and master in D.C. So I have given you this time to prove this assumption correct. Identify, now!"

After a few seconds, the voice hollered back, "Oregon Partisan Rangers, Captain Gomes."

"Enter! Slowly!" Asno hollered back. "Keep those hands where I can see them."

Gomes and his team, two men and one woman, tied their horses to trees close to the river and entered Asno's camp. They all seated themselves by his fire pit, still aglow from the evening before.

"Thanks for letting us join you, Colonel," Gomes said, warming his hands by the dimmed coals in Asno's fire. "We've been–"

"Listen, Captain. I know you are tired, but you can spend no time here. You must take the trail across the river and up the mountain to the south before taking the river road again. There will be an unfriendly contingent coming up the road soon in at least one ᴦmored Scout Vehicle, a government paramilitary unit, and I need you to avoid them."

"And you are just waiting here for them? Colonel, I have heard of your reputation and your ingenious tactics at Fort Peck all the way from Oregon, but you're gonna need our–"

"I don't need any help in this ambush, Gomes." Asno gave the man a smile. "I need to lull these people into a false sense of security, and adding your numbers to my party would undermine that false sense of security. What I need from you is two of your horses in trade for my Armored Scout with the heavy weapons onboard. I need you to take the Armored Scout and your team to Fort Peck. I've heard the recent updates, and I have heard chatter that the Tolerance Corps is gearing up again. The Fort Peck dam must be held from the invaders at all costs. But for now, take your people and horses up the mountain and stay out of sight. While you are at it, take some of these damned government rations with you." He handed over a box of bagged kale. "Know that I'm going to fire off a green flare when it is safe to come back down. It may be a day or two. Stay quiet up there."

Vaccination Patrol Juliet Juliet: 133 January 0039

BEGIN TRANSMISSION:

08:15:12:1:133:0039: Vaccination Patrol Juliet Juliet to Overseer of Sacajawea: Plans for 900 locations and 3 kg in gold bars delivered to subject Intolerant collaborator. Our Dear Friend accepted payment. Vaccination Patrol Juliet Juliet has withdrawn from vicinity, despite evidence of animal abuse at location. We are prepared to reengage. Awaiting instruction. VPJJ out.

END TRANSMISSION.

BEGIN TRANSMISSION:

10:09:33:1:133:0039: Overseer to Vaccination Patrol Juliet Juliet. Overseer in receipt of your transmission. VPJJ is not to engage subject. Repeat. Patrol is not to engage subject. Rendezvous with Vaccination Patrol Hotel India. Await further instruction. Switch to DETA Band 19 cipher code AG72. Overseer out.

END TRANSMISSION

BEGIN TRANSMISSION:

12:42:07:1:133:0039: Overseer to VPJJ. Overseer directs VPJJ and VPHI to track movement of subject Intolerant using MQ Wildfire inventory. Report immediately when subject Intolerant enters terrain suitable for air strike by DETA iTolerator. Require zero response to this message. Begin radio silence immediately. Overseer out.

END TRANSMISSION

Asno the Tracker: 133 January 0039

On the morning of January 133rd, Asno finally had his meeting with Jones-Jones, who wore her retro U.N. powder blue helmet as some sort of fashion statement. She brought along her driver, a lackey named Rohm. After handing over the incendiary rockets he had kept from the Seattle Cod Protests in exchange for the plans to 900 bunkers throughout the Not-East and gold bars, Asno shot off a green flare up into the hills. This signaled for his new friends from the Oregon Partisan Rangers to come back to his camp. It was quite fortuitous they had arrived. They would certainly be of great use to him in warding off interference on the road ahead.

During his long stay along the Salmon River, Asno had honed his skills at smoking fish. When Captain Gomes and his men entered camp about an hour later, Asno greeted them with a hot breakfast of smoked rainbow trout and reused broken orange pekoe tea.

"Welcome back, troops. Sorry to hide you up there for a while." Asno smiled. "But my Armored Scout Vehicle will more than help make up for your lost time. Care to make that trade we discussed? My vehicle with the weapons for a couple of your horses?"

To sweeten the deal, Asno let Captain Gomes keep half of the gold bars onboard with the idea that Gomes would take it to Fort Peck. Gold was one sure way to continue the funding of the rebellion. For himself, Asno kept half of his gold bars, the designs of the bunkers, and his gear pack of personal equipment. This consisted of his tent, his solar panels, his tablet, his satellite phone, a lever-action .308 rifle, a .45 caliber pistol, his fishing pole, his fishing gear, a set of camp tools, some ropes, and enough rations to last him a few days. He planned on eating what he could gather, what he could shoot, and what he could catch along the way, but the rations would make a decent insurance policy in the event of bad luck or bad weather.

After waving Gomes and his men goodbye, Asno loaded his ₅ent, most of his gear, and the gold onto one horse. "Your name is Cargo," he said to the horse while loading him up. Cargo had the privilege of wearing Asno's solar panels on his back while they rode. Asno placed himself, his weapons, and his gear pack on the other horse. "Your name is Meego," he said to his riding horse, giving him a pat on the neck as he mounted him.

Although the Armored Scout could travel much faster than he could ride on Meego with Cargo in tow, Asno was confident he could keep tabs on it well enough. In fact, it would be quite easy for him to track the Armored Scout over mountainous terrain and the limited amount of roads it could traverse. In addition, Asno doubted the vehicle would get too far very fast with Jolly's GPS transponder aboard and with Jones-Jones shadowing it.

As Gomes and his men disappeared in a cloud of dust down the canyon road, Asno gave Meego a soft kick and rode slowly after them. He wondered to himself, would it be an ambush? An air strike? An anti-vehicle mine buried in the gravel road? What did Jolly and Jones-Jones have in store for him? He would find out sooner or later. Gomes and his men would find out sooner. If they survived and managed to take out Jones-Jones, good for them. If they didn't, he had sacrificed far greater numbers for lower stakes. Four men, six horses, and a dog would be an acceptable amount of casualties given what was at stake now that he had the plans in his hands.

As he rode, Asno was monitoring all DETA radio bands with his portable scanner. There was no radio communication, which was very unusual. There should always be some chatter back and forth among vaccination patrols. On occasion, he could hear what sounded like digital interference – likely drone-to-drone communications. But he could only make an educated guess. He had not yet had the opportunity to replace the descrambling catch drives needed to store and decipher encrypted radio messages since the loss of most of his equipment at the Seattle Cod Protests.

Asno had assumed that Jolly and Jones-Jones had no idea what they had just given him. If they knew what he could do with the design plans and access codes for those bunkers, they would never have given them to him so easily. One way or the other, they were almost certainly planning to kill him. That is, they were either planning to kill him, or they had given him fake plans.

But had they given him fakes? This question burned in Asno's mind.

It would be difficult to fabricate the plans for 900 bunkers scattered across the country, but not impossible. It was much more difficult for Jolly to put together the payment in gold than it was for her to use her DETA connections to obtain copies of the department's files on obscure locations scattered across the country.

Asno was counting on Jolly to confuse the effort needed to put together the different aspects of her payment with the importance of those payments.

Asno did have a significant advantage on his side. He had been to the important bunker in question and would be able to verify the accuracy of the plans. Two years ago, when he thought he had nearly completed his mission, he had thoroughly explored the exterior of the Nebraska bunker known as Carhenge.

He knew Carhenge's rather unusual layout very well. After all, not every bunker complex was built out of abandoned automobiles that were arranged to be an exact replica of Stonehenge. Based on his past exploration of the area, he knew the layout, he knew where to find the access panel needed to gain entry to the bunker, and he knew that the access panel was rigged to detonate if any attempt was made to open it with brute force.

When he first found Carhenge, Asno had a good idea of what sat beneath it. His investigation up until that point indicated a strong connection between Carhenge and the Nebraska Compromise. But he knew he needed access codes to get into the Carhenge bunker to confirm his suspicions.

His investigation since last seeing Carhenge only gave more weight to his theory. His long conversations with Fred Palmer and the sensitive records Fred shared with him strongly indicated that the bunker beneath Carhenge concealed President Tolerance from the world.

Carhenge was quite an unusual place. When it was first built near a now-abandoned Walmart near the now-abandoned city of Alliance, Nebraska, the local people were told that Carhenge was simply an avant-garde monument to the absurd.

For many years, it was just that. However, the political maneuver known as the Nebraska Compromise gave Carhenge a much more important purpose.

Shortly after the Nebraska Compromise, the Alliance community welcomed the construction of a new Carhenge visitor center with a great deal of fanfare. While the visitor center was completed, an old 1962 Cadillac positioned outside the main circle of abandoned cars received a special upgrade in its trunk. This '62 Cadillac stood outside the main circle of Carhenge, in place for the Heelstone in the original layout of Stonehenge. It was in its trunk that Asno found the access panel for the bunker beneath it.

After trailing Gomes' tracks for most of the day, Asno stopped Cargo and Meego, tied them to a juniper tree, and began to pore over the documents he had received the night before while he could still do so in daylight. After scanning through more than 200 of them over the course of an hour, he finally came across a design that looked familiar. He compared the diagram labeled with the code name CVW-1322-B with notes he had taken from his personal inspection of Carhenge. The longitude and latitude coordinates matched his notes: 42.142 by -102.858.

Furthermore, the bunker plans indicated that three separate 16-digit alpha-numeric access codes needed to be entered in sequence on a keypad hidden in the bunker access panel. The Heelstone Cadillac's trunk was quite demanding.

Everything appeared to be a match. "So Jolly and Jones-Jones are planning to kill me after all," Asno said with a sense of elation.

He was so close to success that he felt drunk with excitement. Soon, very soon, he would be meeting President Tolerance face to face. Soon, he would complete his mission.

He committed a basic encryption cipher to memory: JA8P. Then he spent the next few minutes storing the alpha-numeric access codes in encrypted files in his tablet.

After encrypting the codes in his tablet, Asno set about securing the plans for all 900 bunkers and silos. He walked up the canyon wall and found a small crevice. He did not want these plans to be easily found, but he did not want to destroy them either, when he thought of just how much they had cost him in terms of lives and gold to get in the first place. And should his tablet ever be damaged or destroyed, he could not comprehend how difficult and expensive it would be to get replacement copies.

After hiding the plans and the codes, and feeling secure in the knowledge he would soon be meeting President Tolerance, Asno jumped back onto Meego and trotted after the tire tracks in the gravel and sand until the sun ducked behind the Sawtooth Mountains.

As night began to harden around him, Asno dismounted Meego and continued on foot, pulling the reins of the horses behind him. Staying close to Gomes and the armored transport would only be possible by continuing to travel while Gomes' group rested at night. The next few days and nights would be light on sleep for Asno and his horses, but tracking Gomes would be easy thanks to tire tracks and the occasional piles of dog turds and horse apples in the road.

With each dogpile Asno walked by, he felt a twinge of remorse. Gomes' dog was an interesting little orange mutt. She looked a lot like an Australian Cattle Dog, a breed good at herding cows as they moved through the outback. How an Australian cattle herder found her way to a relatively quiet battlefront in a North American civil war tantalized Asno as a quiet little mystery to keep his brain alert while his feet unconsciously walked up the canyon road in pitch black of night.

But the more he thought of it, the more he realized that the presence of the son of a Monterrey baker and a Miami postal worker walking through the dark of night, pulling Cargo and Meego and a lot of gold, in a remote canyon on the far side of the continental divide at this particular moment in history would appear just as mysterious to a detached observer.

Asno knew his long and twisted journey up until this point had put him on the cusp of greatness. Should he succeed in his mission, he'd reclaim his family name and make his mark in history. He'd have in his power the ability to take down the Tolerance Administration. "Take down … *or take over*?" Asno whispered quietly to himself.

Around midnight, Asno heard the first roll of thunder. Rain began with a drizzle. By 0100, rain poured into the Salmon River canyon as lightning sporadically illuminated Asno's path.

Asno and his horses walked all night as he noticed the tracks and animal droppings becoming fresher and fresher. But the road became wetter and wetter with the rain. He was a decent tracker and estimated he was now about two and a half kilometers behind Gomes and the Oregon Partisan Rangers, but he could not be sure with torrents of rain rapidly altering their tracks. The cloudy sky to the east began to change from the greyish pink that clouds took on at nighttime to more of a reddish grey. The sun would rise soon. Asno looked at his watch – 0530. Now would be a good time to give Cargo and Meego a rest.

As Asno began to tether his horses to a sturdy-looking lodgepole pine tree, he jerked his head eastward at a sound in the sky. This was not thunder – this was the unmistakable sound of jet engines. Victor Papa Juliet Juliet was making its move. He mounted Meego, gave him a swift kick, and trotted up the canyon road with Cargo trotting behind. He knew he had to arrive on scene shortly after the damage was done. He'd have to finish things with Jones-Jones and her partner.

Vaccination Patrol Juliet Juliet: 134 January 0039

BEGIN TRANSMISSION:

07:23:47:1:134:0039: Vaccination Patrol Juliet Juliet to Overseer of Sacajawea. Report successful air strike on Dear Friend's Armored Scout Vehicle. Kills indicated. Plural. Kills indicated. Based on drone photography, Dear Friend appears to have been traveling with members of a rebel army unit.

We have linked up with Vaccination Patrol Hotel India detachment of four agents. Now traveling over land to site of air strike to confirm kills and obtain genetic sample of deceased for identity confirmation with Dear Friend. Will recover of gold bars belonging to Overseer. Estimated time of arrival on scene is 2-3 hours. Road conditions to the canyon are bad due to storms. Request drone coverage of site in interim.

END TRANSMISSION

El Asno the Spotter: 134 January 0039

Just as Asno could see the smoke on the morning horizon, a trail of black tar smearing the reddish-grey sky of sunrise, he knew the DETA iTolerator aircraft had done its work. He also knew that traveling by road was no longer safe. He would need to stay out of sight for quite a while.

After finding a spring that fed into the Salmon River, Asno guided Cargo and Meego up the hillside. It looked like a safe spot; it was along the spring but away from the river and the road that hugged it. He did not know how long he would be gone, but he wanted to make sure his horses had enough food and water. He tied them, using the full length of two of his ropes, next to the spring near enough to low-hanging cottonwood branches to keep them well fed. They'd last a few weeks like this before hunger motivated them to bust through their ropes.

Asno placed his radio in his shirt pocket, secured his pistol in his holster, wore his binoculars around his neck, clipped his canteen to his belt, and carried his .308 rifle and scope in his chilled morning hands. He knew he could be stuck watching the site for some time, so he took four ration bags and threw them into his gear pack before strapping it to his back.

Staying in the trees lining the canyon, Asno made his way toward the smoke and flames. iTolerators were frighteningly effective, but only when guided by people or surveillance drones. There had to be combat controllers or drones in the area, so he could not let himself be seen.

Asno knew Jolly would not let Jones-Jones order the airstrike, then return home to the coast. She would demand a positive DNA identification and the return of the gold bars. Sooner or later, Jones-Jones would need to get to the bombing site. Asno would have to get there first.

Step, step, step, jump log, step, step, step, jump rock, step, step, step. Asno carved his way through the canyon through mud and over and around obstacles as quickly as he could. He had to beat

Jones-Jones there. He needed to secure a proper vantage point that gave him a view of the airstrike site but was out of sight of the MQ Wildfire drones he knew were buzzing above.

By 0830 that morning, Asno had secluded himself from the rain beneath a stand of pine trees. Through his binoculars, he had a good view of the burnt-out hulk of his old transport and the burned bodies of Gomes' rangers and two of his horses. He scanned the canyon and its walls – no sign of DETA personnel, but he could hear the whirling of Wildfire Drone rotors hovering in the air. No sign of Gomes' remaining horses or his cattle dog, either. They must have escaped the shrapnel and flames of the iTolerator strike.

Asno estimated he was now about 200 meters from the destroyed vehicle. He needed to be closer. Crouching and slowly creeping along the canyon wall, he made his way closer and closer for 10 minutes until he found a proper vantage point. About 50 meters from the destroyed Armored Scout, Asno found a set of boulders he could use as a shield and a sniper position beneath the cover of tall pines and flanked by shrub yews. He would be concealed and protected here.

At this point in the morning, the sun emerged from behind the clouds for the first time of the day. But the storm had dropped a tremendous amount of water in the mountains surrounding the canyon, and the Salmon River had begun to swell.

Observing the burnt-out Armored Scout from his new vantage point in the full light of day, Asno heard and saw turkey buzzards circling overhead, as he had expected. But he also heard and saw something new: barking. Gomes' orange cattle dog stood on a boulder in the river, barking in Asno's direction. This dog was going to be a dead giveaway if Jones-Jones arrived soon. He needed the element of surprise to pick her and her lackey off cleanly.

Asno had killed many people and animals in his day. But his count of dead dogs stood at zero.

He readied his .308 rifle and adjusted the rifle's scope to about 70 meters. *Click, click, click.* He lined up his shot and moved the scope's crosshairs right over the barking dog. He took a deep breath and held it, feeling his heart beat in his chest, preparing to take his shot between beats as he had done a hundred and fifty times before. As he looked through his scope and prepared to take his shot, Asno paused, a quiver of nerves shaking through his hands. Heartbeat one. Heartbeat two. Heartbeat three.

He set his rifle down.

"Dog!" he called out. "Quiet yourself and get over here!" He stood and waved his arms toward himself.

Within a minute, Asno had a wet Australian cattle dog by his side. "Keep your mouth shut, dog," he said to his new companion as he gave her a pat on the head. "You have a name – I never bothered to ask your old owners." He put his binoculars up to his face and surveyed the canyon. "We'll figure a name out for you later, Orange Dog. Stay quiet, girl. We're going to be here a while."

Turkey buzzards screeched and growled as they circled above.

DETA Agent Jones-Jones: 134 January 0039

"All right, Patrol. This should be an easy one." Agent Jones-Jones briefed the five DETA Agents under her command now that the members of Vaccination Patrol Hotel India had joined her ranks. "We just had an iTolerator take out the subject's vehicle, a subject who was witnessed by myself and Agent Rohm torturing fish yesterday, so ... we did what we needed to do from the air."

In the 32 hours since Jones-Jones had last seen Asno, she had linked up with a larger DETA Vaccination Patrol of four agents. The five agents under her command were looking to her for guidance and inspiration on the verge of their first real taste of a combat situation. Jones-Jones surmised it was likely their first paramilitary duty since joining DETA. After all, they had been vaccinating grizzly bears and bison against the hoof pox a few hours earlier. She addressed her team as they gathered just over the crest of a hill covered with scrub bushes and just out of direct line of sight from where the iTolerator did its business that morning.

"So, extreme animal cruelty is why I had to pull you off routine vaccination duty, so ..." Jones-Jones said as she looked over the new arrivals. In addition to Agent Rohm, she now had Agent Irvinston, Agent Mosly, Agent Fenceminder, and Agent Martez all under her command. Given Asno's reputation, she had thought she was going to need all of the personpower she could muster, but now things seemed to have been settled nicely.

"So, now, we've hit this target about zero-five-thirty this morning. And we have had eyes on it since that time with Wildfire drones still hovering overhead. And we ourselves have had eyes on the scene since twelve hundred hours and it is now sixteen hundred hours. The sun is going to set in a few hours and I would like to start driving back to Seattle soon, so ..."

Jones-Jones paused. She knew she needed to get down the hill and to the bombed-out Armored Scout in order to take DNA samples and recover the gold bars she had given Asno yesterday. She looked over the new Agents under her command. Agent

Irvinston, a typical male, slouched with bad posture and likely had struggled past eighth grade at his public school in whatever southern backwater he had come from. Agent Mosly, another typical male, stood upright too tall and wore the greasy mustache she had seen on all too many East Coasters. Agent Fenceminder, yet another typical male, cocked his head to his left and squinted while keeping his mouth open while he listened like so many other ignorant hicks she met from flyover farms. But Agent Martez would do nicely. She was about the same height as Jones-Jones, but her hair was a little lighter in color than Jones-Jones' – an almond color compared to Jones-Jones' hazelnut. But Martez would work out well.

"Agent Martez, Agent Rohm. I am appointing you with the honor of driving down to the burnt-out Armored Scout. Once onsite, you will gather DNA from the bodies there using the forensic kits in the trunk. You'll also recover the gold bars these Intolerants have, err, had, y'know, stolen from DETA. We can fund a lot of vaccinations with this gold, Patrol. So, are you ready?"

"Yes, Ma'am," Rohm and Martez echoed nearly simultaneously.

"Good. One more thing, Martez." Jones-Jones put her arm around Martez's shoulder and walked her off to the side. "I want you to do me an honor and wear my helmet. I know it's in violation of regulations, but I decorated it in blue, like the old United Nations helmets. It's for, you know, good luck. I think you should wear it on your way down, so ..."

"Yes, Ma'am," Agent Martez said, handing her helmet to Jones-Jones with one hand and holding out her other hand, ready for the trade.

"Thanks, Martez," Jones-Jones said, while handing her blue helmet to Martez. "You are doing the Department of Equally Treating Animals proud!"

El Asno: 134 January 0039

Asno checked his watch. Hours and hours had passed as he had scanned the Salmon River canyon with his binoculars. He could see no activity. But the whirling of at least two Wildfire drones in the air above him continued. Asno took this to mean Jones-Jones was only waiting for the right time to inspect the results of her handiwork and to confirm that he was one of the corpses she would find.

He checked his watch again. 1615. "When will these assholes get here?" he asked aloud, gaining a slight stir from Orange Dog, who raised her head and looked around from the crouched position she had taken next to him.

But Orange Dog did not lay her head back down as she had done the last few times Asno had talked to himself. She rose to her feet and leaned up against the boulders they had been lying behind. She looked up at the hilltop across the canyon, her tail pointed straight backwards, and she gave a brief growl.

Asno looked upwards with his binoculars and could see a movement and shaking in the shrub branches on the hill across the river and to the south. The movement wound its way through the shrubs, heading down to the river. "They're here," he said to himself.

Asno checked the bolt and magazine on his .308 rifle and double checked that the scope was set to 50 meters. He gave the lever action on the rifle a couple test pulls, ejecting two rounds of ammunition before loading them back into the linear magazine. He had eight bullets ready to go, counting the one in the chamber and the seven in the magazine, but he should only need two shots to take care of the immediate business at hand. The pain-in-the-ass Wildfire drones hanging out overhead would need to wait until his human targets were eliminated. And after that, he'd be on his way through rebel territory, then on to the demilitarized territory of Western Nebraska – on to Carhenge and success.

Through his scope, Asno carefully watched the movement in the bushes as it descended down the hill. Waiting and watching, he followed the movement in the trees until he saw Jones-Jones' Armored Scout Vehicle emerge from the tree line and drive straight down the road on its way to the burnt-out vehicle.

Asno took a deep breath and exhaled, practicing his deep-breathing exercises. He felt each beat of his heart. With the excitement, he was clocking more than 90 beats a minute, which would not make do for a steady shot. He breathed deeply, exhaling at an excruciatingly slow pace. With each deep inhalation, he felt his heart speed up momentarily. But with each slow exhale, he felt his heart rate drop. Soon enough, his heart rate was back around 75, giving him enough time to squeeze a trigger pull in between beats.

The armored vehicle crossed the river, which stood about a meter deep at its center. It then stopped about 10 meters beyond Gomes' resting place, which now stood in between Asno and his targets. The driver's side door faced Asno's direction. It opened.

"Quiet, Orange Dog," he whispered proactively, feeling the tension from his canine companion. "Easy, girl."

Asno could see Rohm get out of the driver's side door and walk toward the burned hulk. Asno could see the passenger side door open and close, with Jones-Jones' blue helmet peeking over the top of the vehicle as she made her way back to the trunk. Rohm met her at the back of the trunk and began to reach in for some gear. The moment was perfect – they were standing right next to each other with a clear line of sight. If Asno could get the angle right, he could send one .308 round right through Rohm's neck and into Jones-Jones' sanctimonious blue helmet.

Breathe, rest, breathe, rest, breathe, squeeze, boom!

Asno squeezed his trigger and let his bullet fly. Through his scope he could see a red mist as both of his targets collapsed and fell to the rocky ground. He pulled down the lever on his rifle, ejecting the casing for the bullet he just used, then pushed the lever back up, moving the next bullet into the firing chamber. "Quiet, girl," he said, patting Orange Dog on the head. As the echoing in his ears faded, he could hear the impassive whirling of the Wildfires above him. Whoever was watching the video feed from those drones would be in for quite a treat.

By nightfall, the drones above him would be useless. But Asno did not want to wait until nightfall to get back to Cargo and Meego and continue his journey to Nebraska.

Asno looked at Orange Dog and sternly said, "Stay, dog." He slowly crept down to the tree line that separated the wooded area from the exposed gravel bar lining the river. Orange Dog gave a brief whine, and Asno turned and gave her a *shush*. He continued, creeping and crouching down the hill to the edge of the trees until he concealed himself behind a patch of fir trees. He could see one of the Wildfires moving closer to what remained of Jones-Jones and Rohm, angling its camera for a closer look.

Asno angled his rifle through the branches, placing the belly of the Wildfire, where its power source was stored, in his crosshairs.

Breathe, rest, breathe, pull, squeeze, boom, hit!

Down went one MQ Wildfire. Asno pulled the lever on his rifle as a brief outburst of machine gun fire erupted from the other Wildfires in the canyon, apparently firing rather indiscriminately into the trees that surrounded the river. A few rounds peppered trees and rocks around him. Orange Dog turned tail and ran up closer to the canyon wall, but Asno remained concealed.

That was odd, Asno observed. But once the Wildfires had expended their ammunition, his ears told him there were two more of the drones still circling above the canyon. They were climbing higher to take a vantage point. This was not good. He pulled out his satellite phone and tablet, taking a quick look at the sort of radio signals they were sending out.

This was guidance behavior. The drones must be guiding in larger aircraft for a bombing run.

Figuring that the Wildfires had just expended their ammunition and abandoning stealth, Asno ran out into the middle of the canyon, taking cover next to the remains of Gomes' vehicle. He needed to take out those Wildfires immediately.

There was one farther up the canyon, about 100 meters east and 80 meters in the air.

Breathe, rest, breathe, rest, breathe, squeeze, boom, hit!

He released one bullet into the drone's belly. The Wildfire caught fire and spun uncontrollably before crashing into the swelling river below. Asno pulled on his rifle's lever to move the next bullet into the firing chamber.

"There is still one more up there," Asno said to himself, twisting his shoulders and neck and trying to get a look at it. Suddenly, the remaining Wildfire flew past him just meters over his head before climbing up toward the mountains to his north. He needed to take this drone out before he found himself facing an iTolerator or, worse, a B-75 Acceptor. He pulled up his rifle to his shoulder and lined the last drone up in his crosshairs.

Breathe, squeeze, boom, miss!

Asno pulled the lever on his rifle to reload and propped himself up against the fender of the burnt-out vehicle.

Breathe, rest, breathe, rest, breathe, rest, breathe, squeeze, boom, hit!

That round found its mark and the Wildfire spun out of control and crashed into the canyon wall.

Asno exhaled deeply, continuing to lean against the burnt-out vehicle. He turned south and walked toward the bodies of Jones-Jones and Rohm to confirm they were taken out. He took a few steps before hearing Orange Dog barking in the trees behind him. He looked up – movement and noise in the bushes on the hill across the river. Something else, another armored vehicle perhaps, was now moving down the hill from the same direction Jones-Jones had just come from. Time was short.

Asno ran over to Jones-Jones' vehicle to confirm his kills. He saw the two bodies and could immediately recognize the face of Agent Rohm, the lackey he had seen yesterday. He turned to the other body, her idiotic blue helmet smashed, partially covering her face where she had fallen to the ground. He kicked the helmet aside. *Not Jones-Jones.*

Orange Dog continued to bark from the north side of the canyon. "What is it, dog?" Asno yelled out.

And that is when he heard it, the unmistakable roar of jet engines coming from the east. He looked up to the sky just in time to see an iTolerator release its payload of laser-guided bombs.

Asno strapped his rifle over his shoulder and ran across the gravel bar, sprinting for the trees, turning his back to the bodies and the Salmon River.

Step, step, step, step, almost there, he thought, when the canyon burst into flames behind him with a deafening explosion.

"Hit! Hit!" Asno growled out instinctively as he had heard so many other soldiers call out before him. But unlike those other soldiers, Asno was alone and no one would hear his cry for help. He crawled his way across the gravel toward the trees on the north side of the canyon, his hearing muffled and his head swirling from the concussive impact of the iTolerator's bombs. As he crawled across the gravel bar and into the trees, he felt a burning in his left calf, just below the knee. Shrapnel had torn through him and he was losing blood. He took rope from his gear pack and began to tie a tourniquet around his wounded leg. Then, the situation worsened for Asno. Through the smoke and flame of the iTolerator's bombs, he saw a new armored vehicle stop just on the other side of the river. Four people jumped out and began to fire their weapons in his direction.

Asno hid himself behind a pine tree and finished tying his tourniquet. The sky above him began to turn from bluish grey to reddened grey. The sun would be setting within a couple of hours.

With a badly wounded leg and four goons shooting at him, he would never survive the night. He had to even the odds a bit. He peered around the pine tree and saw the four figures wading slowly across the river. He readied his rifle and he held it to his chest, his head swirling, his eyes twisting.

Asno laid himself prone on the ground, using the tree to shield the bulk of his body. Just as he was about to put one of the soldiers into the crosshairs of – *his scope* – he now could see the scope on his rifle had been shattered. "Not good," he said to himself.

He pulled his .45 caliber pistol from his holster and sighted up his adversaries, who steadily made their way across the swelling river, now chest-high on them. They were now about 60 meters from him. This would be a miracle shot with his pistol, and he was in no condition to be working miracles.

Asno put his pistol down and began to detach the scope from his rifle, his multi-tool frantically clawing at the screws that held it to his rifle barrel. He'd have to take this shot analog. The paramilitaries were now spread out, walking abreast from each other, negating any linear shot opportunities like he had had against the first two he had taken out. They were now about 50 meters from him.

He pried the wrecked scope from his rifle.

He took aim for the largest target.

Breathe, rest, breathe, rest, breathe, rest, breathe, rest, breathe, click! Misfire!

Asno pulled the lever on his rifle and ejected the dud bullet from the chamber. He had just spent the sixth bullet of the eight he had loaded into his rifle and now only had two bullets left before he had to refill the magazine. Growling at himself for not refilling his magazine when he had had a chance, he patted his gear pack. Thankfully, it felt like his extra ammunition was still inside.

He again sighted up the largest opponent, now about 40 meters from him.

Breathe, rest, breathe, rest, breathe, boom! Hit!

His bullet found its mark, but Asno needed to take his next shot while his opponents were still slightly surprised he was fighting back.

Breathe, boom! Miss!

"Damn it," Asno growled as he fumbled into his gear pack for more .308 caliber bullets. If his opponents rushed him now and used their automatic weapons for suppression fire, Asno knew he'd be dead. But something curious happened.

From out in the river, he heard the familiar voice of Agent Jones-Jones call out, "Fall back! Fall back to the Armored Scout," as the body of Agent Mosly floated down the river.

Asno took the time to reload his magazine and crawl a little deeper into the trees to protect himself. He would need to be ready for Jones-Jones' next advance.

After about 15 minutes, Asno realized that Jones-Jones was not making another advance. He heard the all-too-familiar roar of iTolerator engines coming from over the mountains. Within a few moments, the iTolerator opened up its 29 millimeter machine cannons into the entire north side of the canyon, ripping trees apart and bursting branches above him.

Asno pulled himself as close to a large boulder as he could. He furiously piled up rocks, tree branches, and anything he could reach around him to give himself as much protection as he could muster.

A few minutes later, an iTolerator repeated the strafing run, sending burning chunks of lead into the area. One thing was clear – Jones-Jones had an idea of his position but did not know exactly where he was.

Another three or four minutes later, yet another set of jet engines roared up the canyon. *Hit! Hit!* Asno felt the burning pain of something hot striking him in the face.

Can't see, Asno thought. He felt around his head with both of his hands and found a six-inch chunk of pinewood jutting into his head where his right temple met his cheek. He tried to pry the pinewood free, but the pain was excruciating. He could not budge it. At this moment, Asno deduced he would likely die in the Salmon River canyon, his mission unfulfilled.

Asno wiped blood from his face and found he was at least able to see from his left eye. Orange Dog howled in the distance.

Before the next strafing run could begin, he took his satellite phone out of his gear pack and held down the phone's voice command button. "Dictate message to codename …" He paused to breathe. "Horned Rims."

The phone beeped and its automated voice responded, "Commence."

"Horned Rims, Codename Special Friend here. It has been too long. I have nearly completed the mission without your help and without creating exposure for you. I have the codes to access our objective. But I am pinned down, wounded, and near death or capture at the hands of DETA paramilitaries. They have iTolerators pinning me down. Request air support and medical assistance. My coordinates are," Asno said, pausing to look at his tablet, "four-five, point four-zero-five, cross minus one-one-three, point niner-niner-seven. Special Friend out."

Asno never really thought it could have come to this. He never thought he'd pull in this favor. But about 10 minutes later, as another set of jet engines came thundering down the canyon, he covered himself with more and more rocks and debris until he was fully covered. He wiggled to move his tablet beneath him, shielding it with his body from any glancing blows. He braced himself as the next strafing run began. Tree trunks and limbs burst above him, rocks and boulders fragmented around him.

Strafing run followed strafing run.

How many more of these could he survive?

Asno did his best to maintain his awareness and avoid going into shock. But his head wound and blood loss were taking their toll on him. If Jones-Jones and her goons were to wade across the river and attack him at this point, he had his .45 pistol and his rifle, but he doubted his ability to aim either of them. He shimmied his way deeper into his pile of rocks and debris, leaving only small cracks of daylight above him. The sky was becoming red. Daylight was running out. Asno clung to consciousness but began to lose his concept of time.

Beneath his rock pile, Asno could hear one more iTolerator's roar from east to west, strafing the canyon. But on this run, he heard something unusual. Multiple sets of jet engines drummed up from the south at the same time. The rare, but unmistakably acrid, sound of air-to-air lasers pierced the atmosphere. An explosion filled the skies above the canyon and echoed off the canyon walls.

Just a little bit after the new jets circled back into the canyon, he heard 29 millimeter cannons open up, but this time on the south side of the river. An explosion signaled the destruction of Jones-Jones' Armored Scout Vehicle.

The skies fell quiet. All Asno could hear was Orange Dog barking more than 100 meters away and the echoed yelling of Jones-Jones and her men. If they figured out what they were doing, they'd be putting their infrared night-vision goggles on as soon as the sun went down. Then, they'd be able to find him by his heat signature and finish him off.

Asno began to fade in and out of consciousness. Each time he awoke, he'd look at the sky. Each time, it would get darker.

As he stirred back to consciousness one last time, he knew he needed to hold onto consciousness as long as possible this time around. If he passed out one more time, he'd likely stay gone. He gripped the rocks around him, digging them into his palms. He needed noise to stay awake. He began to hum *Tolerance Marching Toward Victory* to himself.

His eyes began to drift shut, but each time, he'd squeeze the rocks harder and hum louder. This created the risk Jones-Jones would find him, but he had to hold on. He had to hold on a bit longer. Help would surely be coming.

As the sun started to set, through his own humming Asno abruptly heard the deep rumble of large jet engines, the largest he could remember ever hearing. The rumble was coming from high in the sky to the southeast. The rumbling ceased, followed by a horrifying screeching sound, a sound like the sky itself being ripped to shreds. Over the screeching sound, the low growl of payload rockets began to reverberate through the canyon. A series of explosions ripped through the canyon as the rockets detonated one by one, each explosion getting closer and closer to Asno until a forceful detonation resounded just meters above him.

His eyelids fell shut.

Light evaporated from Asno's world.

Captain Leroy T. Hazard: 134 January 0039

"Fatal uniform defects," Captain Hazard muttered to himself. "Fatal frackin' uniform defects."

Hazard looked out the window in the hallway outside Major Manos' office in Echo Company's administrative building. Through the window and in the reddish glow of sunset, he could see Sergeant Cornwall berating Alfa Platoon for their failure at the parade grounds. Hazard had been summoned to Major Manos' office shortly after the parade, where he had been waiting patiently for several minutes while hearing muffled voices from inside.

Hazard had been stewing the whole time he was waiting. He had busted and worked Echo Company, specifically Alfa Platoon, into one of the finest groups of trainees in the history of Fort Freeperson. But one backwards cap had negated 100 days of good training. And here he was, on the cusp of greatness, about to be sent to build up the new 138th Airborne Division, about to shape a company in his own image, about to lead that company in the conquest of Norway from the air. But instead of preparing for battle, he was standing in the Echo Company administrative building, waiting for what was likely to be a formal reprimand from Major Manos.

The door to the major's office opened. "Hazard, get in here," the Major Manos' voice called out.

Captain Hazard walked into the office and raised his salute at the chair behind the desk as he had done so many times before. But he found himself saluting at the thick-rimmed glasses of a civilian in a civilian's suit, with the Major standing to the man's side.

"At ease, Captain," Major Manos said as he quickly returned Hazard's salute. "We have a visitor from D.C. who would like a word with you."

"Hello, Captain," the civilian behind the desk spoke. "I'm Chief of Staff Fillburn Wickard, Department of Internal Security. Major Manos here has recommended you for a sensitive DIS mission, and I hope you are ready for action."

"Yes, Sir, Mister Wickard, indeed I am," Hazard responded with a smile and a nod. "I understand I am heading for Operation Norwegian Emancipation."

Major Manos injected himself back into the conversation. "About that, Hazard. Chief Wickard has something more immediate, more urgent, in mind. A dark op – the details of which are on a need-to-know basis."

Hazard shook his head briefly as he processed this turn of events. "A dark op. Yes, Sir." He swallowed as he spoke.

Wickard put his hands on top of a folder lying on the desk marked "*eyes only*" and smiled. "Yes, that is of course if you are up for the challenge and willing to accept the risks of going dark for a while in the service of those who *put* you here," Wickard said with a short nod at Major Manos. "The DIS is calling in a favor from you and from your Major. Care to learn more?"

Hazard was coming to the realization that this meeting was not about the clusterfrack of Trainee Gumbo's backwards cap. This might be welcome news and a turn of events that would have him seeing action even sooner than he had thought.

"Absolutely, Sir." Hazard looked Wickard in the eye. "I am all ears."

"Good, Captain. Good. I see the Major here has an eye for talent, but I want to advise you of the risks of taking on a dark op on behalf of the DIS. Now, I would normally have you pull up a chair and have a seat for a conversation of this nature, but the fact is that time is of the essence. We have a very valuable DIS asset out in the Not-East. He's in the disbanded dominion of Idaho, to be precise. He's been wounded in a confrontation with rogue paramilitary personnel from DETA. He's alone and pinned down in a canyon along the Salmon River. He's holding off enemy advances with cunning, fire, and guile, but he is badly wounded and will not last the night. Considering how far away he is from our nearest base in Oregon and the presence of hostile enemy air and ground units that could take out a chopper, he can only be rescued by a Screaming Eagle airborne insertion. With me so far?"

Hazard nodded his head as he processed what Wickard was telling him. Wickard was referring to the CJX-245 Screaming Eagle jet transport plane that was now in the later stages of experimental operations. Fort Freeperson's aircraft hangar housed several of the planes under lock and key, and Hazard had seen the delta-winged craft take off only a handful of times during his stint at Fort Freeperson. The CJX-245 was cutting-edge technology and had some of the loudest, most powerful engines to ever come out of the Bureau of Lockheed's Skunkworks. Built for rapid insertion of ground troops into hostile territory anywhere in the world on short notice, it was the only troop transport plane that could travel at more than two-and-a-half times the speed of sound.

Chief Wickard continued. "On paper, your transfer to Combat Command and to the 138th Airborne Division will be delayed. You will continue to report to Major Manos for the duration of the operation. The same will be said for your team. You'll pick your team from the enlisted personnel here at Fort Freeperson. The Screaming Eagle's drop glider cage, known as the Baby Eagle, can deliver only four soldiers at a time. And you are going to need one medic to medically stabilize our asset. So on paper, your troops, they'll be assigned to a special detail here at the fort. Officially, you all will be training new recruits here. Officially, your rescue mission does not exist. How does this sound so far?"

"Well, Sir," Hazard responded confidently, "I'm up for it. I think I know who I'd want on my team. Sergeant Hamilton immediately comes to mind, and he can help me assemble—"

"Hold on there, Hazard," Major Manos interrupted. "I'm not giving you any of my NCOs. You need to pick from the raw recruits. This whole mission depends on the presence of people who will not be missed for weeks and weeks on end."

Hazard nodded, understanding why Major Manos had volunteered him for this mission – he was officially non-essential.

Chief Wickard, sensing the Major's misstep, added, "The reality is, I need a crack team pulled from personnel who are in transition. People who can go dark without raising any red flags in the Tolerance Corps. You fit the profile because you are being transferred to a unit that does not yet exist. And the recent graduates fit the profile because there is never any guarantee that they will graduate and leave this place. But I assure you, this mission is of highest priority. And I have read your files, and you are exactly who I am looking for to lead this rescue mission. So, Hazard, do you accept this offer?"

Hazard straightened up his spine and looked Chief Wickard in the eyes. "I do, Sir."

"Good!" Chief Wickard clasped his hands together as if he were giving himself a congratulatory handshake. "Your first job is to pick your team. A medic and two riflepersons. And get them to the hangar. You will need to leave as soon as we are done here if you are to get there before night sets in out in the Mountain Time Zone."

"Yes, Sir. Do you have a briefing file that I can review along the way?" Hazard asked, looking at the folder sitting on the desk in front of Chief Wickard.

"About that, Captain." Wickard smiled. "This mission does not exist. No one, and I mean no one, in the Department of Internal Security knows about it other than me. And other than you, Major Manos here, and the officer prepping the plane, a Lieutenant Khouri who your Major vouches for, no one in the Tolerance Corps knows about it either. I'm going to give you all the information you need verbally. Are you ready to remember everything I tell you?"

"Yes. I am, Sir."

Wickard opened the folder and pulled out a photograph of a man and pushed it across the desk to Hazard. "Pick that up, and commit this face to memory," Wickard said.

Hazard studied the photo a moment. The man was in his late 40s or early 50s, clean shaven, brown eyes, with salt-and-pepper grey and black hair. He wore the sort of double-breasted faux Italian wool suit Wickard was wearing, which appeared popular with most of the DIS agents Hazard had seen before.

"Well, Hazard," Wickard continued. "Keep in mind this photo is several years old now, and this asset has been in the field for three years. So do not focus on the superficial. Focus on the eyes, the nose, the mouth. His hair and his clothes, especially his clothes, will be different. He has been deep undercover for years, and his alternate identity is that of a rebel officer. So make sure your team knows not to automatically kill any rebels on sight."

"Understood, Sir," Hazard responded.

"Good," Wickard said, holding his hand out. Hazard returned the photo to Wickard's outstretched hand.

"What is his name, Sir?" Hazard asked.

"He has no name. His mission is even darker than yours. And the less you know about his mission, the easier it will go for you and your men. Your job is to arrive on scene, eliminate any remaining rogue paramilitaries, and render whatever aid to this man he needs to help him get on his way. Stabilize him onsite, but ping me, and only me, if you need a medevac chopper after we get the air power situation under control out there. And ping me, and only me, if he dies. I'll need to secure his belongings. Our man out there has a sat-phone you can use to reach me discreetly if need be."

Wickard opened his folder again and pushed several laminated red cards across the desk to Hazard and continued, "Once you have helped this man get on his way, whether it takes a day, or whether it takes three hundred days, you'll return to the nearest Tolerance Corps base or the nearest DHZ. These cards are your re-entry visas and your all-expenses-paid travel passes back to Fort Freeperson. No questions will be asked of you or by you. Understood? Just help my asset out there and get back here quietly."

Hazard picked up the cards and held them firmly in his hands. "Understood, Sir."

Wickard added, "Save my guy out there, and you'll save the whole country."

"Yes, Sir." Captain Hazard saluted.

"The whole damned country." Chief Wickard gave a brief nod and looked over to Major Manos.

Major Manos walked over to the door and opened it. "Walk and talk with me, Hazard," he said tersely. Hazard followed Manos through the doorway and back into the hall. As Manos escorted Hazard out of the Echo Company administrative building, he informed him that Fort Freeperson's quartermaster would be delivering the weapons, ammunition, medical supplies, field supplies, and rations to the transport jet.

Manos held his hand out to Hazard for a handshake, the first time Hazard could remember the Major ever doing such a thing.

As they shook hands, Manos quickly looked around, then leaned in to Hazard and squeezed his hand with the firmness of a twisted vise. He whispered, his voice like gravel in Hazard's ear, "So now you see why I treated you as I did. No one could know. They could not see we are both cut from the same cloth and that we both have the same friends in high places." Manos let go of Hazard's hand and resumed speaking in a normal tone of voice. "It's about time for you to get over to one of the barracks and pick your team. I'll have a jeep and driver on standby to get you to the airstrip. Let the sergeants know who you are taking, and I'll handle the paperwork."

"Yes, Sir." Hazard saluted.

Major Manos saluted in return, before adding, "And Hazard, don't make me look bad out there – not in the Chief's eyes."

As Captain Hazard made his way out of the Echo Company administrative building and walked to the barracks, he had a decision to make. Which three soldiers would he take? He had to admit to himself that he did not know the soldiers very well and knew only a handful of them by name. And most of the trainees he did know by name were the exact sort of soldiers he did not want to take with him on a dark mission – a mission without any backup. Once the Baby Eagle glider cage was dropped from the Screaming Eagle, it would just be him and his men. They'd be alone and in hostile territory, certainly dealing with rogue paramilitary fighters and potentially dealing with rebel Intolerants. He needed to choose wisely. His life would soon depend on these soldiers.

As these thoughts rolled through Captain Hazard's mind, he made his way to Alfa Platoon's barracks and saw that no transport buses had arrived yet. *Good news*, he thought to himself.

Hazard unlocked and opened the barracks door himself, not wanting to deal with door guard games. He then asked Sergeant Cornwall to bring Corporal Bowperson to him while he took a seat and waited in the barracks office.

After a few moments while Sergeant Cornwall barked out a call for the Corporal to report to the office, Bowperson entered the office and saluted Captain Hazard.

Captain Hazard quickly returned the salute and said, "Stand at ease, Corporal. I have a mission for you. I hope you are ready for action."

"Yes, Sir," Bowperson responded without any facial expression.

"I can see I have not sold this very well, Bowperson. The fact is, this is a very exciting mission we're about to go on together. We're about to ..." Captain Hazard paused, catching himself mid-sentence before turning to Sergeant Cornwall. "Sergeant, would you give us a few minutes alone?"

"Yes, Sir." Sergeant Cornwall saluted and left the office, closing the door behind himself.

"Well then, Corporal," Hazard resumed. "We're about to go on a dark op out in the Great Not-East. It's a rescue mission of sorts, and we are going to go on a supersonic paradrop to help a very important person get out of a jam against some rogue DETA paramilitaries who we have to take out."

The idea of going against DETA paramilitaries appeared to have gained Bowperson's interest. "Count me in, Sir. What do you need?"

"Who's the best medic in the company?" Hazard asked.

"That would be Doc Newton – umm – Private Newton, Sir. He was a doctor back in Boston before getting sent here."

"Newton," Hazard said aloud as he wrote down the name on a notepad. "Thank you, Corporal. Now, other than yourself, who is the best fighter in Echo Company? The best killer, a killer not likely to freeze up in action?"

"That's going to be Hackberry, Sir. They've got him slotted in for EastProtComm, but he's the best shot at the range and is one of our main fire watch guards."

"Well then." Hazard wrote the name down as well. "This is our four-man team. Go get those two men and meet me outside in your battle uniforms."

Captain Hazard left Sergeant Cornwall the names of his team, Bowperson, Hackberry, and Newton, and ordered him to get the list to Major Manos immediately. After pondering the nature of his mission for a few minutes, Hazard walked out of the barracks and found his team waiting for him – his first real combat command.

"All right, men. In just over an hour, we are going to be in a battle. The details are on a need-to-know basis. So here is what you need to know. Without saying too much, I have been handpicked to lead a vital mission. And I have handpicked you all to be on my team to rescue someone very important, someone who matters to the highest tiers of the government, if you get my meaning. We're going to be paradropped via supersonic transport jet into Idaho. We'll be riding the experimental Screaming Eagle jet and dropped in its glider cage, known as the Baby Eagle. We'll be rescuing a VIP from rogue paramilitaries from the Department of Equally Treating Animals. Our VIP is wounded, outnumbered, and pinned down. We three," he gestured to himself, Bowperson, and Hackberry, "are going to take out the rogue DETA personnel, and you, Newton, will stabilize our VIP medically. Hooyah?"

"Hooyah, Captain!" the three men yelled.

"Very good. Sergeant Cornwall will be gathering your things in the barracks and putting them into storage. The quartermaster is loading up the Screaming Eagle with all our weapons, ammo, and gear right now. Our job is to get to the landing strip immediately. Now," he gestured to the jeep parked nearby, "get your asses into that vehicle and let's go bonk some heads!"

Private Hackberry: 134 January 0039

Hackberry had never seen a CJX-245 Screaming Eagle up close until Captain Hazard scorched pavement with vulcanized rubber from their jeep's tires the whole way to Fort Freeperson's hangar. Along the way, Hazard gave a second briefing to the team on their rescue mission and reminded them that they'd be dropped from a supersonic jet, that they'd be rescuing a VIP who shall remain nameless, and that they'd be helping him along his way. He reminded them of who they would be rescuing, who they would be killing, and not to automatically kill anyone dressed as an Intolerant.

"Troops, there are going to be medals and commendations for all of you men if we pull this off," Hazard said. "But this is a dark op. Not a word to anyone of what we're about to do out there, hooyah?"

"Hooyah, Captain!" Bowperson seemed to be taking the idea of killing some DETA paramilitaries in stride, but Doc Newton seemed a little nervous – certainly, he was not looking forward to this jump. Hackberry took the idea in stride as well. Getting dropped in a cage from a jet aircraft was a slight improvement over protest duty, in his mind.

The CJX-245 was an unusual sight for a troop transport aircraft. The Screaming Eagle's triangular delta wings spread about 20 meters apart, but the fuselage in which they would be flying was only about seven meters long by three meters wide. The cockpit was a small, windowless, pointed knob at the front of the aircraft, and it was only large enough to hold the flight computer that would be guiding them to their destination. But the engines – it had the largest jet engines Hackberry could remember seeing. Each engine was nearly the size of a train car, and each wing had three engines mounted underneath. From an opening in the rear of the plane extended a ramp to the ground that served as both entrance and airborne exit.

Without a pilot, the CJX-245 Screaming Eagles and those who flew inside them were commanded by a loadmaster. This particular CJX-245 took its orders from a loadmaster in the form of the diminutive but resoundingly boisterous Lieutenant Khouri, who stood next to the loading ramp, directing traffic as her ground crew guided the Baby Eagle glider cage into the belly of the aircraft while they simultaneously loaded gear into the cage's undercarriage.

As their jeep pulled up, Hackberry stared at the small Baby Eagle cage, wondering how they would all fit inside its confines and how it would somehow get them safely onto the ground from a screaming jet. In all of their training drops and in their drop during Operation Manhattan, they had always jumped out of relatively slow-moving propeller-driven aircraft – and they had jumped out as individuals. But now, they would be dropped in a padded cage.

The cage was less than a meter wide, about four meters long, and a little more than two-and-a-half meters tall. Seeing as how the cage had a series of harnesses strapped to vertical uprights, it looked like they would be standing in a single-file row on the way down. Khouri's crew loaded rations and equipment into the series of storage compartments in the cage's undercarriage. Four thick roll bars reinforced the top portion of the cage, in case the cage did not land right-side up. *A lovely death trap*, Hackberry thought to himself.

When Captain Hazard stopped their jeep and jumped out, Lieutenant Khouri popped a salute at him and shouted as though the Screaming Eagle's jet engines were already flaring. "Welcome to the Screaming Eagle, Captain! Any friend of Major Manos is a friend of mine!"

Captain Hazard returned the salute and walked up to the Lieutenant. He whispered something in her ear while Bowperson, Hackberry, and Newton waited in the jeep. She quietly said something back as Hackberry tried to read her lips when she spoke but could only make out the words "to know."

Captain Hazard waved at his team, and the three newly minted Tolerance Corps graduates jumped out of their jeep and walked up the ramp of the Screaming Eagle.

The Screaming Eagle's six jet engines sparked to life a few moments after Hackberry and the rest of Captain Hazard's fire team had harnessed themselves into the seats bolted to the starboard wall of the aircraft's main compartment. As the engines rumbled, they donned their radio-synchronized jump helmets that would allow them to communicate over the commotion and thunder of their flight.

Hackberry continued to stare at the glider cage sitting in front of them. The Baby Eagle stood on a set of sliding rails, ready to be ejected from the rear of the aircraft as soon as it received its human payload.

The g-forces on Hackberry's previous flight climbs paled in comparison to what he felt when the Screaming Eagle's landing gear left the safety of Fort Freeperson's concrete runway. The plane lurched into a 60-degree climb and held the steep angle until about 10 minutes into the flight.

"Stay with us, Doc," Bowperson called out, looking at Newton, who was sweating bullets and pale as a sheet. It was clear he was about to let his Graduation Day lunch fly all over the fuselage. "Stay with us!"

"Feeling ill?" Lieutenant Khouri called out as she unharnessed herself from her seat at the command terminal at the front fuselage wall, clutching a carabineer-like hook in each hand. Hackberry was slightly awed; what the hell was this crazy woman doing? Using her hooks, she latched onto what Hackberry could now see were pipes in the fuselage's ceiling. She then kicked off the fuselage wall and slid across the ceiling to them. She pulled out a jet injector from her utility belt as she came to a stop in front of Newton. "Nothing a little spray of Loadmaster's Helper won't cure! Show me your neck, paratroop!"

"Ma'am," Newton looked up at Lieutenant Khouri, who was suspended from the ceiling. "What drug is this that you are giving me?"

"Your neck!" Khouri shouted. "Troop!"

Newton had been in the Tolerance Corps long enough to know an order when he heard one and tilted his chin up. Khouri injected him with the medicine with one hand while holding her hook to the ceiling with the other. The Lieutenant then kicked the wall above Newton's head with both feet and slid back to her seat at the plane's controls. A few seconds later, Newton appeared to be back in control of his bowels.

"Whatever that was, Ma'am, I think it worked," Newton said, his voice echoing through everyone's helmet speakers.

"Did I tell you to talk, paratroop?" Khouri shouted from her control station, her voice crackling through the electromagnetic interference from the Screaming Eagle's massive engines. "I need radio silence in my aircraft! Hooyah?"

"Hooyah, Ma'am!" Newton yelled.

"Quiet, Doc!" Captain Hazard chimed in. "The Lieutenant is working."

"Please shut the frack up, Sir!" Khouri crackled over the comm as she wrestled with the inputs on her control station.

A few minutes later, the aircraft felt like it was leveling off. After about 30 minutes more, Lieutenant Khouri detached herself from her harness, hooked herself to the ceiling pipes, and slid over to and on top of the Baby Eagle, facing Captain Hazard's seated team. "You can unharness yourselves now, chiefs! Right now, we are soaring somewhere about fifteen kilometers over the Des Moines DHZ. Have a look at the Baby Eagle while you're up and about." She gave the top of the cage a kick. "Your weapons, night-vision goggles, zip ties, and enough ammo to eliminate your targets are strapped to the uprights you'll be harnessed to. And the medical kit is strapped to the upright at the back. All of your other gear, rations, etcetera, it's down in the storage compartments below."

Hazard, Hackberry, Bowperson, and Newton rose from their seats and began to look around the cage they would soon be plummeting from the sky in.

Khouri sat on top of the cage and gave it a shake before continuing, "Gents, this plane is still classified as experimental. And so is this here Baby Eagle. But I will tell you fellas that this plane is solid as a buffalo's head, while this cage shit is hyper-experimental. The idea is I drop you all out the back of this plane while the plane points a laser at the desired landing spot. We already keyed that spot into the system based on pre-existing satellite imagery and the coordinates our rescue target sent in." She paused to smile. "If all goes to plan, you'll have a nice easy landing right next to your VIP on the banks of the Salmon River. Now, if it doesn't go to plan," she shook the Baby Eagle again, "experimental is experimental. Oh, and Captain, sorry about the 'Shut the frack up, Sir.' No offense intended."

"None taken, Khouri." Hazard smiled as he leaned inside the Baby Eagle and looked around. He looked up at her. "This is your craft. I'm just thankful for the ride. Now about air support, what sort of weaponized payload does this craft have to offer?"

"Oh, Sir. Now that is the sweet part, Captain!" Khouri waved her fists in front of her as though she were boxing a goblin. "Right before I drop you out of this Eagle's rectum, I'm letting fly about 30 concussion rockets! Any bird, bug, critter, or rogue-ass-paramilitary is gonna be knocked right the hell out for a good ten or twenty minutes. You boys'll have a nice head start on them bad guys down there. Kick a few in the teeth for me!" She gave a jump kick to her side and into the Baby Eagle, propelling herself along her hooks and her ceiling pipes back to the control center. "Oh, don't mind the cage. She's pretty indestructible! Unreliable as shit, but pretty well put together. I mean, one time we did a test drop with goats inside instead of crash dummies or prisoners like we're supposed to. You know, just to piss off a DETA functionary who had been giving the Skunkworks trouble, and the damn thing flipped upside down on the way down. I mean, the goats were baahing and baahing or whatever it is that goats do, all the way down to the ground but–"

"We get the picture, Lieutenant," Hazard jumped in. The jet engines continued to roar and the aircraft shook around them. "How about you tell us how we are supposed to survive in this thing dropped at supersonic speeds from fifteen kilometers?"

"Well, Sir," Khouri scratched her neck and spoke into her helmet comm over the vibrations reverberating throughout the plane, vibrations she appeared to be immune to. "That is where the screaming comes in with the Screaming Eagle. This baby was originally developed as a dive-bomber, but the payload was too small for bombs. So they converted her into a high-speed insertion aircraft. She's gonna swoop down from on high, the g-forces are gonna pull your face back something sweet! And on the way down, we're gonna let loose our dive breaks – these big-ass, honking flaps that extend both down and up from the wings. Four layers of twenty-meter-long flaps are gonna come down and slow our airspeed to a crawl. And the beauty of it is, when they thought this was still gonna be a dive-bomber, the fellas at the Skunkworks put some enormous air-raid sirens on the flaps. They make it sound sort of like the sky itself is being tortured, just to scare the shit out of anyone and everyone below."

"Sounds impressive, doesn't it, team?" Hazard looked at the men with a smile.

"Hooyah, Captain!" they responded.

"Well, Captain," Khouri announced. "We're now over Central Wyoming – hostile territory. We're almost there. One important thing. Who is gonna take the steering position in the Baby Eagle – the person who steers this puppy and deploys the 'chute if something goes wrong?"

"That's going to be me," Hazard said with a firm nod.

"All right, then. You take the front spot in the Baby Eagle; it's the closest one to the drop door at the back of the plane. So, which one of you is the medic?"

Newton raised his hand.

Lieutenant Khouri smiled with a sense of recognition. "Okay, you, Pukey McDontMessUpMyPlane, you get in the back spot, farthest away from the drop door. You've got a field medical kit strapped to your upright, and all the med gear is going to be in storage under you."

"You," Khouri pointed at Bowperson, "take slot number two behind your Captain. And you," she pointed at Hackberry, "take slot number three in front of Pukey. Don't get drenched!"

The men entered the cage through small doors on the sides and harnessed themselves against the four uprights inside the cage's padded steel bars.

"Paratroops, just remember." Lieutenant Khouri's voice echoed through their helmet speakers above the din of the aircraft. "Stay put and don't mess with your harness until you hit the ground. Your weapons are strapped to your uprights. Once you are down there, grab those smoke wagons and radio me. I'll come in for another pass and run a thermal scan so I can get you all a location for your targets. Then you can wipe those shitheads out and do Chief Wickard proud!"

"Who is Chief Wickard?" Doc Newton cried out.

"Lieutenant! A word with you?" Captain Hazard shouted from the front of the Baby Eagle.

"No time, Captain! I need to pay attention to these controls! Just one more thing. Once I let you go out the back of this beast, you have exactly three seconds of freefall before the autopilot on this Baby Eagle thing engages. It should engage automatically, and you'll know it when you see the steering flaps come out from the sides. But if those flaps do not come out, you need to count three more seconds and hit the emergency parachute release. The red button right in front of you. Do you understand me, Captain?"

"Yes. Yes, absolutely I do," Hazard said hesitantly.

Khouri slid back across the fuselage, grabbed the cage, and shook it next to Hazard's head. "Listen, Captain. I know it is hard to count to three or to count to six while falling out of an airplane, but I have to put this thing into dive mode in about three seconds. So here is how we count to three on a Screaming Eagle Drop! We yell, 'Hooooooh-leeeee dog doo!'"

With that, Lieutenant Khouri pushed off and glided back to her control station, then harnessed herself in. "When you are done hollering that out, you just spent three of your precious seconds. All right, it is six minutes to show time, boys! I'm putting her into dive now!"

Hackberry felt the Screaming Eagle roll downwards as he and the other men in the Baby Eagle started to face upwards at the back of the plane. As the plane entered what was a controlled crash, he saw Bowperson's arms float out in front of him as he cracked his thumb knuckles with his fists. "We're weightless!" Bowperson yelled out into his helmet microphone.

"Shut the frack up, Corporal!" Lieutenant Khouri yelled with a smile. "It's Screaming Eagle time!" she yelled as she lowered the dive flaps on the plane.

Gravity returned. The sense of weightlessness dissipated into an acute awareness of g-forces pulling against Hackberry's face. "Fucking death trap," he mumbled softly.

"Shut the frack up, person with name I do not know!" Lieutenant Khouri yelled. "Your helmets are still hooked up to radio and will be until you go out the back door, and I am trying to concentrate." Her voice crackled above the wailing of the dive flaps.

Suddenly a series of low-pitched rumbles screamed from both sides of the fuselage above the noxious scream of the dive flaps. "That sound, those are the concussion rockets paving your way," Khouri announced without turning from her controls. "Everyone down there is about to get knocked the hell out! Get ready for depressurization now!"

With a few strokes of her fingers, the Lieutenant opened the rear door. A flood of red light from the evening sky entered the fuselage. She yelled, "In three, two ..."

The Baby Eagle entered a sea of crimson and grey clouds. The deafening roar of massive jet engines replaced the sound of the Screaming Eagle's dive flaps as Khouri turned the plane back up, higher into the sky.

Freefall, weightlessness.

Hackberry could not wait to get down to the ground. At his next opportunity, he'd take his freedom back and take Bowperson and Newton along with. Then he'd take care of Captain Hazard.

Hackberry noticed they were still in freefall. What was the Captain doing?

"Holy dog doo!" Captain Hazard yelled out.

Another second of freefall passed.

"Holy dog doo!" Hazard yelled out again.

"Holy dog doo! Holy dog doo! Holy dog doo!" Captain Hazard yelled out amid the freefall.

"Hit the button, Cap!" Hackberry yelled.

"Holy dog doo!" Captain Hazard yelled again for good measure.

Hackberry looked around himself. To his right, he saw the Baby Eagle's steering flaps deployed. To his left – to his left he had the uninterrupted view of a river, a canyon, and a canyon wall racing up to meet them.

"Hit the button, Captain!" Hackberry yelled out again as he felt his cheeks pushed upward by the wind.

"Might miss the target!" Hazard cried.

"The red button, Captain!" Bowperson joined the chorus.

"Whoah, dog doo!" Captain Hazard yelled as the glider cage began to enter a slow horizontal roll, with the right side of the Baby Eagle beginning to face skyward. Through the cage's left side, Hackberry could see the canyon floor getting closer and closer. The cage began to vibrate uncontrollably.

"The button, Captain! Hit the red button!" A cacophony of voices rang out from the Baby Eagle as the canyon floor raced up to meet them.

With a violent shake, the left steering flaps on the Baby Eagle finally extended, stopping the vertical spin. The cage's parachutes extended out and flapped above. Hackberry felt like he weighed 400 kilograms when the parachute expanded above the Baby Eagle. Gravity returned to his world with a crush.

"I told you we did not have to hit the button! But we're coming in a little hot!" Captain Hazard yelled as the Baby Eagle fell downward. "We're about thirty seconds from impact. Brace yourselves!"

"We're off-target. We're gonna miss the canyon floor!" Bowperson yelled. "We're heading into a wall of those ripped-up tree trunks! Hold onto the cage uprights!" Behind Bowperson, Hackberry looked around beneath them. Trees stood but were ripped apart. The whole canyon appeared to be a smoldering, shattered ruin.

"I see the tree wall, Corporal – hang tight!" Hazard yelled. "I have a plan!"

Moments later, Hazard pulled hard to the right on the steering stick, pivoting the Baby Eagle just before impact. "I'm going to use the flaps to take some of the impact," Hazard called out moments before the left side of the glider cage smacked into the burning remains of a set of lodgepole pine trees about eight or nine meters above the ground.

Hackberry lurched to the left upon impact. He clutched his harness as the cage crashed into the trees. His head slammed into the roll bar to his left and he felt a twinge of pain in his left leg as the Baby Eagle fell to the ground beneath them. The cage reverberated like a steel drum when it collided with the rocky surface of the canyon floor. As the cage rang around him and the deep vibrations echoed through his bones, Hackberry felt his head grow foggy. He could hardly keep his eyes open. He groggily patted himself on the helmet and shoulders, checking for injuries, then looked down at his leg, where he felt a stab of pain. There he found a two-inch-thick piece of pine snapped off at the glider cage's bars, but jutting into his thigh.

"Stabbed by a tree," he mumbled aloud with all the voice he could muster before slumping forward in his harness. "I'll be damned," he rasped, "I'm hit."

Corporal Bowperson: 134 January 0039

"We made it! We frackin' made it!" Captain Hazard screamed with joy as he unharnessed himself. "I'm pulling out coordinates, but I think we're off by only a few meters. Not bad. Now, everyone – out of the cage! We've got paramilitaries to kill and a VIP to rescue."

Hazard shoved the gnarled and dented side panel of the Baby Eagle's steel cage open and jumped out while the rest of his men were still struggling with their harnesses. Bowperson, regaining his bearings as the ringing in his ears subsided, started to unharness himself.

Captain Hazard pulled his radio from his belt clip as he surveyed the destruction in the valley around them. Holding the transmit button on the radio, he called out, "Ground team to Screaming Eagle. Do you have a thermal reading on my targets?"

A moment later, his receiver came to life with the raucous voice of Lieutenant Khouri. "Circling back for a pass now, Captain. Thermal scanners are active. ETA for those scans is three minutes. Hang tight, ground team. I'll find your bad guys!"

Hazard transmitted back, "Roger. Understand."

As Bowperson found his way out of the Baby Eagle and reached back in for his weapons and field pack, Hazard turned to his team and barked, "Time is of the essence, men!" He put his hand on the pistol in his hip holster. "Get your asses out of that cage. Once we get direction from Lieutenant Khouri, we need to be moving like hungry ants toward a cupcake contest at the DHZ fair. Our targets are likely going to be regaining consciousness in about ten minutes when those concussion bombs wear off. And our rescue target needs medical help ten minutes ago!" He pointed over Bowperson's shoulder toward the rear of the cage. "Doc Newton, you're on me. We're going to find our VIP and patch him up." He then pointed at Bowperson. "Corporal, you take Hackberry and eliminate these rogue paramilitary shitheads with extreme prejudice. Hackberry, get your ass in gear and get out of that cage! The

Redcoats are coming! We will take no prisoners – Newton, what the hell are you doing?"

Bowperson quickly shifted his eyes from Hazard, standing in the twilight settling throughout the canyon, and turned to the rear portion of the Baby Eagle – looking in that direction for the first time since their crash landing. There, he saw Hackberry slumped forward in his harness. He wasn't moving.

"Sir," Newton called out, having just exited. "Hackberry is unconscious, Sir."

"Wake him the hell up, Doc!" Hazard walked over to the rear of the cage.

"He's bleeding, Sir!" Newton called out. "There's blood all over the bottom of his compartment. Bowperson, help me get him out of the harness."

As Bowperson reached into Hackberry's compartment to release him from his harness, he found the harness clip was badly mangled. "It's gonna take some doing, Doc. His harness clip took a beating in the impact."

From about a meter behind, Hazard called out, "Stop fiddling with him. Our priority is our rescue target."

"Sir," Bowperson yelled out while still working with Hackberry's harness. "He needs help! And we don't have our scans from the Screaming Eagle yet. We don't know where our targets are. We have time to help him – we need to help him or he'll die!"

Hazard walked over and stood immediately behind Bowperson. Hazard grabbed Bowperson by the shoulder, spinning him around to face his Captain. "Very well, troop. You've got until we hear from Lieutenant Khouri to patch your friend up. But disrespect me by yelling at me with your back turned again," Hazard wagged his finger in Bowperson's face, "and I'll have you harvested. I will personally supervise the cutters who harvest you. And I will personally smoke your fracking spleen, if you know what I mean."

"He's got a chunk of wood in his thigh," Newton called out. "It's in the location of his femoral artery. Based on all the blood loss, I think the artery is severed. Tourniquets won't do any good here. I've got to find the artery and clamp it closed." He reached into his medical kit for his clamps. "If that artery is severed and if I can't get a clamp on it, he won't last." Newton looked up at Bowperson and Hazard, still standing face to face as if they were about to come to blows. "Bowperson!" Newton yelled out. "Forget the harness for a second and put pressure just above his wound while I get my clamps!"

Bowperson turned back to Hackberry, still slouched forward in his harness, growing paler by the minute. "Stay with me, buddy," he said to Hackberry as he leaned down to reach his injured leg. "We'll help you out of this."

As he put pressure on Hackberry's leg, just above where the chunk of wood was jutting out of it, blood continued to spurt out – splashing all over Bowperson's hands, arms, legs, and boots.

"I've got my clamps. Give me some breathing room," Newton barked out. "Move your hands up here, Reggie." He tapped a higher portion of Hackberry's inner thigh. "And push hard! Hard!"

As Bowperson put as much pressure as he could onto Hackberry's leg, he saw Doc Newton tear Hackberry's pant leg wide open; then he pulled the chunk of tree limb out of Hackberry's leg. A large glut of thick, dark blood fell onto the Baby Eagle's floor. Newton started reaching around inside the wound.

"Damn," Newton grunted while his hands felt around inside Hackberry's wound. "The artery is cut and it snapped. It's retracted up higher into his leg. But ... but I think I can reach it," he said with a grunt.

At that moment, the roar of the Screaming Eagle's jet engines started to thunder down the canyon. Lieutenant Khouri's voice boomed in over Hazard's radio. "Okay, ground team. Coming in for my thermal scan run now. Hang onto your hats!"

The roar of the jet engines drowned out any other sound. Doc Newton yelled something out as he continued to work furiously. Bowperson could not quite make out what he said and yelled back, "I'm putting as much pressure on the leg as I can, Doc!" He could barely hear himself over the roar of jet engines.

As the jet engines subsided, Newton yelled out, "I got it! I frackin' got it! The artery is clamped!" He stood up. "Bowperson, help me unharness him. We need to get him flat. There's a good chance the blood pressure could overwhelm the clamp, especially if we leave him up upright in his harness. I need to get him flat then look inside the wound and do some field surgery to make sure he survives."

Captain Hazard's radio chirped with the voice of Lieutenant Khouri. "Scans complete. I have vectors to your targets, ground team. I see three heat signatures, all immobile just across the river from your position. They are out on the gravel bar. One hundred twenty-eight meters from the Baby Eagle, bearing two-zero-zero degrees. I see a fainter, but human-sized, heat signature, likely our VIP. He's up in the woods a bit more. Looks like he is under a pile of rubble. Just eighteen meters from the Baby Eagle, bearing three-four-zero degrees. Happy hunting, ground team!"

"Acknowledged, understand," Captain Hazard said, turning to Bowperson and Newton. "You heard the Lieutenant. And you've saved your friend's life. But it's time to do what we came here for."

Bowperson yelled out, "But Sir, he could still die–"

Captain Hazard put his hand on the 9 millimeter pistol in his hip holster. "No buts, Corporal. Get across that river and do your job. Doc has Hackberry stabilized, but Doc has another patient now. So, move!" He gestured across the river. "And Doc, keep your medical kit handy. You are on me."

The water in the Salmon River was much colder than Bowperson had expected for this late in the spring. Back home on the Chariton River, he would have been able to take his first swim well before January 134. But as the rapids swirled hip-high around him, Bowperson felt a distinct mountain chill in the water surrounding him. He held his M8 rifle above his head to keep it from getting wet while red streaks of blood trickled off his uniform, swirling downstream.

Bowperson knew he would need to take care of his task quickly. Captain Hazard would no doubt be forcing Doc Newton to spend all of his efforts on the very important person they were here to rescue. Bowperson had to kill these rogue paramilitaries and get back to Hackberry. He had to get Hackberry out of that damned harness inside that psychotic flying cage and onto a folding cot inside a tent so Doc Newton could save his life.

Bowperson trudged through the cool current around him until he emerged on a gravel bar littered with debris from obliterated trees and the remnants of a shattered armored vehicle. He looked around for his targets in the twilight of the evening but could not see them until he put on his night-vision goggles.

Once he put his goggles on, there they were: three glowing globs of light propped up against a downed tree amid a darkened background. Bowperson took his night-vision goggles off now that he knew where they were and ran over to the fallen tree that they had been using as a makeshift bunker.

He stopped running about 10 meters away from the tree and readied his weapon, walking the rest of the way to his unconscious targets. *Targets*. That is what he kept calling them in his mind, but they were little more than incapacitated, sleeping knuckleheads from DETA at this moment in time, thanks to the Screaming Eagle's concussion rockets.

As he approached his targets, his prey, Bowperson could see a radio and a set of laser guidance binoculars still sitting on the fallen tree's trunk. He smashed the binoculars with his rifle butt so that they would not guide any more drones or bombers to this location.

The sound of the smashing stirred one of the three unconscious paramilitaries. A groggy groan in a female voice filled the air as if one of them were starting to wake up. Bowperson looked more closely at the paramilitaries. Two male, one female.

They were wearing DETA uniforms, sure enough. "Turn away from the sound of my voice," he growled at them. "Turn away from the sound of my voice!"

The memory of DETA agents arresting him at his home and the allure of a little revenge had helped him take part in this filthy mission enthusiastically and willingly volunteer his friends to join him on it. But shooting three unconscious people hardly felt honorable. "To hell with Captain Hazard," he muttered to himself.

He reached for his zip ties. He would tie them up, binding them together and to their tree trunk. And then the thought crept back into the pre-frontal lobe of his brain. *But what about Hackberry?* He had to get back soon to make sure Hackberry survived.

"Hell with it," Bowperson said quietly to himself.

One.

Two.

Three.

Bowperson put three bullets into three unconscious heads.

The radio lying on the downed tree trunk chirped, "Overseer to Victor Papa Juliet Juliet. All aircraft lost. But I can have two reinforcement patrols on the way. They are about two days out. Do you require backup to complete your mission? Come back, Victor Papa Juliet Juliet. Over."

He picked up the radio, then turned and ran back to the river, wading across its rocky bottom and through its surging currents as quickly as his feet would take him.

The Trial of Reginald Bowperson: 134 January 0039

Shaking his legs dry, Corporal Bowperson emerged from the Salmon River and trotted back to the Baby Eagle. With each step as he ran in the dim light of dusk, he could more clearly make out Hackberry's silhouette, still suspended upright in his harness inside the glider cage.

It was not until he was about 15 meters away that Bowperson realized – Hackberry was still not moving, and he was in the exact same position he had been in before.

Bowperson slung his M8 over his shoulder and sprinted the rest of the way to the Baby Eagle. Skidding his boots in the gravel at his feet, he grabbed the bars surrounding Hackberry's compartment with both hands. "Hackberry?" he asked, looking closely inside. "Hackberry?" he asked, louder, shaking the Baby Eagle's cage wall.

Bowperson reached his hand out to Hackberry's face and gave him a light slap – no response. He put his finger to Hackberry's neck to take his pulse – no movement. He wetted his finger and held it out in front of Hackberry's mouth – no air.

"I … I don't … believe … he's gone," Bowperson said as he leaned against the cage, then slid downward to the ground. He held his helmeted head in his hands.

First it was his home and family. Then, his freedom and his name. Now, Gumabay and Hackberry. What would they take away next?

As these thoughts coursed through his mind, he felt the heat of a steady, slow boil rising within his chest.

"Nice work, Newton!" Bowperson could hear the unmistakable voice of Captain Hazard about 20 meters away. Bowperson could even hear the blithe smile on Hazard's face stain the vibrations of his voice as they crackled through the canyon. "Keep him stabilized while I get back to the Baby Eagle to grab a tent for us to set up. He needs shelter."

Loud footsteps crunched through the trees and the rubble. Bowperson climbed back up to his feet. He unslung his rifle from his shoulder, holding it in both of his hands.

Captain Hazard emerged from the trees and came around to Bowperson's side of the cage. He stopped walking about three meters from Bowperson, pausing when he saw him. "Nice work, Corporal! We saved our target. The Doc is stabilizing him now. I heard three shots earlier. Did you take care of business with the rogue DETA agents?"

Bowperson stood in silence a moment, holding his M8 at his chest. "Gone. They are all gone."

Just now, Hazard looked into the glider cage and saw Hackberry still suspended in his harness. "Umm, well done, Corporal. And don't worry about Hackberry there. Doc can see to him in a few more minutes."

"He's dead, Captain."

"Dead, you say?"

"Dead," Bowperson growled, keeping his eyes on Captain Hazard.

"Well, Corporal. It is always hard to lose a man under your command and this is no– What the hell do you think you're doing, soldier?!" Hazard yelled out while Bowperson put his rifle butt into his shoulder and aimed the muzzle directly at him.

"Shut your mouth, Hazard."

"Troop, you are under a lot of strain, I can see that," Hazard said, reaching slowly for his pistol in his belt holster.

"*Stop*!" Bowperson screamed, aiming his rifle at Hazard's forehead. "Stop reaching for that weapon, Hazard. And stop – stop talkin'. You are gonna listen to me now."

"Reggie, listen to me." Hazard put his hands out to his sides, away from his holster. "Hackberry knew the risks when he joined up for the Corps, we all did. You've been through a hell of an experience today. But we'll be back to base soon. Listen, Bowperson, I–"

"That is *not* my damn name." Bowperson raised his chin; his eyes widened. "I want you to know something, Hazard."

"What, what's that, troop?" Hazard asked as his face grew pale, his hands starting to shake out at his sides.

"I'm going to put a bullet into your VIP's head right after I put one in yours," Bowperson said, squeezing his trigger.

Four.

Hazard's body, his hands still out at his sides, fell backwards and hit the gravel below. A bullet hole shattered the bridge of his nose.

Bowperson squeezed the trigger again, then again, and again.

He looked over at Private Hackberry, then down at Captain Hazard. It was the VIP's turn.

Bowperson stormed into the woods, calling out, "Newton! Newton!"

"Here, Reggie! Over here!"

Bowperson came upon Newton as he crouched next to a large boulder and worked on his unconscious patient. The Doc hovered over his patient, hooking some intravenous bags to the man's arm and chest.

The man's shirt was unbuttoned, exposing his chest. One pant leg had been cut off and replaced by a series of bandages. He had a grey beard, but a pile of bandages on the right side of his head prevented Bowperson from getting a decent look at him. Newton looked up at Bowperson, seeing the wild look that must have been in his eyes. "What did you just do, Reggie? What did you just do, man?"

"Hackberry's gone, Doc. Not breathing, no pulse, dead."

Newton lowered his head at the news and held one hand to his forehead as he stood and said, "I'll check on him right now, there's still a chance–"

Bowperson interrupted, "I know dead when I see dead, Doc. And so is Hazard – dead. And I know you are not gonna like this one bit, but I am going to park a five-point-five-six millimeter slug right in your patient's heart now."

"But, Reggie!"

"But nothing! Hackberry is dead because of this piece of shit. And I am going to finish off what those DETA paramilitaries started."

"Bowperson!"

"Not my name, Doc!"

"Reggie, I'm sorry Hackberry's gone. The Captain kept his hand on his pistol the whole time and would not let me leave this patient to go tend to him. But you'll want to see this, Reggie. Before you shoot this guy, just have a look."

Bowperson continued unfazed. "Doc, you and I are going to take the tracking chips out of each other's necks, and we are going to head for Montana. Hackberry told us the rebels were doing well enough out there, so we are going to go join them."

"About Hackberry's stories from Montana, Reggie! Listen to me!" Newton was adamant. "Just look at something before you kill this man. Look at his shirt. Remember Hackberry's stories? Look at his shirt pocket." He pointed.

Bowperson's hands involuntary released his rifle; the sound of the M8's gun barrel striking gravel and bouncing on blood-splattered boots pinged throughout the canyon.

A row of triple-barbed brass fish hooks dangled from the man's shirt pocket.

Just above the fish hooks, he wore the name "*El Asno*."

Epilogue

Supra Agent Sulla: 135 January 0039

"Did you see the score on the WWFL match last night?" Supra Agent Mackey yelled out in the conference room as everyone was settling in to take their marching orders from Subdirector Ombudsperson. "I was the only one among you chumps who took the over! But the Giants and the Societans scored more than two hundred points in the first Megalopolis Derby of the season!"

"A record by two points, thanks to the defensive tag-team end sacking the punter, then carrying him back twenty yards! Amazing!" Supra Agent Radom smiled. "I have him on my fantasy team!"

"And some people think it's rigged," Supra Agent Sulla said loudly, with a sardonic smile.

"Sulla," Radom shook his head. "Don't be a wet blanket just because you owe me about twenty cases of whiskey on over-unders and because your Pioneers are in last place once again this year – about to be relegated to tier two with the Good Louis Lambs!"

The 10 Supra Agents of Purge Division gathered in their conference room got a chuckle out of Radom's remark. The banter about professional football wrestling continued for several minutes more.

But Sulla found himself lost in his thoughts again. Ever since he had been pulled off the investigation of Leonard's forbidden question and the whereabouts of El Asno, he had been clearing purge after purge at a record rate.

For all outward appearances, he seemed to be doing quite well. He had even arranged for Doctor Armida to be transferred to D.C. and things between them were moving along quite nicely.

Yet Sulla felt hollow.

Eliminating corrupt bureaucrats from the Department of Protests or the Bureau of Public Safety was one thing. But up until quite recently, Sulla had been hot on the trail on a case that actually mattered.

Sulla had taken a tiny remark from a Tolerance Corps trainee and pinned down the source of seditious thoughts to a known dissident. He then had gone a step further and had identified a subject who was likely acting on seditious intelligence.

Sulla still kept the notes of his forbidden-question case. The diagrams of Fred Palmer's circle of knowledge still sat pinned on the ceiling of his 12th-floor apartment. In his pocket, he kept his moleskin notebook – still filled with questions unanswered.

As the banter of professional football wrestling continued in the briefing room, Subdirector Ombudsperson flung the door open and slammed it shut behind her, silencing the room.

"All right, you over-pampered shitheads," Ombudsperson began. "It is time for some field work! Who among you has the stones to get your team together for a likely purge outside your usual territory?"

The professional football wrestling conversation had now completely died down. Ombudsperson looked across the room and continued, "The Overseer of Sacajawea–"

"I'm your man." Agent Sulla surged to his feet.

Subdirector Ombudsperson paused before continuing. "The Overseer has made unauthorized use of paramilitary units to interfere with–"

Wasting no time, Sulla said as he walked out the conference room exit, "Get my flight ready. I'm already there, boss!"

APPENDIX:

The Rise of President Tolerance

The tolerant and advanced Unified Society of America straddled North America as an expanded, but a more thoughtful, superstate than its predecessor had been. It was a superstate that had been built upon the foundations of the old United States. Much of what existed in 0039 could be directly traced back to the events that happened in the last few years of the old U.S.

For example, the National Tolerance Policy Act (NTPA) of 0005 B.E.E. marked not only the high point in tolerance of the old American republic, but helped lay the foundation for the new society. This brought about a guided transition to a more perfect and fully enlightened system of governance. It was a rare law in its relative brevity, and this brevity helped lead to its eventual adoption as Article One of the Unified Society Constitution in 0000 E.E.

The National Tolerance Policy Act of 0005 B.E.E.:

§ 1. Congressional declaration of purpose.

The purposes of this Act are: To declare a national policy, which will encourage tolerant and enjoyable harmony between people and their fellow persons; to promote efforts, which will prevent or eliminate the insidious evils of intolerance; to establish racial, gender, and demographic categories for all residents and assign each resident of the United States a demographic category in order to monitor the continued progress of tolerance; and to stimulate the health and welfare of humankind.

§ 2. The Tolerance Czar
   (a) There is hereby established the Cabinet Position of Czar of Tolerance.
   (b) The President of the United States shall appoint a Tolerance Czar with the Senate's advice and consent.
   (c) The Tolerance Czar (1) shall develop priorities in the new field of tolerance and (2) shall have supervisory control over federal administrative departments and agencies in order to ensure compliance with tolerance.
   (d) The Tolerance Czar shall serve for a term of life with removal only for good cause.
   (e) The Tolerance Czar shall create and direct a Tolerance Enforcement Administration, which shall monitor continued progress in tolerance and enforce and implement this law.

§ 3. Limitations on Federal Agency and Executive Action
   (a) Tolerance Impact Statements: Before undertaking any action, every agency, department, or official (1) shall assess that action's possible impact on tolerance, (2) shall prepare a detailed impact statement explaining the action's possible

impacts upon tolerance, and (3) shall prepare a list of alternatives to the course of action.

(b) This impact statement shall be prepared and submitted to the Tolerance Enforcement Administration, and every government actor shall await approval by the Tolerance Czar before any action is taken or any resources are irrevocably committed to such action.

(c) With the Tolerance Czar's approval, Federal action shall consist of the course of action the Tolerance Enforcement Administration finds to be most likely to maximize Tolerance. (Added by section 15 of the Freedom and Liberty for Everyone Act of 0003 B.E.E.)

§ 4. Limitations on Congress

(a) Congress shall make no law without assessing that law's impact upon tolerance.

(b) To this end, Congress shall establish in both houses a Tolerance Committee, which shall review all legislation before submitting such legislation to the full houses of Congress.

(c) Veto power for the Tolerance Czar: Every Order, Resolution, or Vote to which the Concurrence of the Senate and House of Representatives may be necessary shall be presented to the Tolerance Czar; and before the law shall take effect, shall be approved by him, or being disapproved by him, shall be repassed by two thirds of the Senate and House of representatives before becoming law. (Added by section 19 of the Milk for Children Act of 0002 B.E.E.)

§ 5. Judicial Review of Cases and Controversies Arising Under This Law

(a) Review of cases and controversies arising under the provisions of this Law by the courts established under Article III of the U.S. Constitution shall be precluded.

(Added by section 38 of the Wagner Dairy Act of 0001 B.E.E.)

(b) Cases and controversies arising under this Law shall be heard by a secret nine-person tribunal, which (1) shall consist of nine judges appointed by the President subject to the advice and consent of the Senate (2) who shall serve for a term of life (3) with removal only at the discretion of the Tolerance Czar. (Added by section 39 of the Wagner Dairy Act of 0001 B.E.E.)

Tolerance Czar Tolerance:

In the last years under the old Constitution, the broad interpretive powers vested in the Tolerance Czar made the appointment process for the first Czar hotly contentious. The President suggested 14 appointments, but none would be confirmed by the Senate. Confirmation hearings often devolved into months-long debates as to how the term tolerance should be defined and how tolerance could best be served. Some lawmakers expressed concern as to whether tolerance was an end in and of itself, rather than a means to another end. These lawmakers were rightly decried as tolerance deniers. After careful background checks, many nominees were rejected because they simply were not tolerant enough. Others were rejected because they proposed complicated mathematical formulas for ascertaining tolerance levels, which included the controversial use of fractions.

After two years, the government ground to a halt. Agencies could not comply with the National Tolerance Policy Act (NTPA) because there was no Tolerance Czar to inform everyone what tolerance was. They could not submit their Tolerance Impact Statements and therefore had to stop functioning. The TSA stopped searching old ladies' shoes, the FCC ceased regulating television and radio broadcasts for content, the Department of Agriculture stopped cross-breeding horses, and the Department of Energy stopped cross-breeding horses with horseflies. Even the media declared that the war on drugs was about to be lost. Not many people noticed until the first month Social Security checks were not deposited. Civil disorder broke out and a few states threatened secession. A compromise had to be made.

The Nebraska Compromise provided for the appointment and confirmation of Tolerance Czar Tolerance. Tolerance Czar Tolerance, as his first order of business, prevented civil war by courageously ordering that Social Security checks be issued immediately. Hailed as a genius, Tolerance saw his career take off.

Capital T versus Small t:

In the last years of the old United States, the case of *Rhyddid v. Tolerance* involved a congressional challenge to the Tolerance Czar's veto powers that were given to him by Section 19 of the Milk for Children Act. A nearly unanimous Supreme Court issued an anonymous opinion, upholding the constitutionality of the Tolerance Czar's veto power over Congress.

Opinion of the Supreme Court, Per Curiam:

The Tolerance Czar exercised veto power over the Equal Opportunity Act, an act passed by a radical legislature that would purport to prohibit the use of all government classifications that would place people into demographic groups based upon religion, disability, race, gender, or sexual orientation. The Tolerance Czar stated that he was exercising his veto power in order to preserve the collective rights guaranteed to the classes of people of the United States.

Speaker of the House Rhyddid brought a lawsuit to stop Tolerance Czar Tolerance from exercising veto powers granted to the office of the Tolerance Czar by Section 19 of the Milk for Children Act. Section 19 has added Section 4(c) to the National Tolerance Policy Act as presently codified. Rhyddid contends that Section 4(c) violates the Presentment Clause of the U.S. Constitution, which requires presentment to the President for ratification of all bills and laws, whereas Section 4(c) requires presentment to the Tolerance Czar. We cannot agree with Rhyddid's contention of unconstitutionality.

We hold that the recently passed 30th Amendment to the U.S. Constitution is the clear authority on this matter.
Amendment XXX:
Tolerance, being proven by enlightened political discourse to be necessary to the tolerance of a

tolerant state, Congress shall make no law that impedes the progress of Tolerance.

The amendment clearly states that "Congress shall make no law that impedes the progress of Tolerance." Rhyddid argues that the word "Tolerance" is at best an ambiguous term that requires definition and explanation by the court. We disagree.

We find that because the final word of the 30th Amendment uses a capital "T" for Tolerance and because Czar Tolerance was already a public official at the time of the Amendment's drafting and ratification through plebiscite, this clause is textually and correctly to be interpreted as protecting both tolerance, the ambiguous but normative concept, as well as Tolerance, the public official serving as the Tolerance Czar, from interference from Congressional legislation.

Because the 30th Amendment, therefore, must refer specifically to Tolerance Czar Tolerance, we hold the definition of tolerance to be a non-justiciable political question assigned to the Tolerance Czar for interpretation. Because the definition of tolerance is contingent upon what Tolerance Czar Tolerance determines tolerance to be, and because Congress can make no law impeding the progress of tolerance or Tolerance, we hold that Section 19 of the Milk for Children Act is not only constitutional, but it is necessary and proper to fulfill the purposes of the 30th Amendment.

Dissenting opinion by Justice [He Who Never Existed] stricken from the public record.

He Who Never Existed:

Department of Free Speech Regulation 9:

The Department of Free Speech, empowered by the 1st Amendment to the Tolerant Constitution of the Unified Society, the guarantor of both the freeness of and tolerance in speech, is hereby authorized to prohibit the utterance, publication, or dissemination of the identity, name, or any description of [He Who Never Existed].

Ignorance as to the identity of [He Who Never Existed] is not a defense for violating this Department of Free Speech regulation. Any violation of this regulation shall be punished by loss of speech privileges for not more than 15 years, or reparations, or both.

Consent to this and all Department of Free Speech regulations is to be implied by partaking in the regulated activity of free speech.

The Nebraska Compromise:

PARTIALLY DECLASSIFIED

The Nebraska Compromise came forth as the brainchild of Senator Wagner of Washington and Congressman Cabeza de Vaca from the Third District of Nebraska, the politicians who served as the heads of the Senate and House Tolerance Committees. This compromise conclusively ended the political stalemate over the appointment of the first Tolerance Czar.

According to the terms of the compromise, the Tolerance Czar would ███████████████████████. █ ████████████████████████████ analyzing media broadcasts and internet publications in order to divine the objectively true meaning of the key term: tolerance. ██████████████████ at that time ██████ ███████████████████████████████ ███████████████████████ and █ ███████████████████████████████ ███████████████████████████████

Tolerance Czar Tolerance was even-handed and open-minded. ██████████ compiled data and answered tough political questions when prompted. Giving so much discretionary power ██ ███████████ was a tough political sell. Thankfully, the National Tolerance Policy Act, the NTPA, did not expressly call for the Tolerance Czar's identity to be public information. Nor did it specifically call for the Tolerance Czar ████████████████. When a compromise was announced, no one cared to know who the Tolerance Czar was; what mattered was that a solution had been reached and the U.S. Government could resume depositing checks.

Tolerance ████████ in a secure underground bunker █████ ██████████. The ██████████ explanation was that such a powerful official with a term for life needed to be protected from terrorists.

Slow Boil Rising

This ███████████████ explanation had the added bonus of explaining why the Tolerance Czar ██████████████████████ ██████████. After all, the American Hero Act of 0002 B.E.E. prohibited the disclosure of the identity of all cabinet-level officials in order to protect them from terrorists. In protected seclusion, Tolerance Czar Tolerance was able to answer tough questions by carefully analyzing the NTPA's call for the advancement of tolerance and acceptance. Tolerance Czar Tolerance was able to analyze Tolerance Impact Statements at an incredible rate. Whenever a tough decision had to be made in the Congressional and Senatorial Tolerance Committees, the committees delegated the decision to the Tolerance Czar. Tolerance Czar Tolerance was so effective, talk of a presidential run sprung forth. Tolerance became the great arbiter in Federal politics. In 0002 B.E.E., the Tolerance Czar was given the additional task of tabulating the electronic votes required in all federal elections so that the mistakes of past elections would never be repeated. ████████████████ would never taint the ballot count again. In the momentous year of 0001 B.E.E., Tolerance Czar Tolerance tabulated the votes in a successful call for a new Constitutional Convention. More impressively, Tolerance received the nominations of both major political parties for the office of President, the votes for which he was not even in charge of counting.

Tragically, shortly after these historic votes, Senator Wagner and Congressman Cabeza de Vaca were both killed in a devastating attack by Curaçaoan terrorists, an attack that wiped out a conference meeting of the House and Senate Tolerance Committees.

Made in the USA
Lexington, KY
18 September 2015